WHITBY VAMPYRRHIC

WHITBY VAMPYRRHIC

Simon Clark

severn House

This first world edition published 2009
in Great Britain and 2010 in the USA by
SEVERN HOUSE PUBLISHERS LTD of
9–15 High Street, Sutton, Surrey, England, SM1 1DF.
Trade paperback edition published
in Great Britain and the USA 2010 by
SEVERN HOUSE PUBLISHERS LTD

British Library Cataloguing in Publication Data

Clark, Simon, 1958-
   Whitby Vampyrrhic.
   1. World War, 1939-1945–England–Whitby–Fiction.
   2. Hotels–England–Whitby–Fiction. 3. Motion picture
   industry–Employees–Fiction. 4. Vampires–Fiction.
   5. Horror tales.
   I. Title
   823.9'2-dc22

ISBN-13: 978-0-7278-6831-2   (cased)
ISBN-13: 978-1-84751-204-8   (trade paper)

All Severn House titles are printed on acid-free paper.

 Mixed Sources
Product group from well-managed
forests and other controlled sources
www.fsc.org Cert no. SA-COC-1565
FSC © 1996 Forest Stewardship Council

Typeset by Palimpsest Book Production Ltd.,
Grangemouth, Stirlingshire, Scotland.
Printed and bound in Great Britain by
MPG Books Ltd., Bodmin, Cornwall.

*To Whitby, its people, its legions of dedicated visitors —
and to its exquisite spirit of enchantment, which is
difficult to describe, but is impossible to forget.*

{Anonymous graffiti, circa 1940}
HELL IS A STREET IN WHITBY

THAT FIRST TIME IN THE CAVE

{*From the* YORKSHIRE EVENING MERCURY,
October 1, 1924}

*Buried gold, a sea monster and an invasion of gulls. It's not often a
newspaper reporter is gifted the opportunity to write about such marvellous
things. However, all three presented themselves in just one night in
Whitby – a coastal town that is famous for its windy shoreline and
smoked kippers, rather than a welter of unexplained mysteries.
On Friday evening, Mr Walter Parks of Fishburn Road, a retired
farm labourer, decided to harvest the last of the potato crop from his
backyard. Instead of lifting the common-or-garden spud, he unearthed a
dozen gold amulets of Viking origin. Mr Parks confesses to being
on 'the rough side of the poverty line', but now he and
his family will be assured a comfortable future.
Later that same evening, a huge flock of seagulls descended on Whitby
town. Like vengeful demons they did their level best to swoop down on
men and women in the streets, then these vicious creatures flew into the
windows of St Mary's Church, cracking several panes of glass.
And to complete this trio of miracles: just after midnight, an enormous
creature swam into Whitby harbour. It slammed into fishing boats, causing
mooring lines to break. One local gentleman insisted the creature to be a
hundred feet long with a snake-like neck. Others reasoned that the creature
was a whale that had mistakenly entered the confines of the harbour.
Then, who are we to question what manner of creatures spawn in the
depths of the ocean? Or, for that matter, the depths of the Earth?*

One

Fear of Falling

Eleanor Charnwood ended the argument with her mother by slamming the front door. Then she raced into Whitby's tangle of narrow streets. The argument had been an old one. The same angry words received an airing at least once a week. Eleanor wanted to leave this out-of-the-way English town at the edge of the ocean and find work at one of the new advertising agencies, springing up all over London. And after London? Who knew? Paris? Berlin? New York? But Eleanor's mother always shook her head. 'No. Not ever.'

The October sun hung low in the sky as Eleanor strode out in all her righteous fury across the swing bridge that spanned the River Esk. Her long black hair fluttered in the sea breeze; the heels of her ankle boots clicked against the pavement.

'I'm nineteen years old,' she seethed. 'I'm not going to be trapped in this prison forever.' The rush of anger turned into something near gloating. 'I'll show her. I'll prove I'm not some stupid child.'

On the bridge, she saw Gustav Kirk. At eighteen, he had a lot in common with Eleanor. Although he lived in Whitby, he seemed adrift from the town somehow. A doctor's son, slightly built, fine blond hair that looked as if it would blow away in the wind, he enjoyed his own company. More than anything, he liked to tuck himself into some corner or other to read books about Norse mythology, visionary tales by Machen, Stoker or Poe, and the bone-chilling ghost stories of Edith Nesbit. He also enjoyed an eccentric dress style. Under that heavy overcoat, he'd be wearing his customary tennis whites. And instead of a belt around his waist, he'd always use a red and white striped necktie. Oh . . . and another thing . . . a deep shyness of girls made it nigh impossible to hold a conversation with him. He'd nod politely, offer a shy, 'Hello.' That's just about it. Then he'd back away so quickly that he'd often stumble into passers-by, which would result in him stammering, 'I'm so sorry,' and, 'I do beg your pardon.'

So, when Eleanor blocked his path across the bridge, his blue eyes met hers with a startled flicker.

'Eleanor? Good evening.'

'Gustav. Do you ever feel like doing something *forbidden*? Acting in a way that's so *wrong* that your parents would cover their eyes and scream in horror?'

'Oh? Erm.'

'Even though you were born in Whitby, you don't feel as if you belong, do you?'

'Well . . .'

'We went to the same school. We grew up in these streets, yet we still feel like strangers here, don't we? As if we really belong somewhere else? And to other families?'

'Well . . . I'm sure I don't have much in common with, ahm . . .' His shy blue eyes darted over men and women bustling across the bridge; they were busily attending to their own lives, which revolved round work and families, and chatting to the same friends about the same old thing. Or so it seemed to Eleanor.

'This is 1924, Gustav. Nearly a quarter of the way into the twentieth century. It feels as if we're trapped in the past here.' Eleanor Charnwood surged on, gripped by a searing passion. 'Damn Whitby, I tell you. Damn everyone in it. What do you say?'

'Eh, you have strong opinions, Eleanor. Hmm, have you seen your brother?'

'By that, Gustav, you really mean you want Theo to save you from this wild woman who's confronting you now.'

'No, that's not, ahm—'

'Where are you going?'

'Oh—'

'Usually, you've got an armful of books. What's in the sack? *A shovel*! Crowbar. Rope. Satchel. You're going to break into a house! Whose?'

Gustav fluttered in shock. 'No. Not burglary.'

'I know, you're going to the cemetery to rob graves.'

Her accusation made him appear light-headed. 'No. Nothing like—'

'Take me with you.'

'I . . . I don't think that would be really—'

'Alright. If you don't let me come, I'll take off all my clothes.'

The shy youth backed away in horror.

'Starting with my blouse.' She undid the top button. 'When I take off my stockings you'll have to put your arm around my waist, because I always fall over when I slip those off.'

Despite his embarrassment, his eyes rolled down to her calves, which were clad in black silk.

Grinning, she undid another button of her blouse.

'Alright, alright!' His voice rose so much that pedestrians on the bridge shot him quizzical glances. 'You can come with me. But I warn you. It's not safe. Not safe at all.'

'Good. That's what I wanted to hear.'

Suddenly affectionate, she linked arms with Gustav. His slender limb quivered beneath the coat sleeve.

They crossed the bridge together back into the old half of Whitby town, with its amazing profusion of red-roofed houses that climbed up the hillside towards the church on the headland. To Eleanor, it seemed as if the town had crashed into England from another mysterious realm. Despite the fact that there were motor cars, steam engines, electric lights, and Woolworth's had stocked the first wireless sets, there was something unearthly and disturbing about the way Whitby clung to sides of the estuary. Certain buildings employed the jawbones of whales to frame doorways. Fish aromas filled the air, courtesy of dozens of herring boats that docked in the harbour each day. And there was always the restless vista of the ocean. This was where two worlds collided – the world of deep, dark waters and the dry world of humanity.

From an early age, it struck her that these two worlds were at war. Whitby was the battlefield. There were dangers everywhere. Tides raced in fast over the sands. Often huge waves would explode over the piers. Down through the years, many a person had been swept away. Vicious currents swirled around the timber posts that supported the wharves. Underwater, discarded nets lay in wait to trap unwary swimmers. The cliffs were towering, precipitous rock faces. And always, in the twist and turn of dark alleyways, she was convinced that one grim night she'd come face to face with something monstrously inhuman.

They passed by the Leviathan Hotel on Church Street. Owned by Eleanor's father, the big red-brick building boasted starkly white window frames that reminded her of bones snatched from a tomb.

From Gustav's expression, he clearly hoped she'd tire of teasing him and return home to the hotel. But this was no tease. This was serious. Today, she was determined to commit a reckless act. Whitby be damned. Caution be damned.

Seeing the doorway she'd stormed from just minutes ago made

her decide to air her grievances before an unprepared Gustav, the pleasantly shy man, who loved nothing more than to read his books about Viking gods and demons.

Eleanor began. 'I told my mother that I wanted to move to London to work for a company that make advertisements for magazines. This is 1924, not the dark ages. Women can have professional careers, too. But, no, my mother won't have it. She says I'm too fearful of people. That I'm far too timid to live in a big city. Mother says I must stay here and learn the hotel trade, so I can take over from my father when he retires. Charnwoods are doomed to be hoteliers. We even have one up in godforsaken Leppington.'

'Oh . . . and your brother?'

'My brother can escape Whitby. They're happy with him enlisting in the army. Then, the pair of you are the best of friends so you'll know that already. But I'm a prisoner. In Whitby! The bloody town!' She saw that he appeared to regard her with genuine sympathy. 'So, Gustav. Where are we going with your shovel and crowbar? To do something illegal, I hope?'

By way of answer, he pointed at a piece of paper pasted to a municipal notice board.

> Whitby Town Council, October 3, 1924
>
> The Council receives requests from members of the public to reopen the cave known as 'Hag's Lung' near the abbey ruin. The police have objected to its reopening on the grounds that it has always attracted individuals of unsound mind. Indeed, there are well-documented cases of self-injury and suicide occurring within the cave. Therefore, the Council hereby resolves to keep 'Hag's Lung' closed, and access by the public is strictly forbidden.

His shy demeanour evaporated as he grinned. 'Turn back now, Eleanor, if you're afraid.'

Two

Benighted Place

Their route took them further along Church Street: a thoroughfare lined with houses that faced each other across a street so narrow that they were almost close enough to kiss . . . or, maybe, bite each other, if they were so minded. Soon they reached a flight of stone steps that rose up a cliff face (the stairs always reminded Eleanor of a knobbly stone spine). They climbed these to the graveyard of the church, then they followed the path to the other side, which, in turn, took them by the vast towers and archways that formed the ruined abbey. To their left, the cliff edge. The ocean stretched away into the distance, a metallic blue in the late-afternoon sun.

Gustav Kirk, with the sack over his shoulder, headed for a clump of trees.

Eleanor eyed the man with new-found respect. 'You're so shy, Gustav.'

'I like to keep myself to myself,' he replied softly.

'But you saw the council notice. You're not allowed into Hag's Lung Cave. It's dangerous.'

He shot her a grin again that raised a sparkle of delight in her veins. 'You're right, we are alike. Every so often, the boredom here threatens to break me in two. The only way to beat it is to do something crazy. This morning I thought to myself, shall I run through the streets, yelling rude words? Shall I kick the mayor in the backside? Or should I raise Satan, just so I can talk to someone with interests outside of that town back there?' The grin widened. 'Or shall I break into Hag's Lung and see what it's really like?'

'You're insane.'

'No. I'm inspired.' He laughed. 'Then madness and inspiration are different sides of the same coin.'

I want to kiss him. Here's my soulmate. But she must bide her time before making a move. And wasn't love merely a trap lying in wait for free spirits? Goodness! Her heart thrashed against her ribs. *Make conversation, or I really will kiss him.* 'Why do they call the cave Hag's Lung?'

'Not been here before?'

'Never.'

He led her through the trees to a bulge in the earth. Just as in a fairy tale, a timber door had been set into the earth. It was padlocked. Not just once, but four of them. Great rusty blocks of iron that locked their iron loops into corresponding lugs in the door frame. No one comes in, it seemed to say. Keep out. Go away. No entry. Not ever.

'They call the cave Hag's Lung because . . .' Instead of completing the sentence, he touched his ear. 'Listen at the door.'

Eleanor did so. She heard a faint breath of air blow through gaps in the timber. Air so cold it caused her breath to turn ghostly white. All of a sudden, the blood-chilling draught stopped; a moment later it started again. Only the air was being sucked inwards. It drew her long black hair with it.

'My God! Gustav, it's breathing. The cave is really breathing!'

'Actually, no. But geologists believe a tunnel connects it to the sea. The action of waves gushing into a cavity at sea level causes it to mimic respiration. It pushes air out – then sucks air in. Hence the name, Hag's Lung.' That grin again. 'Nobody's been in there for fifty years. Until now.'

As the sun dropped towards the horizon, Gustav wielded the crowbar to snap each of the massive padlocks. Metal broke with the sound of gunshots. Eleanor flinched, covering her ears with her hands at the shocking punch of sound.

'Strange things have been happening,' he told her as he worked the hasps free. 'Did you read in the paper that old Mr Parks found Viking gold in his garden?'

'Good. He deserves it. Have you seen how decrepit his cottage is? And his wife is crippled with rheumatism.'

'And did you know he only eats half his dinner every night? The rest he offers to Tiw on the old altar stone up on the moor.'

'Tiw?'

'A Norse god – mysterious, unknowable. Tiw is more ancient than Odin and Thor. His origins lie in a horrific and violent spirit that haunted the tundra when mammoths still roamed.' He smiled as he threw open the door. 'Tiw. Long gone. Forgotten. But we speak his name every week.'

'Gustav, you're starting to frighten me.'

'Tiw? He has a day of the week named after him. Tuesday.'

He lit a candle, set down the sack at the entrance, then went down into the cave.

I'm entering the jaws of a monster, Eleanor thought. *But there's no going back.* Air blew into her face one moment, then was sucked in against her back the next. For all the world, it felt like being in the trachea of a huge creature that aspirated – and had done so for ten thousand years. Back to a time when a princess would be selected from the tribe that lived in these borderlands between mountains and ocean. A princess to be married to the god of this cave . . . by the simple act of opening a vein in her neck. Then tumbling her into the velvet darkness below.

Gustav stepped into the body of the cave. His candle revealed its dripping interior of black rock. There was something organic about the stone. It appeared slick with mucous. It smelt 'animal' too. His voice shimmered from the walls. 'There are other strange things, too. Can't you feel the tension in the air? Like an approaching storm? Flocks of seagulls have attacked the town. Then there was the creature that came into the harbour to break ships' moorings.'

'A whale.' Her voice sounded tiny. 'Just a lost whale.'

'Believe me, something strange is happening to Whitby. Can't you sense it? As if the atoms in everything you touch are tensing. Almost like everything's going to explode.' He indicated a hole in the cave wall. At shoulder height, perhaps four or five inches in diameter, it was roughly circular. From the way the candle flame flickered, as he approached, this was where the air gushed in and out. Once more, she was struck how 'biological' it all seemed, rather than geological. It made the earth a living, breathing thing. This was the airway, the throat, the channel into which it sucked life-giving oxygen, then expelled cold, damp vapour. A vapour that smelt of the sea, and of something else she couldn't quite place.

'Do you believe the Viking gods are dead, Eleanor?'

'If not dead, definitely replaced.'

'Then they'd be angry. For thousands of years they were worshipped, then came Jesus Christ, so we slapped Thor, Odin and Tiw in their faces. We've spurned them.'

'I'm going back outside. I don't like it in here.'

'Scared?'

She glared at him with a blazing savagery. 'I'm not scared of anything. My mother said I'd be too timid to leave Whitby. I'll show you who's timid.'

With that, she crossed the cave floor, then thrust her hand into the blowhole. Cold air gushed round it. Sucking then pushing. The force of it was extraordinary. The blast rippled her clothes, tugged at her hair, and chilled her body.

Triumphant, she turned to Gustav. 'See? Am I frightened? Am I too scared to put my hand inside?'

His eyes gleamed at her in the flickering candlelight.

Her voice rose. 'How's this for courage?'

Laughing, she forced her arm deep into the hole. She felt the narrow, rocky gullet enclose her limb tightly. She kept on pushing.

'Eleanor!'

She didn't know whether he wanted her to withdraw or push harder.

But she forced her fist ever deeper. Just as her shoulder met the rock, her hand broke free of the other side. She flexed her fingers.

'I'm through.'

Her eyes snapped wide.

'Eleanor, what's wrong?'

In both horror and wonder, she began, 'I can feel—'

Then pain. Pure agony, a heart-wrenching agony that overwhelmed her as she screamed.

For, at that moment, a set of teeth bit her wrist. She felt their points slide through skin, through muscle, before stabbing into bone. Eleanor tried to push the mouth away that must lie at the other end of the miniature tunnel. Her fingers alighted on flesh; she felt a nose, eyes; this was a human face . . . or some creature that wore a face that might pass for human in an ill-lit place.

The candle went out. Darkness engulfed her. She heard feet scrambling away.

'Gustav, don't leave me alone . . . Please don't leave me!'

PART ONE

{*From* THE FILM & THEATRE GAZETTE, *January, 1942*}

WANTED ~ Experienced Actors and Actresses, ages 21-31, to play North-Country working-class civilians in Govt. sponsored motion picture. Must travel. Apply in writing, with current photograph, to: Cromwell-Sterling Presentations (Casting), PO Box 71, Denham Studios, England.

One

'What have we got to lose? It's either act in this film, or slave every hour God sends in a munitions factory making bombs. You do know that the chemicals in TNT turn your hair green? You'll never marry the man of your dreams with hair the colour of cabbage.'

'But we have to go to Whitby to film it.'

'So?'

'Whitby's on the East Coast of England. If the Nazis invade that's where they'll come ashore.'

'Don't you worry, Sally. I've protected you from rampaging men in the past: if the Nazis come, I'll do it again.'

At twenty-seven, Beth Layne was two years older than her friend, Sally. Ever since they'd met eighteen months ago, Beth had found herself in the role of friend, mentor and guardian. Sally Wainwright was a warm-hearted, amiable woman; she possessed an open face and a ready smile; however, she had the knack of attracting personal catastrophes as lovers gather wild flowers in spring.

Beth Layne, however, realized that her own relationships were often problematic for a different reason. Sally was *too* trusting. Whereas Beth tended to be more cautious in her dealings with people. Character traits in others came under her close scrutiny. Constantly, she found herself analysing conversations with acquaintances. To her own irritation, she realized that, unconsciously, she searched for hidden motives the moment someone developed emotional ties with her. *Does that make me a cynic? Am I overly suspicious of people who want to be friends with me?* Questions that would keep her awake at night.

This morning they waited in a screening room at Denham studios. Basically, the screening room, its ceiling and walls painted black, was a cinema in miniature, with twenty comfortable seats set in front of a ten foot by ten screen. In those seats, a dozen strangers. Beth knew these were the actors and actresses, aged between that magical 'twenty-one to thirty-one' range reserved for youthful, romantic roles. They'd clearly replied to the same advertisement in the *Film & Theatre Gazette*. At present, they were all beautifully poised, nonchalant, even blasé about their surroundings – that untroubled, 'Oh, darling, this is just so routine for we actor types.' Beth, however, sensed the undercurrent of excitement. Surreptitiously, everyone glanced at each other. No doubt envious of each other's looks, comparing footwear and hairstyles, and desperately worrying who would win the lead role.

Sally Wainwright also had a tendency to be incredibly gullible, so she whispered excitedly about a mystery famous actor, who was supposed to play the male lead. As the speculation had only been overheard on the bus ride to the studios, Beth dismissed it as simply the kind of garrulous rumour that flies from many a young actor's lips.

Sally's eager words were so breathy in Beth's ear that it tickled outrageously. 'American, it must be an American; failing that a British actor. Or Australian.'

Beth shook her head, smiling. She was fond of Sally, but she could be so dizzy at times. Even so, Beth noticed the way other young hopefuls strained to hear what Sally murmured.

At that moment, Beth couldn't restrain herself. Just as would-be starlets in neighbouring seats imagined themselves playing opposite a world-famous star, the screening room door opened, and Beth uttered with shocking loudness: '*Cary Grant.*'

A dozen heads spun at once in the direction of the door; a dozen mouths gaped with astonishment. They were halfway out of their seats, eager to welcome the most handsome man in the world. Cary Grant. The king of fashion, the lord of elan. However, the man entering now walked with a stoop. Untidy strands of grey hair wormed their way from beneath a flat cap. All in all, he could have passed for Cary Grant's seedy-looking uncle.

Beth couldn't stop grinning. The expression on all those eager hopefuls' faces had been priceless. 'Yes, Cary Grant,' she continued in a voice calculated to be heard around the room, even though she pretended to be chatting to Sally. 'Definitely one of my favourite actors. Did you see him in *Bringing Up Baby*?'

Nearly everyone realized they'd been the butt-end of a joke. Half smiled in Beth's direction, as they recognized they had someone in the troupe with a sense of humour. The humourless, however, glowered.

The man in the cap shuffled to a set of light switches on the wall.

The door opened again.

Sally took it upon herself to continue the joke. 'Bela Lugosi!'

This time, even those who'd been amused by Beth's Cary Grant leg-pull were embarrassed by the entrance of a man wearing a black eyepatch.

Briskly, he strode towards the cinema screen with the words, 'Bela Lugosi? I'm afraid not. I'm a lot less Hungarian than our esteemed Mr Lugosi.' The rich Scottish accent of rolling Rs would have been hard to miss.

Blushing furiously, Sally stared down at her knees.

'Good morning, ladies and gentlemen,' he continued, 'my name is Alec Reed. I have written the script and will direct you to the best of my ability to act brilliantly. Congratulations on being selected to play in the film. I'm sure we'll all do our best to work professionally. But hear this: I have at least one good eye. And one thing I know is when people are slacking. I can spot the work-shy a mile off. I won't tolerate anyone trying to rob me of an honest day's work.' He glanced at Sally, still red-faced and cringing in her seat. 'Together we will forge *This Midnight Realm*; a story to melt hearts. It will remind audiences at home and abroad why we are fighting this war with Hitler. As well as entertainment, its purpose is to explain what it is like to live in the Britain of 1942. A Britain at war with an evil lunatic, who loves nothing better than to drop bombs on our heads every night.' He touched the eyepatch. 'The damn dog nearly got me last week. And I daresay he's tried to kill you, too, and the ones you love. So . . . consider this as your part in the fight against Fascism, which threatens democracy itself. If our film can help persuade neutral countries to side with us, we will have won a battle – one just as important as blowing up Nazi tanks. If you're not prepared to surrender your home comforts, your film-star egos, and even your lives for this film, then haul your stinking backsides out of those seats and trudge back to whatever hole you crawled out of. Do I make myself clear?'

A good many in the audience shuffled uncomfortably at the man's suddenly aggressive tone. But nobody challenged what he'd said. Nobody, however, but one.

Beth Layne raised her hand. 'Mr Reed, a question?'

'Oh, our American actress, or so I detect from the accent?'

'Yes, my name is Beth—'

'Layne. I know that, madam. I personally rubber-stamped your application.'

'You've asked us to surrender ourselves body and soul to this motion picture.'

'Indeed I have, madam. I demand it. Freedom demands it.'

'Then will you surrender the liquor bottle for the sake of the film?'

He glared at her. *If looks could kill . . .*

Everyone's jaws dropped at her words. Beth pressed on. 'I know the scent of gin, Mr Reed, and plenty of it followed you into this screening room.'

Sally looked ready to die of embarrassment.

'And, Mr Reed, the aroma of freshly imbibed gin at ten in the morning is a sorrowful thing in my estimation.'

The man's face quivered. That single eye of his blazed. Then something that was as shocking as it was unexpected. A bead of red liquid, quick as a tear, emerged from beneath the eyepatch to roll down his cheek.

Taking a deep breath, he spoke in a low, controlled voice – a little too controlled, 'You will now see the prologue to *This Midnight Realm*. It explains what dangers we are experiencing. After the presentation you will receive your scripts, together with your allotted roles.' Then he turned to Beth. 'Miss Layne. I wish to speak to you before the scripts are handed out.' He nodded at the man in the cap. 'Lights, if you will, Stan.'

The moment the screening room plunged into darkness, lights flashed on the screen. Numbers scrolled downward in silence: 10 . . . 9 . . . 8 . . . 7 . . .

Beth whispered into Sally's ear, 'No prizes for guessing what Mr Reed wants to tell me after the film.'

Sally hissed back, 'You idiot, Beth. You're going to wind up in a factory making bombs, after all.'

Those nearest shushed Sally with unconcealed irritation.

Beth thought, *I guess we've got off on the wrong foot, alright. The omens aren't good.* Feeling her spirits droop into the soles of her 'sensible' lace-up travelling shoes, Beth focused on the screen in front of her.

The title blazed, accompanied by a heroic fanfare of music:

THIS MIDNIGHT REALM
A Cromwell-Sterling Presentation
Written & Directed by Alec Reed

Following that, shots of London streets, Big Ben, the winged statue of Eros in Piccadilly Circus, children on swings in a playground.

Then a siren rose over the music. Beth sensed a sudden stillness amongst the audience. The shots of London were repeated, but each one quickly faded. The screen crashed to black. Only the siren continued.

Slowly, it faded as the voice-over began: '*Ladies and Gentlemen. That dreadful sound you are hearing is the siren that warns every man, woman and child that enemy planes are approaching their homes.*' Beth recognized those softly modulated tones. Alec Reed had narrated the introduction to the film. He spoke with a measured dignity – unrushed, precise, yet with a special clarity, as if he wished with all his heart to be understood. '*Ever since 1939, Britain has been at war with Hitler's evil Nazi empire. We are an island under siege. Enemy submarines sink our ships. Enemy planes pour fire and explosives on to every city.*' Images again: this time of bomb craters in a children's playground, of burning ships in a harbour, of ruined homes with dazed survivors sitting on the rubble. Alec Reed's voice-over continued. '*The war kills people like you and I. Bombs destroy homes and factories and schools. But this war has brought something else. It has engulfed us in a great tide of darkness.*' Once more, footage of wrecked houses faded to black.

'*Darkness, darkness . . . all encompassing. There are times we believe that the darkness will flood our minds and drown our souls. Because, ever since the war began, British people are strictly forbidden to show any kind of light at night. Lest that light act as a guiding beacon to enemy bombers. After all, even a lighted cigarette can be seen from five thousand feet above your head. So . . . at night . . . that long, dreadful night . . . windows are shrouded by cloth: dark cloth, funeral black.*' Scenes of men and women pulling swathes of blackout material over windows. '*If the light still shows through the drapes and curtains and blinds, then we must paint even the window glass. Show no light. Not a glimmer. Not a twinkle. Otherwise the bombs will fall. Bombs are death to you and your neighbour, and to her baby sleeping in its cradle.*' More shots of cities at night, the buildings reduced to ghostly silhouettes. '*So we blunder about in darkness. Even in the middle of our biggest city. No street lights . . . No headlamps on cars must be visible. If they are, the Nazi death machine will come. This, then, is our night. When darkness is king.*'

Sally couldn't stop herself whispering in total admiration, 'Isn't he poetic?'

From all around, people shushed.

The narration rose in volume as music surged in to carry his words to the climax. '*And so, ladies and gentlemen, I invite you to spend a little while with me . . . to watch how ordinary families, from an ordinary street, not only cope with life in this new midnight realm, but how they rise up, conquer it, and make darkness their domain . . .'* Music boomed in triumph. A map appeared of a coast. *'Here is the little English seaside town of Whitby. Come with me now and meet these ordinary − yet, as you'll see − extraordinary men and women.'*

The film ended abruptly.

'Lights please, Stan.' The room lights revealed the narrator of the film standing by the screen. His fingertips touched the eyepatch, as if he'd become even more conscious of it. 'So far, that's all that has been shot of *This Midnight Realm*. This is where you enter the story of our film, ladies and gentlemen. You will play those ordinary men and women of Whitby, a town at war. It will be your role, *your quest*, to show the rest of the world how we carry on with our ordinary lives, despite the hardships of air raids, food rationing and the blackout.' He checked his watch. 'We'll now take a break. Please be back here for ten forty-five. Thank you.'

The audience applauded. They were excited, enthusiastic.

Beth applauded, murmuring as she did so, 'He knows how to work a crowd, doesn't he?'

Sally didn't pick up any note of sarcasm. Breathlessly, she gushed, 'I can't believe I'm going to be in my first movie. All I've ever done is shows in village halls. It's wonderful. Will they style my hair . . . Oh? Do I have to buy my own make-up? But I will be in black and white, won't I? Don't we have to wear black lipstick, so it shows up on screen? Just imagine, Beth! We'll have our faces in big, shining close-up! Big as giants! And we'll be in cinemas all over the world.'

'Just wait until Hitler begs for your autograph.'

Sally's eyes went wide. 'Oh, he might see me. I hadn't thought about that.'

'Don't worry. I'm sure *This Midnight Realm* won't play in down-town Berlin.' Beth put her arm around Sally to give her friend an affectionate squeeze. 'I'm really pleased you've got the part. And I'm sorry that I won't be with you in Whitby.'

'But you will. You've signed the contract.'

'And I'll be fired before I even get the script. Me and my big mouth, eh, kid? But Mr Big Guns Director there, Alec Reed, made me so angry. He shouldn't talk to us like we're lazy no-gooders.'

Already the young actresses had formed a half circle in front of Alec, so they could vie to flatter him, laugh at his jokes, and beam winning smiles.

Beth said, 'You best make sure your face is seen down there by Mr Reed. Otherwise all the pretty girls will get the best parts.' She stood up.

'Beth, where are you going?'

'Oh, I'm going to get some air before he fires me.'

'Beth—'

'Sally, don't worry. I'll stick around and look after you today. Men in film studios prowl round like hungry wolves when pretty young actresses are about. Later, I'll play the big sister and give you a list of do's and don'ts before you go off to Whitby. There's no need to fret about costumes and make-up; they have people to take care of that for you.'

'I'm scared, Beth. I don't know what to say to anyone.'

'You'll be fine. Because you're a golden-hearted sweetie, and everyone will recognize the good in you.' She stood up. 'Ciao.'

Two

Beth Layne relished her current sense of utter relief. A hothouse of thespian egos always oppressed her. *Don't get me wrong,* she thought. *I love the job of acting. It's just that some actors and actresses can be so damn annoying. I'd love to see them in a big factory with clanking metal presses making turrets for tanks. Would they last the week? A day? No, I think not.*

'Now I'm being bitchy,' she murmured to herself, as she paused at a mirror by a studio door to adjust a lock of hair that hung down over her forehead. 'And I'm being as vain as they are.' Beth, an American by birth, had left the States to find work in the English film industry five years ago. She figured her American accent, and hair as golden as a Nebraskan cornfield, would win her lead roles. Also, she had served Cary Grant a cocktail in one of his Hollywood movies. That kind of gem on a résumé could get a girl decent acting parts in the old motherland. Only, the war had come along to complicate things.

Roaming wolf-packs of German submarines made Transatlantic crossings for civilians a near impossibility, so she couldn't return home to the US of A. Add to that, America had entered the war against Japan and Hitler's Germany just a matter of weeks ago. And, dear God in heaven, she did want to aid the war effort. If it wasn't for landing a role in *This Midnight Realm*, she would have presented herself at a munitions factory and begged to make bullets for allied soldiers. Beth told herself firmly, *One thing I'm not afraid of is to get my hands dirty.*

She gazed into the mirror. Now she wanted to kick herself for lousing up this opportunity. *I must have been out of my mind to accuse the director of being a gin-sodden lush.* But the moment he'd opened his mouth he'd annoyed the hell out of her.

'Fresh air,' she muttered. 'Get fresh air and plenty of it.'

Beth headed down a long corridor. Doors off carried signs like *Edward Birks, Senior Producer* or *Kathleen Miller, Script Supervisor.* Everywhere, on the drab green walls, there were reproductions of the Cromwell-Sterling logo, a female warrior carrying a shield and a spear. She paused. She couldn't remember if this corridor led to the exit. After all, it was her first time at this particular studio. A pair of secretaries, hugging armfuls of scripts, rushed from a door in front of her. Their red lips were the brightest slash of colour in the corridor.

'Excuse me,' she began, 'can you tell me—' But they vanished through another door marked *Production Accountant.* 'That's it,' she muttered darkly. 'I'm doomed to wonder the studios for all eternity.'

She longed for a lungful of cold winter air. Her head felt muzzy. A pain flared behind her eyes. *Great, just great, now I'm going down with flu. But the symptoms don't occur so quickly, do they?* Suddenly, the air in the corridor of a million doors – at least that's what it seemed like – became thunderously oppressive. Pain speared her eyes. *Good grief. My skull's going to explode.* She gritted her teeth. For some reason it seemed like a huge charge of energy had invaded the building. Dizzy, she placed her hand on the wall to steady herself. Lights dimmed. As there were no windows, the corridor grew so gloomy that she could barely even see those doors leading off; what's more, the doorways became suggestive of churchyard headstones – tall oblong, shapes that breathed the words *grave, tomb, cemetery* and *death* into her ear.

A sudden gust of air raced down the passageway. The gale came from nowhere, but its scent reminded her of the sea. Posters fluttered on the walls. The studio's logo of the she-warrior writhed on a poster that was the size of one of those damned doors (which could have led to hell for all she knew).

Then a figure. Beth glimpsed a man in the shadows. A burly individual who swept by her. He pushed open a pair of doors that admitted light into the corridor. Thinking the way led outdoors, she followed the man. Moments later, she found herself bathed in light. Only, it was a thin, grey light. A poor excuse for daylight really. Beth closed her eyes, kept them scrunched shut, then opened them again. She stood in a street. One paved with cobbles. Ahead of her, a line of ancient cottages. Their red-brick walls bulged, and the windows were tiny openings that resembled the eyes of reptiles. Doorways were low, stunted things, seemingly constructed to admit goblin men into their dwarfish houses. An iron plaque fixed to the front of one cottage spelt out: CHURCH STREET – BOROUGH OF WHITBY.

'Ah.' Beth rubbed her throbbing forehead. 'Whitby. It makes sense now. They've built a replica of one of the streets.' She frowned. The detail of the set was extraordinary. Dozens of houses had been built. Smoke rose from chimneys. 'So why are we going on location, when they've gone to the trouble of building this?' The authenticity took her breath away. She'd seen many a studio set. This, however, had to be the biggest, the best and the most realistic ever. A cat, a live cat, stood on a mound of lobster pots. *Why, I can even smell the scents of the sea and the fish in the market.*

Drawn by the extraordinary craftsmanship of the set designers, she moved further along 'Church Street'. She rested her palm against the wall of a cottage. The dull red-brick under her hand felt solidly real, not the papier mâché or plywood that was the usual choice of carpenters when they built a mock-up of a town. What's more, these buildings didn't resemble flimsy free-standing 'flats'. They had all the substance of being rooted into the earth for the last five hundred years. Once more she asked herself why the actors and crew were being sent to Whitby, on the English coast, when they could film right here. She looked up at the ceiling of the studio, which would be around thirty feet above her head. Clouds hung there, or something that resembled clouds. Beth figured that a gauzy material had been suspended from roof beams to create the effect of natural cloud. And even as she gazed at it the light dimmed on this magnificent recreation of Whitby town. Perhaps one of the exterior doors was being slowly drawn shut?

Now the gloom closed in. Shadows spilled from authentic-looking alleyways. Darkness crept along Church Street. It seemed as if a black mist engulfed the houses, until they became indistinct shapes that assumed the menacing aspect of hunched figures. Windows were dull eyes that watched. Just as if they expected a terrible fate to befall her. Now they were curious to what that fate would be . . . and how much she'd suffer before she died.

Stop that, she told her rogue imagination. This flu bug, or whatever it was, was clouding her mind. Her stride became increasingly unsteady. Her eyes blurred, so the already gloomy town became even more murkily indistinct. *No, not a town*, she thought. *This is a set made out of plywood and paper in a film studio.* She pushed at the door of a cottage, expecting it to flap open in that flimsy way that is the province of studio scenery. Only, this robust slab of timbers remained locked solidly shut.

On impulse she rapped on the door, as if challenging it to be just a copy of a cottage door that would have been cobbled together in a studio workshop. Her knuckles rapped solid oak. A moment later she heard footsteps. The owner of the house had answered her call.

But who owns a strange, goblin cottage like that? What would they look like? Would they welcome a stranger at dusk? Not wishing to meet the denizen of such a weird little abode, she fled before the door could be opened. She rubbed her forehead. That sense of energy building inside the studio came back to her. A huge storm's worth of charge. Something huge and violent and terrifying just about to break. Tiny, skittering objects ran across the cobbles in front of her. Rats. They had to be. Loathsome, disease-bearing rats.

To avoid being in the rodents' way, if they decided to rush back at her, Beth turned left into an alleyway that boasted the bizarre name of Arguments Yard. She passed through a narrow, echoing passageway to a tiny close lined with equally tiny houses. And at that moment Beth sensed eyes staring at her. Yet she didn't see a single person.

She moved deeper into the strangely named yard. Above front doors, house names had been chiselled into solid stone lintels: *Nag's Cottage, North Star Lodge, Twixt Heaven & Hell, Jack O' Bones* . . . Beth felt herself drawn deeper into this narrow gulf. It seemed like a huge hand pressed against the back of her neck, pushing her forward. But forward to what? Her destiny? Her one true end?

Her eyes tried to penetrate the gloom in front of her. Now that darkness had the rich velvet intensity of red wine. The harder her gaze tried to penetrate the veil of shadow the more the optic nerves compensated by conjuring purple patterns into her field of vision. They were slow moving shapes, twisting, undulating . . .

I'm going to die in here, she told herself. *I'm going to die and no one will ever know.*

Her normally cool, rational nature had abandoned her. Only a primordial occult terror remained: that instinct to imagine that monsters lurk under your bed, that there are phantoms in your closet, and that the man following you along the street at midnight is a killer with a bloody knife in his hands . . . and lustful eyes focused on your softly delicate throat . . .

Then a figure stepped out of the shadows. A young man, his face as pale as ancient bone. Beth retreated along Arguments Yard, aiming to retrace her footsteps to the exit. She reached the passageway that led to the street. The top of the passage, formed by the upper story of a house, dragged at her hair; an old, blackened timber snatched away an entire lock of blonde. Her gasp of pain must have triggered what happened next.

Fast-moving figures erupted from the shadows of the yard. This time she didn't see any detail, other than bright, glaring eyes. Bizarrely, they didn't possess coloured irises, just a fierce black pupil dominated the white.

Beth ran. She hadn't the luxury of debating what was actually happening. Why a studio set looked so solidly real, or just who those menacing figures were. A mist had made the cobbles slick. Even in this gloom they glistened, as if they oozed their own inner moisture. Beth raced along the street. It seemed to extend forever into darkness. A derelict tavern stood at the corner; the sign over the door read *Blessing on the Drowned.* Such a grimly macabre name; the image that accompanied the words emphasized it: a human skull with the incoming tide lapping around it.

Beth turned a bend; as she did so her feet slipped from under her. An agonizing pain exploded through her nerve endings as she slammed on to the ground.

'Damn, that hurt!' The words were born of frustration and fear as much as pain. Because right now she wanted to scream her distress out to the world. Then she glanced back the way she came. Light-footed figures, nothing more than silhouettes that possessed whitely staring eyes, raced towards her. Something about their eagerness spoke volumes about lust and hunger.

In a heartbeat, she scrambled to her feet. Once more she rushed down the never-ending street. One lined with tiny shops, cottages, and strange-looking chapels from which protruded grotesque carvings of heads with bulging eyes.

The footsteps grew louder as her pursuers closed the gap. Already, she could imagine fingers reaching out to grab her hair, then bring her to a screaming, pain-filled stop. After that . . . what then?

All of a sudden the houses were gone. She burst through twin doors and into the grasp of a tall, rage-filled man.

'*Where the hell have you been? We've been waiting for you.*'

Her gaze locked on to the eyepatch beside the good eye. The flesh surrounding the patch had puffed outwards with a reddish inflammation.

She panted out some words. They meant nothing to him . . . nor to her.

'I recommend you catch your breath, then try again,' Alec Reed said in his cold Scottish accent. 'Then maybe I can let the others go for their lunch.'

'Back . . .' She turned to the doors, expecting them to burst open and admit those monstrous figures into the corridor. 'In there . . . someone attacked me in the town.'

'The town?' His one good eye registered surprise.

'Yes, on the Whitby set!'

'Are you making fun of me, Miss Layne?'

'No, I'm trying to tell you that I was attacked. Look at my elbow.'

'You've got a heroic graze there, I'll give you that. Did your assailant do that?'

'They were . . . I don't know. Demonic.'

'And it was someone in there?' Alec indicated the studio doors.

'Yes, you idiot. Listen to what I'm saying.'

'And in there is the Whitby set?'

'Yes. The Whitby set.' Beth could have cursed with frustration. It took the man an age to understand what she told him. 'There's a long road lined with cottages called Church Street. My God, that's a hell of mock-up. That's big budget stuff – cottages built of brick; there are chapels, a cobbled street, even an authentic smell of the sea, but why go to that trouble for a film? Where nobody can smell any . . . Wait, where are you going?'

'To check for myself and find those men. Nobody roughs up my actors. I mean . . .' He gave a grim smile. 'You'll vouch for the fact that it's me, Alec Reed, who gave you a hard time.' He strode towards the twin doors.

'Wait. Get help first. There were a whole bunch of—' The rest of her words trailed away.

Beyond the doors, there it was. In all its glory . . . well, what would be glorious once the set was lit and dressed correctly for the camera. Beth followed Alec Reed into a decidedly modest studio. A better description than 'modest', however, would be 'pokey'. The room had little in it other than a flimsy wall of hardboard, painted to look like brick. A mat of dark material had been laid out, which should pass for a road. A horse-drawn cart (without the horse) stood before the 'wall'.

'But the set for Whitby was amazing. Really, really good. So authentic.' Beth shook her head. 'If I didn't know better, I'd swear I'd walked into the real town.'

'There's only this set, Miss Layne. And this is for a dramatization of a Charles Dickens' story being filmed here this week.'

'There must be a door to the other set.'

'There is no other set, Miss Layne. That's why we're filming on location in Whitby. I fought tooth and claw to do that, otherwise we'd have ended up with piffling cardboard cut-out houses, that are as authentic as this so-called London street.'

'I've gone mad,' Beth said with absolute clarity. 'Mad as the March hare, because there were streets here, and cottages. Even smoke came out of the chimneys – inhale: you can still catch some of it.'

'That smells like pipe tobacco to me, Miss Layne. It's wafting in from the executives' boardroom next door.' His single good eye focused on her face. 'Even though I don't believe in your manifestation of Whitby in this very building, I do believe you've had a nasty experience. Your elbow looks quite sore, you know.'

'I had noticed, thank you.'

'You really have worked with Cary Grant?'

'I served him a dry Martini in a movie. Now I wish it had needed a dozen takes. We did it in one. But I have my five seconds on-screen with the great man himself. He even smells as good as he looks. Acqua di Parma; an aftershave; it—'

'You're trembling.'

'I'm also babbling about Cary Grant, aren't I?'

The anger left him now. 'Come on, we'll go somewhere quiet for a coffee.'

'If you're firing me, do it here.'

'Firing you?'

'For suggesting you're a raging liquor lover.'

'No. I've a proposition. One, I trust, that you will find as irresistible as it is fascinating.'

He held open one of the swing doors for her. In the back of her neck blew a cold, damp breeze. *What if I turn round and I can see Whitby again? If I can, that proves I'm mad, doesn't it?* Salty ocean scents, laced with odours of raw fish, crawled up her nostrils. She could almost hear the distant whisper of surf. At that moment, she knew Whitby's Church Street would be there waiting, as cold as a tomb, if she glanced over her shoulder. Clenching her fist, and resisting the urge for that last backward look, she walked out into the corridor. She only allowed herself to breathe again when the door closed firmly behind her.

Three

Alec Reed ushered her into an office so flamboyantly untidy she wanted to describe it as sexy. A pair of typewriters faced each other across a large table, as if eager to fight a duel. Scripts were piled on shelves. One wall was devoted to large sheets of paper on which had been drawn the storyboard of the script. And above that, a banner proclaimed *This Midnight Realm*. On the table: empty cups, beer bottles, ashtrays crammed full of cigar butts. Tellingly, a bottle of gin, half empty, stood by a typewriter. Beth could still smell that particularly distinctive spirit on Alec's breath.

Alec invited her to take a seat, vanished from the office for a while, then returned with two cups of coffee.

'Thank you,' she said, 'but isn't all this an overly elaborate way to fire me?'

'Coffee's as rare as a good night's sleep these days, what with the air-raid sirens screaming fit to burst. Cheers.' He sipped the coffee. The action of swallowing caused a drop of red liquid to emerge from beneath the eyepatch and roll down his cheek. He dabbed it away with a knuckle.

Beth set her cup down on the table. 'Well?'

'Well, what?'

'Fire me.'

'Don't be ridiculous.'

'Ridiculous?' Her anger rose.

'Drink your coffee. You won't believe how severely rationed it is now. Ships bringing it across the Atlantic are targeted by submarines. Crews drown by the hundred.'

'So there's blood in the coffee. Is that what you're trying to say?'

'Peppery, aren't you?'

'Why are you treating me like your personal enemy?'

'You really could smell gin on my breath from, what? Three rows back in the screening room?'

'Absolutely. Now fire me for making that crack about you being liquored up, and stop playing games. I don't like it. What's more, I won't tolerate it.'

Once more his fingertip rested on the eyepatch, as if still coming to terms with it being attached to his face.

'Miss Layne. Permit me to confess what happened ten days ago. It may help you make up your mind about me. Then act according to your conscience.'

His manner irritated her, but she nodded. 'Go on.'

'Ten days ago I sat in a café in London. There was an informal meeting, you see, with the director and location manager for the film I'd just finished scripting. We sat there with slices of cherry cake, cups of tea, and the director smoked his favourite tobacco. All profoundly normal. A waitress brought sandwiches to a young couple sitting at a table opposite. He wore a blue Royal Air Force uniform. She was a nurse. They were holding hands. I suggested to the director that wherever possible we film on the streets of Whitby and dispense with rickety cardboard sets, then . . .' A stillness crept over him. 'Then the café didn't exist any more. Everyone was dead. The young sweethearts, my colleagues. The walls had vanished. Tables pulverized to splinters. There I was standing in the rubble, smoke and fire all around, and no sound whatsoever.' He took a mouthful of coffee; as he did so, his eye alighted on the gin bottle. 'A bomb had struck the building. Everyone died but me.'

Beth said, 'You must have been saved for a higher purpose.' Then she clenched her fist. *Did I really say that?* The glibness of her own comment shamed her. 'I'm sorry. That sounded crass.'

'No . . . I've had plenty of time to consider it. An eighty-kilogram bomb, containing high explosive, fell ten thousand feet from a plane on to the building. Everyone reduced to a smear of bloody red. An awful description, but it's true. Yet all I suffer is a gash in my eyelid.' He gave a grim smile. 'A nurse needed a long needle and a lot of thread to reconnect that flap of skin. And I have to wear this pirate's eyepatch for another week or so, but they tell me I'll be good as new. I'd just begin to 'see' the location manager, or date her as you Americans would say.'

'She was your girlfriend? I'm sorry, Mr Reed.'

'Alec, please.' He held eye contact with her. 'Do you think I have been saved for a higher purpose? Did God intervene, so I might achieve great things in order to aid a victory over Hitler? Or have some ancient gods, who are bitter and twisted through neglect, decided to save me for their own evil purposes?'

'Ancient gods? Why do you say that?'

'I've been troubled by such strange dreams. Every night, when I close my eyes, I find myself in Whitby. A place I've never been. In the dream, I walk through the streets. It has become a ghost town.' He stared at the coffee cup, as he remembered what must have been disturbing nightmares.

'Alec, listen to me. In wars, strange things happen. We've all heard tales of soldiers who are shot, but a Bible in their breast pocket stops the bullet. That's the mythology of battle. You hear stories like that all the time. Shells hit a trench, killing every soldier bar one – he escapes without a scratch. Something like that happened to you. Maybe some individuals are spared for a higher purpose. Maybe not. But it does no harm to believe we've been given a second chance, so we can make the most of life. Turn over a new leaf. Be a better person.'

'A better person? Last night I was tortured by the same old nightmare. My eye stung like fury. Worse, I wallowed in self-pity. My friends were dead. Better people than me gone. So, this morning, I swallowed a heck of a lot of gin before I could bring myself to stand in front of those actors and actresses.'

'After what you've been through, it's understandable.'

He gave a grim smile. 'If I had been saved from the explosion in order to perform mighty deeds, all I did this morning was prove to you, and everyone else, that I'm weak as water. A flimsy, paper cut-out of a man. A coward who needs booze before he can bring himself to speak to his fellow man and woman.'

'Now you are sounding sorry for yourself.'

'True. And I promise to do better. I want to make this film work; it has a mission to inform other countries about the hell this nation is enduring in order to oppose the Nazi barbarians.' He leaned forward, hands clasped together on the table. 'Now to business, Miss Layne.'

'Beth.'

'Thank you, Beth. I want you to replace my girlfriend.'

'*You want what!*'

'Sorry. Bad choice of words. The gin's made me fuzzy around the gills.' Alec took another swallow of coffee. 'Lorna was the location manager. It's hard to find replacements. Most people who could do this kind of work are now either in the military or munitions factories.'

'I couldn't. I'm an actress.'

'Oh, too good for that kind of work, are we?'

'I meant I'm not qualified.'

'You have a good head on your shoulders. That's the only quali-fication you need.'

'I wouldn't know where to begin.'

'My director is dead. I'm the writer; I'm having to step into his shoes.' He pulled a file across the table. 'Here is your résumé. When you had the opportunity to return to America, before it became unsafe to make the Atlantic crossing, you decided to stay here to perform in hospital shows for our wounded troops. You participated in ENSA concerts in France before the British were forced to retreat. It demonstrates you are prepared to do what you can to help the war effort and thwart mad Herr Hitler and his villainous regime. As you Yanks say "you are not a quitter".' He studied a sheet of paper. 'You have a great list of screen credits, too, so you understand the mechanics of film-making. Therefore, I am not firing you, Beth Layne. You will act in my film. What's more, I need you to go up to Whitby to scout out locations. We start shooting in twelve days.'

'Alright. But I insist on my friend, Sally Wainwright, coming with me.'

'By all means.'

'And she gets paid, too.'

'You'll both share the same wage as Lorna would have received for scouting locations. Later, you'll both be paid acting fees as set out in the contracts. Those fees begin the first day of shooting. The government are funding this production most handsomely.'

'We'll need to go back to our rooms in London to pack. We only brought clothes for an overnight stay.'

'Beth. This is war. Be it military or civilian work, when we are deployed we must obey instantly.'

'What do you mean?'

'I want you to leave for Whitby this very minute.' He handed her slips of paper from the file. 'Here are your rail warrants. They'll get you to Whitby by midnight.'

'Our clothes are—'

'I have every confidence you'll use your considerable initiative to find more clothes when you're there. As well as wonderful, atmos-pheric locations for our film.'

'I'll find them,' she told him firmly. 'But if you ever intimidate your actors and actresses, in the misguided belief it gets the best out of them, I'll launch my own personal war on you. Understood?'

'Understood.'

He held out his hand, which she shook.

'See you in Whitby, Beth.' He smiled, and just for a moment she wondered if his confession about the near-death experience in the café had been intended to disarm her.

'I' m sure interesting times lie ahead for both of us,' she told him. 'Ciao.'

When she'd gone, he picked up his coffee cup and took a hearty swig. 'Beth Layne sees a phantom Whitby in the studio. I see it in my nightmares.' He toasted the picture of Whitby on the wall. 'You're getting into our blood, aren't you old girl?'

Four

Flying Officer Benjamin Green knew he'd been born a fortunate man. As a child, he'd beaten death when he'd escaped a burning schoolroom that had claimed the lives of everyone else in there. His terrific parents had encouraged his ambitions to become a musi-cian. When war came they hadn't discouraged him from joining the air force. They were so proud of their son. His death-defying abil-ities allowed him to escape two bad crashes during training flights. That trick of spitting in the Reaper's eye had happened all over again an hour ago when anti-aircraft shells had struck his aircraft. True, his co-pilot and navigator lay dead in their seats. And one engine burnt so brightly that his aircraft must have resembled a fiery shooting star, streaking through the night sky.

But his charmed life still held true. The engine on the other wing ran well, if not that smoothly. The blood that soaked his flying suit, goggles, oxygen mask and leather helmet wasn't his. The Essex kid, who'd joined him as co-pilot yesterday, had taken a shell fragment the size of a tennis ball in the centre of his face.

Half of the kid's head had landed in Benjamin's lap. Gently, he'd placed it on the slumped body in the seat beside him.

'I've beaten death,' Benjamin murmured. 'I'm going home.'

He nursed his reconnaissance aircraft westward. Germany receded behind him. England lay beyond the nose of the plane. He'd cheat that harvester of souls again; the Grim Reaper wouldn't claim Benjamin Green. Not this time. There'd still be enough fuel to get him back to the airfield. Wiping his comrade's blood from the goggle lenses, he peered out through the side window. A mile below, the ocean resembled beaten silver in the moonlight. Those seemingly tiny dimples in the surface were, however, substantial waves. If he had to ditch the plane in that, it would test his knack of giving Mr Death the slip.

He checked the blaze on the port wing. So far, so good. The flames were confined to the engine itself, so sparing damage to the structure of the wing.

'A wing falling off wouldn't bode well,' he murmured dryly. He checked the radio. That had died, too.

Taking a deep breath, he concentrated on holding the machine steady. The stars above shone with their customary eternal steadfastness. The moon's full disk glowed with a calm radiance. The heavens had witnessed humanity slaughter its own kind too many times to reveal any dismay at the fools doing it all over again. He glanced at the two bodies. Although they were stone dead, they flinched as the lone motor sent shudders through the aircraft. Guy Forester, in the back seat, even patted his fingers against his lap, as if impatient to get home to see his wife and children.

'Patience, Guy, I'll get us back.' He tightened his grip on the quivering flight stick. 'Gentlemen, you're going home.'

With growing tension, he peered through the blood-speckled glass in front of him, searching for the coastline. The flight stick's convulsions told him that the remaining engine had begun to misfire. Its violent shaking made the plane jerk like a beast in pain.

'Come on, my sweet,' he cajoled the aircraft. 'Get my brave boys home. Courageous British bones deserve to rest in British soil.'

The engine coughed. Sparks began darting from the exhaust manifold. He leaned forward again to search the way ahead. At last. Silver ended at a line of black. That must be the coast. He dipped the nose a little so that the plane would increase in speed. As soon as he was over solid ground he'd cut the engine then glide down. He could land this thing in a cabbage patch if need be.

Even as he sighed with relief at the sight of the cliffs by moonlight, a huge snap of a sound came from his right. He turned his head to see the remaining engine toss out a ball of fire. Simultaneously, the sound of the last motor slowly died away. Soon the air rushing over the fuselage was the only noise that reached his ears. Guy's corpse still tapped his leg as if impatient to see home. The hunched back of Pat Craig juddered in imitation of panting. Benjamin knew these signs of life were fake; a result of the machine's vibration as it bounced along on turbulent air.

Still, he willed the aircraft on. Below him, an opening in the coast resembled a yawning mouth. That must be the River Esk where it flowed into the sea. So the blacked out town of Whitby had to lie beneath him.

'Told you I'd do it! You're nearly home, boys.'

Benjamin glanced at the port wing. It had begun to flap in such an exaggerated way that it resembled the flight of desperate gull. The fire had spread. Now the timber ribs that normally kept the wing rigid must be burning through.

He undid his harness. 'Sorry to leave you like this, boys. I'll see you again when we've got different kinds of wings, eh?'

Benjamin didn't want to bail, but he knew the instant that the wing broke away from the plane then he'd be dead, too. Adrenalin powered his limbs. In a blur of movement he scrambled to the back of the aircraft, kicked open the hatch, then tumbled out into the cold night air.

Benjamin Green awoke. He swayed gently. A stillness enfolded him. Cool air played over his face. After the turbulent, flaming hell of the plane, a seemingly indestructible serenity eased his mind. On opening his eyes, he saw first of all that his parachute had caught in the branches of a tall tree. The ground lay ten feet beneath his dangling boots. Moonlight illuminated the side of a valley that ran down to a sparkling river. In the distance, he could make out the ruins of Whitby Abbey, bathed in silvery radiance.

The plane had gone, of course; it had probably crashed on the hills. At least the bodies of Guy and Pat would be recovered for their funerals.

'You've done it again, Benjamin, old buddy,' he said aloud. 'You've cheated old Mister Death.'

Then he looked down to see four upturned faces. Immediately, he knew they weren't right. Strike that. They weren't even human. Their eyes were pure white, except for tiny black pupils. This imbued their gaze with a ferocious curiosity. The moonlight revealed the gaunt figures to be human-like, yet the way they stood, and the aura they radiated, was nothing less than demonic.

From his boots, blood dripped. It wasn't his; he knew that. Blood from his comrades had soaked his flying suit during the homeward journey. Now it pit-patted on to the dry soil below the tree.

The creatures stared at the drip-drip of crimson. This was a wonderful sight. It enchanted them. Then something triggered their cravings. They fell on to the blood to lap at it like thirsty lions at a waterhole. That taste excited them. They shivered with pleasure. Gasps erupted from their lips. A moment later, they leapt to their feet; they tried to reach Ben's feet to drag him from where he dangled in the tree.

Yet, they couldn't quite reach. They leapt upwards, yet always fell short.

'Get away from me!' Ben pulled his revolver from its holster.

But the idea of firing on them appalled him. *What if these are patients from a lunatic asylum? Yet their faces . . . Surely, these things aren't even human?* Confusion swirled through his mind.

Then the branch above him dipped. He glanced up to see one of the men had scaled the tree. The climber didn't bother trying to untangle the parachute harness. Instead, he simply worked his way along the branch that it had wrapped itself in. The creature's weight on the branch forced it downward. Benjamin descended with it.

The creatures below grabbed his feet. Now he did fire. The bullets pecked holes in white flesh.

The creatures flinched, but their bloodlust overrode any sensation of pain. *Him!* That's what they wanted. Nothing else mattered.

Seconds later, their combined weight broke the branches that had snagged the parachute. The instant he struck the ground, the monsters' teeth sank into his body. Hard, sharp incisors punctured his skin. The heat of their mouths burnt through the fabric of his flying suit. It felt like hot metal being pressed to his flesh. Then they sucked hard at him. Their mouths pulsated. He felt it distinctly. They were draining his blood. Waves of darkness swept through him. His limbs sagged; he could no longer fight back. Powerless to even attempt an escape, he lay limp on the ground. The pilot's friends lay dead in the mangled wreckage of the aircraft up on the moor. Soon they'd lie in peaceful sleep within the embrace of Mother Earth. But Benjamin Green would be denied even that final reward.

PART TWO

{Extract from a letter to the Whitby priest, Father Donald Mercer,
circa 1941}

Is there nothing you can do to prevent the continuation of occult practices in
the town? The innocuous sounding festival of 'Bonny Pie' that is 'celebrated'
on the first Thursday in October every year is, in truth, continuing the
ancient Norse rites of human sacrifice, albeit in a symbolic manner.
The 'Bonny Pie' was originally known as the 'Bony Pie' or, more grimly,
the 'Bone Pie'. In ancient times, this monstrous dish contained the
pulverized fragments of human skeletons.
To permit even a small number of local people to make these pagan
offerings of the 'Bonny Pie' will, without a shadow of doubt,
invite evil into our town.

One

Beth Layne thought, *We travel in darkness. We arrive in darkness.* The train journey had taken the best part of ten hours. As soon as the winter sun had set during the afternoon the train's conductors had closed all the blackout blinds in the carriages. For all they could see of the world outside, they might have been confined to a cave deep underground. At least her demands had been met by Alec Reed. Beth travelled in the company of Sally Wainwright, so sparing her a friendless journey into the north of England.

After changing at York station for the train that would take them to the Yorkshire coast, they'd had the compartment to themselves, apart from a grey-haired soldier, who spent most of the time shooting coldly disapproving glances in their direction. *Maybe our clothes are too brightly coloured for his Puritan tastes*, Beth told herself.

Sally had tried to make conversation with the soldier. 'We're going to Whitby to act in a film. But first we'll be finding the locations. Have you ever been to Whitby, sir? Can you tell us what it's like?'

He'd found her questions so shocking that he'd pointed at a poster on the compartment wall. Above a cartoon of Hitler and Mussolini hiding under a café table, where a pair of women talked about their husbands' military postings, glared a stark warning: CARELESS TALK COSTS LIVES!

The frosty soldier left the train at a place with the intriguing name of Robin Hood's Bay. After that, they were alone in the compartment for the next twenty minutes until panting, hissing, and spitting, like a bad-tempered mule, the loco hauled them into another station.

The conductor walked along the corridor calling out, 'Whitby. End of the line. Whitby. End of the line.'

'End of the line.' Sally giggled nervously. 'I hope that isn't an omen.'

Lamps inside the station building were so dim as to be near useless. Several passengers from the other carriages bumped into one another or into the pillars that supported the roof.

Sally exclaimed, 'It's so dark I can hardly see my hand in front of my face.'

'Then best not put your case down or you'll never find it again.'

Silhouettes milling round them, searching for the exit, were little more than phantom shapes in the gloom.

'Make your way to the red lantern,' came an authoritative male voice. 'You'll find the exit that opens on to Station Square. There are no taxis so you'll have to walk.'

Sally groaned, 'My case weighs a ton. And do we know where the hotel is?'

'Just a five-minute walk, or so Alec's memo tells me.' Beth's heart sank. Being dumped in a strange town at midnight, with all the street lights blacked out, threatened total disaster. 'Excuse me.' She approached a silhouette that appeared to be in uniform. 'Sir. Can you tell me the way to the Leviathan Hotel?'

'Do you know Whitby?'

'No.'

'Then God help you.'

'Pardon?'

'The Leviathan got shut up at the start of the war. You might as well wait here for the next train back to wherever you came from.'

'We're not on vacation. We're here to work.'

'You're a long way from America.'

Do I detect a note of sarcasm? Forcing herself to remain calm, she pressed on, 'Sir, my friend and I have been instructed to go to the Leviathan Hotel.'

'Your funeral. The place has been closed these last two years.' He turned to another figure. 'George. Get those mail bags on the train. She's running late as it is.'

The man began to move towards the locomotive, which gushed steam out on to the platform.

Beth persisted. 'Excuse me, I know you're busy. But will you *please* give me directions to the Leviathan Hotel?'

Even though darkness left her blind to her surroundings, she knew the man didn't even turn to face her when he snapped, 'Exit the station, turn right, then right again over the harbour bridge. If you find Church Street, you're as good as there.'

'Church Street?' Beth shuddered, recollecting that strange incident this morning, when she'd wandered into what she'd believed to be a film set of Whitby. There'd been a mock-up of Church Street, or at least she'd believed she'd seen one.

Sally tugged her arm. 'Come along, Beth. Let's get out of here. Oh, I've dropped my umbrella. I can't even see it on the ground. Damn this place. It's as dark as Hades.' Her voice quivered.

'Don't worry, Sally.' She squeezed her friend's hand. 'I'm here. We'll get you safely to the hotel, just you see.'

'But the man said it was closed.'

'He must be mistaken.'

'Beth, I hate it here. It feels all wrong. Like a bad dream . . .'

'Look, I've found your umbrella. Come on, it's time we found a nice warm bed. We'll feel better in the morning.'

They left the station to find mist creeping through the town. Turning right, as directed, they followed a road that ran alongside a river. Bitterly cold air nipped at their exposed faces. A spiky ocean scent filled Beth's nose. To avoid drawing the attention of enemy bomber pilots, the town had been completely blacked out. No lights showed through the windows. Street lights had been extinguished. No cars ran along the streets. The few people who had disembarked from the train had already vanished into alleys that led off the main road.

As they walked, arm in arm, lugging their baggage best they could, Beth tried to make out some of her surroundings. To her right, a greasy-looking river oozed towards the sea. It carried tree branches: skeletal arms that thrust outwards from its glistening surface, seemingly grasping for a route back to life, not the deep, dark grave that was the waiting ocean. Rags of mist ghosted over the waters. Although darkness engulfed the place, Beth formed an impression that they were at the bottom of a narrow, steep-sided valley. Box shapes emerging from the valley slopes, suggested a profusion of houses. Yet they were chaotic somehow. As if a demented god had flung an entire town into the valley. Now they were tenanted by a mysterious people, who accepted the crazy, higgledy-piggledy nature of their borough as being normal.

Through this ghost town of a place came a forlorn groan.

Sally stopped dead. 'Oh, God, what's that?'

'It's just the foghorn.'

'Thank goodness, I thought it was sea monster.'

A church clock announced the midnight hour.

'Sally. Don't let your imagination run away with you, or I'll end up seeing demons again.'

'*Seeing demons again?* What do you mean, "again"?'

Beth gently tugged at Sally's arm to get her walking. 'Oh, just me and my overactive imagination. Anyway, it's too late at night for spooky stories. Come on, let's find that hotel.'

'Knowing our luck it will be a witches' lair. They'll boil guests' heads for soup, and fry fingers and call them sausages.'

'And human beings will become human beans.'

'Idiot.' But Sally's tone had become lighter. 'Just remind me, are we really going to be acting in a film?'

Beth saw an opportunity to raise Sally's spirits. 'You signed the contract, didn't you? You'll be seen in cinemas here and in America. All over the place. And people will cry, "Wow, who is that beautiful brunette? She must come and star in our movies in Hollywood."'

'It's amazing. Only, I'm sure I'll forget all my lines. What is it? What's wrong?'

'We've found the bridge. And we've got our welcome party, too.'

'What do you mean?'

Beth nodded at the bridge. Around a hundred feet long, built from iron, with latticework fences, the structure spanned the river. Clearly, the bridge had a formidable mechanism that would cause it to swing open when ships needed to pass upstream. But the bridge itself wasn't the problem. Something else blocked their way.

Sally had seen it, too, for she gripped Beth's forearm. 'Maybe we can find another way across. I don't like the look of this.'

Ghostly strands of mist veiled the lone figure on the bridge. Again the foghorn cried out, long and low.

'It's just a person,' Beth insisted. 'They're not here to do us any harm.'

'How can you be sure?'

'Come on . . . we'll be alright.'

'Beth, I'm scared.'

'Sally, we must only be a minute from the hotel.' She stepped out on to the bridge. The figure at the other end took a step, too.

Beth paused. The figure halted. Beth took another step. The figure moved forwards too, as if this was a game to mirror Beth's advance across the bridge.

'They won't hurt us.' Beth spoke firmly, yet her heart clamoured. Only too vividly did she recall her encounter on the film set earlier that day. Those swift demonic figures. But all that had been imagination, hadn't it? No mock-up of Whitby had been built in the studio. Probably she'd fainted, then dreamt the whole thing. Her hand went to her head, where a lock of her hair had been caught in the passageway to Arguments Yard. The pain had been real. Her scalp still stung.

The foghorn cried out to the eternal once more. Its sound shimmered over the blacked-out town to die alone in the wilderness beyond.

'Where is everyone?' Sally uttered. 'Surely there must be some people about – going to work, that kind of thing, and why aren't there policemen out on patrol?'

'Keep walking,' Beth ordered. 'We're not going to be stopped from crossing over to the other side.'

'But I don't like her.'

'*Her?*' Then Beth noticed the female cut of the figure. Albeit one that was as tall as a man, yet brutally thin.

They continued to walk forward. The woman advanced steadily, until they faced each other in the centre of the night-time bridge.

Now Beth saw the woman clearly. The sight did nothing to ease her alarm. The thin woman wore trousers. On her top half, a jersey in dull-green wool clung tightly to her narrow torso. She wore her hair short. The leanness of her body matched the gauntness of her face. A face as white as milk. A pair of black eyebrows formed forbidding arches above her eyes. And, dear God, those eyes?

The foghorn called again. When the sound died, the silence that replaced it managed to be oppressive.

An uncanny stillness made the stranger appear to be carved out of stone. Her physical appearance suggested someone of around twenty. Yet the eyes were older than her years. This was someone who'd witnessed terrible events. Those eyes were distant, brooding – haunted by the phantoms of past experiences.

Beth and Sally attempted to ease their way past the woman; their luggage clunked against their legs. However, that silent guardian of the bridge sidestepped to block their way.

'Excuse me,' Beth said at last. 'Please let us pass.'

The figure was perfectly still once more.

'We must cross,' Sally insisted.

Beth added, 'Or is there a reason you don't want us here? Are you frightened for us? Do you want to protect us from harm?'

Sally gasped, 'Beth, why did you ask her that?'

Beth shook her head. 'A sixth sense? An instinct for self-preservation?'

The woman's lips parted; she tried to speak.

Sally cried, '*Her teeth! What's gone wrong with her teeth?*'

The foghorn flung its warning of danger over their heads.

Beth continued, 'Why don't you want us here?'

'Because nobody in their right mind would *want* to be here.' The harsh female voice didn't belong to the gaunt woman. It came from a hunched shape that bowled out of the mist. A woman of around sixty, a shawl dragged tightly around her humped shoulders, bustled up to the bridge's guardian. Roughly, she turned the thin woman round, then pushed her towards the houses on the other side. 'Whitby's no place for visitors. This ain't no pleasure resort, you know. Not in wartime. Get home, while you've got a chance.'

'Have you suffered much in the way of bombing raids?' Beth asked.

'Bombing raids? They're the least of our worries. Now get out of here. I won't tell you again.' The woman turned aggressively on the pair now. 'Why are you wandering around here at night, anyway? Menfolk here wouldn't give you a penny for whatever you're offering.'

'We're not prostitutes.'

'Could have fooled me. Decent women don't put that red muck on their lips, like you two.'

'We're actresses,' Sally told her.

'Actresses, tarts – one and the same.'

During this exchange, the gaunt woman didn't react. She remained in that trance-like state.

'We're trying to find the Leviathan Hotel.'

'Best of bloody luck to you. It's been shut these last two years.' The woman spat on the ground. 'You won't find space in a man's bed round here, even if you give it away for nothing. Now get back to the station, or I'll black your eyes!' The woman bunched her fist.

'You'll do no such thing, Mrs Brady. These are my guests.' Yet another figure emerged from the mist.

'Oh, Miss Charnwood. I shouldn't be surprised that you're in thick with these two hussies. You're the cause of this town's woes as it is.'

The new stranger murmured smoothly, 'Mrs Brady. You're letting your tongue run away with you. Of all people you should know better than to antagonize me.'

'I speak my mind. If the truth's got to be said then—'

'Goodnight, Mrs Brady. You get yourself and Victoria back home.'

Grumbling, shaking her head, while shooting the three venomous glances, Mrs Brady led Victoria over the bridge, where they soon vanished into the mist.

The tall woman, aged around forty, with a swathe of long, dark hair, held out her hand. 'Welcome to Whitby, Miss Layne. Miss Wainwright. My name is Eleanor Charnwood.'

They shook hands.

'You're expecting us?' Beth asked in surprise.

'Whitby hasn't fallen off the end of the world yet, ladies. Your director, Mr Reed, sent me a telegram to say you'd be arriving on the 11.30 train. And as I saw it pull into the station I decided to do the civilized thing and come meet you.'

Sally frowned. 'Why did the thin woman try to stop us crossing the bridge to you? And just what on earth's happened to her teeth? They were like—'

Beth interrupted, 'Standing on a fog-shrouded bridge at midnight isn't the place to discuss a stranger's dental condition.'

Smiling, Eleanor said, 'Absolutely. Now, can I help you with those cases? The hotel's just along Church Street there.'

'The Leviathan?'

'Of course.'

'But everyone here insisted it was closed for the war.'

'Not closed, only sleeping.' Eleanor's smile broadened (and Beth decided she liked the woman). 'Your film company asked me to reopen it so we could accommodate the artistes.'

'We're artistes,' Sally added quickly.

'I know. Last month I saw Miss Layne here on the silver screen at the Whitby Picture House. She served the delicious Mr Cary Grant a Martini in a tall glass, with lots of ice.' The smile became a grin. 'In these parts we get precious little Martini.'

'Or Cary Grant,' Sally exclaimed.

'Absolutely. Now come along, my dears, you must be frozen.'

'And call us Beth and Sally.'

'And I'm Eleanor, to friends, which I sincerely hope you will become. Others round here have different names for me: Wicked Witch of the East, Devil Woman, "that bloody hag".' She helped them with their baggage. 'Now, we turn left here on to Church Street.'

Beth shivered as they walked along it. The street was just as she remembered from the film set this morning. So narrow, it would barely admit a car. The upper stories of the houses leaned towards one another, as if eaves on opposing sides of the street could steal kisses from one another in the middle of the night. Beth glimpsed ancient taverns in the gloom. Cottage windows were narrow – oddly reminiscent of coffin lids standing on end. A mad comparison to be sure. Yet an impression lingered of an avenue of tombs. Even the low doorways appeared as if they'd only allow inhuman goblin creatures to enter.

Beth couldn't stop herself asking, 'I might be going insane, but I've got a question.'

'Fire at will.'

'Is there an alleyway called Arguments Yard?'

Eleanor raised a dark eyebrow. 'That's not an insane question. The answer's "yes" – it's just there on your left.'

Shock snapped along Beth's nerves. Even in darkness, she could make out the grave-black mouth of the passage, which pierced the face of a building. The entrance, low as she remembered it, exerted a formidable pull. A morbid curiosity tugged hard. Just like standing on the top of a cliff, and a voice in the back of your head murmurs, *Jump, jump, jump* . . .

'I'll be right back.' Beth darted into the Argument's Yard tunnel, which was filled with a distillation of pure night. A liquid darkness that seemed to run into her eyes and ears and mind, making her feel she might drown. Quickly, she searched for what she knew – against logic – would be there. Darkness forced her to search with her fingertips; they scurried over the timbers that supported the building; her hands resembled white spiders running back and forth against the black wood. Then . . . *Got you.*

Beth emerged to hold up her prize.

'What have you got there?' Sally asked.

'A lock of hair.'

'Hair?'

'Happens all the time.' Eleanor awarded Beth an extremely curious stare. 'The low timbers catch women's hair. It's a wonder that Whitby ladies aren't all bald.'

'You'll have to excuse my friend.' Sally tried to make a joke of the hair foraging expedition. 'She's had a very long journey. She needs her beauty sleep.'

'Then we'll get her tucked up snugly in bed. After a warming noggin of something. This way, ladies.'

Eleanor led the way to a tall free-standing building that rose from the very edge of the sea. 'Welcome to the Leviathan Hotel. I hope your stay will be a happy one.'

Beth followed. The strand of hair in her fingers resembled her own – the colour of sun-ripened wheat on a summer's day. Or in this perfidious gloom was that a trick of the eye? She paused, wondering if there was time to turn back. *This is my last chance to escape* . . .

'I've been here before.' Her voice came out strained. 'I know I have.'

'When?' Sally looked puzzled.

Eleanor unlocked the hotel door. 'Don't worry,' she said softly, 'Whitby's that kind of place. Some visit it in their dreams. Plenty have described it as an enchanted town. The old abbey on the hill is reputed to be . . . Oh no, here we go again.'

The chilling note of the air-raid siren rose into the air. It warned that enemy planes were approaching the coast.

'Instead of the comforts of the bar, all I can offer is the protection of the hotel's basement. Follow me, please.'

Eleanor carefully closed the hotel door, then she switched on the light. After that, she ushered them by the reception desk, through another door, then down a flight of stone steps into a cold tomb of a vault underground.

Two

The air-raid siren's cry rose after midnight. Its notes clawed their way to heaven before falling back to earth with a sigh. Whitby's maze of streets lay deserted. The long harbour walls extended out into the ocean – crocodile-like jaws that waited to swallow ships into the throat of the River Esk. The river waters had flowed down from the North Yorkshire moors since the end of the last Ice Age ten thousand years ago. The sirens' call, which warned of incoming aircraft, laden with murderous bombs, carried upriver, beyond the edge of town, to the ancient crossroads that had once been the site of the gallows. Here, criminals had danced at the end of the rope. After the death throes, they'd continued to swing wearily back and forth until moorland crows whittled them down to size. Often locals would steal body parts to create magic talismans, just as their Viking ancestors had done twelve hundred years ago. On the north side of the crossroads, a small field contained scabs of black stone. These were the tombs of the hanged men, the suicides, and the men and women who had died, for whatever reason, beyond the embrace of the Christian church.

As the siren continued to bray its warning, he scrambled upwards through the gap between the slab and the earth. There, he found the dog that waited patiently for him to emerge every night. Once he'd drawn himself free of the tomb, he raced, as was his habit, towards town.

Every night the boy promised himself he'd return home. The cottage, deep in the heart of Whitby, exerted an irresistible attraction. Yet, whenever he arrived there, his nerve failed him. For the people in the cottage didn't bear any similarity to his family. True, a long time ago, an old lady there had resembled his mother. Yet his mother had been young. Her red hair had been a flash of fire in sunlight. That old woman had been a shrivelled thing, with such sad eyes. Her white hair had, however, contained strands of dull orange. Then, one night, he realized she'd gone. The boy had stared at the black ribbons tied to the door knocker without understanding.

Yet he still returned to his old home in the hope he'd glimpse his parents and his sister. Then he'd rattle that big old iron knocker, while crying out joyfully, 'It's me, it's Tommy! I'm back!'

But it hadn't happened yet. The only friendship in his life was the dog he'd named Sam. This black dog, which stood nearly as high as his hip, sported a blaze of white fur running from its bottom jaw down its chest. One night, he'd seen a man tie the animal to a rock and throw it into the river. Tommy had dashed forward to shout angrily at the man (knowing he'd get a slap for his troubles), but the man had taken one look at Tommy's face, then screamed in fear. After that, he'd fled so fast that, when he'd fallen flat on his face, every last coin in his pockets had shot out on to the ground. Yet, he'd been so scared of Tommy that he hadn't stopped to pick up his money.

Tommy had jumped into the river after the dog. For a long time he'd remained underwater as he'd searched amongst the rocks. Strangely, he'd had no need to breathe. He'd found that the deep, dark waters no longer scared him (as they had done in that past time, when he didn't occupy that little hollow beneath the stone). Tommy had rescued the dog from drowning. Now they were friends. He knew that during the day the dog stayed close to the stone slab in the field near the gallows' crossroads. At night, they followed the lane into town. Frantically, he'd search the streets for his parents. Always, he'd find himself trying to look through the windows of his home. But there were only strangers indoors now. He wondered if Dad would be annoyed that they'd stayed there so long. What's more, those trespassers had changed the colour of the walls. The furniture had been replaced, too. Strange. Tommy just couldn't understand what had happened.

Tommy raced through the night-time streets. Sam effortlessly kept pace with him. Tonight, a wailing sounded over the rooftops. He'd heard it before. Sometimes, soon after the wail started, flying crosses would appear in the night sky. They'd all glide in same direction. A droning sound would come from the flying crosses. He didn't know what they were, but they troubled him. He sensed a danger throbbed inside of them.

In the town, he tried to look through windows, but they were covered with black cloth on the inside.

As he hurried to his old home, he saw that figures approached. A man in white, and another dressed in a strange-looking suit with goggles; four more men and women ran with them. They had white, blazing eyes and were eager to reach their destination. In fact, so eager that they brushed Tommy aside as if they'd not seen him. Sam barked furiously. The runners had already vanished into the alley-ways.

Tommy wasn't hurt. Nowadays, nothing hurt him, unless you can describe missing your parents and your sister as hurting. After stroking Sam for while to soothe him, he sensed he should leave the town behind for tonight. That hole in the ground at Gallows Crossroads could have been calling his name; its pull became irresistible. So he turned his back on the town. Overhead, black crosses appeared. A mournful drone grew louder. As he passed by a cemetery one of the crosses dropped a silver object: a cylinder, which screamed to earth, to plunge into the graves. An enormous bang followed.

Tommy watched the explosion rip open tombs. Coffin wood, skulls, bones – they all rushed into the sky. Up, up went the dark pall of debris before cascading back down again. The boy observed all this without any real interest. Strange events occurred all the time now. It was as if he'd become separated from the ordinary world and from reality. Nothing really impacted on his life now. That is, apart from Sam, so he hugged the frightened dog. Soft fur pressed against the side of his face as he murmured, 'Don't worry, boy. I'll look after you.'

Once the dog had stopped trembling, Tommy left the steaming crater in the cemetery and trudged back to his resting place beneath the stone.

Three

Beth Layne woke the moment the bomb fell. There first came a deep thud. Just after that, something that resembled thunder. Beth sat in an armchair in the hotel basement. Sally had gone to sleep on a bench against one wall. As always, when Sally woke with a start (as she did now), she looked as anxious as a child. The unfamiliar surroundings startled her.

'Beth . . . Beth! Where are we?'

'Don't worry, you're safe. We've arrived at the hotel in Whitby.'

'Uh . . .' Sally rubbed her eye. 'I dreamt we were still on that train. I thought we'd never get here. Where's the owner?'

'I don't know. The moment I sat down here I fell asleep. I can't believe how exhausted I was by the journey.'

Sally sniffed. 'There must be something in the sea air. I can't even remember closing my eyes. Uh, my shoulder's sore from lying on this hard wood.'

Beth checked her watch. They'd been in the basement for more than an hour. The sirens no longer wailed. The falling bomb, however, had been shockingly loud. *It must have been a close one*, she thought, with a shiver, *but I won't tell Sally that. There's no point in scaring her.*

'I hope we won't be down here much longer.' Sally shuddered. 'It's a scary tomb of a place. I keep expecting Boris Karloff to walk in.'

'At least we're safe from the air raid, that's the important thing.' Yet Beth had to agree. This was one creepy pit, alright. The basement roof and walls consisted of dull red-brick from which cobwebs fluttered. *It would make the ideal dungeon,* she told herself. She could just imagine half-starved prisoners chained to the walls. The only light came from a bare bulb fixed to the ceiling. Even the light didn't want to venture into the corners, lest it find something frightening there. She'd not seen shadows like these before, which pooled in the recesses of the walls. They possessed a liquid darkness. *Shadows in Whitby aren't like shadows found anywhere else,* she thought. *Whitby shadows can pour out of their lairs to engulf victims. Whitby shadows drown you . . .*

She clenched her fists. *Why am I letting my imagination run away with me like this?* Her mind swam with the strange events of the day. The Whitby set in the studio that never actually existed. Her being

pursued by those demon creatures (which couldn't have existed, either
– could they?); then the arrival at this strange coastal town. One that
seemed to have landed here from some occult realm. Then she'd
found the hair in the entrance to Arguments Yard. What if . . .

'Beth? Anyone home?'

'Pardon?'

Sally shook her head. 'You were miles away.'

'Sorry. I can hardly keep my eyes open.'

'Only you could sleep through a bombing raid.'

'The planes must have gone by now.'

'Did you hear me? When I told you what I'd found? Look.'

Beth saw that Sally had bent at the waist to examine an object
on the floor. It resembled another of those liquid-looking shadows.
Sally's eyes were wide with wonder. And what was happening to
her hair? The curls fluttered. Some were straightened out to stream
upwards.

'Isn't this weird?' Sally exclaimed. 'Where do you think it goes?'

Fully awake now, Beth left her armchair to approach the puddle
of shadow. To her surprise she saw an iron grate set in the floor.
The thick rust suggested its great age. And the size of it? Easily as
large as a house door, it could have served as the barred gate to a
prison cell. Sally crouched in order to gaze down through the bars.

'Feel that air rushing through?' Sally exclaimed. 'It smells of the
sea. Do you think it leads down to the harbour?'

A voice cracked across the basement, 'Keep away from that. It's
dangerous.'

They turned to see the owner of the hotel sweep towards them.

'You! Sally!' she snapped. 'Get back from it. Right back. I don't
want you anywhere near it.'

'But I only wanted to see if—'

'Keep away! I won't have your death on my conscience.'

Sally appeared so stung by the flurry of stinging words that Beth
flew to her defence. 'Stop that! Sally was only curious.'

'Believe me, curiosity in this town gets you into serious trouble.'
Eleanor advanced from the shadows, carrying a tray on which there
was a silver coffee pot and mugs. She set them down on the table.

Beth continued, 'So you own this hotel, it doesn't give you the
right to berate my friend like she's a stupid child.'

Eleanor jabbed a finger at the grate. 'I hate that bloody thing. It
scared me to death as a child. Every time I came come down here
on an errand I convinced myself that either I'd fall down it, or a

great hulking Frankenstein thing would push open the grate and grab hold of me.' She steadied her evidently jangled nerves with a deep breath. 'There is a horrible monster down here.' A smile played on her lips. 'And that monster is Miss Eleanor Charnwood, hotelier, spinster, and thoroughly bad-tempered woman.' She offered Sally a hank of her hair. 'Go on, pull. Pull it really hard. I deserve it.'

Sally appeared startled at being invited to torture the woman. Then she laughed when she realized that Eleanor was making a joke of her own outburst. 'No, I'll do no such thing, Eleanor. You were frightened for my safety, that's all.'

'Then we're all friends again?' She positioned the mugs on the table.

Sally gushed, 'Oh yes, absolutely.'

Beth nodded. *This is an unusual woman,* she decided. *She's got a wacky sense of humour, but she seems to be wearing a mask. The real Eleanor is concealed underneath. I'm sure of it.* Allowing herself a smile, also, Beth decided she must remain on guard. Something didn't ring true about Eleanor Charnwood. Beth glanced around the basement. 'So – this is where you dispose of the bodies?' A joke with a serious question in the centre. Not that Beth suspected Eleanor to be a murderer, but that macabre quip might help dislodge the mask.

'Oh, definitely.' She picked up the coffee pot. 'At night I hoist up the big iron trap-door and drop them into the tunnel below. All those men who told me they loved me, but had every intention of sneaking out of the back door, never to return. No coffee, alas, but I have made hot chocolate.' She poured steaming liquid into the mugs.

'Eleanor.' Sally beamed. 'You've got a devilish sense of humour.'

'Indeed I have, my dear. It keeps me sane in this insane world. Well, this insane hotel, really. Every night I say a little prayer to the patron saint of bomber pilots to drop a five-hundred-pounder on the bloody roof. Then freedom, delicious freedom.'

'But you said you lived here as a child?'

'Indeed. Born here, I was. Along with my brother. Hotels are in the Charnwood blood. My cousin runs one in Leppington, just a few miles from here. My brother and I inherited when Mother died.' She tilted her head, listening. The cool flow of air from the iron grate toyed with her hair. 'The bombers must have got tired of Whitby and gone home. Anyway, we should be safe here. The masonry's awful thick. Thicker than a tomb, no doubt.'

Sally accepted the hot chocolate with a grateful sigh. 'So where does the tunnel go? The one you chuck your lovers into?'

'Beneath the grate is a pit that goes down seven feet, or so. It connects to a tunnel that runs about twenty yards in that direction.' She pointed at a wall. 'It opens out under one of the harbour quays. In years gone by, boatmen used it to deliver French brandy into the vaults of the hotel. Whitby was a haven for smugglers way back when. At high tide the sea comes rushing in to fill the tunnel – don't worry, it doesn't come up the shaft very far. You won't wake up to find your beds floating, or sharks biting your toes.' Beneath the ironwork, those liquid shadows filled the pit. 'My grandfather used to joke that you could dangle a baited line down there and catch a fish for your supper. Come on, drink your chocolate while it's hot. Brrr, cold as the grave down here, isn't it?'

'It must be lonely living in a hotel when it's not in use,' Beth said.

'Oh, I'm not on my lonesome, dear. Theo, my brother, lives here, too.'

Sally's eyes widened in shock. 'Then why isn't he down here? We don't know for sure if the bombing has stopped.'

'Wild horses won't drag him down here.' Her smile became artificial.

Ah ha, Eleanor, the mask is starting to slip.

The woman covered her change in expression by topping up their mugs again, while telling them it was difficult to get drinking chocolate, now the rationing of groceries was becoming severe. She added it was also near impossible to buy timber, because she wanted to lay stout boards over the iron grate in the floor. 'It's badly rusted. I don't want my guests falling through.'

'And joining your old lovers.'

'Sally, my thoughts exactly.' The easy smile returned. 'And you're to star in a film? And my hotel will be home for an entire troupe of actors? How exciting. Have you learnt your lines yet?'

Beth said, 'We've got the scripts, but Sally and I also have the task of finding locations for the filming.'

'By all means, use the hotel. And let me know if I can be of any help in helping you scout suitable places to shoot your picture.'

'Perhaps you could be in it?' Sally gushed.

'Really?'

'And your brother.'

Again, a slip of the mask. 'Ah, no, he's not the acting sort.'

'Camera shy, Eleanor?' Beth wanted the question to dig through the mask.

Eleanor simply shrugged. 'He's not in the best of health, unfortunately. He stays in his own place. A little cottage in the hotel yard.' She set her mug down. 'So what's your film about, ladies?'

Beth told her, 'It's called *This Midnight Realm*. The government want to show the rest of the world how ordinary British families cope with day-to-day life in wartime. In this case, the families will be from Whitby.'

'And you'll be playing these ordinary Whitby folk?'

'Yes.' Sally grinned. 'I'm playing a wayward daughter – she lives for dancing the night away.'

Eleanor gave a long *Hmm*. 'I would be careful what you tell the locals. One thing they won't take kindly to is what they see as pampered actors and actresses from London pretending to be them.'

'I'm not from London,' Sally protested. 'I'm from Wakefield, and that's Yorkshire, too, like Whitby.'

'Nevertheless. I'd keep the film's plot a secret, if you can, otherwise the locals will think you're making fun of them. Then, believe me, they'll turn hostile.'

'We'll deal with it,' Beth told her.

'Good, because once they turn nasty on you they'll try and wreck your filming.'

'We saw some of the hostility tonight,' Beth said.

'Ah, Mrs Brady and her daughter.'

Sally exclaimed, 'The poor girl's teeth. They looked so strange. I mean . . . they were really tiny in her mouth. Like a baby's milk teeth. And I've never seen teeth as white as that before.'

'Ah . . .' Eleanor collected the mugs on to the tray. 'When Victoria was eighteen she got some kind of fever. She never fully recovered. There was an outbreak of it in the town about twenty years ago.'

Beth raised an eyebrow. 'Twenty years ago? But Victoria didn't look much more than twenty herself.'

Another siren sounded. This one differed to the rising and falling cry that warned of imminent attack. The alert started with a very low note that rose into a sustained call across the town.

'There goes the all clear.' Eleanor clapped her hands together. 'I'll get you to your rooms.'

Sally checked her watch. 'Two o'clock in the morning. At least we should be able to get a few hours' sleep. God willing.'

Four

Mary Tinskell needed to escape her husband. If only she could put on her best coat, then walk smartly down to the station and board a train that would take her from him and his wearying obsession. Harry played darts. Only, it went beyond that. Those diminutive arrows were his life. Once she, Mary, had been his life, and the children, of course. But now darts, darts, darts. That's all he ever thought about, talked about and probably dreamt about. Oh, he played well, no doubting that. Harry challenged men in the local pubs. Invariably, he won the wagers of beer, which pleased him no end.

'I went out with exactly the same money I came back with,' was his proud boast (accompanied by waves of beery breath).

Only, it had reached the point where he'd come home, after the pub had closed, to practise darts for hours in the front parlour of their cottage on Henrietta Street. That monotonous thud-thud-thud of darts hitting the board at gone two in the morning had driven Mary outside in desperation. She had to escape that sound; the infuriating man would send her crazy!

So, as the clock hands crept beyond a quarter past two, Mary stood in a calf-length nightdress in the cold winter air in the rear yard. This row of houses backed on to the cliff, which soared eighty feet or so above her, to the graveyard. The night lay still after the air raid (such attacks didn't discourage Harry from playing darts; his new monotonous refrain was, 'If Hitler wants my darts, he'll have to cut my bloody fingers off to get 'em'). She inhaled the chilly sea air. If she got herself cold enough, then even the *clump* of darts, coming from downstairs, might not seem that bad once she'd slid beneath warm bedclothes.

Mary smoothed the white cotton of her nightdress. At forty years of age she had an enviable figure. More than once, it had occurred to her if Harry's dart obsession grew too much she'd be able to find another husband.

Mary moved around the tiny yard, which was enclosed by high walls. The moon had emerged once more. It revealed the bulbous swellings in the rock face. She blew into her numbed hands. *This is insanity*, she told herself. *I can't let Harry drive me outside. Even yard dogs have kennels. Here I am, freezing in a nightdress.* Probing fingers of air slid around her bare legs. Her skin went bumpy across her chest. Shivers darted down her backbone. The cold grew just too intense. She couldn't stand it any more. When she exhaled, a gust of white blossomed round her head.

As she crossed the yard towards the cottage door, she happened to glance upwards. Moonlight had emphasized those raised bumps in the cliff face. The rocky protrusion seemed to hang directly above her head.

Then the rocky outcrops did something they'd never done before. They moved.

Mary Tinskell stepped into the centre of the yard, staring upwards; only, the harder she stared, trying to identify what those shadowy bumps were, the more the cold made her eyes water. Was the cliff falling? Images flashed through her head of boulders crashing down on to her cottage.

Yet the moving objects made no sound. She blinked until her eyes were clear. Her vision snapped into sharp focus. Those objects clung to the cliff face as they swiftly climbed downwards.

And they descended towards Mary in the yard.

She moved backwards, keeping her gaze locked on the four figures climbing down the cliff. But they climbed head first. And with such speed. Twenty feet above her one of the climbers paused. It raised its head to look at her. She saw a man, wearing pilot's goggles. His face was smeared with a dark liquid. Moonlight made the goggle lenses shine silver. Yet she knew with absolute certainty that he stared at her.

Mary spun round, then raced for the door. Only to find it blocked by a figure. This one she recognized. Dressed in a white shirt, and wearing a striped tie round his waist like it was a belt, was a man she'd seen often in her youth.

'Gustav Kirk?' Her heart raced. 'But you went missing twenty years ago.'

He took a single step forwards. Behind her came soft concussions as the cliff climbers dropped the last few feet into the yard.

'Don't you dare touch me.' Mary had detected the predatory menace in their postures. 'Don't you dare!'

The figures approached, eyes ablaze with ferocity, their faces smeared with a rich, dark liquid that could be nothing else but blood. In the moonlight, there seemed precious little colour to their irises. If anything, each eye simply contained a fierce black pupil.

Gustav reached out to touch the side of her neck. The cold-as-ice sensation of his fingers on her bare skin did it. In an explosion of movement, she raced through the alleyway to Henrietta Street beyond. If the back door was blocked, she could beat on the front door to alert her husband.

Yet the creatures anticipated her move. And yes they were creatures . . . They were inhuman . . . No living humans possessed eyes like that. When she dashed towards the front door Gustav smoothly sped by her to block the way. He smiled. His teeth were tiny yet perfectly shaped. The other creatures possessed the same kind of teeth, as if God in a moment of reckless abandon had snatched up different animals, then moulded them into something that, at least outwardly, resembled a man.

Running became her mission. Nothing less. If her feet pounded the cobbled street, then it proved she hadn't been caught yet. Because that was her intention. She knew they wanted to lay hands on her. To bundle her roughly away. But what then? What would they do with her? Creatures like that? What brought them pleasure?

Mary raced long Henrietta Street. At this time of night, bathed in moonlight, not a soul graced it. Houses to her left lay in darkness. To her right the hillside flowed down to the vast expanse of harbour waters. And behind her, softly padding feet. Gustav and his monstrous companions were in full-blooded pursuit. Maybe they enjoyed the chase? Did they savour her fear as they closed in?

Mary sped down towards town. Ancient cottages grew more tightly clustered. The incline added to her speed so she kept running downwards. Instead of joining the level ground of Church Street, she sped down Tate Hill. Only, this led to the beach. The tide had rolled in, flooding the sands. So Mary dashed out along the stone pier. Little more than eight feet wide, it jutted out into the waters of the harbour. A bridge to nowhere.

Keep running. That's all that mattered. Maybe she could elude her pursuers yet. She raced along the tongue of stone. At the end, she kept running. Her heart had become this huge, pounding engine in her chest. Adrenalin filled her veins with fire. In that heightened state, the moon burnt like the torch of the gods in the sky. The ocean became a luminous silver highway all of its own. Nightdress flapping, hair rippling wildly, Mary leapt, then flew outwards, her face turned up to the stars and the moon.

The sea took her into itself. It embraced her tightly as a lover. Its cold fingers explored every inch of her body in a split second.

For a moment, she tried hard to swim in the direction of the bridge. However, the tide had turned. Roughly, the current bore her back to the stone pier; there, she buffeted against its stone blocks.

Instantly, hands seized her from above. Gustav, the pilot, and the others, swiftly drew her from the water. She lay dripping in their arms, as they carried her into a secret, shadowed place, where they could do whatever they wanted to her.

But there in the night a strange thing happened. Yes, horror engulfed her. No doubting that. But there was something else, too. A thrill she'd never felt before. Excitement snapped through her veins; an electricity of forbidden desires burst through her English reserve.

She moaned as they fought to be first to clamp their mouths on to her body. The bites were a sweet pain of release. Memories of her life with her husband roared through her head. The confinement in the cottage to cook and clean. The dull monotony. The loss of hope that things would change for the better one day. The never-ending thud . . . thud . . . thud of darts in the board, which could have been nails being slowly hammered into the coffin of a loveless marriage.

When those small, razor-sharp teeth released blood from her veins, she roared with a vicious pleasure. Then, as consciousness began to fade, she pictured Harry's face as he admired his beloved darts . . . and the final words that slipped through her soon-to-be inhuman lips were:

'*I'm free . . .*'

Five

Unable to sleep, Eleanor Charnwood descended into the hotel's basement. A clock in reception chimed four in the morning as she gritted her teeth against the icy flow of air within the underground vault. She passed the huddle of chairs, where she'd sheltered from the air raid earlier with her new guests. In the corner of the cellar, she tugged back an old rug she'd used to hide a line of gallon jars in thick glass. Pasted on each one, a label that bore a skull and cross bones sign. Beneath that the word: *DANGER!* Because of the war, everything (but fear and want) was in short supply. It had become increasingly difficult to acquire more stocks of the chemical, but she knew she must. So far she'd bought a dozen gallons on the black market. However, she reckoned on needing at least another dozen more, if she were to stand any chance of success.

Donning thick protective gloves, she tugged the jars deeper into the basement, where she could lock them in the wine cellar. Until a couple of weeks ago, she'd not anticipated that the hotel would be opened up again to paying guests. At first she'd resisted; an official from the Ministry of Information, however, made it absolutely clear to her that if she didn't make the hotel available to the film people it would be requisitioned anyway. That would spell disaster for Eleanor's plans. In a matter of days, the place would be bustling with actors. She couldn't even keep them out of the basement, because it served as the air raid shelter. So, no time like the present to move her precious hoard.

Eleanor had dragged five of the heavy jars to the subterranean store when she heard a voice.

'Eleanor . . . Eleanor . . . It's me.'

She paused only for a second. Then, taking a deep breath to steady her resolve, she continued her work. There was barely enough time to make the preparations as it was. Many a time, she'd find herself becoming increasingly moody, as she worried about all the jobs she needed to do in order to carry out her plan. The enormity of the task left her anxious, flustered, in fact so on edge that she wanted to yell at anyone who called at the hotel.

Now that voice . . . She'd heard it at least once every twelve months for the last twenty years. It started just weeks after she visited Hag's Lung Cave with that shy, dreamy youth. The one who loved nothing more than to find some sheltered corner of the beach to read his treasured books.

'Eleanor?'

She continued working. *Go away*, she thought. *I'm busy. I'll never get this done.*

'Eleanor. I know you're there. Why have you never spoken to me? For twenty years I've come back here in the hope you'll discuss what happened.'

She dragged more of the hefty jars full of that fiercely toxic brew to the storeroom.

'Eleanor.' The voice shimmered from some other world, or so it seemed to her. 'Do you remember what happened that night at the cave? You put your arm into the hole; something bit you on the wrist.

When you fainted I carried you outside. Then I went back into Hag's Lung. It was a stupid thing to do, but I wanted to know what lay beyond the hole in the cave wall. I widened it with the crowbar, then I put my eye to it to try and see inside. What a foolish boy I was, Eleanor.' He paused. 'Will you tell me about your wrist? What happened?'

In the shadows of the basement, she couldn't stop herself sliding back the sleeve of her pullover. On her wrist, eight open wounds. They'd never healed since she'd been bitten there twenty years ago. The punctures resembled tiny open mouths, with delicately pink lips. The holes, arranged so − :::: − extended deep inside the flesh. Most nights they itched . . . a furious itching.

'They bit me, Eleanor. But you were never infected. Not like me and the rest. Why do you think you're immune, Eleanor?' A pause. 'Please talk to me.' The soft, whispery voice continued until it resembled the throb of surf on the beach just yards from the hotel. 'Please talk to me. I want to see your face. You were the only girl who didn't make fun of me at school. Listen, I've told you this before. Myself, and the other ones, have tried so hard not to feed. If we ingest human blood it speeds the transformation in our bodies. We have tried to resist. But it's getting difficult. Bodies of sailors are washed up on the beach, the blood still fresh in their veins. It's this war. It delivers prey to us. We try not to feed on it, but it's difficult to resist. Sometimes airmen fall out of the sky. It's like a hungry child, standing in an orchard, with ripe apples dropping from the trees into its hands. Help us, Eleanor, we need you.'

Don't do it, don't do it! You've promised yourself you'll never talk to him.

But those incessant pleas − 'Talk to me. Help us.' − and the power of the sheer sorrow in those words overwhelmed her self-restraint. She set the jar down, then marched to the iron grate. And there he was. Gustav Kirk stood beneath it. His hands clenched about the bars. His bone-white face peered up through the gaps at her. The fierce black pupils locked on hers.

'You left me in the cave!' *Traitorous mouth.* She'd tried so hard to ignore Gustav all those times before, when he'd crept along the tunnel. 'You abandoned me to them!' She flashed the wounds at him. 'They've never healed. So how could I ever marry a man with these marks of damnation?'

'I didn't leave you. The candle went out so I had to go get my bag. The matches were there. Eleanor, I saved you.'

'Saved me for a life of hell, you mean!'

She fled to the stairs.

'Eleanor! Help us! We're going to do something terrible – and we can't stop ourselves. Eleanor! Don't go!'

Six

The milk-white eyes of the Vampiric men and women had adapted well to darkness. And though not so much as a glimmer escaped the houses of Whitby town, these night creatures saw the buildings spread out beneath them perfectly.

There were six now. They stood in the cliff-top cemetery that overlooked the harbour and the chaotic scatter of tightly clustered rooftops. The pilot rested his hand on a tombstone and realized he'd cheated death once and for all. Mary gazed down at her old home eighty feet beneath her. In her heart of hearts, she knew she'd escaped the drudgery of everyday life. Changes were taking place in both her body and her mind, yet the overriding emotion was one of pleasure. She was free. And she loved that sensation. No more domestic chores. No more being tied to the house. Licks of white, glistening ice formed on the gravestones. Grass became crisp underfoot. Mary's nightdress still dripped from her fall into the sea. Cold couldn't reach her now. The crunch of frosted grass against her bare toes didn't bother her one jot.

Behind them, the squat, block shape of St Mary's Church. And behind that lay the ruins of the abbey. This monastic relic consisted of skeletal structures, bereft of a roof, yet containing vast arched openings that had once been the abbey windows. Keen Vampiric eyes glimpsed spiral staircases in the remains of the abbey's towers, which had once taken the monks that bit closer to heaven; now the broken staircases led to nowhere. Those ferociously sharp eyes also detected subtle mounds in the earth where the ancient Viking temple stood.

Gustav, even in the days when he was still human, sensed that the old gods had returned to the temple site in the hope that humanity hadn't forgotten them. But now Odin and his clan were shunned. They hadn't lingered long, and they'd soon returned to wherever spurned gods dwell. But a yet more ancient deity, the one known as Tiw, was as mysterious and unknowable to the Vikings as it was to modern Man. And Tiw was psychotically tenacious.

Often Gustav had stood up here in the cliff-top cemetery. In his mind's eye, both as a human and the vampire-like creature he'd become, he imagined Tiw pacing between this high point above Whitby and the abandoned, and very much neglected, pagan temple.

Tiw's rage poisoned the soil. It made even the worms bite like vipers. Fury blazed itself into the very rock. The profile of his brooding face could be glimpsed in the cliffs. Tiw — bitter from neglect, insane from anger — nurtured plans of revenge against the human race. They were fools to scorn this primeval Viking god. They ignored him at their peril.

The creatures were still hungry. Tiw now ensured that never again would they be satisfied with a mouthful of crimson from a sheep's vein. Tiw inflamed their appetites.

Driven by hunger, the six moved by instinct. The path took them through the graveyard to an anti-aircraft gun in a meadow beyond the abbey precinct.

Something would happen soon. The six Vampiric minds could sense it. Gustav had felt this tension in the air before. As if electricity had begun to spark across its very atoms. Did it herald Tiw reaching from his world into this one? *Soon . . . It's coming . . . Hurry . . .* The six moved swiftly now. They could almost smell the approaching event, just as wolves catch the scent of an injured deer in the wood. Their mouths became wet. They would feed again soon. They were sure of it. But where exactly?

Two hundred yards away, the crew that manned the anti-aircraft gun began to move ammunition back to the bunker some thirty yards from the emplacement. Sunrise lay just an hour away. It was unlikely that the Nazi bombers would attack now, as it would require a daytime return journey to their bases in Germany. Daylight would leave them vulnerable to attack from allied fighters. Therefore, by day, only a minimal amount of ammunition would be kept near the gun itself.

The corporal picked up the heavy shell. At over a foot long these brass cylinders, full of explosives, could only be moved one at a time. You carried them just as you would a newborn baby, cradling it gently in your arms. The corporal had followed this route dozens of time. The pathway had been marked out by white posts on to which had been painted spots of luminous green paint. The green dots resembled little gleaming eyes in the darkness. Yet they would guide the soldier safely to the ammo store. One of the men behind him hummed a song that was irritatingly tuneless.

The corporal's stomach rumbled as hunger pangs set in. Dear God in heaven, he could almost taste his morning plateful of bacon, fried eggs and mushrooms. To that, he'd add hunks of bread, a mug of tea. Then the first glorious cigarette of the day. He longed for that dizzying rush to the head as he inhaled deeply, gratefully, blissfully . . .

The corporal stopped dead, the shell lying heavy in his arms. *Strange.* That had never happened before. He'd been so engrossed in such an enticing image of breakfast that he'd wandered off the path marked by the white posts. He blinked in the darkness. The green, luminous spots on the posts all lay off to his left. Nearby, a soldier still hummed the odd-sounding ditty.

'Hey, is that you, Sparky?' he called.

The soldier continued to hum without answering.

'Who is it, then? Yes, you, laddie. The one who's grunting the God-awful noise.' Wrapped in darkness, the humming figure consisted of shadow, nothing else. 'Well, whoever you are, go back to the gun and tell them to bring the torch. I'm off the pathway in rough ground. I'm not risking carrying this thing back.' He hugged the shell to his chest. 'It's about as flat as a flaming mountain range here.'

The figure stopped humming. Then, as if his presence was no longer required, he retreated into the night. A smooth withdrawal, like the man, if indeed he was a mortal man, didn't need to use his legs.

The rest of the gun crew had returned to pull a canvas sheet over the weapon. Like bats and nightwatchmen, the anti-aircraft guns usually slept by day.

'Hey. Shine a light, boys.' But for some reason they couldn't hear the corporal. 'You all gone deaf?' Although only forty yards away, not one man showed any sign of hearing his shout. 'They're playing silly beggars,' he said. 'Just wait till I get back. I'll roast their ears off.'

The corporal took a careful step towards the line of white posts that marked safely level ground. So far so good. He took another step. And another.

The next step robbed him of the earth beneath his foot. A hollow, or a rabbit hole. He managed a curse of irritation. Then he lost his balance and fell forward.

The weight of his body on top of the high-explosive shell slammed it down hard. His last impression, the curved cylinder smacking against his ribs. Then came the detonation. It cast his body parts for more than fifty yards. Blood joined the frost to paint the grass in the meadow, long streaks of red and white.

As the gun crew ran to get help from their comrades further along the cliff, six figures raced into this scene of gory devastation. The man's blood had been widely dispersed, for sure, but they relished every sip of the red stuff.

Gradually, the sun rose over Whitby. The start of an extraordinary day.

Tuesday.

PART THREE

{*Lady Catherine Fitzroy's letter to her sister, December 15, 1851*}

*Such a barbaric act! The entire household is in clamour. You should see
the expression on our dear Uncle's face — for, as magistrate, he had to
preside over the execution. I sincerely hope there are no more public
hangings in Whitby. Even though the wretch was delivered to the gallows
before sunrise, the townsfolk appeared en masse. They laughed and
caroused as if it were a piece of theatre. They did not cease their vulgar
merriment until the entire proceedings ended in disaster.
You see, a certain young man had been condemned to death for breaking
into houses on the waterfront and biting the occupants. When the jailors
brought him, hands firmly shackled, to the scaffold platform, the crowd all
began to shout very loudly at once, 'VAMPYRE! VAMPYRE!' The
very instant the priest asked him to accept Christ as his saviour
he snarled with the ferocity of a demon. Well, the hangman placed the
noose around the prisoner's neck, and the fellow tried to bite his hand.
After that, the hangman didn't even try and hood the man. Instead, he
pulled the trap lever. Down went the prisoner! The rope snapped tight!
Often that kills instantly; you see, the neck is broken, indeed the wrench
of the noose can often decapitate. Yet, the young man writhed at the end of
the rope. Again, this may occur when a person is hanged. However, the
death throes that produce that 'dancing on air' soon subside. Not in this
case, dear sister. The hanged man writhed at the end of the rope. His feet
kicked. The grimacing of his face made a number of ladies swoon fully
away. Twenty minutes later, he appeared more vigorous in his bodily
contortions than ever. He even freed his wrists from the manacles. Now
there was a real danger he'd escape from the noose to unleash his
fury on the crowd. Men and women fled back into town.
The cries they made! The panic!
That's when Uncle ordered his men to unsheathe their sabres. Such a
brutal aftermath. I withdrew to the carriage. But those shouts, my sister!
Those screams! They'll remain with me until my hour of dying. Later, I
overheard the servants say that parts of the Vampyre still squirmed in the
sacks, as they were cast into the sea. May God preserve us.*

One

He bowled into the hotel with all the grandeur of a victorious general.

'Good morning, Beth. Good morning Sally.'

Alec Reed had spotted the pair through the open doorway of the dining room, where they were eating breakfast. He marched through the doorway, sweeping off his broad-brimmed hat as he did so. The black eyepatch still covered the wounded eye. Today, enthusiasm roared through him, adding a decibel or so to his Scottish accent.

Beth found herself smelling the air for the tell-tale whiff of gin, a spirit that might account for his grandiose manner.

'Any sign of the hotel staff?' he boomed. 'I've left my luggage in the doorway.'

'Best bring it in yourself,' Beth told him. 'There's only a staff of one, and I think the lady is with her brother.'

'Any chance of a cup of tea? I'd swear all those hills and moors have been piled up round Whitby to keep outsiders from ever getting here. It took the trucks over an hour to cover ten miles.'

Beth poured him the tea. 'So you've arrived with your battalion of film-makers? Add your own sugar, Alec.'

'Isn't it exciting?' Sally scrunched her shoulders. 'But how on earth are you going to get those trucks full of cameras and lights along this little street? You can hardly get a wheelbarrow down it.'

'Thank Providence we did our research. The crew are staying in a guest house in the wonderfully named Boghall. There's a secure yard for the vehicles, too. We can't have those expensive cameras vanishing into the hills.' Swishing his hat against his thigh to remove drops of moisture, he kicked a chair away from the table and sat down. 'Ye Gods. We had to sleep in the trucks at Malton last night. The police wouldn't let us cross the damn moor at night. I'm whacked.' He took an interest in the breakfast plates. 'Is that toast going spare?'

Sally beamed. 'Help yourself. There's the butter. I'm sure I can find eggs in the kitchen if you'd like—'

'Don't go usurping Eleanor's role, Sally.' Beth smiled as she spoke firmly. 'I'm sure she won't allow our esteemed film director to starve.'

He layered butter on the toast. 'You've both settled in?' He surged on without waiting for a reply. 'Today's Tuesday, isn't it? Good.

The cast will arrive a week today by train. They're lodging here with us. Any luck in finding those shooting locations?'

'Hardly. We only arrived here last night,' Beth told him.

'All locations have to be fixed by Thursday at the latest. By then, I'll be having the cameraman shoot some establishing shots of the town. Mainly the picturesque stuff – harbour, churches, quaint taverns, cute bairns playing hopscotch. Any more tea? My throat's become a veritable Sahara.'

'Don't worry, Alec.' Beth's voice hardened. 'It's all in hand.'

Sally added, 'Eleanor's kindly agreed to give us a tour of Whitby this morning. She knows some lovely places to film.'

'I didn't know Eleanor was on the payroll.'

'She owns the hotel.' Beth's irritation grew. Alec Reed had become bombastic again. She sniffed for gin. 'She's also very nice and very helpful.'

'Good. Because I need her to provide an office. I want access to a phone and a typewriter. The Ministry require a major change to the script. It seems our film of ordinary men and women being the heroic embodiment of the British bulldog spirit has become *too* ordinary for them. They want me to introduce a larger-than-life hero: a lifeboat man, who has to brave a storm in order to rescue passengers from a torpedoed ship. It will add five days to the shooting schedule. Thank goodness, the government are funding the overrun. Is that the last of the sugar?' He emptied the remaining grains from the sugar pot into his cup.

'Sugar's rarer than pearls, remember? Along with just about every-thing else.' Beth added, 'You need to hand your ration book to Eleanor when you check in.'

'You've just finished our day's sugar ration.' Sally grinned. 'But it doesn't matter. I want to keep off sugar. It goes straight to my waist.'

Alec leaned towards Beth as if about to kiss her. 'Check for yourself.'

'Excuse me?'

'Yesterday, you accurately detected the whiff of mother's ruin.'

'It's not my job to dry you out.'

'But I shouldn't be boozing at nine in the morning, even if it was medicinal.' He touched the eyepatch.

'How is it?'

'The eye? Want to look for yourself?'

'Ugh!' Sally pulled a face. 'Is it really bad?'

He raised his hand to the eyepatch, as if to flip it up.

Beth dabbed her mouth with a napkin. 'I suspect Alec is showing us our place in his team. He wants us to know that he is our lord and master.' She stood up. 'And he wants us to be afraid of him.'

Sally shuffled uncomfortably in the seat, knowing that the seeds of another argument had been planted. 'Beth. We should be getting ready.' The sound of a door shutting gave her another reason to divert the confrontation. 'That must be Eleanor. Alec will have time to check into his room before we leave.'

As Sally stood up, so did Alec to give a polite bow. 'Ladies. Thank you for your company. And I'll see you get the sugar back.'

Sally laughed, relieved that the impending awkwardness had been avoided. 'Oh, we're sweet enough.'

'I'm sure you are.'

'Come with me, I'll introduce you to Eleanor. You'll love her.'

'Indeed?'

The pair left the room.

Sally laughed at everything Alec said, Beth realized. The same kind of giggle schoolgirls use when they have a crush on a teacher. She decided to wait for Sally so they could go up to their rooms together to collect their coats. For a while, she examined framed photographs on the walls. There were scenes of old-time Whitby: sailing ships in the harbour; a paddle-steamer being smashed to pieces on the rocks by enormous waves; lifeboat men wearing bulky cork lifebelts; women in long skirts, lugging baskets of freshly caught fish. Then there were pictures of the Leviathan Hotel as it was in years gone by. Beneath one, a date fixed it as having being taken on Christmas Day, 1921. Outside the front door, standing in a neat line, were four people. A middle-aged man and woman, and then probably the son and daughter. Beth studied the features of the young woman. Eleanor, it had to be – yet an Eleanor of twenty years ago. Those features were unmistakable. Her brother smiled broadly. He possessed a healthy robustness. In his hand, a fishing rod. No doubt a Christmas present that he'd insisted on displaying proudly.

Eleanor had told them that her brother suffered ill health. So, if this photograph of a strong, young buck full of vigour didn't lie, then his sickness must have struck him down later. After she'd glanced at the other photographs (all ships with masts), she gazed out of the window. From the reception area came the deep rumble of Alec's Scottish burr, mingled with Sally and Eleanor's voices. Sally's laugh would often rise above the others' conversational tones.

This window didn't open on to any grand vista, unlike her

bedroom, which revealed the waterside hotel had perfect harbour views. All she could see from here was the small cobbled yard hemmed in by walls six feet high. Tucked in one corner, a little cottage in the same deep red-brick. Its frontage presented a door, two windows at ground level, then another pair of windows on the upper story. As her eyes alighted on the upstairs windows she noticed one had its curtain parted by just six inches or so. At that moment, a thin, weak-looking hand fumbled for the edge of the curtain. *He can't see it*, she told herself. *Eleanor's brother must be blind. The poor man . . . and he looked so healthy in the photograph.* That prolonged fumbling at the fabric, the long, pale fingers searching desperately for a fold to grasp, saddened her so much that a lump formed in her throat. She wondered if she should warn Eleanor that her brother might need help. However, after a moment's scrabbling, he seized the fabric, then shut the curtain so quickly that she could almost feel his desperation to keep the world out of sight.

Sally appeared at the doorway. 'Didn't you hear me?'

'Sorry, I was just . . .' *Spying on Eleanor's brother?* 'I'll be right there.'

'Get your scarf and gloves. It's freezing.' Sally clutched Beth's arm as they headed for the staircase. 'Our first day in Whitby. Can't you just feel it in the air! Something really amazing is going to happen today. Just you wait and see.'

Two

At the reception desk, Eleanor handed Alec Reed a pen. 'If you can sign the register, please, Mr Reed.'

'Call me Alec, please.'

'And I'm Eleanor. Ah, a left-hander, I see. An indication of artistic sensibility.'

Alec wrote his name in the book. 'Your last guest before Beth and Sally signed in was two years ago.'

'The war stopped people holidaying at the coast. They were afraid that Hitler's Storm Troopers might come ashore here. So I decided to simply keep the front door locked until hostilities ended. I'll get your cases.'

'No bellboy?'

'He's on a minesweeper out in the Atlantic. And our chef is

making his wonderful beef and ale stew for the garrison down in Portsmouth. Young men are hard to find in Whitby these days, Alec.'

He returned her pen. 'So you'll be wondering what a six-foot Scot, of thirty years of age, is doing in your nice safe hotel. The man should be marching with a rifle in his hand, isn't that so, Eleanor?'

'We all have our reasons for what we do, whether they be public knowledge or utterly secret.'

He held up his right hand. 'This has all the dexterity of a crab's claw. The bus I was travelling in, when I was ten years old, rolled off the road. It did such a good job of busting the ligaments that my right hand, though it's strong, acts like a pincer – nothing more. Hence, the military rejected me and my crab-claw hand.'

'You must be frustrated that you can't join the fight.'

'So you'd think, but when I received the letter telling me that I'd spend the war as a civilian I celebrated for twenty-four hours straight.'

'Oh.'

'Can I be confessional, Eleanor?'

'If that's what you wish.'

'Well, I confess this fact: I've never done a useful thing in my adult life. I lived for pleasure. Let everyone else do the dull chores. If you work for a living you're a fool.'

'Is that what you think?' Eleanor put the register back on its shelf.

'It was my mantra. I told everyone I was a writer. In truth, I wrote very little. All my creativity went into finding routes to pleasure.'

'Alec Reed, *Soho Square and Beyond*.'

'You've read my one and only novel? You belong to a tiny elite, Eleanor.'

'And it is an extraordinary book. You are a very talented writer.'

'You're too kind.'

'Not at all. I'm not one to flatter for no valid reason.'

He picked up his suitcase. 'A production company hired me to write a script for a patriotic film. One that shows neutral nations how life is lived under siege here in Britain.'

'Then it's a laudable film to make.'

'I wrote the script. And I hated it. Hated it with a passion. And I resented being forced to work the nine to five. Then I happened to be discussing its production with my colleagues in a café that, as bad luck would have it, took a direct hit from a bomb. Everyone was killed but me. It's where I got the . . .' He touched the eyepatch.

'But I'm told it will heal.' He shrugged. 'As there is a shortage of directors I've now been given the job of directing the film I scripted.'

'Fate is a contrary mistress, Alec.'

'Indeed.'

Eleanor regarded the tall man with that black eyepatch, which seemed to concentrate the force of his other eye – as if it peered into her soul. He continued staring at her.

'Is there a problem?' she asked.

'I just wanted to add that I'm happy to be here. And that I'm going to try my utmost to make this a good film. Maybe even a great film. If *This Midnight Realm* can encourage neutral nations to stop supplying the Nazi war machine it may shorten the war. And if my film helps shorten it by even one hour then I will have succeeded.'

'And all your past sins will be wiped from your soul?'

'You may think I'm ridiculous, Eleanor, but until a few days ago I was an idler. A heart stealer. Overfond of the bottle. And in other people's eyes, an infuriating wretch.'

'Then this is your opportunity to prove yourself. Genuinely, I do admire your change of heart.' She plucked a key from the wall cabinet. 'Follow me.' Eleanor climbed the stairs. 'Welcome to the Leviathan. Breakfast is served between seven thirty and eight. Dinner is seven prompt. If you hear the air-raid siren take shelter in the cellar. The entrance is next to the reception desk. And I do understand that this film is important to you. If I can help, in any shape or form, then my door will always be open to you.'

Eleanor continued to the next floor. Alec followed. He'd confessed to her; would there be a time when she confessed her secrets to him? And she wondered if he watched the shape of her figure with interest as she led him to his room.

Three

Beth, Sally and Eleanor climbed the stone steps that clung to the almost vertical hillside.

'Great exercise for the calf muscles.' Eleanor breathed hard. 'And what man doesn't like a firm calf muscle in a woman?'

Sally panted. 'Phew, there must be a hundred steps at least.'

'To be precise, one hundred and ninety-nine.'

Beth paused where the steps had been punctuated by a short level section before the next flight started. Although the cold pierced her clothes, the sun had driven away the last of the mist. She jotted a sentence in her notebook. These amazing steps cried out for a dramatic scene in the film. Perhaps where the character played by Sally rushes to tell her family she is to be married.

Eleanor indicated the level section of stone slabs. 'In days gone by, pall bearers would carry coffins up to the graveyard on the cliff top. These breaks in the steps allowed them to get their breath back. Ye Gods, they'd have needed it. That fragrant scent of burning wood you can smell comes from the sheds down there. That's where they cure herrings and turn them into kippers. Ready for the final push to the summit?'

Eleanor led them upwards. To Beth, it felt as if they were flying free over Whitby. The roofs below formed patches of different shades of red from the earthenware tiles that covered them. The narrow streets were swarming with people. She glimpsed a postman. Fishermen headed off to their boats. Women carried bundles, baskets, or pulled along children who were late for school. Mixed into the stew of men and women were soldiers in their characteristic pale-brown uniforms.

Mrs Brady appeared at the foot of the steps, the lady they'd encountered on the bridge with that silent sentinel of a daughter. She glared up at the three of them. Beth decided there must be an ongoing feud between Mrs Brady and Eleanor Charnwood. Then again, Beth had noticed the way people had moved out of Eleanor's way, even in the narrow confines of Church Street, as if she carried a nasty germ. In fact, not a single person had offered Eleanor a courteous 'good morning'. *Outcast.* That's the word that had sprung immediately to Beth's mind.

'All those seagulls,' Sally exclaimed. 'There's thousands of them, and, gosh, aren't they raucous?'

'They follow fishing boats into the estuary. They know that once the gutting starts they're in for a feast. Come on, nearly there.'

Eleanor ushered them up the remaining steps to the cliff top. The squat church dominated the immediate area, yet beyond it were the tall, mysterious ruins of Whitby Abbey, which cast an other-worldly spell over the place. The graveyard itself bristled with dark, weath-ered gravestones. Ocean gales had not only erased inscriptions on the older stones, but had worn away their once precise geometric shapes, leaving them with a weird, undulating appearance, as if a magic spell had solidified wraiths of smoke and left them here, standing in the grass.

Beth drank in the beautiful view. Whitby was truly extraordinary. Beneath her, the higgledy-piggledy cluster of cottages by the dozen. The doors were painted bright reds, greens and yellows. To her right, the vast expanse of the ocean. A pair of long harbour walls extended out to sea. Each one ended with a tall stone tower. Between the walls seawater flowed into the harbour to mingle with the fresh waters of the River Esk. The river itself cut the town into two distinct halves. Far away upstream, hills formed vast, smooth mounds against a bright blue sky.

'This side is considered to be the old town,' Eleanor told them. 'Over the river, the newer, more orderly part. See the big, posh buildings on the cliff top? They're the hotels for the smart set, though most are now occupied by soldiers stationed here to deal with any attacks from the sea.'

Beth jotted notes. 'If we can get permission, it would be ideal to film up here, for establishing views of Whitby, and there're bound to be some great scenes that can be shot in the graveyard.'

Sally beamed. 'Later in the film, my husband is killed rescuing me from a burning house. This would be an ideal spot to bury him.' She pretended to dab away a widow's tear. 'Alec will shoot me in this huge, great close-up, so my face fills the screen, and you will be able to hear the gulls crying, and it will seem like they're crying for poor Nathan.'

Eleanor said, 'I'll give you the telephone number of the verger. He looks after St Mary's Church. If possible try and get permission to film inside. Ships' carpenters produced the interior woodwork, so parts resemble a boat. Now, if you'll follow the cliff-top path, I'll show you the abbey ruin. The monks built the first phase almost fifteen hundred years ago, but it was burnt down by the Vikings in AD 867. Earlier, in 664, the Abbess Hilda held what is known as the Great Synod of Whitby. That's when she merged the Celtic Church and the Roman Catholic Church.' She smiled. 'See, my dears, we women have played a bigger role in humanity than many think. The Abbess Hilda, in that building on the cliff top, changed the course of the Western world. If she hadn't united the two rival Churches, Europe couldn't have resisted invasions by pagan armies. Without Hilda, the Vikings might have destroyed Christianity. Instead of celebrating Christmas you'd have been offering sacrifices up to

Odin and Thor.' She touched Sally's arm. 'You, my dear, might have been that offering.'

'Don't! You're making me go all goosey!' Sally squealed with laughter.

'Well, thanks to Abbess Hilda, you're safe from that at least, and snakes.'

'Snakes?'

'According to legend, the Abbess Hilda confronted a plague of snakes here. She beheaded them all with a whip. That's why there are no snakes in Whitby.' She gave a knowing smile. 'Try putting a nun with a whip in your film, especially one chopping up serpents.'

Beth smiled back. 'I doubt if such a scene would escape the censor's scissors.' *Eleanor has such a wicked sense of humour. I bet she has lots of naughty stories to tell.* She found herself liking this charismatic woman more and more.

'Oh, flick my ear.' Their guide stopped at the edge of the cemetery. 'Something's happened. I'm sure they won't let us go further.'

A soldier, armed with a rifle, stood by the gate. In a meadow, some way beyond the abbey ruin, the barrel of an anti-aircraft gun pointed at the sky. However, not far from the weapon was a military ambulance, its rear doors open wide. On a scorched area of grass, a number of men searched the earth; they had large, brown paper bags in their hands. Every so often, one of the searchers bent down to gingerly pick up a scrap of something, which he then deposited in the bag. Invariably, the man would wipe his hand on a rag afterwards.

The soldier advanced in a leisurely way towards them.

'You can't go any further, ladies.'

Sally asked, 'What happened?'

'You know I can't reveal military affairs, miss.' In order to avoid appearing officious, he added with a grin, 'For all we know, Hitler himself might be hiding behind that headstone.'

'Of course,' Eleanor agreed. 'We'll go back the way we came. Good day.' When they reached the top of the steps, Eleanor said, 'It's like that all the time. The army have turned the town into a fortress, which is the right thing to do, of course, considering the Nazis might invade at any time. But we always have to pretend we don't see anything, if, say, they cordon off streets for no obvious reason. Sandgate has been closed for over a week, and nobody knows why. And that's the quickest route to the hotel from the swing bridge. Naturally, the shopkeepers complain to the mayor, as they have to stay closed, and they're losing trade. But, all in all, the soldiers are welcome. Not only as protectors; they've brought a lot of money into the town. Hundreds are billeted in the boarding houses. And those smart young men in uniform are very popular with the local girls as well. That church back there is busier than ever with weddings.' She shrugged. 'All we have to do is pretend we don't see any soldiers or the big artillery guns that are popping up along the cliffs.'

A plane swept through the sky above their heads. Beth saw its grey underbelly and the black Swastika on each wing.

Anxious, Sally backed towards the cemetery wall. 'Shouldn't we take cover?'

'A lone German aircraft usually means reconnaissance. He's just taking a peek to see what naval ships we've got in the harbour or if there are any more artillery guns in the fields.' Then in a darker tone Eleanor called up at the enemy pilot, 'Just you come and invade us. You might defeat the soldiers . . . You might capture the town. But you'll soon wish you'd never foot set in Whitby.'

Sally gave a nervous laugh. 'He can't hear you, silly.'

Before the anti-aircraft crews could even fire a shot at the trespasser, the plane banked over the abbey ruins, then screamed away over the sea, eastwards, back home to the Fatherland. Without speaking, they descended the one hundred and ninety-nine steps into the bustling town. When they reached Church Street, Beth put her hand on Eleanor's wrist to gently attract her attention. The woman quickly drew her arm away, as if that light touch had stung her.

'Sorry, I didn't mean to hurt you.'

'It's nothing, Beth. I injured it a few years ago. Sometimes it plays up.'

Sally went to admire jet necklaces in a shop window.

Quietly, Beth said, 'You made a very strange comment up there, Eleanor.'

'Strange comment? I'm famous for them.' She smiled.

Eleanor's wearing the mask again. The one that claims: 'Look I'm just a carefree woman, with a risqué sense of humour and nothing to hide from the world.' Really, Eleanor? You've no secrets?

Slowly, they strolled side-by-side.

Beth murmured, '*You might defeat the soldiers . . . You might capture the town. But you'll soon wish you'd never foot set in Whitby.* Those were your words, Eleanor. If the enemy succeeded in capturing Whitby, why would they then regret it?'

Once more, local people stepped aside from Eleanor without looking into her face. *Unclean . . . Unclean . . . Is that what they're thinking?* One middle-aged lady even inadvertently bumped into Eleanor. When she recognized her, she flinched back, shocked to have made contact. *You have a secret, Eleanor, dear. A deep, dark secret. What is it?* And, what's more, Eleanor didn't appear to have any intention of answering Beth's question.

'We'll go down by the quays,' Eleanor said. 'If you need to film close to the boats that's the place to be.'

'Eleanor?'

The mask of frivolous normality stayed firmly in place. Eleanor made a joke of the answer. 'Because if the Nazis occupy the town, I'll personally make their lives a misery. Hitler daren't take me on.'

'Ah, you're good at evasion, Eleanor.'

'Pardon?'

'Perhaps this strange dream of a town is sending me crazy. But I wonder if what you called up at the plane is tied in with me finding a lock of hair caught in the passageway to Arguments Yard, even though I've never been here before.'

'That could be anyone's hair. You're not blonde exclusively, you know. Come on, I'll treat you to coffee and cake.'

'And is it connected to the fact that everyone in the street shies away when they see you? It's like they know you're carrying a time bomb or something. You scare them.'

'I can't control what they think about me, Beth.' She attracted Sally's attention. 'Come on, we're going for coffee and cake.'

Sally rushed after them. 'Did you see that lovely jet brooch? It's like a big black diamond.' She cast longing glances back over her shoulder at the jeweller's. 'When I get my first pay cheque that brooch is mine.'

'You're a girl after my own heart, Sally. Keep up, Beth. We don't want you getting lost in Whitby's dark labyrinths. Sometimes, if you take a wrong turning, it's hard to find your way back to the real world again.'

Four

Eleanor Charnwood happily offered Alec her own office. A door beside the reception desk led to the room, which she'd comfortably furnished with thick rugs, an antique desk, and shelves of books.

A tall window opened out over the estuary. In fact, if a boat moored here at the harbour wall, freshly caught fish could be handed through the window.

Beth spent the afternoon in the office with Alec. Together they went through the locations that Beth had found on her walk that morning with the enigmatic Eleanor. Alec didn't hide his admiration that she'd completed the list so quickly.

'Whitby's a beautiful place, even in war,' he said as he rolled paper into the typewriter. 'It's a remarkable setting for the film. Thank goodness I persuaded the bosses to allow me to shoot on location, not in a studio in some London suburb.'

Beth found herself warming to the man again. He'd told her about the problem with his 'blasted crab-claw' of a hand, and she knew he'd also shared the story with both Eleanor and Sally. Even though it didn't look any way out of the ordinary, she appreciated that it didn't work as a hand should. He could operate the return lever on the typewriter with it, but could only type with his left hand. She sensed his growing trust of her. Because, after they'd finished compiling the schedule of locations, which now matched scenes in the script, he then started to discuss the extra plot strand that the Ministry required to be woven into the story.

'What do we do with our hero lifeboat man?' he asked. 'Is he a character separate from the rest? Do we dip into his life every now and again?'

'If he stands outside the lives of everyone else in the film, it wouldn't be as satisfying for the audience. After all, if none of the other characters care for him, why should the cinema-goer?'

'Good point. A cousin of our family, then?'

'Cousins are neutral.'

'Oh?'

'A cousin is there by default. Nobody has to like their cousin; they just show up at weddings and whatever.'

'I see.' He adjusted the black eyepatch. It looked itchy. 'Then you're talking about that magical thing, then?'

'You mean the magic of love?'

'Absolutely.'

She sat down on the chair opposite him. 'Make your lifeboat man a former boyfriend of Sally's character. He returns from active service.'

'Then he's on leave?'

'No – wounded in a sea battle. But he's determined to do his bit in the war, so he volunteers to skipper the lifeboat.'

Beth realized that Alec had quietly accepted her role as co-author of this additional segment of script. The hours flew, and by the time they'd finished typing the outline she noticed the sun had, at last, set.

Five

At seven that evening, the three sat down to dinner. Eleanor Charnwood, dressed in a smart dark jacket and matching skirt, served them freshly caught Whitby cod with boiled potatoes. They asked her to join them in the otherwise deserted hotel dining room. However, she politely excused herself and left. Beth, Sally and Alec chatted about what they'd seen of Whitby town. They all agreed on how much they liked the place. Alec revealed that he planned to shoot general panoramic views in the morning, weather permitting.

Even by that relatively early time, Whitby was in the grip of utter darkness. Because no lights could be shown outdoors, nobody risked venturing out into the narrow streets. Eleanor had told them that to even reach the end of Church Street on a moonless night meant groping your way along, touching the walls as you went, to avoid bumping into obstacles. She also warned that men and women of a libertine disposition used the cloak of darkness to plot brief encounters. 'If you leave your window open at night, you're bound to hear sighs of rapture coming from the alleyway,' she'd told them. 'Of course, whether or not you want to listen is up to you.'

By the time they'd finished the meal, Alec had begun to explain to Sally that her character would be involved in a love triangle. He was describing the lifeboat man's dramatic return when the hotel's back door gave an almighty bang.

In alarm, Sally all but leapt out of her chair. Eleanor appeared in the hallway. Her mixture of panic and downright fear brought all three to their feet.

'Eleanor, what's wrong?' Beth called.

Eleanor didn't reply. Instead she rushed from room to room on the ground floor. Then she ran to the dining room doorway to rake the interior with a shockingly wide-eyed stare. After that, she bolted towards the kitchen. Beth hurried after her, Sally and Alec following. She found Eleanor anxiously searching the big walk-in pantry.

The woman's face had gone completely white. Her hands trembled as she unlocked a storeroom door.

'What's happened?'

Panting, Eleanor rushed to another room, fumbled with a bunch of keys, dropped them, then after snatching them from the floor tried to get the key into the door.

Alec stepped forward. 'What's the matter?'

All three were shaken by this normally composed woman's collapse into panic.

'Tell us, Eleanor,' Beth urged. 'Please.'

'We don't like to see you so upset,' Sally cried. 'Let us help.'

Eleanor opened the door to a laundry room. After scanning the interior, she slammed the door shut again. She seemed determined to rush out of the kitchen without even acknowledging they were there.

Beth caught her by the arm. 'Eleanor. You must tell us what's wrong.'

For a moment she struggled to make a decision. Then: 'It's my brother, Theo. He's gone.'

'Is he a child?' Alec asked.

'No, he's a year younger than me.' Eleanor's words tumbled out. 'But he's not at all well.'

'You've searched his cottage in the yard?' Beth asked.

'Of course! Every room!' She pressed her hand to her forehead. 'Oh, my God. I'm so worried for him.'

'Is there anywhere in Whitby he's likely to go?'

'He never goes out. I've got to find him. He hasn't had his treatment tonight. If he doesn't . . . If he doesn't . . .' She couldn't even bring herself to finish the sentence.

'Then we'll help you find him,' Beth told her calmly. 'Everything will be alright. You'll see.'

'*My God, I hope so!*'

'It's too dark for him to go far,' Sally ventured. 'He might be nearby.'

'I can't understand it. My brother dreads the idea of going out into the town. Something must have made him.' She shuddered. 'Or taken him against his will.'

'We will find Theo,' Beth assured the woman.

Alec eased the curtain aside a fraction. 'It's as dark as Hades outside. You wouldn't see to the end of your own nose.'

Beth took charge. 'So we'll search the hotel first. Eleanor, where are the keys to the rooms?'

'I'll get them.'

'Sit down here; catch your breath.'

'No. He'll need me.'

'Alright. Sally, stay by the reception desk, just in case he comes in from the street.'

Eleanor grabbed the keys from the wall cabinet then all three rushed upstairs.

'There are guest bedrooms over three upper floors,' Eleanor told them. 'My quarters are on the top floor. There are also linen stores, staff rooms — they're disused now, oh . . . and a rear staircase.'

Alec paused. 'Is your brother likely to do himself harm? Or try to harm anyone else?'

'Theo? No, he wouldn't; I'm sure of it.' Eleanor ran upstairs, if anything, her anxiety increasing by the moment.

The footsteps reached Sally as soft thuds on carpet. Her eyes roved over the ceiling as she tracked the sounds the three made as they opened doors to the rooms. Her heart thumped painfully hard. Even when she sat on the sofa in the reception area, it showed no signs of easing. Nerves taut, she paced in front of the desk. Every so often, she climbed a stair or two in case she could see anything of their search. Yet by now even the sound of their feet had faded so much that all she could hear was the clamour of her own heart.

Just what's wrong with Eleanor's brother? she wondered. *Why did he need the medicine so badly? Why does he have such a fear of leaving his cottage? And what had made him go and do just that?*

Even to look at the big front door of the hotel troubled her. She expected it to fly open to reveal a maniac. All too easily, she pictured the wild hair, the staring eyes, the hooked fingers, the crazed leer — and poor Sally Wainwright, all alone in reception. He'd be on her in an instant, hands at her throat.

Plucking up courage, she hurried towards the door to check that it had been locked. To her relief, she saw a couple of hefty bolts were firmly pushed across the frame. Even so, when the clock struck eight she spun round with a cry.

Silly girl, she scolded herself. *It's only the stupid clock.* She listened hard. But now she could hear nothing of the three upstairs. *The maniac will have slit their throats by now.* Sally told herself to shut up. And even put her hands over her ears. But that didn't stop disturbing thoughts about the maniac slipping under her bed. He'd lay there grinning until she went to sleep then . . . *Stop it!* Sally prowled from the reception area into the dining room. But all those empty tables seemed just too ghostly, as if they waited for phantom diners. Sally quickly returned to the reception desk.

Got to keep myself busy, she told herself. *Besides, I'm an adult now.* Taking a deep breath, she composed herself. Sally decided to take a firm grip on her courage and search for the missing brother on the ground floor. A quick check of the office revealed no brother (a lunatic one or otherwise). She checked under the reception desk. There. All done. No brother here.

Then she noticed the door tucked behind the desk. Ah . . . the basement. Last night they'd sheltered in it during the air raid.

But did she really, really have to go down there? *Don't be such a coward, Sally Wainwright. Soon you will star in a feature film. Famous actresses aren't scaredy cats.* She found the door to be unlocked. *Which makes sense. You don't want to be hunting for keys when the air-raid siren starts.* Straightening her back, as she'd seen Beth do when gathering her resolve, she switched on the light, then descended the stone steps.

Just like last night, there were the chairs they'd occupied when the siren sounded. Here it was: a vault of cold silence. And there, set in the floor, the big, iron grate. Eleanor said it connected with a smuggler's tunnel that led to the sea.

So: nothing to be afraid of. She walked across the floor slabs, her heels clicking. *Just look in the corners at the far side, then go back upstairs. Job done. Nobody down here. I'm alone. There's no one.* As she returned to the steps, she kept up the mantra. *Nobody here. I'm alone. Everything's normal down here. No problems. Nothing to be afraid of.* She repeated that mantra to block out her sudden eruption of terror. For there was something to be afraid of. A man stood beneath the iron grate. He watched her through the bars, his face nearly level with her feet. He didn't move. The eyes were very white. Yet in their centres lay fierce black pupils.

'There's nothing there,' she whispered, heart racing. 'I'm imagining it. There is nobody under the grate. I'm going back upstairs now. Everything is fine. I'm not scared . . .'

'*Who are you?*'

Sally screamed and clutched her stomach. 'You're not real, you're not real.' She planned to dash for the steps, only now she couldn't; fear had locked her muscles tight. She couldn't move an inch.

'Who are you?'

Sally shook her head.

'Come here. Talk to me.'

She found herself turning to stare down through the iron bars. There he was. *Oh no, I don't like this.* Her heart slammed against her ribs. She could barely breathe. Purple shapes flashed across her eyes. Shock had made her so dizzy she swayed. Yet her attention locked on that pale face beyond the bars. A cold flow of air gushed up from the pit in the floor.

'Please talk to me,' whispered the stranger. His eyes locked with hers.

'Can't,' was all that Sally could say.

'Oh, you look nice. Very beautiful.' He worked a pale hand through the bars, so that it appeared to grow from the floor like a white flower. 'If you won't tell me your name, then shake my hand.' Fingers flexed. The nails were pale blue. An even blue like the sky in spring. 'Shake hands. Please.'

She swayed. Shock always did this to her. It made her feel faint. Now she was sure she'd topple over at any moment. What's more, she realized she'd fall on to the grate. The intruder's face would only be separated from hers by that inch-thick lattice of iron. His hands could easily touch her.

'Tell me your name, beautiful. Go on, just open those ruby lips. Form the vowels. Say it.'

The basement grew darker as the blood flow no longer reached her brain. She felt top heavy. Slowly, slowly, she began to topple – towards the abomination.

'Sally! We've found him!' The voice came from behind. 'Sally? What's wrong?'

Sally's knees folded. Dizzily, she turned her head. Eleanor had grabbed hold of her. However, her eyes returned to that bone-white face in the pit of shadows.

'I've got you,' Eleanor panted. 'I won't let you fall.'

The stranger beneath the grate spoke conversationally, 'Eleanor. I'm sorry it happened to Theo. Victoria didn't know what she was doing. If I could turn back time . . .'

Eleanor put her arm around Sally's waist and guided her up the steps to the reception area. Then she closed the door on the cellar. And whatever it was that intruded there.

Beth Layne stood beside Alec at the open attic window. At that moment, Eleanor arrived with Sally. However, when the women entered the attic Beth sensed all hadn't gone well. Alec had been obliged to kill the lights, so as not to breach the blackout. Even so, in the midst of this gloom, she could tell that the colour had drained from Sally's face. And was that a flash of fear in her eyes? Her friend shot glances back at the door, as if expecting to see a figure blunder in.

'Everything alright?' Beth whispered to Sally.

'Yes . . . I think so . . . but . . .'

Eleanor declared, 'My brother's out there on the roof. I've got to bring him in.' Immediately, she rushed for the open window.

'Wait,' Beth hissed. 'You can't just go clambering out there.'

Alec agreed. 'You're forty feet from the ground . . . It's pitch black out there.'

'I'll be fine. The moon's coming through.'

Beth had to grab the woman to stop her climbing out. The drop would be lethal if she slipped. 'Eleanor, wait. Plan the route first.'

'She's right,' Alec said. 'Now there're four of us we can bring him back safely.'

Beth positioned herself so she could see Theo Charnwood. He was a shockingly gaunt man; he possessed an angular face, high cheekbones, and strangely gleaming eyes, which stared up towards the cliff-top cemetery. For some reason, he'd decided to climb out of the window, then stand on the low wall that ran around the edge of the roof. He didn't move. Didn't speak. The roof itself sloped steeply. That rim of stone, which topped the brick wall, presented the sole level part of the structure. In front of him — and below him — was only cold night air, until it reached the equally cold and unforgiving hard slabs of the yard.

'Try calling him,' ventured Sally. She seemed to be recovering her composure.

Once more Beth glanced at her, wondering just what had happened downstairs. *Good grief, there might be fifteen hotel rooms, but there's no place for guests: this entire building's choc-a-block with secrets.* She didn't intend the thought to be flippant. Without doubt, this hotel reeked of mystery. Its walls oozed strangeness. The hotelier hid her true self behind a mask of normality. *And her brother climbs out on to the roof. To admire the view? To throw himself to his death? Who knows?*

'Why don't you just call him?' Sally suggested again.

'When he's like this he won't respond to commands,' Eleanor said. 'I'll have to go out there and bring him in.'

'I'll do it.' Alec slipped off his jacket.

'No, it's got to be me.'

The moon peeped from behind a bank of cloud. Its glow revealed the brother. He stood perfectly still and perfectly straight. He wore black trousers, while on his top half a white shirt, open to the waist, fluttered like a shroud in the breeze. Beneath them, Whitby's lanes were deserted.

Eleanor climbed out on to the parapet.

'Easy does it,' Alec murmured. 'It's a big drop.'

'I know.'

Beth said, 'If you wait by the window we'll follow you . . . form a human chain.'

'No, the three of you stay here.'

'No deal,' Alec told her. 'We're helping. I'll go next, then you grab my hand.'

Beth turned to her friend. 'Sally, you stay inside the window. Just hold on to my belt as tightly as you can. Do you think you can?'

'I'll do it. Trust me.'

The parapet had a five-inch span. Eleanor had to shuffle along it like a tightrope walker. To one side rose the steep pitch of the roof; the other side, a deathly drop to the ground. Alec joined Eleanor. With his right hand, impaired though it was, he could tightly grasp her left hand. Then Beth climbed out. She stood with her back to the edge of the window frame. She found Alec's hand, then held it tight. His powerful fingers encircled hers. She could feel Sally clutching her belt. And so forming a human chain, the three stood at the edge of the roof. Sally performed the role of anchor inside the attic. Sometimes they were in moonlight, which revealed clustered roofs of cottages and the face of the cliff, then the silver orb retreated behind cloud, and they were engulfed in darkness.

Beth closed her eyes to concentrate on her balance. Fingers of cold air trailed over her face. *Don't slip*, she told herself, *just don't slip*. When she opened her eyes again, Eleanor had reached her brother. His shirt rippled in the breeze. With calm eyes, he gazed at the cliff-top cemetery. It seemed as if he heard a voice calling his name from far away; it entranced him. His eyes never strayed from the night-time gravestones.

For a while . . . a long while it seemed to Beth . . . Eleanor patted Theo's arm to attract his attention. She even stroked the side of his face, as if she were trying to gently wake a sleeping child. Eventually, he stirred. Without any fuss, or even a word, he consented to be led back to the attic window. Nobody spoke as they carefully retraced their steps. Then, thankfully, one by one they re-entered the safety of the attic.

Still with utter gentleness, Eleanor guided her brother away to the cottage in the yard.

Beth, Sally and Alec regrouped in the hotel bar. Nobody had spoken since Theo's rescue.

That is, until Sally regarded them with troubled eyes. 'His shirt was all open. Did anyone see his chest?' She took a breath. 'It was covered with teeth marks. Dozens and dozens of teeth marks.'

Six

The three had only been in the bar for a few minutes when the siren began its wail over the town. The people of Whitby would be making their way to their own cellars, or underground shelters built in their gardens, or, if they lived in apartments, they'd head for communal shelters. After months of hearing sirens calling them to take shelter, this migration to the bunkers had, at least, lost its element of panic. Most people would sigh that their night's sleep was going to be interrupted, as they ambled to their subterranean dens.

Alec grunted and said, 'Don't those Nazis ever take a night off?'

As the siren faded they all listened for the distinctive bark of German aircraft motors overhead. At the moment, however, nothing could be heard.

'We should take shelter in the basement,' Beth told them. 'That's what Eleanor told us to do whenever the warning sounded.'

Alec hesitated. 'Perhaps I should help her get her brother to the basement.'

'Oh, he never takes shelter during air raids,' Sally told him.

Beth stood up. 'But *we* should. If Eleanor goes down to the basement, and we're not there, she'll feel obliged to search for us. And after the evening she's had that wouldn't be fair.'

'I'm staying here.' Sally shuddered. 'I hate that rotten hole.'

Beth took her friend's arm. 'Sally, you'll do no such thing. I promised you I'd look after you in Whitby. I'm not going to leave you up here if the bombs start to fall.'

'But it's horrible down there.'

'Alec and I will be with you.'

He smiled. 'I'll sing old Scottish ballads to you. My voice is guaranteed to take your mind off bombs and horrible old basements. Ladies?' He held open the door for them.

Sally went grudgingly. 'But will it take my mind off Eleanor's brother? Who do you suppose made all those scars on this chest? They were bite marks, weren't they? And made by human teeth?'

Beth guided her friend with a firm grasp. 'Now isn't the time to speculate. Those bombers could be here at any moment.'

Alec opened the basement door. 'We can talk to our hearts' content once we've got that protective masonry over our heads.'

Despite having been in a café that took a direct hit from a bomb just a couple of weeks ago, Beth realized the man was remarkably calm. All he'd suffered was a cut to the eye. She gazed at his face. The eyepatch must be a constant reminder to him of the event that had cost his colleagues their lives. And the female casting director was more than a colleague. *Because the man escaped death, does he now believe he's invincible? And is he convinced that he's been spared in order to fulfil some great quest?*

They entered the basement. A single light bulb illuminated the vaulted ceiling. Just as before, the chairs were clustered together. As they crossed the floor, Sally froze. She stared at that forbidding iron grille set into the stonework. Beth noticed the expression on her friend's face, as if she'd suddenly remembered something that appalled her.

'Sally? What's wrong?'

'Earlier, I came down here, when we were searching for Theo. I . . . Something wasn't right. I . . .'

Alec turned a chair towards her. 'Sit down, dear. You've turned very pale.' Sally's eyes bulged, as they remained locked on that pit of shadows, one from which frigid air rose.

Beth put her arm around Sally. 'What happened? You can tell me.'

Sally refused to sit, her muscles so tense that her entire body quivered. 'I came down here. Then I had a dizzy turn. I would have fainted dead to the floor, if Eleanor hadn't caught me. She'd come to tell me that you'd found Theo.' She swallowed, as if an unpleasant taste leeched across her tongue. 'I blacked out. Only for a few seconds, but I dreamt that a man was in there.' She pointed at the iron bars. 'He stood beneath the grate . . . He was looking up at me and saying things. His eyes were so . . .' She shuddered. 'He wanted to shake hands with me. He even pushed his hand up through the bars. All I can think about are those eyes . . .'

Alec brought a straight-backed chair to her. Gently, he encouraged her to sit. 'You'll feel better in a moment. And, remember, a dream can't hurt you.'

Sally gripped Beth's hand. 'Only, I'm not so sure now. It's too clear for a dream. And I'm certain I remember seeing the man *before* I fainted. But what with the shock of Theo being out there on the roof it all got jumbled inside my head. In fact, the more I think about it now, the more I'm convinced I saw a man standing down there in that hole in the floor. He wore a white shirt. His eyes . . . Beth, there was no colour in them. No irises. Just whites, with black pupils in the centres. He looked just awful. And he wanted to shake my hand. But there was more to it than that. He . . . He planned to do something when he got hold of me.'

Alec went to stand over the grate. His eyes widened in surprise, as he looked down at something beneath the bars. 'My good God.'

Beth joined him. Cold air vented up into her face. She heard a flurry of whispers.

Sally blurted in panic, 'What's wrong, what's happening!'

'It's the sea,' Alec marvelled. 'It's flowing into the bottom of the hole.'

Sally cried out in fear.

'Hear that whispering sound?' He sounded full of glee. 'It's the waves washing against the stonework.'

Groaning, Sally looked as if she'd faint again.

Beth rushed to comfort her. 'It's nothing to worry about. Remember, Sally, Eleanor told us that sometimes, if the tide was really high, seawater would flow along the tunnel.' She turned to Alec. 'It connects with the harbour.'

'Splendid.' He grinned. 'It's bound to be one of those old smuggler tunnels. They'd have unloaded tobacco and brandy, and all that naughty contraband from the boats, and brought it up here to be hidden. Ah, I wonder if there's a nice bottle of Cognac still secreted here?'

'If the tunnel leads to the harbour, someone might have got in.' Sally's anxiety grew. 'He could creep up the tunnel and break into the hotel.' She grimaced. 'And I never want to see his rotten eyes again. They made my blood run cold.'

'Sally, it was a dream; you must've been in a dead faint for longer than you thought.'

'Or some local peeping Tom.' Alec crouched in order to study the grating. 'He sneaks into the tunnel, so he can look up ladies' skirts.'

'Alec,' Beth scolded.

He became serious again. 'There's nothing to worry about, Sally. See this grate?' He stomped his boot on it. 'Solid as a rock. One man couldn't lift that. Even if some local lad managed to get into the tunnel he wouldn't get any further than this.' He laughed. 'It'll even keep Adolf himself out and all his ruddy Storm Troopers.'

Beth tilted her head. 'There goes the all-clear siren.'

'So, nothing to worry about. Back to the bar, ladies.' Alec now adopted a jovial all's-well-with-the-world persona, evidently to re-assure Sally. 'Maybe we can persuade Eleanor to serve us all a snifter or two. I daresay we could do with a tot of the strong stuff.'

Beth told Alec to lead the way with Sally. The woman still shot fearful glances back at the grate. When the pair had left the base-ment, Beth returned to the grate. Below her feet, dark waters swirled. The smell of brine prickled the sensitive membranes of her nose. From this angle, she could just make out the throat of the tunnel through which the waves entered. Certainly, it would be big enough for a man to pass through. Then she transferred her attention from the pulsating body of water to the bars themselves. A moment later she plucked something from a flake of rust.

How did you describe him, Sally? A man wearing a white shirt? Between her fingers a strand of white cotton fluttered in that blood-freezing updraught.

Seven

Through Whitby's dark and deserted streets they came. Six figures moved swift as panthers along narrow canyons formed by unbroken lines of cottages. Not a light showed through the blacked-out windows. Clocks struck midnight. In gun emplacements on the cliff top, soldiers had to clap their heavily gloved hands together to chase away the cold. For now, the sky remained empty of Nazi bombers. Though the troops were alert to threats from both sea and air, they did not see the boy run silently by the abbey ruins in the direction of the graveyard of St Mary's Church. Loping alongside him, a sleek, black dog.

Many a time the boy had watched the pack of figures led by the man in white. The predatory way they moved had always persuaded him not to get too close. But he noticed that now more people had joined the group. Tonight, a lady in a pale nightdress ran with them. Their eagerness to reach their destination, coupled with an air of excitement, encouraged the boy to follow, albeit in secret. Swiftly, the pack descended the long flight of cliff-side steps to the houses below. For now, they seemed no more substantial than flitting shadows. When they reached the Leviathan Hotel, they didn't even pause. They climbed the smooth walls, with the same ease they'd raced along Church Street. There, they went from window to window, trying to peer in past the heavy blackout material. When that failed, they pressed their ears to the glass panes to listen to whatever occurred within.

Accompanied by the dog, the boy followed as far as the wall that encircled the rear yard. There he concealed himself in all-engulfing darkness to wait and see what the strange, predatory figures did next.

In the cottage, Theo stood in the dark, the light out and the curtains open wide. His eyes were fixed on the figures swarming over the hotel's exterior. They moved across the walls with fluid grace, their fingertips hooking into the gaps between the bricks. Moving swiftly from window to window, they appeared to be searching for someone. One figure, in a pilot's uniform, complete with goggles and leather flying helmet, tried to see through Eleanor's bedroom window. A woman in a billowing nightdress climbed up to the roof to where he, himself, had stood earlier. Then, Theo had been listening to the call of the *many* from the cave. They were growing restless. They'd been trapped for centuries. They wanted out.

Theo heard their call, which sounded like a song shot through with a haunting melody – such yearning; such an unquenchable desire that excited them yet pained them, too. The woman ran lightly, and utterly without fear, around the low wall that separated the hotel roof from forty feet of thin air. The pale nightdress fluttered.

Theo saw another figure. This one he recognized as Gustav Kirk . . . or at least it had been once. On all fours Theo scurried up the brickwork to Eleanor's apartment. There he tried to work his fingers into the gap between the frame and the window in order to slide it open.

Theo sensed Gustav's longing. He sensed it in the other men and women, too. Still gazing at the intruders, he ran his fingers over the scars on his chest. Dimly, he recalled the sensation of teeth crunching through the skin. How they'd gnawed at his torso in excitement. How the vampire's mouth had pulsated, as she sucked hard. Viciously, she'd drawn the blood from his veins. Those memories made the bite-marks tingle. Theo longed to join Gustav and his friends, but Eleanor had made sure that he wouldn't run with his kind.

He closed his eyes, fingered the tingling stigmata on his chest, and listened to the song of those still trapped in the cave. But not trapped for long. Theo was certain of that.

Sally worked in her room, the film script in front of her. Lines always gave her trouble; sometimes, shamefully, she'd corpsed in the plays she'd performed in. Yet she was determined to memorize her part to perfection. Heaven help her, she'd be word perfect. If she made a success of this, her first film, she'd be hired for other roles. Since she'd been a little girl she'd dreamt of being an actress. Whenever she sat in the cinema all her worries evaporated the moment the titles rolled up on the screen.

Sally knew people thought she was overexcitable, giggly, and sometimes downright scatterbrained. Her father had been forced to retire from work when he'd hurt his back at the factory. When she played the fool, or got ridiculously excited over something as trivial as her mother baking a cake, it made her disabled father smile. So, through her childhood, Sally had developed the habit of being silly and scatterbrained in order to distract Dad from that gnawing back pain. To her, it was the right thing to do. And what others thought of her? Well, they could go scoot; this was a small price to pay, if she could shine a little happiness into her father's life. Now she'd do everything in her power to make a career in films. Already, she could send money home from time to time.

Sally went to the mirror to act out the scene. 'Nathan, I don't care that our families have been feuding for fifty years. I'm going to marry you. Your parents will have to accept me as their daughter-in-law. See this ring on my hand . . .' *No, get it right!* 'See this ring on my finger. It means . . .'

Sally paused. Wasn't that a tapping at her window? A bird, perhaps? She shook her head, drew a deep breath, then launched herself back into the role. 'See this ring on my finger. It means we're betrothed. If I'm not going to let those Nazi nitwits stop this wedding, I'm not going to let our families stop it, either.' *Nazi nitwits?* Would Alec agree to the phrase being changed? Maybe 'Nazi henchmen'? The 'nitwits' phrase made it too much like comedy.

The tap sounded again on the window. An insistent tapping. But she was three floors from the ground. Curious, she approached the window, wondering what could be causing it.

Eleanor continued her preparations. In her self-contained apartment within the hotel, she worked steadily. She'd barely noticed the hands of the clock creep past midnight as she wielded the sharp knife. Carefully, she cut along chalked lines on the sheet of black rubber. Because the material couldn't be sewn she had to hammer brass rivets through it when she needed join the pieces together. Utterly focused on the task, she connected strips of black rubber that would serve as belts, so she could fasten the garment at the back. It had been tempting to simply add fabric strips that could be quickly tied, rather than fiddling with cumbersome buckles. But she knew that no cotton-based fabric could be used in the garment. It must be rubber and metal. Lastly, she riveted the section that would form a high, protective collar around the front of her throat. Not that it could be too high, as she'd have to be able to manoeuvre her head freely in order to see either her next phase of works, or, later, her prey. She set down the hammer, then absently ran her fingers over the puncture wounds that so steadfastly refused to heal on her wrist. Tonight they tingled. A permanent reminder of a past tragedy. Sighing, she put the sensation to the back of her mind. Nothing must distract her. *It's taken me twenty years to decide to act. I've been a fool to leave it so long. Nothing, but nothing, must stand in my way.*

As she went to the mirror, to don the heavy rubber apron, she heard scratching on the window pane.

'Go away, Gustav,' she whispered. 'I know it's you.'

Of the four in the hotel, Alec had been the only one to fall asleep. He'd sat down in an armchair with the script on his lap. The uncomfortable night spent in the lorry had exhausted him. One moment he'd been writing *Long shot of arriving lifeboat*, the next, in his dreams, he floated along Whitby's streets; a phantom-like presence. In a café he found the original director of the film (a powerfully built man with a shaved head), the casting director that he'd just taken on their first date (her lips were bright red, just like in life, yet her eyes were full of darkness); the director pushed out a chair for him to sit down and join them.

However, still wrapped deeply in the dream, Alec left the café to ghost through the night-time town. When fingernails tapped on his window, he never heard them.

Beth Layne lounged on her bed. It'd be so tempting to slip under the sheets. But like so many people now in wartime Britain, to allow oneself to relax in bed almost seemed to invite an air raid to start. Beth didn't relish the thought of scurrying down to that icy basement in her nightgown. What's more, so many thoughts swirled inside her head. They all had that irritating quality of a stone in a shoe. She wanted rid, yet they wouldn't quit. So she replayed memories of Eleanor's brother standing out on the roof, his open shirt revealing dozens of scars that resembled bite marks from human teeth. She doubted if any explanation of his injuries could be prised from Eleanor. And Sally had claimed a strange figure had lurked beneath the cellar grate. Since Beth had found a strand of white cotton caught on the bars, it quashed any hope that the intruder had been a product of Sally's dream. Thoughts of the sea washing in through the tunnel to swirl around the bottom of the pit unsettled her, too. *Whitby's a strange place*, she mused. *It occupies an other-worldly borderland between heather-covered mountains and the ocean. And in this mysterious town sits an equally mysterious hotel. Whitby isn't real. Whitby is a dream dreamt by the spirits.* The sound of the window creaking made Beth sit up straight. She realized she'd begun to drift asleep. Now, however, a draught disturbed the heavy curtains. Yet she was convinced that the window had been locked shut.

Frowning, she stood up, before advancing warily towards the curtained opening.

Concealed by darkness, the boy and his dog watched those predatory forms scuttling over the face of the hotel. They were probing the windows, searching for a weak point. Now they were joined by the woman in the nightdress who looked like a pale flame in the night. She tapped a long finger against a glass pane.

Crouching, the boy put his arm around Sam.

The dog lightly pressed the side of his head against the boy's cheek, a gesture of affection and reassurance, and shivered. Those creatures swarming over the building alarmed him. Yet he wouldn't desert the boy. The pair were fiercely loyal.

As the boy watched, one of the windows slid upwards. For some reason it didn't rise very far. It appeared to have jammed. Or was the opener of the window being cautious? Perhaps afraid that something was amiss?

A hand reached out, then ran from left to right as if checking the window ledge. The woman in white crawled spider-like across the wall to the window and darted at the extended hand.

Sally Wainwright had convinced herself that a piece of newspaper, or something, had become stuck outside her window. It must be flapping in the wind – that was causing the tapping on the pane. So, switching off the light to ensure she didn't breach blackout regulations, she parted the curtains. Beyond the glass lay the inky totality of night. Not even the cottages over the way were visible. Sally heaved at the sash window. It juddered, creaked; grudgingly, the heavyweight frame slid upwards about four inches, then stopped dead. It probably hadn't been opened in years. Never mind. This should do. Cold air gusted in. Dozens of feet beneath her lay the hotel yard. Merely the thought of her friends on the roof, just a few hours ago, made her shudder again. They could so easily have fallen to their deaths.

Sally slipped her hand through the gap. The iciness of the stone ledge. Air currents tickled her fingertips. No . . . she couldn't see any newspaper, or anything that could have caused the tapping on the pane. Maybe a mischievous gull had been to blame? She pushed her hand out further, as far as the bend in her elbow. Nothing but sea air played around her bare fingers.

Wait!

An object softly brushed her exposed flesh. A word flashed through her head: *lips.* Then: *mouth!* Before she could even wonder why someone was outside her window, it happened. Sheer agony blasted up her arm. Sally screamed. The pain grew worse, it seemed to set her nerve endings ablaze, and she screamed again.

At the sound of the scream from the next room Beth raced into the corridor. A shaken-looking Alec Reed stumbled, blinking, from the room opposite.

'*Was that you?*' he thundered.

'It's Sally. She's in the room next to mine.'

Before they'd even reached Sally's door, it flew open and the woman hurled herself from it. Her eyes were wild. For some reason she'd acquired a splash of freckles across her face. Then, to Beth's horror, she realized those freckles were bright, glistening red.

Sally held her right hand level with her face. 'They bit me,' she wailed. 'Look, I'm bleeding!'

Another figure flew along the corridor, eyes wide, long hair streaming out. 'What's happened?'

'It's Sally,' Alec began. 'She says something bit her.'

'In her room?'

'Yes. No.' The shock had obviously confused Sally. 'I thought something had got stuck on the window frame. Tap, tap . . . it drove me mad, so I opened the window. I put my hand out to feel . . . Ouch, ouch.' Tears rolled down her cheek. 'It really does hurt.'

Eleanor shoulder-charged the door to Sally's room. Then she went to the window, slammed it down, twisted the lock shut, then closed the curtains.

'I'm bleeding.' Sally turned white.

'My God,' Alec exclaimed. 'Blood's gushing out of the poor girl.'

'Good!' was Eleanor's surprising comment.

Beth told her friend, 'I'll get a towel and stop it.'

'You'll do no such thing,' Eleanor snapped. 'She's got to bleed it out.'

Alec shook his head. 'Bleed what out?'

'Just get her to my room. Quickly.'

'But I've been bitten,' Sally cried. 'I'm bleeding to death.'

Eleanor gripped her hand so she could examine the wound. A series of puncture wounds like so ::::

'Oh, my dear God,' Eleanor groaned. 'They *have* bit her.' Suddenly, she raged at the top of her voice, 'After all these years! I thought I'd managed to stop it happening again! It's my fault! I should have destroyed them! But I couldn't. I didn't have the guts . . .' Her chest heaved with fury.

Sally shrank back in terror. 'What's she talking about? And what's bitten me?'

'Some animal . . .' Alec began.

'No animal,' Eleanor contradicted. 'I wish to heaven it were.'

Beth grabbed Sally's arm. 'Your brother has the same bite mark. Only his body is covered with them.'

Eleanor seized her long blouse sleeve. 'And the same as this.' She yanked back the cuff. The electric light shone down hard on to the wounds there. The same :::: pattern. They resembled tiny, red roses. The edges of the wound could have been miniature petals.

Beth shoved the woman's arm away. 'My friend's gushing blood here. I'm going to stop it.'

'No, let her bleed.'

Beth put her arm around Sally to guide her to her room.

Eleanor, with formidable strength, grabbed hold of Beth and swung her against the wall. 'I said: LET HER BLEED!'

'You're insane.'

Alec stopped Beth swinging her fists at Eleanor.

'You want to fight for your friend's life. Good!' Eleanor pointed to the staircase at the end of the corridor. 'Then bring her to my apartment. I've medicine.'

'Medicine for bites.' Alec floundered. 'But you need to staunch the bleeding before she has any drugs.'

'It's important to bleed the contagion out first.'

'Contagion . . .' Sally crumpled against the wall.

'I've got her,' Alec assured them as he swept her into his arms.

Beth pleaded, 'Let me wrap her arm in a towel; she's losing blood fast.' Eleanor didn't answer. She led the way at a run.

Alec nodded after the woman. 'She seems to know what she's doing. Trust her.'

In moments, they arrived at Eleanor's apartment, where she instructed Alec to lay Sally on the dining-room table. Then Eleanor went to work. With swift efficiency, she examined the wound. Blood coursed from the bite marks. It pooled, rich and red, on the wooden table top. 'Good. This flow is cleaning the wound.'

Cleaning the wound of what, exactly? Beth glanced at Alec and knew he was asking himself the same question.

Eleanor checked Sally's pulse, then studied the woman's eyes, as if searching for telltale symptoms.

'Beth, over there by the tailor's dummy,' Eleanor began. 'You'll find a clean bed sheet on the shelf. Tear it to pieces – use them as swabs to wipe the table. I need an area clear of blood so I can work on Sally.'

Beth didn't question the order. Eleanor really did appear to know what she was doing. But what, in God's name, had bitten not only Sally, but also this enigmatic hotelier and her brother in the past? Lord knew, she craved answers, yet she began shredding the cotton sheet.

'Alec. Open that cabinet in the corner of the room.' Eleanor pointed at the tallboy. 'You'll see glass jars full of white powder in front of you. Bring one to me.'

He opened the cabinet door to reveal a line of tall jars with glass stoppers. 'But which one?'

'Any will do, they all contain the same medicine. Then bring me a jug of cold water from the kitchen – it's through that door there. Quickly! I might be able to catch it in time.'

Again, those mystifying references to . . . what precisely? Catch it in time? Contagion? Beth wiped blood from the table, only it kept flowing from the punctures in her friend's flesh. She tore another strip from the sheet then folded it into a pad.

Eleanor guessed what she planned, 'Don't touch the wound yet, Beth. Blood loss is the least of our worries. Thank you.' She took the jar from Alec, unstoppered it, then shook a generous dusting of white crystals on to the bloody wrist. Sally lay there in a daze; she hardly noticed all the activity around her. 'Beth, pass me the scissors from the top of the sewing box. Thank you.'

Alarmingly, in what seemed a shocking act of sadism, Eleanor dipped the point of a scissor blade into the powder then pushed the tip of the blade into one of the open wounds.

Sally screamed.

Beth couldn't take any more. '*Stop it!*'

Eleanor repeated the procedure. The white-coated point of the blade penetrated the wound, just the tip, true, yet the pain of cold metal being forced into the injury made Sally convulse upwards from the table with a heart-rending shriek.

'I'm sorry,' Eleanor cried. 'You've got to trust me. This is for your own good.'

Beth had to steel herself from punching Eleanor. This procedure of driving the white powder into the bite wounds seemed utter madness, yet instinct told her to allow Eleanor to work. That same instinct told Beth, loud and clear, that a battle for life and death was being fought in this little room tonight.

'There.' Eleanor set the bloody scissors down. That done, she dusted the bite area with the white stuff again. As it mixed with the blood it formed a lurid orange. 'Beth, on the shelf beneath the glass jars are packs of sterile bandages.'

Alec returned with the jug of water. 'Quite a first-aid kit you've got there.'

'It looks more like a stock cupboard for an alchemist,' Beth commented as she handed over the bandages.

'It looks strange to you,' Eleanor said. 'Nevertheless, it saves lives. And it should, God willing, save your friend, too.'

Alec frowned. 'Does this mean Whitby is plagued by diseased animals? And that they are in the habit of biting people?'

'Something like that.'

'Shouldn't you be informing the police, Eleanor?' He watched her bandage Sally's wrist. 'After all, there are procedures for dealing with rabid dogs.'

'A dog – rabid or otherwise – never made that wound,' Beth told him, angrily. 'Sally put her hand out of a window that was more than twenty feet from the ground.'

'Now isn't the time for discussions.' Eleanor carefully measured a quantity of the same powder into a glass; that done, she added water to produce a liquid that sparkled. 'Help her to drink this. She has to take all of it.'

'What then?'

'Say a prayer; it might help. If I've done my work correctly then Sally will be back to her ebullient self in the morning.'

Sally appeared much calmer now. Though blood loss might have left her with that languor. However, she managed to sit up on the table in order to drink Eleanor's medicine. Although Beth found herself thinking of it as a 'witch potion'. The crystals sparkled with extraordinary brightness in the water. It appeared as if Sally were drinking a glass full of twinkling stars.

'Help me get Sally back to bed. That's where she needs to be right now.'

Alec gently supported Sally while she eased herself from the table. The woman appeared half asleep. Beth realized that the wound didn't seem to hurt her now.

'So what did bite her, Eleanor?' Alec asked.

'We need sleep, too, Alec. We're all exhausted. It's long past midnight.'

Beth, realizing that Eleanor wouldn't answer questions relating to the bite, fired an unrelated question. 'That's an unusual garment on the tailor's dummy. A coat made out of rubber?' In the white-heat of activity, when they were treating Sally, Beth hadn't noticed the strange garment, consisting of sections of heavy-duty black rubber fixed together with brass rivets. It was only now that it became strikingly obvious.

Eleanor simply pressed her lips together. No answers would get through that blockade of pink flesh.

Alec lacked subtlety. He simply fired off a salvo of direct questions: 'What bit the girl, Eleanor? Are we safe in the hotel? Shouldn't you describe the animal, in case we see it? What is the powder you used in the wound? Why do you need a coat made from industrial-grade rubber? Aren't you going to answer me, woman?'

By this time, they were in the corridor that led to Sally's room. 'It's too late to be debating this. Frankly, I'm too damn exhausted to give you any coherent answers.'

'When then?' Alec fixed her with his single good eye.

Beth nodded at the door to her own room. 'Take Sally in there. She can spend the night with me. I'll make up the second bed once we've got her settled.'

'Eleanor? When?' Alec's voice resembled the warning growl of a dog. The man needed answers.

'I'm going to Leppington in the morning to fetch more of the medicine. Meet me in the foyer tomorrow at five p.m. prompt.'

'You'll tell us then about all this?' Beth asked.

'No.'

Alec nearly erupted with anger.

Eleanor continued smoothly, 'I'll take you across to the cottage. You'll find out what you need to know there. In the meantime, keep your windows locked. And Beth?'

'Yes?'

'Sally should sleep until morning. But if she wakes and behaves oddly, or in any way out of character, lock her in the room, then come to find me. And make it fast.' As Eleanor withdrew, she turned to Alec. 'And it isn't a rubber coat, it is a protective apron. I designed it in order to save my life. Goodnight.'

After Eleanor's departure, the pair simply looked at each other, not knowing how to even begin commenting on what she'd just told them. Sally, meanwhile, had drifted into a deep sleep. Even so, her head turned from side-to-side; what's more, her lips moved, as if she tried to reveal some facts that frightened her.

Alec sighed. 'That woman, Miss Eleanor Charnwood. What on earth is she planning to do?'

Beth shivered, as if she'd just dipped her toe into an open grave. 'Whatever it is, she intends to make us part of her plans. That's right, Alec. She's going to use us. Whether we like it or not.'

The boy still watched the hotel from the darkness. Sam whimpered softly. Even the dog realized something was amiss. He was troubled by the sight of men and women climbing over the face of the hotel on all fours, as if scaling vertical walls was as easy as running up and down a gentle incline.

'Don't worry, Sam,' murmured the boy. 'I won't let them hurt us.'

Cold winds sped through Whitby's deserted streets. The hotel sign, which projected from above its door, creaked as it swung to and fro. In the distance, the soft roar of surf. The tide had, at last, turned.

For some reason, the six figures that swarmed over the hotel lost interest in the building – and its occupants. Fluidly, they descended to the ground, before speeding off into the night; they had all the predatory menace of panthers hungry for fresh prey.

Once more, the boy felt the tug of home. 'Come on, Sam.' He lightly touched the dog's back to attract his attention. Then the pair of them ran into the maze of streets that led to the cottage he'd once shared with his family. That was more than half a century ago, when the boy had been still really a boy, and not the creature that loped alongside his flesh-and-blood canine friend.

Eight

In this war, the fate of just one small ship would never be headline news. On the same cold February night that Sally felt those teeth sink into her wrist, other terrible events unfolded around the globe. Before sunrise put an end to yet another cruel night, Nazi aircraft bombed London. Tons of high explosive rained down on the houses of ordinary families. Direct hits on shelters obliterated people by the dozen. A bomb fractured the water main above a London Tube station, where three hundred sheltered. The deluge cascaded into the subterranean station: one hundred and fifty drowned. In the deserts of North Africa, armies clashed during the night. By the time Beth had settled down into bed at the Leviathan Hotel, the desert battlefield blazed with destroyed tanks. In Russia, the SS burnt an entire town. When the night retreated before the rising sun, it carried three thousand ghosts with it.

So what happened to the ship off the Whitby coast wouldn't trouble future historians that much. Nor would the loss of the *SS Banwick* have much of an effect on the course of the war.

The ship steamed northwards. It hugged the coast to avoid enemy submarines, prowling the shipping lanes. But the slow steamship, with its fifteen strong crew and contingent of a hundred and twenty-one troops bound for a garrison in Iceland, made an irresistible target for the German dive-bomber. Before any of the crew even saw the machine plunge through the dark clouds, it had released its armour-piercing bomb. It pierced the deck, passed right through the galley, where Cookie fried bacon for breakfast. A second later, it exploded in the coal hoppers that fuelled the ship.

As the blaze took hold, the captain ordered the helmsman to drive his craft aground, just half a mile from Whitby's harbour. Even if the ship couldn't be saved, its surviving passengers and crew would be able to scramble ashore.

Just fifty yards from the ship ramming the beach, the fire on-board reached the ammunition store. In a blossoming rose of igniting shells, the *SS Banwick* was torn apart. The explosion flung what was left of the men over a hundred acres of ocean.

When the sun peeked over the horizon, it had never seen an ocean as red as this. Bloody waters turned the surf pink. Waves carried what had flowed through men's hearts, until just minutes ago, to the base of Whitby's cliffs. There it poured through fissures in the rock. Soon, it found its way into the cavern that lay beneath Hag's Lung Cave, where both Eleanor and Gustav had been bitten twenty years ago.

Gallons of blood swirled into the great, hidden sump cavern. One that contained dozens of pale figures that had, in the main, lain sleeping here for a thousand years. Now the blood washed over the pale, naked men and women. The second the tide painted crimson splashes on cold skin the figures' eyes snapped open. The touch of the blood electrified them, energized them; it brought them alive again.

For now, they were contained in this prison of a cave. But as they excitedly licked the blood from each others' bare flesh they knew they'd be free soon. What's more, they'd woken properly for the first time in generations. And after such a long sleep? They were hungry. Relentlessly, furiously, searingly hungry. The time had come.

PART FOUR

{Caedmon's verse, circa AD600, translated from the Anglo-Saxon}

I sang to you of heaven's roof that protects us all
From Satan's storm
Now I warn of these lowly dales
Where the ghosts of Whitby town
Devoured the blood of King Oswy's soldier men . . .

One

The day began with rumours. Townsfolk were saying that a ship had been destroyed somewhere along the coast. Soldiers closed the cliff-top steps to deter sightseers. In the main, people just shrugged. 'It's wartime,' they told one another in Whitby's maze of ravine-like streets. 'Hitler himself could have been drinking in the Duke of York pub, but the army would hush it all up. We're told nothing.' Plenty had heard a huge detonation, though. For a while, there'd been real anxiety in certain quarters that a Nazi invasion had begun. By lunchtime, however, the soldiers that could be glimpsed on the cliffs merely stood about bored. Life soon returned to normal.

For Whitby's residents, that is. Beth had spent the morning with the distinct impression that a huge event was poised to happen. Something strange was in the air. Eleanor had already left for the Leppington train by the time Beth had gone downstairs. A note invited the three guests to make their own breakfast. None of them minded. They knew Eleanor didn't have any hotel staff.

Beth repeatedly asked Sally the same question, 'How's the wrist?'

And got the same reply, 'Fine. I don't know what the fuss was about.'

'Don't you remember what happened?'

Sally gave one of her carefree smiles. 'It's all a bit fuzzy really. I must have got light-headed after losing the blood.'

'Are you sure you're alright?'

'I'm fine. Really.' To prove it Sally waved her hand in a theatrical way. The bandage bore a brown smudge; the only visible reminder of last night's drama.

Alec took charge of making tea and toast. He strode into the dining room with a laden tray. 'Well, we're getting to the bottom of the biter tonight. Eleanor promised to tell all.'

Again, Beth figured that Eleanor planned to draw them into some scheme of hers. And today they would have to kill time until Eleanor revealed her secrets. This felt like waiting for a birth . . . or a death. It made her restless. *I want to know now,* she thought over and over. This air of mystery cranked up her nerves to screaming point. She needed a task to occupy her mind.

'You're going to take those establishing shots of Whitby today?'

Alec munched his toast. 'The boys should be out of the B&B now. They'll be loading the camera on the truck. Why?'

'I'm coming with you,' Beth told him.

'And me,' added Sally.

'I'll just be squirting off a few hundred feet of film to catch some pretty views. The harbour, a few boats and those old buildings on the waterfront.'

'After what happened last night – Theo on the roof, Sally being bitten – I'm too on edge to sit still.'

Alec appraised them. 'Alright. But wrap up warm, it's going to be Arctic out there.'

It became one of those days when everyone strove in a very deliberate way to be ordinary, and to do ordinary things. So they ate breakfast, washed the dishes, brushed their hair, put on thick overcoats, chose scarves. They talked about the weather. Alec pondered aloud, wondering whether to get footage of waves breaking over the harbour wall. From a hotel window, they could see boys larking about, trying to dodge cascades of water after they burst over the quay.

Beth knew that they were all trying hard to avoid imagining what mysteries would be revealed by Eleanor at five o'clock. *The purpose of the rubber apron? The cause of the bites? The nature of the white crystals in the jars? Stop it!* she fumed. *We'll be told everything tonight.*

She shared a mirror with Sally to apply lipstick.

'I can't wait until I'm in make-up for the filming,' Sally bubbled. 'Then someone will do this for me. And I've learnt my lines. Do you want to hear them?'

'Tell me on the way. I can already hear Alec's big boots clomping downstairs. He'll sulk if we're late.'

Ordinary, so ordinary . . .

Beth could almost believe that the dominating factor of their lives for the next two weeks would be the film shoot. Not the fact that something deeply and profoundly strange had occurred in this little coastal town. And that just hours from now the lives of Beth Layne, Sally Wainwright and Alec Reed would change forever.

Two

Beth, Sally and Alec gathered in the foyer of the Leviathan Hotel at five minutes to five. They'd spent the day working with the camera team to film Whitby's picturesque streets, its port crammed with boats, and views of the river winding down from the hills. By this time, the winter afternoon had surrendered to the night. Shadows flowed from alleyways. The harbour waters were the colour of dull iron.

Every so often, Sally scratched at the bandage around her wrist. Beth saw, to her relief, that the wound didn't unduly bother her friend; if anything, it seemed to be a little itchy, nothing more. Alec stared out of the window, as a naval gunboat glided out through the harbour mouth. No doubt it was departing on a night-time patrol, hunting for enemy U-boats. Because one eye still remained covered by the black patch, it seemed to imbue the other eye with a burning intensity. Perhaps he imagined what it would be like to be a member of the gunboat's crew. Out there, in cold waters, death might be waiting for the sailors. This might be their last glimpse of dry land.

The clock struck five. As the final chime shimmered on the still air a figure swept downstairs. Eleanor Charnwood, dressed in a calf-length black skirt and a black sweater. She'd plaited her long, black hair. It hung over one shoulder in a darkly glossy rope.

Instead of a greeting, she announced, 'I'm warning you all. What you'll encounter in my brother's cottage is going to disturb your peace of mind. I daresay it will frighten you. So, if you decide not to come, I shan't blame you.'

Alec boomed, 'You've got us hooked, Eleanor. We crave answers. After all, what on earth attacked Sally last night?'

Beth added, 'And was it the same thing that hurt you?'

'I could tell you –' Eleanor opened a door – 'but it's better to show you living proof. Although "living" is debatable.' She led the way. 'Follow me. Stay close; it's too dark for comfort.'

They followed Eleanor through the hotel kitchen to a rear door. This opened on to the walled yard. In one corner, her brother's cottage. The deepening gloom made it hard to see where they were stepping in the yard. And the hotel behind them had turned into a forbidding silhouette that loomed over their heads like a raised fist.

'Stay close,' Eleanor repeated. 'If I yell "run" don't question me. Just follow.'

Alec began with, 'Eleanor, what will be running from? If there's—'

She hushed him, then covered the remaining few yards to the door of the cottage. Made from heavy, black timbers, studded with iron, it possessed the disquieting appearance of the entrance to an ancient tomb. Eleanor produced a key; unlocked it. Quickly, she ushered them inside before closing and locking that grim door. That done, she switched on the light to reveal that the entire ground floor of the cottage consisted of an archaic kitchen, complete with a table and chairs that might have been roughly hewn from drift-wood. Human comforts were in short supply. The floor was starkly bare – no carpet, not even a hearth rug. A biting cold filled the place. When they exhaled it manifested ghosts of white vapour.

Sally spoke in a doubtful tone. 'Eleanor? Your brother really does live here?'

Again, she evaded the question. 'Come with me.'

Eleanor ascended the stairs to a tiny window that remained uncov-ered by blackout material. Carefully, she slid the cloth over the panes to ensure that no light escaped. The stairs didn't open on to a landing. Instead, they emerged directly into a single large room. At one end, a double bed.

Eleanor spoke matter-of-factly. 'There he is.'

Nobody approached the bed, with the exception of Eleanor. She went to her brother, who lay there, his eyes fixed on the ceiling. He showed no sign of noticing their entrance. What's more, he remained absolutely still.

'Oh no,' Sally gasped. 'He's died.'

Eleanor rested her palm on Theo's forehead. 'No. Not death. Not strictly speaking, anyway.'

Beth said, 'You didn't have to show us your brother like this. He won't want us gawping at him like he's a freak.'

'You wanted to know what was happening here, Beth. So I'm showing you.'

They took cautious steps forward. Theo remained perfectly still; he stared upwards from where he lay flat on his back. He wore black trousers and a white shirt; the top buttons of the shirt were open. *Maybe Eleanor has dressed him for this occasion*, Beth told herself. *But it's so bizarre to reveal your sick brother to strangers like this. What does she want out of it? What's her angle?*

'This is scaring me,' Sally whispered. 'What's wrong with him?'

Alec took another step closer. 'I can see the scars on his chest. They're the same as the ones on you, Eleanor, and on Sally's arm.'

Eleanor merely assented with a shrug.

Beth said, 'Theo is mid thirties. But he'd pass for twenty. Has the illness arrested the ageing process?'

'That's perceptive of you, Beth. Indeed it has.'

'So what now?' Alec asked. 'What are we supposed to glean from this display of your sibling?'

Eleanor eased back the curtain. 'The sun has set. It should be fully dark in a few moments.'

The gaunt figure didn't react to the sound of his sister's voice.

Sally took a cautious step towards the bed. 'What about his blankets? Isn't he cold, lying there like that?'

Again no answer passed through those formidable red lips of Eleanor Charnwood. Instead, she pointed at the stairs. 'Go back down into the kitchen. I'll follow.'

They retraced their steps to the frigid room below. Their feet on the stairs echoed. The sound of footfalls in a tomb. Alec and Beth exchanged glances, both knowing what the other was thinking. *What is Eleanor up to? She's planned something for us, that's for sure.* Sally trembled, scared-looking.

Silence descended on the kitchen. Eleanor went to a timber cabinet fixed to the wall. Producing a key from her skirt pocket, she unlocked it. Inside were more jars of the white crystals.

'I went to Leppington in order to replenish my stocks,' she explained. 'A family there make it from an ancient formula.' She measured an amount out into a glass, then added water from a jug. Once more, it resembled stars in solution. 'What it is exactly, or how it's made, I don't know. The family keep its ingredients a closely guarded secret. They merely refer to it as Quick Salts.'

Beth said, 'Quick meaning "life" rather than "fast". At least, in relation to these powders?'

Eleanor nodded. 'Alec, you have an extremely intelligent lady working for you. She invariably hits the nail on the head. Yes, this stuff could be termed "Life Potion".'

Sally screamed. '*Look!*'

The figure – tall, thin, gaunt-faced, with a terrible light burning in its eyes – stood at the foot of the stairs.

Eleanor said, 'Don't show any signs of panic. Just keep perfectly still.'

Sally's eyes roved anxiously around the kitchen. She was obviously searching for an escape route from this uncanny totem.

Theo didn't appear to notice them. He said nothing to Eleanor. Nor did she speak to him. He crossed to the table. His burning eyes fixed on the glass of medicine – the Quick Salts. A thin hand extended towards the glass. The fingers appeared unnaturally long; the fingernails were pale, with a whisper of blue. Before he could pick up the glass, Eleanor put her hand over it to block his grasp. At last, he made eye contact with her. She gave a shake of the head.

He didn't register any emotion at being prevented from taking the glass. Instead, he merely took a couple of steps towards the locked door to the yard. Then stood still. His eyes remained fixed on the door. If anything, when he turned his head ever so slightly, Beth guessed that he listened to sounds that she and the others failed to hear. A distant calling, perhaps. A summons – one so faint that only gaunt Theo, with the haunted eyes, could catch it on the cold night air.

Alec reacted with anger. 'Eleanor? Is this medicine important to your brother?'

'Of course.'

'Then why are you depriving him of it, woman?'

Near to tears, Sally cried, 'Don't leave the poor man to suffer. Have a heart!'

Eleanor remained calm. 'He'll drink the medicine. But all in good time. First we must wait for him to wake.'

'But he is awake,' Alec said.

'Properly awake. You're going to hear the story from his own lips.'

Three

Perhaps five minutes had elapsed since Eleanor's promise that they would 'hear the story from his own lips' when Theo changed. He'd stood a few paces from the door that led from the kitchen to the hotel yard. It still seemed to Beth that he appeared to be listening to sounds they couldn't hear. All of a sudden, he hunched his shoulders. Tremors ran through his body. He spun round to sweep a blazing stare over everyone present in the room.

'Eleanor. Naughty sister. Why didn't you warn me that we were having guests, hmm?'

'As a rule, Theo, you're not the listening type.'

'No?'

'No.'

'But then how long is it since you've allowed me to rise to the surface, so to speak?'

Beth saw that they weren't being unpleasant with each other. It struck her as the sibling banter that they'd grown up with. As if testing each other's affection for one another. He paced the kitchen. His movements were quick now. A darting wasp of a man, taking a sudden interest in his surroundings and his visitors.

Theo clicked his fingers. 'They're still fighting the war?'

'Yes.'

'How long now?'

'Almost three years.'

'Any bombs fallen on us?'

'No.'

'On Whitby?'

'A few. We've been luckier than lots of places. London's been hit hard.'

'Our handsome guests . . . who are they?'

Everyone had been too surprised to speak. Theo's transformation from inert statue to this lively, inquisitive man had been astonishing.

Then Sally blurted, 'We met last night. You were on the roof of the hotel.'

'The roof!' He eyed her with close interest. 'How extraordinary! How utterly nuts! What was I doing on that bloody roof?'

Daunted, Sally turned to Eleanor for help.

'You had a bit of a wander, Theo. Everyone here helped bring you back to safety.'

Beth started probing for information. 'On the roof you appeared to be listening to a faraway sound. One that you found irresistible.'

'Ah, I remember now. At least a little. I can hear their song. They're all like me now. Awake!' Theo paced around the table, eyeing the glass that contained the sparkling potion. 'You don't want me to drink it, Eleanor?'

'Not yet.'

'Then might I skip my medicine entirely for one night?'

'That's not a good idea.'

'Pleased to meet you. I'm Theo Charnwood.' He held out his hand to Alec.

Alec shook it. 'Alec Reed.'

'Ah . . . a man of Scotland. And?' He held out his hand to Beth. 'Charmed, dear lady.'

They shook hands as Beth told him her name.

'An American. How cosmopolitan. And the fairest of them all?' Smiling, he extended his hand to Sally. 'And you must be a Russian princess.'

Sally giggled. 'From Yorkshire, actually, just a couple of hours – oh!'

Instead of taking a hand, he seized her forearm and raised it to his face.

Alec lunged forward. 'Leave her!'

Eleanor called out, 'Alec. Don't touch him!'

Sally stared at Theo in shock, not knowing what he'd do to her but fearing the worst.

Theo moved slowly now, raising the bandaged wrist to his nose. He sniffed. 'Quick Salts . . . blood . . . and can I smell my old friends on you?' Glancing quickly at Eleanor, he asked, 'When did they bite her?'

'Last night.'

'You managed to treat the wound in time?'

'Yes.'

'Ah . . . it's coming back to me. I remember standing at my window and watching them climbing all over the walls of the hotel. Like rats, they were. Scurrying, prying, sniffing. Wanting in. Wanting something tasty between their teeth. Something like this!' His mouth pressed against the back of Sally's hand.

The woman sagged, close to fainting dead away. Then she sighed as she realized he'd simply kissed the flesh – quite lightly, a courteous formality.

'You know what kind of animal attacked Sally?' Beth asked.

'Animal. We haven't described them as such, have we, Eleanor, dear? Demons, monsters, and if you're feeling wicked call them vampires. That's what the locals would say, isn't it, Eleanor? Fierce, blood-hungry vampires.'

Beth shot Eleanor a quizzical look.

'No, he's sane, my dear. My brother's mind works perfectly, once the drug's cleared out of his veins.'

Swiftly, Theo pulled back chairs from the table. 'Sit down. Sit down. Your friend here suffered an attack by people who were once my friends.'

When they were seated (and still shooting wary glances at Theo) he began to talk. 'I don't have much time. So, I'll tell you what happened to Eleanor and me as quickly as I can. Please save your questions for the end.' His smile was surprisingly pleasant, turning that gaunt face into one that was strikingly handsome. 'My old school friend, Gustav Kirk, loved to read. You know, the visionary, fabulous stuff by the likes of Poe, Arthur Machen, Le Fanu and William Hope Hodgson. He also had an insatiable appetite for old Norse legends. Fables about Odin, Thor, Freya – in fact, all the pantheon of gods. His favourite was the god Tiw. From his name we get Tuesday, of course. Gustav had a fanciful nature. Even back as children, he liked to speculate that Tiw, an ancient and mysterious deity, even to the Vikings who worshipped him, had become angry at human beings for rejecting him in favour of the Man from Nazareth. If a boat sank, or if a car crashed off one of the moorland roads, or if some local tyke fell under the wheels of a train, Gustav would hold his finger up like this and say, "Ah, Tiw strikes again!"' Theo spoke with fluid ease; he barely resembled the zombie of a man they'd seen just moments ago.

Alec shook his head. 'You're saying that an old Viking god, with a taste for revenge, is responsible for whatever attacked Sally?'

'Save your questions for later, sir. Time is running out. But, yes. That's what my old friend would claim. That behind all the rotten things in this world, including the war and the hurting of the beautiful lady here, Tiw is to blame.' Theo extended his hand towards the glass of sparkling liquid. He seemed to have a love-hate relationship with those nightly doses of medicine. Sighing, he withdrew his hand. 'Well, that is Gustav's theory. An angry, vengeful god called Tiw. One so bitter as to be deranged. A deity with one purpose left: to make life a living hell for men, women and children everywhere. But especially Whitby. The location where Christian churches were united in the seventh century. Which, ultimately, resulted in the containment of the Viking hordes and their conversion to the Roman Catholic faith. So, if Tiw really can launch his crusade against humanity where better place? Whitby will be his battlefield. His Armageddon.'

'All very interesting,' Beth remarked, 'but where's the proof?'

'You have proof in the form of teeth-marks on dear Sally's flesh. More proof will come your way very soon.' He smiled. 'But you will keep interrupting.'

Eleanor said, 'Theo. Tell them what happened to us.'

He nodded, then, in that smoothly polished voice of his, he

unfurled past events that sent goosebumps popping up on Beth's spine.

'Eighteen years ago, Gustav Kirk decided to break into a cave known as Hag's Lung. Firstly, it fascinated him because so many legends attached themselves to it. Secondly, he was an intelligent and imaginative young man, who'd become so bored of this quiet little town that even to be reckless and foolhardy was preferable to spending another dull night at home with his parents. So, one evening in 1924, armed with candles, crowbar and a rope, he headed in the direction of the cave, which lies behind the abbey ruin. On the way, he met Eleanor. My sister was a formidable female. Even as a nineteen year old. When she insisted she join Gustav, he had no choice other than to accept her as part of his expedition.

'The cave had been sealed up on account of its dangerous reputation. More than one person has come to harm there down through the years. The pair broke open the big old timber door to the cave. Inside, they found the reason why the cave is known as Hag's Lung. A hole in the rock connects it with a sealed cavern. Geologists believe that fissures in that cavern run down to the shore at sea level. The action of the waves compresses the air in the hidden void, causing air to flow through the blowhole into Hag's Lung. It imitates perfectly the respiration of an animal. The air flows in and out. And, for reasons known only to my sister, she thrust her arm into the narrow opening. It was then . . .' He turned to regard her. 'It was then that something bit her on the wrist. Gustav should have simply got them both back into town. But Gustav couldn't stop from indulging himself with a closer look at the blowhole. A burning, uncontrollable curiosity drove him. If Gustav was here right now—'

'Heaven forbid,' whispered Eleanor.

'Gustav would put his finger in the air and claim, "Ah, Tiw strikes again."'

Sally frowned. 'You mean to say, this Tiw creature got inside his head and made him act nuts?'

'Absolutely. Anyway, as my sister slowly returned to her senses outside on the grass, Gustav used the crowbar to chip away at the narrow aperture in the rock to enlarge it. He succeeded only too well. When it was large enough, he managed to force his limb through the opening he'd made. A snug fit, I'm sure, but he did it. An act of madness. After all, he'd witnessed the attack on Eleanor, so it was hardly rational. And that's when mouths clamped on to his forearm. After that, Gustav wasn't Gustav any more – at least, not the man who'd been my best friend.' Theo stood up; a restlessness drove him to pace the kitchen. The surf attacked the beaches. A muted roar, as if a beast had woken from a deep sleep.

Eleanor said, 'I don't remember a great deal, other than I must have staggered home.'

Theo's edgy manner quickened his voice. 'Gustav underwent a fundamental change. He never returned home. As far as everyone was concerned he'd vanished into thin air. Oh, the police discovered that the cave had been broken into and found the crowbar that belonged to Gustav's father. The authorities concluded he'd entered Hag's Lung in a fit of insanity, then thrown himself off the cliff into the sea. No . . . that's not what happened at all. Theo underwent a biological transformation. Whether that was down to vengeful old Tiw, or some Darwinian evolutionary twist, I don't know. What I do know is that Gustav isn't human now. I don't normally use the word Vampire to describe him, but I wholeheartedly and passionately refer to him as Vampiric. A night creature. Sleeping by day. Searching for blood after dusk.'

Beth shook her head. 'But how can you know what happened to Gustav if he disappeared? You said he was—'

'Disappeared from sight, yes.' Theo moved faster. He seemed to be building himself up to reveal some secret . . . or maybe even to commit a wild act. 'Vanished. Gone. Not a sign. Not a glimpse. Until ten days after his visit to the cave. Then he called on Victoria. I understand from Eleanor that she tried to stop you crossing the bridge. He attacked her. Biting her through her clothes, then supping her blood. Sucking at it, like you'd suck juice from an orange. Not a pretty image, eh? One to revolt and to horrify. Later, he attacked more of his friends the same night. Then, just before dawn, I heard a tap at my bedroom window. Back then, I lived in the hotel. I opened the window, and Victoria rushed in at me. A flurry of limbs, open jaws, pain; I couldn't shout for help. All I felt were the teeth . . . They ripped through my skin.' He ran his fingers over his chest. Beth could glimpse the same pattern of scars on the skin beneath the open collar. A :::: effect.

Alec digested what he'd heard. 'And yet you weren't transformed.'

Theo ran his hands through his hair. 'Rumours spread about the attacks. It's happened before here in Whitby, and in Leppington up in the hills. A family there, who pass down certain secrets from parent to child, knew what to do. They visited Victoria and myself

– fortunately, we hadn't vanished from sight, unlike Theo and the others. They administered the same treatment as Sally received from Eleanor last night. Because of the delay between the attack and them reaching us, the treatment was only partially successful. The infection had reached too deeply into our systems.'

Eleanor added, 'Victoria and Theo's condition is held in check by the Quick Salts.'

'However, as you see, we lead lives that are greatly diminished. Basically, we're reduced to husks that merely resemble our past selves.'

This shook Sally. 'Does that mean I'll be like Theo? Has the bite infected me?'

'Trust me, dear –' Eleanor smiled – 'you'll be fine. I applied the powder in time.'

Beth found her eyes drawn to Eleanor's wrist. 'But Eleanor was bitten first. Why isn't she now like Gustav?'

'Ah, that's the great mystery!' Theo's manner had become volatile. 'That's what we'd all love to know! Gustav is bitten. He becomes Vampiric. He attacks a number of his friends. They turn into demonic night creatures. But what of my beautiful sister?' The sheer volume of his voice rattled pans on the stove. 'The skin is breached on her skin. One of the monsters in the cavern suckled. But why didn't Eleanor become infected? Why is she immune? What lies hidden in my sister's blood? A certain something that has kept her clean.'

'I don't feel clean,' she hissed. 'Look.' She pulled back the sleeve to reveal what resembled tiny pink roses budding from her wrist. 'Those are open wounds. They never healed. What's more, they never will heal. My life is blighted.'

'*Afraid a man can never love you, with your skin all punctured like that?*' Theo's voice had become savage – raw emotion coarsened it. 'But you've shared our mucky little secret with your friends here. That Whitby is plagued by vampires. So, now you've told them, what do you intend to do with your comrades in arms? Because that's what you've become. I can see it. You four people have forged a bond. You are a team. You care for one another. But will you die for each other?' He raked his fingers through his hair.

'Theo, calm down.'

'How can I be calm? I know too much, Eleanor. Do you know, at night I watch from my bedroom window? I see Gustav and his Vampiric friends swarming through town. They race through the streets like hungry panthers out on a hunt. Gustav has added more to his squad. There's a man in a pilot's uniform. He's also recruited

Mary Tinskell. And you know something? They excite me. I want
to run with them. I want to feed. I want to taste what they taste.'
The black pupils in his eyes grew more pronounced, fiercer. His
gaze raked over the people in the room. By now, he obviously
couldn't remain still if he tried. His hands ran over the timbers of
the door. When he spoke, the sentences came out fractured, guttural,
as if a transformation was taking place inside his head. 'I see everything. I know everything. There's a boy who runs with a black dog.
The dog is as alive as you warm, healthy people. Yet the boy is
Vampiric. He was taken seventy years ago. He searches for a way
back home. His parents? Oh . . . his parents are long dead. Instinct
drives him. Home is what he hungers for, not blood. Home, home
. . . Strange that, isn't it?' He paced the room again. 'Then not
everyone bitten becomes Vampiric. Isn't that the truth, dear Eleanor!'

'Theo,' Eleanor said firmly. 'Drink the medicine.'

'Oh, you want me to drink now. To imbibe! To revert back to
the tenth of a man I once was! You only dragged me back to my
senses so I could reveal your horrific secrets for you. Because you're
still afraid to admit that this tragedy ever occurred.' He sucked air
through his nostrils. 'And do you want to know something really
horrific? I hear them in the sump cavern. All of Tiw's vampires. You
know, he raised the dead from a battlefield over a thousand years
ago. Hundreds of dead Viking warriors gathered up into Tiw's super-
natural embrace . . . He breathed life back into them, then left them
in the sump cavern. There they bided their time. Waiting. Now a
war is raging. The country is forced to remain in darkness by night.
A mandatory blackout. And isn't the blackout a perfect environment
for the vampire?' He listened again. 'I hear them singing. Last night,
a ship blew up near the cliffs. The blood of all those men washed
through fissures into the sump. Picture it: a broth of crimson surging
in with the tide. It painted the bodies a glorious, living red. They
bathed in blood. And they exulted. The vampires sing about their
excitement. About their lust to be free. To join Gustav and to drink
the blood of Whitby men and women dry.'

'Theo, take this.'

'Alec. Ask me how I know. Interrogate me, Beth. How can I
know all this . . .?' He pushed his fists against his temples. 'But I do.'

Alec and Beth moved towards Theo. Sally pulled back one of the
kitchen chairs. Eleanor picked up the glass that contained the glittering liquor.

Theo's nostrils flared. 'I can smell it in your veins. All that red nectar . . . it's pounding through your heart. And I know Gustav and his kind are worming their way out of holes in the cliff face. Those are their lairs, you know. During daylight, that's where they sleep. High in the cliff where nobody will find them. The boy will be pushing himself out of his tomb to join the dog. They'll be running towards Whitby soon. I know all this . . . but I've not set foot outside the hotel boundary for years. So – how do I know? As Gustav would say, "Ah, Tiw strikes again!"' He turned to face the door.

Beth sensed the man's eagerness. What's more, tension sizzled in the air. She'd sensed it in the studio when she'd wandered into the set of Whitby that had never existed in the first place. *Perfidious Tiw. Is he going to meddle in human affairs again? Is he planning another calamity to befall us?* She blinked hard, trying to squeeze the unsettling thoughts from her mind.

Alec took another step towards Theo.

Without looking back at him, Theo said, 'Alec, a few days ago you were spared death. You must be wondering why. Ha, no doubt you'll find out very soon.' Theo whirled round. 'I knew that you'd become a warrior band. You don't even realize it yourself, but see how you can almost read one another's minds? Sally has the chair ready. Alec and Beth plan to grab me. Then, when they force me into the chair, my dear sister will pour that elixir into my mouth.' He grinned, but his face no longer seemed handsome. A monstrous quality distorted it. Whatever it was that the drug normally suppressed, it was beginning to surface. 'Ladies and gentleman. You have become a pack of hunters.'

Alec reached out to take Theo's arm. The gaunt man flinched back so quickly that his back slammed against the door.

'Don't worry, my friends. I'll drink the blessed potion.' He struggled to maintain self-control. 'Because if I didn't take my medicine, the thought of what I will become terrifies me.'

His movements were jerky rather than graceful now. Quickly, he sat at the table, took the glass from Eleanor; drank it down in one. By the time he placed the glass back on the table, the tremors had stopped in his limbs. His features relaxed. His air of relaxation even reached out into the room as a whole. The tension that had been building in the very fabric of the walls eased.

'Theo,' Eleanor murmured. 'Go back upstairs. Why not read for a while?'

Slowly, he lifted his eyes to hers, gave a sluggish nod, then stood up before climbing the stairs.

Beth picked up the silver spoon that Eleanor had used to stir the powder into the water. Sally watched her actions with complete mystification.

However, Eleanor knew perfectly well what she was doing. 'That's quick-witted of you, Beth. You're testing the vampire theory by checking the spoon for my brother's reflection.'

'It's distorted, but he does have a reflection.'

'And according to the myth,' Alec added, 'vampires don't reflect their image in a mirror.'

'That's what happens in stories,' Eleanor agreed. 'But the myth became scrambled through the centuries. Vampires are capable of being seen in mirrors, just the same as you and I. In truth, those creatures that are Vampiric avoid mirrors, because they can't see themselves as they really are. Do you follow? When a vampire looks into a mirror, they delude themselves; they believe they see a beautiful, healthy man or woman. Not a loathsome creature, driven half mad by the desire to gorge on blood.'

Alec gazed very directly at Eleanor. 'So you believe that Gustav is a vampire?'

'The more accurate term is Vampiric.'

'Is that a "yes", then?'

'Yes. I know he's not human. But equally I know that neither a crucifix nor garlic will scare him. A stake through the heart does not kill them. Local legend has it that the Vampiric creatures of Whitby can only be destroyed in three ways: beheading, dismemberment or burning.'

Beth sat down in the chair. 'You intend to kill Gustav and his friends?'

'I've evaded my responsibility for too long. I hoped that someone else would do it for me. But apart from the family in Leppington that supplies the Salts, and my brother, I'm the only one to know. Well, we and Victoria's family, of course, and they keep their mouths shut with regard to that particular issue.'

'Tell the police.'

'And they will take me to an asylum. Who will give Victoria and Theo the Salts? Without daily doses, they will eventually transform.'

'Something extraordinary has happened here, Eleanor,' Beth told her. 'But do you expect us to believe that monsters, with a taste for human blood, emerge from the cliffs every night to attack human beings?'

Eleanor sighed. 'What bit Sally? What did she see in the cellar last night?'

Sally flinched. 'You mean, I didn't imagine that man beneath the grate?'

'No, dear. You met Gustav.'

'Then we're in danger.' Beth eyed the door; all of a sudden, it seemed a flimsy barrier to the yard and to whatever might prowl there.

'Yes, you're in grave danger.' Eleanor's expression was one of pained sadness. 'Gustav returns to try and talk to me at least once a year. Mostly, he enters the tunnel that runs from the waterfront to the shaft beneath the iron grate. You see, he tried so very, very hard to stay human. Gustav was such a gentle boy. A lovely human being who wouldn't hurt anyone, or even say anything bad about people. Even though he craves blood, he uses every shred of willpower to stop himself attacking people.'

'But something happened?'

'The war happened. Suddenly, fresh bodies were being washed up on the beach from torpedoed ships. Aircraft were shot down at night. Gustav and his friends were offered a tempting feast every time a ship sank offshore, or men tumbled out of the sky. The smell of blood stained the very air. If you're as hungry as they are, how long would you resist if tempting food were put in front of you? And they did resist for a long time. But then . . .' She shrugged. 'They could resist no longer.'

'But vampires, or even Vampiric beasts, Eleanor?' Alec resisted the facts that had been lain out before him. 'How can a sane individual believe?'

Eleanor headed for the stairs. 'Your doubt is understandable. That's why I'm going to take you to the cave.'

'Hag's Lung?' Sally trembled. 'I'd be too afraid.'

'You need proof. Firstly, I'll check that Theo is settled for the night.'

'Why should we need proof?' Alec rubbed the patch over his eye. When he became anxious it was obviously irritating to him. 'This isn't our war.'

'Is the fight against Hitler not your war, either? Would you prefer to make friends with him?'

'That's a vile suggestion.'

'So, why can't you help me fight the evil that comes to our very doors?' Eleanor's voice rose. 'People are going missing in Whitby. Because of this war, the disappearances are covered up by the authorities. They don't want to alarm the public. And because we are forced to keep the streets dark at night, Gustav and his kind are free to move around. The blackout is their playground. They can do what they like.'

'So what's it to be, Eleanor?' Beth asked. 'Beheading, dismemberment or fire?'

'Something a little more scientific. But first we'll visit the cave. I'll show you the creatures trapped in the sump.'

'*If* they're still trapped,' Sally added darkly.

'Oh, they must still be locked away in there.'

'How do you know?'

'Because if they weren't, my dear, you would have become one of them by now. And I would have to kill you, too.'

Four

Tommy searched the streets of Whitby for his parents. Even though the town had yielded to absolute darkness, the boy saw every cottage, kennel, alleyway and tavern. The dog loped alongside. Sam's short fur appeared to shine like black glass to the boy's dark-adapted eye. A restlessness to find his family didn't allow him to pause for long. He sensed they called to him. *But where are they? They always seem just beyond my reach.* Of course, Tommy had yet to understand that his parents had died decades ago. His little sister was now an old woman in a nursing home in Scarborough. In a yellowing, faded album, there were photographs of her, her mother and father, and Tommy, a cheerful boy of eleven, who had vanished one winter's night in 1868.

Sam sped alongside Tommy as they ran along Church Street to the market square. The clock's hands touched eleven. No townsfolk ventured out into the darkness. Tommy had seen soldiers with rifles up on the cliffs. But he couldn't understand why they needed to stand guard there. Any more than he could identify those black crosses that rumbled overhead after sunset. The word 'aeroplane' had no meaning for him. Tommy recalled his father would often visit the Black Horse Inn to drink a glass of that rich, amber beer while he discussed the day's fishing with friends. His father never drank as much as the other men, preferring to return to his family before the children's bedtime. Might his father have hurt himself on the

way back from the inn? Maybe he lay in the street, waiting for
Tommy to find him?

Tommy entered the little cobbled area known as Market Place.
Like the streets, it slumbered away the night hours in silence. The
boy and his dog circled the peculiar stone building, which rested
on pillars at the entrance to the yard, where stalls of vegetables
and baked meats would be set out by day. He scoured the stone
pavement, expecting to see the slumped figure of his father. All he
found were discarded cigarette butts, matches, apple cores, shreds
of newspaper – no sign of a man needing Tommy's help to get
safely home.

Every so often, Sam would glance in the boy's direction. The dog
sensed the child's anxiety. And from time to time he picked up on
a yearning to find something precious that had become lost.

As he crossed the square, Tommy cried out in excitement. A man
stood with his back to him. Tommy wanted so desperately to find
his dad that for a moment he recognized the figure as his broad-
shouldered fisherman father. He knew that line of the jaw as the
head began to turn. Already, he could imagine his father's face breaking
into a smile, when he saw his son running towards him.

'Dad!' Tommy ran faster, his arms held out for the warm hug his
father always gave him when he returned to port.

But the figure before him wasn't his father. Sam stopped dead,
his front legs splayed out, a snarl rolled in his throat.

The man lunged at Tommy. A pair of viciously powerful hands
gripped his arms. The face that loomed out of the shadows had the
stark, white quality of bone. The eyes that burnt into Tommy's were
bereft of colour. The pupils were points of darkness.

'A boy . . . A boy in a hurry . . .' murmured a cold voice. The
grin that followed revealed small, even teeth that looked strangely
out of place in the mouth.

Sam launched himself at the man. Before he could sink his fangs
into the man's leg another figure flew from the shadows. It gripped
the dog by the throat.

Tommy tried to kick free as the lady in the pale nightdress pulled
the dog away. 'Save some of the boy's blood for me. You must!' she
hissed.

'Try dog blood,' the man uttered. 'It might be sweeter than you
think.'

More figures flowed into square. One wore strange clothes: a
helmet of leather and goggles that covered his eyes. Alongside him

stood a man dressed in white. For some reason he wore a brightly striped tie around his waist in place of a belt.

The man holding Tommy chuckled. 'Just a sip each from this.'

The man in white approached, his keen eyes studying Tommy's face. 'He's not mortal. You won't find an ounce of blood in his veins.'

'But he's not one of us,' said the man holding Tommy. 'I'd have known.'

The white-clad man shook his head. 'He's older than us. Much older. Maybe he's beyond bloodlust now, or maybe his transformation is different to ours.'

Tommy's captor tugged the boy's wrist towards his face. 'He bears the same scars as we do, Gustav.'

'Nevertheless, he's not the same. Not quite.'

'But he must be. Everyone who is bitten by our kind transforms,' said the woman in the white, as she gripped the dog's neck. Sam still struggled, trying to get his teeth into her hands, his eyes rolling in fury.

'Eleanor didn't.' Gustav took the boy's chin in his hand and raised it so that he could study his face. 'Eleanor received the gift the same night as me, but she never transformed. The gods must have another use for her.' He smiled. 'As I was fond of saying, "Tiw strikes again."'

The captor relaxed his grip on Tommy. 'Then he's no use to us.'

'Keep hold,' the woman hissed. 'If he's not the same as us, he'll become a danger.'

'Just a child,' Gustav declared. 'Doesn't he wear such a sad expression? He's a lost boy.'

'Destroy him.' The woman exerted a crushing grip on the dog's neck. 'Rip him to pieces.'

'How could this little scrap of a thing harm us?' Gustav released his hold on Tommy's jaw. 'He's just skin and bone.'

'Don't underestimate him.' The woman had spite in her eye. 'What if he leads them to where we sleep?'

'Look at the style of his clothes. He must have been roaming Whitby for sixty years or more. In all that time he can't have touched a human being, let alone caused any harm.'

'Did you hear that, boy?' The inhuman eyes of the woman burnt in the darkness. 'You left your mortal self behind over half a century ago. Your mother and father will be long dead. There's nothing for you here now. Just ask us to end your misery, and we'll do it.'

Words spurted from Tommy's lips. 'Ma and Dad aren't dead. You're lying. And get your hands off my dog. Can't you see you're hurting him?'

Sam squirmed in the woman's rough grasp.

'I'm putting an end to the dog,' snarled the woman. 'Both are a risk to us.'

'We're not monsters,' Gustav told her. 'We retain human qualities.' Gently, he asked, 'Boy, what's your name?"

'Tommy, sir.'

'Tommy. We are here for a higher purpose. Not to kill boys and their dogs.'

The woman hissed, 'If you let them go, you'll regret it.'

Gustav shook his head. 'This is nothing but a poor boy and his mutt. Tommy's no longer alive in the accepted sense, neither is he dead. Allow him and the animal to go unharmed.'

Gustav touched the arm of the man who held Tommy. The moment the man released him, the woman threw the dog aside. She flew at Tommy, her fingers hooked into claws, her mouth yawning wide. Gustav darted forward, blocking her way. As she snarled in frustration, Tommy ran to Sam. The dog wagged his tail and licked the back of his hand.

The woman blazed with anger. 'I thought you were intelligent, Gustav. You and all that book learning, and the son of a doctor. But you're a fool. If that boy isn't one of us, then he must be our enemy. Rip him and his mutt to pieces while you can.'

'If Tommy didn't make the same transformation as we did, he has a unique purpose. The gods have plans for him.'

'Plans? Gods? Higher purposes?' the woman sneered. 'You talk about this old Viking god, Tiw, like he's real. It's all imagination. Wake up, scatterbrained dreamer. You're all mixed up in make-believe. Listen. The world is a battlefield. The Allies fight the Nazis. But our war is with mortals. We're fighting for our survival.'

'What did people do to you to make you so bitter, Mary? Why do you hate?'

'I'm a realist. There is no old pagan god tugging puppet strings. We're just hungry vampires who need good, hot blood inside of us. That's all. Blood. Plenty of rich, tasty blood to fill our bellies.'

'Mary. We're not vampires. We're more than that. We have a special purpose.'

'And so have I.' She whirled to where Tommy stroked his dog. 'And one of my purposes is to destroy those two. I'll crush them and bury them out on the moor. Mark my words, Gustav, you can't guard them forever.'

Even as she spoke, all self-restrain evaporated. Once more, she lunged at Tommy and his dog, jaws stretched wide, hands grasping for Tommy's throat. Just in time, Gustav caught the woman. Like a wild cat she writhed in his arms. The other vampires were stirred by the violence. Their expressions grew more inhuman, as they fixed Tommy and Sam with predatory eyes.

Gustav called to Tommy, 'Go . . . they're changing. Even I can't stop them now . . . Go on! Run!'

Tommy and Sam fled into the darkness. Behind them, the man in white tried to calm his companions. But they weren't listening to reason. They wanted blood.

Five

All the town's clocks struck midnight. A cool breeze sighed around the chimney pots. From the direction of the beaches, ocean rollers boomed long and low, as they had done for ten thousand years. Slowly, the moon emerged from a cloud bank to illuminate their way.

Beth Layne ascended the cliff-side steps. At her side, Sally panted. The stiff climb started to take its toll on the pair. Behind and below, the jumble of red roofs appeared to be intersected by rivers of darkness. These were the deep streets and alleyways of a sleeping Whitby. Ahead of Beth, Alec and Eleanor hurried up the steps. An eagerness drew the duo up to the darkness of the cliff heights.

'Sally, we must be mad to have agreed to this.' Beth's thighs burnt from exertion. 'Who on earth wants to break into a cave at midnight?'

'Proof,' Sally gasped. 'Eleanor said we'd find vampires. Like the one that bit me.'

Beth glanced sharply at Sally. The woman's eyes gleamed. She seemed to have fallen under Eleanor's spell.

'Tiw strikes again,' Beth murmured.

'Pardon?'

'Tiw strikes again. That's what the friend of Theo's used to utter when anything bizarre happened. Do you think Tiw's inside our brains, making us tramp up here at midnight . . . Uh . . . these steps – will they ever end?'

Sally giggled. Perhaps the excitement intoxicated her? 'There are a hundred and ninety-nine steps from Church Street up to St Mary's. I've counted a hundred and twenty-two.'

At that moment, Beth felt that she alone retained a shred of sanity. *After all, can't we explore the cave by daylight? Why now? Is Eleanor drawing us into a carefully calculated trap? And what if we're caught? Surely, breaking into locked caves is illegal? So how do you plead, Beth Layne?*

'I'm guilty of rash behaviour.' Her throat burnt from breathing hard. But still she climbed. She'd promised to look after her friend. And right now Sally was hell-bent on following the pair in front.

The others didn't pause for long to catch their breath. And nobody stopped to admire Whitby by moonlight, an eccentric cluster of buildings cut in two by the River Esk. Tonight its waters shone silver in the moonlight. Boats rested at anchor. No lights shone from either vessels or cottages. Once night fell, the town's population retreated into their homes, locked all doors and windows, and waited for sunrise. Did they fear those Vampiric creatures that were reputed to roam the streets?

'Come on.' Sally tugged Beth's arm. 'Haven't you got your breath back yet?'

'I wish to God all of you had got your sanity back.'

'This is so exciting. We're on a monster hunt!'

'Tiw strikes again.'

'Beth, why do you keep saying that?'

'Because we're not acting normally, are we?'

'If we find those vampires, we'll be famous.'

'Yeah – dead famous.'

'Hurry, Beth, or we'll be left behind.'

Despite her misgivings, Beth allowed herself to be guided by Sally along the moonlit path. At either side, ancient tombstones reared from the earth. To their left lay the bulk of St Mary's Church. Ahead, the tall, spindly ruins of Whitby Abbey. A cold breeze made Beth's eyes water. Sally kept their arms linked. This woman, so normally nervous of anything strange, and who yelled at the sight of a spider, now dragged Beth towards a cavern with a sinister reputation. *The war has sent us insane. It's the stress of all the air raids. The threat of invasion. Ye Gods, the world has been turned upside down. No wonder we're acting crazy.* Hundreds of tombstones surrounded them. Eroded into weird shapes, they formed an army of hunched figures in silhouette. Beneath them would be the tombs of generations of Whitby men and women. When she walked by, did skulls in the coffins turn to watch her feet pass above them? Did they beat their coffin lids with bone fists? Were they trying to warn her to go back? To flee from danger? *Or do they call out to me to join them?* Whitby's like that. A town where impossible events became a rock-solid certainty. In Whitby, even the dead don't lie quietly.

Dizzy from exertion, and from the strange thoughts washing through her head, Beth staggered.

'Don't worry. I've got you,' Sally told her.

How long Beth had been in that trance-like state she didn't know. When Eleanor pointed at timber doors set in the grass, Beth had to shake her head to dispel a fog from her mind. She glanced back; already, they were some distance from the abbey ruin. Fortunately, they were also a good distance from the soldiers stationed at the anti-aircraft gun. With luck, the military wouldn't spot these four interlopers.

'Tiw strikes again,' she blurted with a giggle.

The other three laughed. Their eyes were strangely wide. Their movements possessed a buoyant quality, as if gravity here on the cliff had weakened. The moon became unusually bright. Beth found herself seeing it as a glass porthole. One to a room that was brightly lit. A face appeared to press at it. Eyes watched the four humans dancing around the cave doors with malicious interest. Like a nasty old man watching a child wobble on a bike and knowing the child would soon fall – and *willing* the child to fall hard. Very hard, with bone snapping force.

'Tiw! Tiw is watching!' Beth pointed at the moon.

Alec's good eye rolled up in astonishment. 'So he is. The old Viking god has come to take a peek at us down below.'

Sally hugged herself and laughed.

Eleanor handed Alec a tool bag. 'The crowbar's in there. Candles and a torch, too.'

'You think of everything, my dear. You know we must get married. You are beautiful. Our children will be angels.' Alec moved to kiss her.

'Ah, later, my handsome Gaelic prince.'

'May I come to your room, Miss Charnwood, when we're done rummaging amongst your vampires in the cave?'

'Hag's Lung.' Sally recited the name, savouring its sound. 'Hag's Lung.'

'Thank you for bringing us here, Eleanor.' Beth grinned, knowing that her grin was a vast, happy one.

'Eleanor's very generous,' Sally gushed.

Alec pulled out the crowbar. 'Very. Why! Before we left . . . she gave us all a glass of her finest brandy to keep out the cold.' He staggered a little. 'Liquid magic it was.'

'You get to work with the crowbar,' Eleanor told him brightly. 'There are four padlocks. See how quickly you can break them.'

Alec chuckled. 'I'd like to see how quickly I can strip you naked tonight.'

'Padlocks first.'

Sally swayed. 'I've never watched anyone make love.'

Alec saluted her. 'Tonight will be a first, sweetheart. You'll watch me stroke the bare flesh of gorgeous Eleanor. Then I will immerse myself in her beautiful nakedness. Her cool thighs, silky breasts, smooth stomach; she will drench me with her long hair. Then I will drown myself in her beauty.' He pushed the crowbar into one of the padlock hasps. 'The ecstasy I experience will reach Tiw, there in the moon – and it will set his veins afire.' He snapped the padlock.

Beth touched her lips. They were numb. The moon shone so brightly that each stalk of grass blazed with its own green light. Such green. She'd never seen anything like it. A big, juicy green that made emeralds appear dull.

'Eleanor,' Beth said at last. 'You put something in the brandy, didn't you?' Beth found herself grinning, yet her tone was deadly serious. 'You drugged us.'

Sally and Alec laughed.

Eleanor smiled. 'Just a little stimulant. A certain quintessence to keep you alert.'

'You witch, Eleanor. You damn witch.' Beth tried to be angry; however, she started to chuckle.

As Alec broke the last of the padlocks, Beth whirled around, her arms outstretched. She felt so warm inside. So delicious. She longed to be kissed. She could imagine herself sinking back into the grass with a sigh of pleasure, as a bodily weight pressed down on her.

Giggling, Sally hugged herself. 'Alec. When you've finished with Eleanor tonight, will you still have strength to love me, too?'

'There'll be time for all the embraces you desire later,' Eleanor told them. 'First we're going down into the cave.'

Six

They entered Hag's Lung. The cave had a high roof. Milk-white stalactites hung down over their heads – stone swords pointing at them. The cave covered the same area as a tennis court; not at all large. Beth had expected to find stagnant air, yet this had a fresh ocean scent, cold and sharp. Alec and Sally laughed. Their voices were overloud due to the narcotic in their bloodstreams. The immense, echoing din made Beth cover her ears.

Eleanor lit candles, then set them on a boulder; that done, she shone the torch round the cave. 'There's the hole,' she said. 'The one I put my arm through.'

Beth's mind had begun to clear. A sense of outrage burnt. 'Eleanor? What made you put the drug in the brandy?'

'Like I said, you all needed a pick-me-up.'

'Pick-me-up? Whatever narcotic you used has sent us crazy. Just look at those two.' She pointed at Alec and Sally. They sang *lah-lah-lah* at the tops of their voices, as they linked arms to dance round and round in the centre of the cave.

Still twirling, Alec called, 'Eleanor, show us your bloody vampires!'

Sally giggled. 'Where are they? We want to dance with Dracula!'

'You'll pay for this, Eleanor.' Waves of vertigo swept over Beth. 'Spiking our drinks is wrong. It's illegal. It's *immoral*. You—'

'Witch? That's the name you called me tonight. It's what the townspeople call me, too. Eleanor the Witch. Wicked Witch of the East.' Her eyes flashed. 'But I've saved Whitby from the vampires in the past. I treat Theo and Victoria with Quick Salts every night, so they don't turn into monsters. And that's how I'm repaid! By name calling . . . by being scorned. You saw how people avoided me in the street! Whitby doesn't deserve this . . . but I'm going to destroy the vampires once and for all!'

Beth swayed. In her drugged state, those sword-blades of stone that were the stalactites appeared to stretch towards her, as if they'd impale her to the floor.

She shook her head, trying to dispel the fuzzy sensation. 'But why have you waited for so long? You told us the attack on you and Gustav took place here nearly twenty years ago.'

'For a long time, Gustav and his kind didn't bother us. They needed blood, but I suspect they took it from sheep in the hills, or even from rabbits in the fields.'

'You are a spineless coward, Eleanor. You were afraid to go to the police because you were scared they'd call you names, too.' She laughed. 'Mad Eleanor. Crazy Eleanor. Eleanor the nut; she believes vampires visit her hotel. That's what you thought they'd say.'

'I'm not a coward!' She shoved Alec and Sally aside, as they still spun, arms linked. 'What I needed were allies. When you and Sally and Alec arrived, I thought I could trust you.' Tears glistened. 'But you're a shallow woman, Beth Layne. You only have faith in what you can see and touch. You believe in the lipstick you use, the red varnish on your nails. Oh yes, you're happy to make-believe in front of cameras with actor friends – but you refuse to believe in the battle I've fought in here.' She pressed her fist to her breast. 'Twenty years, as near as damn it, I've lived with the secret – that my brother and my friends were attacked by Gustav after he was infected by those monsters. Yes, he is a vampire.' She bared her wrist to reveal the never-healing wound; those puncture wounds in a double row ::::: 'For some reason, the infection didn't take hold in me. But these wounds are always raw, they itch, they keep me awake at night. And they are a constant reminder that I can never marry. Because I'm terrified I will pass on some vile contagion.'

'But you drugged us, Eleanor. That means we didn't come here of our own free will.'

Alec and Sally now held each other, chuckling insanely, kissing each other's faces. The breeze fluttered the candles: mad shadow-dancers swarmed the walls.

'I did it in order to prove to you that the vampires exist.' Eleanor advanced on Beth, her eyes glittering. 'Because I need your help, now I've made my decision.'

'What decision?'

'I've decided that I must destroy those creatures. Gustav and his pack of vampires. They were my friends. I loved them once. Now I have to watch them burn.'

'Look at Alec and Sally. They're so full of your filthy drug that they can barely stand. In the morning, we'll find another place to stay.'

Eleanor lunged at her. 'You want proof? Come with me!'

'Eleanor—'

'You asked for it.'

The woman had formidable strength. She dragged Beth across the cave floor. Sally and Alec still giggled away like dizzy sweethearts. The torch in Eleanor's hand sent giant, distorted shadows leaping madly. Beth struggled. The drug, however, left her disorientated; it seemed nigh impossible to coordinate her limbs, never mind actually fight the woman.

Eleanor seized the back of Beth's head so that she could force her face to the hole in the wall. Barely four inches across, it plunged deeply into the rock. For some reason it reminded Beth of an open mouth, which revealed the throat of a beast. A notion reinforced by air rushing through it. One moment, a chilling blast into her face. Then it sucked inward, pulling her hair into the orifice. The gusts carried rich odours of ocean, kelp, shellfish and a subtle organic odour. It was by no means a foul stench. It possessed intriguing notes that tugged at a nerve.

'Look!' Eleanor hissed into her ear. 'See it? That's where I pushed my arm twenty years ago. See the gouge marks around the opening? That's where Gustav tried to widen it with a crowbar – only, he got too close, and they turned him into one of their kind.'

'*They?*'

'Yes, they!' Eleanor forced Beth's face closer. 'That little tunnel leads to the sump cavern. Fissures in the earth allow the sea to pour into it, but those cracks in the rock are too narrow to allow the creatures to escape into the outside world – for now.' Eleanor pushed harder. Cold lips of stone pressed against Beth's cheek; her eyes watered as air gusted into them.

'Eleanor. Don't do this. Let me go.'

'You must have that proof. I need you to help me. I can't do this alone.'

'Eleanor, please . . .'

'Look through the passageway.'

Eleanor shone light into the darkness. The electric beams sliced away shadows. Beth cried out at the sight that struck her eyes. In the harsh, silver radiance they were revealed with such brutal clarity. Beth gasped, shivers cascaded down her body, as her eyes focused on those squirming forms. The narrow shaft that Eleanor had once forced her arm through was no more than three feet long. It opened into a cave that adjoined Hag's Lung. Inside: squirming, writhing shapes that were moist and pale. With her face to the hole in the rock, it was almost like looking through a keyhole into a room beyond. At first, the figures seemed to consist of the same kind of flesh as shellfish – white, glistening muscular shapes, with no part of the body readily identifiable.

Beth had the impression of hundreds of bodies in there. They filled the cave, just as shrimp are crammed into a glass jar. Then, as her mind made sense of those restless, turbulent figures, she began to see arms, legs, sides of heads, ears, hands. Then it happened. A face slammed to the opening at the other end of the miniature passageway. A face with human proportions, yet utterly *inhuman*.

Eyes. Nose. Mouth. The mouth yawned wide, as the Vampiric face strained forward against the corresponding hole at the other side. *Those teeth? Dear God. They match the wound pattern on Eleanor's wrist.*

Beth screamed.

As she did so, she heard a clatter of footsteps. Suddenly, figures poured through the cave entrance behind her. Hands seized her roughly. An arm encircled her neck. Beth screamed again, then a hand covered her eyes.

Seven

Heart crashing against her ribs, air roaring through her mouth, Beth feared her lungs would explode with sheer terror. For a powerful set of arms dragged her from that peephole into Vampiric hell. Shouts filled the cave. Echoes distorted them so wildly that she couldn't identify individual words. If anything, what occupied her mind the most was the fact that a hand was pulling her head against a man's chest. And the fingers of that hand covered her eyes, blinding her. At any moment, she expected teeth to sink into her throat.

More heavy footsteps clattered down the steps into the cave.

'Easy with her, Sanderson, do you want to pull the lady's head off?'

'She might be a spy, Sarge. I didn't want her to see our faces.'

'Do you think she's going to radio a description of your pretty-boy looks to Gestapo HQ?'

'Sarge. You can't be too careful. The Nazis might parachute in Storm Troopers.'

'Does she look like a Storm Trooper, lad? Wearing lipstick and a skirt?'

'Sarge—'

'Put her down, Sanderson.'

'Yes, Sarge.'

The hand withdrew from Beth's eyes. Blinking, trying to catch her breath, she realized that half a dozen figures had joined them in Hag's Lung. Still groggy from the narcotic that Eleanor had inveigled into her drink, she stood unsteadily. Men in military uniform milled around the place. Two soldiers held Alec at gunpoint. Clearly, the young conscripts were alarmed by the big Scot wearing a black eyepatch. Another soldier held Eleanor by the arm. He looked barely seventeen and the formidable woman made him nervous. The din rose to new levels. Echoes twisted and tangled the sounds into a nerve-shredding maelstrom.

'*Quiet!*' A man, with short silver hair beneath his army cap, moved into the centre of the cave. His air of authority marked him out as leader of the platoon. At his command, the cave fell instantly silent. His stern gaze fixed on Alec. 'What the hell are you playing at, sir? The lights you were shining would have been noticeable from twenty miles away.'

Alec staggered forward. He muttered a sentence that nobody could make out.

'Had a drink or two, have we, sir?' The sergeant maintained politeness towards what he undoubtedly regarded as irresponsible civilians.

Eleanor tried to smooth things over. 'Sergeant. I'm sorry. My friends and I went for a late night walk.'

'A walk? Or was it to indulge in Night Fishing, as the locals term those brief encounters of a certain kind?'

'No, I just wanted to show my friends—'

'I'm not interested, madam, in what you planned to reveal. That kind of thing is best left for indoors. Don't you realize that my men took you for spies? They were a hair's breadth from shooting you.'

Although the sergeant remained calm, if annoyed by gallivanting civilians, his men were still fired up on adrenalin. They held rifles at the ready. Their eyes darted from Alec to Sally to Eleanor and to Beth. Clearly, they'd burst into the cave expecting to find a bunch of gun-toting spies.

Sally found her voice at last. 'We're not drunk, sir. Honest.'

'Madam, we're fighting a war. You and your bunch of merry-makers have taken us away from our guard posts.'

'Sorry.'

'Alright, boys.' The Sergeant let out a sigh. 'Stop pointing your rifles at the ladies and gentleman.'

'Thank you, Officer.'

'Sergeant,' he corrected. 'Now, I'll have to take you to the police station. You're in a restricted area. What's more, you were showing a light from the cave entrance. That's a criminal offence.'

'We didn't mean to,' Eleanor told him.

'That's all well and good, madam, but an enemy pilot could have seen that light from way off. It wouldn't have done us a power of good if Jerry had dropped a bomb on our heads, would it now? The young ladies' hairstyles would have been a heck of a mess.' The joke, albeit a macabre one, suggested that the Sergeant had decided the intrusion into the cave owed itself more to high spirits, and to too much booze, than to covert enemy action.

Sally and Alec were coming to their senses. The narcotic must have been leaving their blood. Sally showed signs of embarrassment. Alec scratched his head, no doubt suspecting he'd misbehaved but unable to remember the nitty-gritty of his misdeeds. He rubbed his cheek, saw lipstick on his fingertips, then his good eye fixed on the smudged lipstick around Sally's lips. The soldiers had begun to relax. They grinned as Alec rubbed lipstick off his face with a handkerchief.

The Sergeant shot Alec a knowing glance. 'Not to worry, sir, we're all men of the world. We shan't mention what you were doing with the young lady. But we'll have to report that you were showing the light in contravention of wartime regulations. My corporal will drive you all to the police station in Whitby.'

'Just arrest me, Sergeant, please,' Alec said. 'It's my fault entirely.'

Beth caught Eleanor's eye, then inclined her head to the hole in the cave wall. She mouthed the words, *I saw them.*

Eleanor gave a tiny nod.

Meanwhile, the Sergeant went to the foot of the steps that led up to the cave's exit. 'Corporal Breen. Bring the truck round. You're to deliver four civilians to Whitby police station.' A pause. No Corporal Breen appeared. Frowning, the sergeant turned back to the others in the cave. 'Sanderson. Scoot up there and find Corp.'

He'd barely finished the sentence when a shape sped into the cave. It didn't even bother with the steps. It leapt from the entrance directly on to the soldier's back, knocking him down.

Everyone stared in shock, as a woman in a white nightdress straddled the Sergeant, her legs at either side of his waist. As she wrestled to hold him down, her nightdress slid up, revealing long, pale thighs, through which a tracery of black veins ran. Before anyone could react, more figures burst into the cave. The candles magnified their shadows against the walls. Beth flinched at the sight of these demonic figures. She counted six of them. One of them wore a pilot's uniform complete with a leather helmet and goggles over his eyes. Then she saw the eyes of the others. They were bereft of colour – not a trace of an iris. Instead, the eyes contained fierce black pupils in their centres.

The young soldiers recovered from the shock. A pair of them dragged the woman from their sergeant. She rounded on them, trying her best to grip their necks. The soldiers started shouting to one another. Once more the cave reduced their words to a swirling babble of echoes. Beth grabbed hold of Sally and Alec, and pulled them back towards Eleanor. She kept moving, shoving them into a narrow recess of the cave, in order to give them the best cover. Just in time. For one of the soldiers fired into the air to frighten the attackers away. The bullet smacked into a stalactite. It shattered into tiny fragments that scattered over the swarming bodies.

'That woman's attacking the soldier,' Sally wailed. 'Eleanor! What's happening!'

'That woman is Mary Tinskell. Or rather she was. She's one of the creatures now. They must have taken her.'

Alec had to shout over the cacophony. 'A vampire?'

'You've got your proof,' Eleanor cried. 'And you've got it the tough way.'

A man in white appeared at the entrance to the cave. He watched the brawl in horror.

'And that's Gustav Kirk,' Eleanor shouted. 'Leader of his pack of blood drinkers.'

Gustav descended halfway down the steps, then he threw out his arms to implore his fellow creatures, 'Don't do this. Leave the soldiers alone.'

They ignored him. Mary, straddling a young soldier, had her teeth in the lower jaw of the man. When she sucked, her eyes rolled in ecstasy.

'We are meant for a higher purpose,' yelled Gustav. 'Don't surrender to your cravings. We aren't monsters!'

Frightened soldiers fired their rifles. One of the bullets struck the pilot. He grimaced, and his mouth drooped to one side, as if the shot had damaged his nervous system. Yet recovery occurred at an astonishing speed. In seconds, he'd regained his strength, and he leapt on a soldier to sink his teeth into the man's wrist – where veins run close to the skin's surface: throbbing conduits of hot blood.

'Stop this!' Gustav dragged a vampire from the Sergeant. 'Stop this. We do not need their blood. We can resist temptation!' Heroic words, noble words. But that appeal to virtuous natures was lost on the vampires. They were locked into a feeding frenzy. Now even Gustav eyed those vessels, full of rich, wholesome blood, that were mortal men. Lust flared in his eyes. He evidently longed to sip from a vein. Yet he resisted – just.

Beth saw that, of all the creatures, he retained a ghosting of colour around the pupil. A whisper of pale blue. And, of all the creatures, he retained a ghost of his former self, too. The gentle, book-loving boy who Eleanor had spoken so sorrowfully about. This man in white, with a striped tie knotted about his waist in place of a belt, struggled not only with his own Vampiric nature. He strove to restrain the others, too.

And he was losing. That expression of sorrow, of pure grief, on Gustav's face melted Beth's heart.

Once more, the surviving soldiers fired their rifles. Bullets struck the walls. They bounced back and forth so fast that they created a cat's cradle of fiery lines in the air. If a vampire was struck, they flinched; their legs would weaken; their eyes would lose their fierce intensity; and the sides of their mouths would drag downwards. But the effects of their wounds would be fleeting. In moments, the strength would pour back into their limbs; their backs would straighten; and their mouths would regain their former shape.

The Sergeant shouted commands. He seized hold of vampires that were swarming over his men and flung them aside. They didn't frighten him. The man obviously had no intention of quitting this battle.

Gustav still cried out for his vampire pack to leave the soldiers. They ignored him. Moreover, his voice became distorted. The hunger that blazed in his eyes revealed that whatever remained of his human side had begun to falter.

His eyes locked on Eleanor. 'I'm sorry. I tried to stop them.'

Another bullet shrieked round the cave, bouncing from rock surfaces, clipping a chunk from a stalactite, then it tore through the Sergeant's shoulder. The bullet's impact flung blood into the air. It atomized in a red mist. Blood settled on everyone, covering the exposed skin of hands and faces in red speckles. Beth tasted its coppery tang.

It sent the vampires berserk. With renewed fury, they attacked the soldiers. Now even Gustav lost all self-restraint. That residual blue in his eye vanished. The black pupils became fierce points of darkness that, in themselves, threatened to draw all that was good and holy from the world. Gustav flung himself from the steps on to the wounded Sergeant. Even as the pair crashed to the floor, Gustav's teeth found the man's shoulder wound. He ripped at already torn flesh. A geyser of blood erupted. Gustav caught the crimson fountain in his mouth, swallowing, gulping . . . sucking it down in his throat. His face became a mask of gratification. His back arched with pleasure.

'Come on.' Eleanor dragged her companions from the fold in the rock. 'Get out.'

Alec paused. 'We've got to help!'

'There's nothing we can do. Run!'

Somehow, they scrambled, in a clump of flailing arms, to the exit. Sally wept. Alec still shouted that they ought to bring help. Eleanor came last, shoving the last one out into the cold, moonlit night.

Eight

Beth Layne opened her eyes to find herself laying in the graveyard. The moon shone down on to a mass of gravestones that ran off to her right and left in lines of black. In the main, each had a similar shape – a vertical oblong with a rounded top. Decades of rain and frost had erased many of the chiselled words that recorded the names, ages and places of those who'd lived out their lives in Whitby and its rural hinterland. Beth lay flat on one such tomb marker that had been toppled on to the earth. Doused by pale moonlight, she found herself faced with a reminder of human mortality: *In loving memory of Thomas Jackson. Master Mariner. Died May 22nd 1901* . . .

Beth raised herself to one elbow. Breezes tugged at the grass, as if invisible claws raked at it. *So, why am I lying here in the graveyard at night? What brought me here?* She blinked. *Have they left me here to be buried?* She extended her hand into the shadows, wondering if she lay beside an open grave. Then came the pad of soft footsteps. They were rapid steps . . . searching . . . hunting for something they knew they'd find here. A flurry of movement appeared over the top of a headstone. A face peered down at hers.

'Beth, are you awake yet?'

'Sally?'

'Oh, thank God!' Her friend knelt beside her. 'I've never been so scared. After we got away from the cave with all those *things* . . . those vampires! . . . we ran through the graveyard. You collapsed here. I thought you'd dropped down dead.'

Beth sat up. 'Dead. I feel half dead. What happened?'

'Don't you remember?'

Beth shook her head.

Sally shuddered. 'We went into that awful Hag's Lung. I remember dancing with Alec . . . and we were *kissing*. My head felt all funny. It must have been that brandy. Soldiers arrived. Then all these monsters rushed in. They must be the vampires that Eleanor told us about. There was shooting – bullets went smack, smack, smack all over the cave. I thought we'd be hit, and then those monsters were on the soldiers . . . biting, and . . . and killing . . .'

Beth's mind suddenly cleared. 'I remember now. My God. Eleanor drugged us. That's why we felt so weird. She wanted to prove that the vampires really existed.'

'They do exist. They nearly caught us.'

'Where are Eleanor and Alec now?'

'I–I don't know. We got split up. It's so dark in those bushes.'

'Sally, we must go back to the hotel. We need to lock the doors.'

Sally was appalled. 'You think the vampires will come for us?'

'I know it for a fact.'

'What about Eleanor and Alec?'

'We can't wait here. Come on.'

Beth seized her friend's hand. The pair hurried through the graveyard to the top of the cliff steps. Moonlight revealed houses on the steep hillside, which rose from the far bank of the River Esk. All the houses faced this way. They rose in tiers, one on top of the other, hundreds and hundreds of them. Beth realized what all those pale buildings reminded her of. The similarity of an expectant audience, sat in rows of seats in a theatre, startled her with its power. Those masses of buildings resembled skull-like faces. The windows were unblinking eyes. They stared at Beth and Sally. Just like an audience watching a play, they expected dramatic events to befall the two women, and befall them soon.

Damn them, Beth thought, *it's as if those houses know something dreadful is going to happen. They've got a perfect view. They want to witness our tragedy. That's true, isn't it, Whitby? You're going to enjoy watching our deaths.*

Sally tugged Beth's arm. 'Look! They're coming after us.'

Beth glanced back in the direction of the abbey ruins. Dark shapes flowed smoothly over the graveyard wall. Then the vampires ran through the tombstones towards them. Metal buttons glinted on uniforms – the Vampiric transformation had been a fast one. Because, surely, just moments ago those had been the soldiers in the cave.

'What now?' Sally asked in desperation. 'We can't go back that way. And we can't run down the steps. They'll see us. Oh, Beth, what are we going to do?'

Beth stood frozen there, with Whitby spread out before them. And she had to admit to herself: *I don't know what to do. Because we can't outrun them. We're trapped.*

Nine

Tommy slunk through shadow cast by the cemetery wall. Sam padded after him. Both were alert; senses keen. Tommy could smell the aroma from the sheds, where the fish were smoked, down on Henrietta Street. He heard waves on the beach a quarter of a mile away. And he saw the undulating shapes of gravestones that had been eroded into fantastic forms.

More importantly, he saw that the vampires sped towards two women, who stood at the head of the steps. They were paralysed with fear. Followed by Sam, he hurried along the cobbled lane that ran in a deep depression beside the graveyard.

'Lady,' he hissed to the woman nearest him. 'Lady. Here.'

Alarmed, she shot him a glance.

'Quickly, lady. Climb down here.'

She hesitated; her eyes were large with fear.

'Please lady. They'll catch you, if you don't.'

The woman glanced back. By moonlight, the approaching pack of hungry vampires must have been all too clear, and all too terrible, to see.

The woman grabbed her companion's arm. 'Sally, follow me.' She swung herself over the cemetery wall, then dropped down into the deep lane. It hugged the same route as the one hundred and ninety-nine steps, yet at a much lower level, into the town below.

Both women were young, and very pretty. Sam wagged his tail

in greeting and sniffed the hand of the blonde lady. The other woman froze.

'Beth! That isn't a boy . . . not a proper boy . . . It's one of those things.'

The blonde spoke to him. 'My name's Beth. You're here to help us, aren't you?'

He nodded.

The sound of feet rushing through the cemetery announced that the mob of creatures wasn't far away.

Beth pulled her friend's arm. 'He's not going to harm us. Come on.'

Tommy whispered, 'Follow me. But you can't outrun them.'

The one called Sally gave a soft sob. 'Oh God.'

The boy led them a few paces down the steep incline. The moment they reached the first line of cottages, he pointed to a narrow gap between a wall and a shed. 'Hide. Don't make a sound.'

Beth said, 'You go in first.'

'No. Sam and me are going to lead them away. We'll make lots of noise, and, if they don't see us properly, the bad men will follow. Hurry, get yourselves in the yard, or they'll hurt you.' The boy snatched up a stone from the lane. Then, pausing just long enough to make sure that the two had concealed themselves behind the high wall, he streaked away at lightning speed. He rapped on cottage walls as he ran. Sure enough, the vampires followed. They were in a state of high excitement. In fact, they reminded Tommy of a bunch of men who'd drunk too much beer and had decided to rampage through town in search of mischief.

Sam ran alongside, his long black legs making easy work of the distance. They avoided the roads and lanes of Whitby, favouring instead the tiny alleyways. Tommy continued to smack the pebble against walls, fence posts and iron railings. The clack, thud and clangs echoed out over the town. To the hungry vampires it could have been a dinner bell summoning them to a feast. They followed, running as fast as they could. But Tommy knew all the hidden pathways and secret routes through back yards. When he'd drawn the creatures safely away from the two women, he cast the stone into the harbour, then he and his companion slipped noiselessly away into the night.

Ten

Beth and Sally hid in the yard. The darkness owned a suffocating, liquid quality. They could see nothing. And the darkness seemed to not only fill their eyes, but to flood into their mouths and nostrils.

Sally pressed herself against Beth for reassurance. Beth flinched at every sound. Any moment, she expected a stark face, with blazing eyes, to rush at them from the gloom. Closing her eyes didn't help. For, if she did, that's when she replayed the events of the night – how they'd entered the cave, and how she'd peered through the hole in the cave wall and glimpsed those swarming creatures. They must have filled the adjoining cavern, like vermin crammed into a tiny cage. They were packed together in a loathsome mass of intertwined arms and legs; their slippery grey bodies rolled over one another. She remembered that pair of eyes that had glared through the dwarf tunnel in the rock. And then there was the attack on the soldiers. She shuddered.

To distract herself from those troubling images, she whispered, 'I'm sure we're safe now. The boy's led them away.'

'Boy?' Sally's faint voice had a tremulous quality. 'Boy? Did you see his face . . . My God, he's one of those vampires.'

'But he didn't try and harm us. He feared them, just as much as we did.'

'Did you see his eyes? They didn't have any colour. The pupils looked as if they belonged to an animal . . . No, not an animal, a monster.'

'He saved our lives, didn't he?' She gave Sally a friendly hug. 'And he had a dog – a real, living dog. That wouldn't stay with him if he was a danger.' For a while, they huddled there in the biting cold of the February night. Eventually, Beth whispered, 'I can't hear them. The boy's plan must have worked.'

'Then God bless him,' was Sally's heartfelt response.

'We should go to the hotel. We'll be safe there.'

They crept from their hiding place. Once more, they found themselves on the steep track that ran some eight feet below the level of the steps, yet still followed its line. Together, they descended into the moonlit town. Beth marvelled at the miracle of their escape.

The smooth blocks of stone were set at an alarming incline. *It's a wonder we didn't slip. If we had, those creatures would have been on us in seconds. And if they had caught us . . .* She decided not to share her thoughts with Sally. The woman had had enough scares for one night as it was.

It took little more than five minutes to reach level ground. This, the junction of Church Street and Henrietta Street, didn't seem much wider than a pathway between the lines of cottages. Beth figured they were just a couple of hundred yards from the Leviathan Hotel – of course, she'd told Sally they would be safe there, but those windows were flimsy things. She didn't place a great deal of faith in them holding Gustav and his hungry pack at bay. So how could they fight these creatures? They didn't retreat before crucifixes, holy water, or garlic – at least that's what Eleanor had inferred.

They'd gone perhaps thirty paces along Church Street, when they encountered the straggler. The moon illuminated him clearly. Beth saw he wore army boots and a dull khaki coat. One of the epaulettes fluttered from his shoulder. The young man wobbled as he walked. From time to time, he rested his palm against the wall of a cottage to steady himself.

Beth whispered to Sally, 'One of the soldiers got away from the cave.'

'He must have been hurt, though. Look, the poor man can hardly walk.'

Beth hurried towards the shambling figure. 'Sir? Let us help you.'

The man turned to them. 'What's happened to me?' Bloodstains formed streaky patterns down the front of his coat. Teeth marks stippled the side of his face.

'You were attacked,' Sally told him. 'We'll get you to a doctor.'

'But why do I feel different inside?' He swayed. 'My blood is on fire.'

The man sucked in a huge lungful of air. His back straightened. Then his eyes changed. The blue of the iris leeched away. The eyes were white – all white. And the pupils became dots of hungry blackness. A darkness that longed to suck the life out of the world.

'Run!' Beth yanked her friend backwards.

'Come here,' he moaned. 'I need you.'

They fled along the street. The soldier took steps towards them, unsteady at first, then with growing confidence. Moments later, he ran – ready to chase them down as a panther chases down a fawn.

The unbroken line of cottages hemmed the pair in. They pounded at doors in the hope some saviour would let them enter. But all the cottages were locked, formidably locked and bolted, as if to seal the occupants from the outside world. No lights showed from windows. Not a curtain moved. A sudden vision struck Beth. The people of Whitby sheltered inside. *They are frightened.* For they knew exactly what event unfurled night after night in these streets. Indoors, families huddled together to wait out the dangers of the night. No power on Earth would entice them into opening so much as a window between sunset and sunrise.

The pair ran hard. Behind them, the soldier's boots created an almighty clatter. When hobnails in the soles crashed against paving stones, a flash of vivid blue sparks shot outwards.

'It's no good,' Sally panted. 'Henrietta Street leads to the harbour pier. It's a dead end!'

A figure stepped out in front of them. A slight figure . . . almost fragile. Beside him, a black dog, with the white, heart-shaped patch beneath its throat. Fur bristled upwards as it saw the approaching vampire.

Beth could barely breathe she was so exhausted, yet she managed to utter, 'Just pray he . . . he can save our skins again.'

The boy pointed to a shed. Pale smoke trailed from vents high in the walls. A sign by the shed door announced, *Kippers Smoked To Order. Enquire 4 Henrietta Street.*

Dazed by the headlong dash, Beth rushed through the gate, then burst through the door of the shed. Sally followed. There, inside, masses of fish hung from rails. The fish had been sliced open, then flattened until they resembled teardrop shapes. The pungent smell of herrings and smoke instantly prickled Beth's throat. Beneath the fish were metal trays the size of table tops; they were heaped with glowing embers. The smoke from smouldering wood cured the fish hanging above. Sally hurried into the far corner of the shed to hide herself. Beth returned to the doorway.

Beth had expected the boy to try and lead the Vampiric soldier away; however, the boy stood his ground.

Beth shouted, 'No – you can't fight him!'

'I have to,' answered the child. 'He saw you go into the smoking shed.'

That's all he managed to say before the soldier was upon him – or what had been a soldier when he woke that morning. Now he was a vampire that raged with bloodlust. Hands extending claw-like, he charged at the boy. Nails in his boots struck sparks from the road.

The dog immediately leapt forward to sink his teeth into the vampire's arm. In one savage movement, the vampire swept the dog from him. The animal struck the steps of a cottage. With a shrieking yelp, he arched his back, then lay still.

The boy turned to his pet with such an anguished expression that Beth's heart lurched. The vampire didn't rush now. He slowly advanced on the boy.

'You don't want him,' Beth snarled. 'You want me.'

The vampire immediately changed course. He approached Beth with lethal intent. Smoothly, she backed into the gloom of the shed, instantly becoming wreathed in smoke.

'Remember? You are a soldier. You serve king and country.' Beth kept a gap between herself and the metal trays heaped with smouldering wood chips that glowed bright orange.

Hungry-eyed, predatory, the vampire passed through the doorway.

Sally whimpered, 'No, no, no,' over and over.

Beth backed away until she struck something that didn't yield. Behind her, a six-foot-high barrier built out of flat wooden boxes, which would be used to ship the smoked fish to market. She couldn't go back. She couldn't go forwards. The vampire's eyes burnt at her through the smoke-filled room. The hundreds of fish oozed oil on to the embers. Each time one dripped into the smouldering mass, the oil would produce a little pop of flame.

'You are a soldier,' she told the creature. 'You have sworn to defend your country against Hitler. You are fighting a war against the evils of Fascism. Now fight what is inside of you!'

He paused. The eyes lowered, as he searched inside himself for a memory of what he once was. Maybe a trace of his identity surfaced. His mouth moved. The blue swam into his eyes to form irises – his eyes were human again.

But only for a second. The blue vanished from the whites. Dark pupils fixed on her. His mouth opened. Already subtle changes were forcing his teeth apart, creating more spaces between them. The gums had become swollen; a bulbous red. He raised his hands, ready to grab Beth's throat. Sally screamed.

A shape darted through the doorway. The boy seized hold of the man's coat. He swung at it, trying to drag him back. The vampire grabbed the boy, glared into his face, then spat in disgust. The boy obviously meant nothing to him – he was useless as a source of food. The man hurled the little figure back through the door with the same contempt as a man throwing out a bad apple.

Beth saw her chance. When his back was turned, she gripped the edge of one of the huge trays full of smouldering wood. Grunting at the exertion, she upended it on to the vampire. The next second he was doused in embers. He blundered back in surprise. The racks of hanging fish brushed against him, coating him with their natural oils. The instant the embers, sticking to his coat, made contact they burst into flame; in turn those tiny spots of flame on his clothes ignited the fabric.

'Get out!' Beth yelled to Sally.

Once the woman had safely exited the shed, Beth shoved the stack of boxes on to the floundering man. The dry wood instantly caught light. And even though he struggled to escape the mound of boxes that now surrounded him, he was bathed in an inferno. Every single inch of him burnt. The light generated by the fire blinded Beth. Choking on the smoke, she found her way to the shed door. Flames crackled like pistol shots. The temperature soared to make the metal ember trays glow, as if they'd turned into luminous yellow disks.

And yet the burning man did not scream. He continued to blunder through the blazing interior – disorientated, blinded, lost, perhaps not even feeling pain as a human would have done.

Out in the street, Beth found Sally with her arm round the boy. Both crouched over the still shape of the dog. The boy's shoulders were shaking as he grieved over his companion.

'Here let me look. That's alright,' Beth said in soothing tones to the child. 'I love dogs, too. I just want to feel his chest.' She swept the dog up into her arms. 'He's still breathing. Come on, let's get him back to the hotel.'

The boy rubbed his eyes with his fists. 'I can't go. I'm not allowed.'

'You want to stay with him, don't you?'

He nodded.

'Then let's get him somewhere safe, so I can check him over.'

As they hurried away, the walls of the shed sagged; flames devoured the wood at a ferocious rate. Moments later, the roof collapsed into the building – a million yellow sparks rose into the air to drift away, like so many freed souls into the night sky.

PART FIVE

One

Beth Layne carried the dog into the yard. Darkness engulfed that area between the perimeter walls and the hotel itself. Beth trusted her instincts to guide her safely to the back door. The dog lay limp in her arms. She hoped that his heart had continued to beat after she'd picked him up from the street moments ago. Sally and Tommy followed. Although the boy's face had many qualities that were utterly inhuman, such as the colourless eyes, the expression of concern for his pet would have been identical on any ten year old whose beloved dog lay close to death.

As they crossed the yard, Beth noticed that Theo Charnwood gazed at them impassively from the upper room of his home. The cottage lay in darkness, yet the man's face appeared to hang suspended in the gloom, like a stark, white skull.

Before Beth had even reached the hotel's back door, it flew open. Eleanor beckoned them frantically.

'Come in,' she hissed. 'Hurry . . . please hurry. Thank God, you're alright.'

They entered the kitchen area before Eleanor could lock the door, then safely switch on a light. That's when she perceived they'd added another to their band of survivors.

She bustled about, filling a kettle with water. 'Who's the boy? Where did you find him? Is that his dog?'

'The dog's been hurt. I need to examine him.'

'Take him into the dining room and put him on the table under the chandelier. You'll get the best light to . . .' Her voice faded; she'd got her first good look at Tommy's face.'

'Oh, my dear God.' She gripped the big kettle as if about to use it as a weapon. 'Beth? Have you seen what you've brought in with you? He's not a boy. He's a—'

'He's called Tommy,' Beth said firmly. 'This is his dog, Sam.'

Sally's posture was defiant. 'Tommy and Sam saved our lives. Not once, but twice.'

Eleanor's eyes swept over Tommy's gaunt body, clad in trousers and a black fisherman's jersey that frayed to a mass of woollen strands at the cuffs; his white face, the shock of hair, the eyes that had been drained of colour. From them burnt a pair of fierce black pupils. 'But you can't . . . He mustn't stay. He's the same as Gustav and the others.'

Alec stood in the kitchen doorway. He must have been listening to the conversation all along. He entered, shaking his head. 'Not exactly like Gustav. He seems to act like a human child.' Alec turned to Beth. 'Has he showed any inclination to attack you?'

'No. Tommy isn't like the others.'

From Eleanor's expression, she'd clearly decided to accept what she'd been told – or at least until the child did something that proved he was dangerous. 'Go through to the dining room. I'll bring the first-aid kit.'

Beth carried Sam to the big room. There she laid him on a table beneath the chandelier. The brightness of the light allowed her to examine the dog thoroughly.

Anxious, Tommy rubbed the neck of the unconscious animal, while murmuring reassurances.

Beth used a clean napkin to dab a cut on Sam's hind leg. This appeared to be a result of striking the ground rather than a bite-mark.

Tommy's voice quavered. 'Is he going to be alright, Miss? Is he bleeding a lot?'

Sally said, 'Should we call a vet?'

Alec's good eye checked Sam, too. 'You wouldn't get one out on a night like this, not for love nor money.'

'Is he going to die, Miss?'

Beth ran her fingers over the top of Sam's head. 'The cut to his leg isn't deep. I'll need to clean it. And he's going to have an almighty bump on his head. But I'd say he's been knocked out cold, that's all.'

Tommy's inhuman eyes roved over the dog and hope suddenly glimmered there. 'Does that mean he's going to get better, Miss?'

'I'm sure of it, Tommy.'

He wiped his eyes. 'I don't know what I'd do if I was to lose him, Miss. You see, I can't find my way home. Sam's all I've got.'

Sam kicked his legs on the table, maybe chasing rabbits in a dream. Then, with a whimper, he raised his head a little. Yet it still swayed, suggesting the animal was groggy.

'We'll fix a bed up for Sam,' Alec said. 'Lots of blankets to make him cosy.'

Eleanor brought a first-aid box. Beth used iodine to cleanse the wound. Sam yelped when the liquid stung raw flesh.

'Don't worry, Tommy,' Beth told the boy. 'If Sam felt that it's a good sign.'

Alec and Sally were happy to be doing something as down-to-earth as fixing up a dog's bed. As they chatted about what blankets they could use from the laundry store, it seemed as if each strove to repress memories of the night's events. Eleanor suggested that they put the bed under the reception counter; Sam might feel reassured if he were closely sheltered by its wooden structure.

Sally chuckled, 'It will be like an indoor kennel.'

Now that Sam had begun to recover, Tommy had taken to exploring his new surroundings. He'd seen Alec switch on the light in the foyer. So Tommy found a light switch in the dining room. He flicked it on and off. From his wide-eyed expression, he clearly found the way that he could plunge the room into darkness, then fill it with light again was marvellous – nothing less than a miracle. He worked the switch up and down: click . . . click . . . click . . .

'How does it do that?' he asked.

'Is this first time you've seen an electric light, Tommy?' Eleanor asked.

'Leck Trick. Is that what's making it go on and off?'

Eleanor shot Beth a tired smile. 'Even though he doesn't look it, I'd say our child of the night is much older then any of us.' Then the smile faded. 'But what are we going to do with him?'

'His dog will need at least a few hours to recover.'

'But we can't let him roam about the hotel tonight.'

'You can't turn him out, surely?'

'No, Beth. But he'll have to be locked somewhere secure.'

'You can't keep him prisoner.'

'It'll just be for tonight. Though what will happen to him at sunrise, I just don't know.'

Tommy still switched the light on and off. By now, the dog kept his head raised to watch his companion with a steady, untroubled gaze. Clearly, the pair were devoted to one another.

'You know,' Eleanor began, 'he is like a real human boy. Because he's become so damn annoying with that light switch.'

Beth saw that Eleanor was smiling, rather than being genuinely irritated. 'Tommy,' she called. 'Leave that and see what I've got here. See this box? It's called a radio. Listen what happens when I twist this knob.'

A light glowed behind the tuning dial. Tommy skipped across the room, excited to see such a thing. 'What will it do, Miss?'

'Wait a moment. It needs to warm up. Ah, here it comes.'

Over a faint hiss, a cultured male voice emerged from the speaker. With perfect diction it declaimed, *'After the four o'clock news, there will be a gramophone recording of a new poem by Mr Dylan Thomas. Following that, the BBC night service will continue to broadcast a selection of light orchestral music for your enjoyment.'*

Tommy exclaimed, 'There's a man in the box!' He rushed to the radio and put his eye to the ventilation slots in the side. 'He's in there, Miss! I can hear him. But how'd he fit himself in that little cabinet?'

A recording of Big Ben's chimes rang from the device. Tommy started back in astonishment. 'And there's a church clock in there, too.'

As Alec gently picked up Sam to carry him to the bed they'd made for him, a siren warned of incoming enemy aircraft.

'I've heard that sound before!' Tommy forgot the radio now. 'When that engine starts its shouting, you see black crosses in the sky not long after. What are they?'

'They're flying machines, Tommy.'

'Flying machines? Nah! There isn't such a thing.' He ran to the window to yank back the blackout material. On high ground, above the harbour, searchlights shot their beams upward. As if the gods of war brandished fiery sabres in the night. The narrow blades of light reached up to pierce a thin layer of cloud a mile above the earth. Carefully, the searchlight operators scoured the sky for Nazi bombers. Once the invaders were revealed, the anti-aircraft gunners would open to fire.

Sally switched off the dining-room chandelier, lest the glow pouring through the gap that Tommy had created in the curtain draw the attention of enemy pilots.

'Why's the town changed so much?' Tommy asked, as he marvelled at columns of light that seemed as if they would sear heaven itself. 'I've seen carts that shoot along roads without horses pulling them. They roar like lions. Now you've shown me Leck Trick light. And a box full of voices and sounds.' He turned, so he could see the adults in the gloom. His face, a ghost-white smudge of a thing, set with eyes that lacked an iris. The little-boy-lost look had leeched away. They were in the presence of an inhuman creature. One that must have roamed Whitby and its surrounding hills for half a century or more. This was sixty pounds or so of muscle, skin, bone and hair that was no longer a child. And all the time, something that resembled a boy's voice flowed through lips that should have been rotting in a grave. 'Miss? Why has the world changed so much? It doesn't seem real to me any more.'

The world hasn't changed, Beth thought. *You have. You aren't human any more. You are undead. You are Nosferatu.*

The four mortals were subdued. They headed down into the shelter of the hotel basement for the duration of the air-raid alert. Maybe it was because they were tired. Or perhaps it was because they knew that what they harboured in the hotel wasn't a lost boy. This Vampiric creature would never grow into a man. He would forever remain this diminutive figure. One doomed to search for his parents. The dog had survived this time. But eventually Sam would grow old and be no more. The boy's love couldn't render the animal immortal. One day, Tommy would be friendless again. Come to that, might the boy still be wandering Whitby's night-time streets a hundred years from now? By then, Beth and her companions, here in the basement, would have left their lives behind. They'd be at rest in their graves, shrouded in eternal darkness. For them there would be absolute peace. Tommy, however, would still be restlessly searching for his family. And still trying to make sense of a world that became increasingly strange to him.

As they sat on chairs in the cold subterranean air, Beth found her gaze drawn to the boy's face. He was that vulnerable, lost child, and, simultaneously, he was profoundly inhuman. A night creature. Just as Eleanor had avoided being transformed into one of the Vampiric ogres, so a quirk of biology had prevented him from lusting after human blood. When Tommy had marvelled over what would be new technology to him – the electric light, wireless broadcasts, and aeroplanes – Beth had found herself believing this could have been some chirpy ten year old getting excited over something new. Yet, in retrospect, the voice emerged from something that resembled a corpse. His skin, although starkly white in the main, displayed patches of deathly blue. Black veins ran up from his hand to the sleeves of his jersey. Rooted in prominent blood-red gums, small white teeth. The white eyes blazed. Centring each, a fierce, black pupil that seemed so non-human and so utterly alien.

Tommy had found a toy soldier amongst old crockery on a shelf. He played with it quietly; the normal action of a youngster. But there was something terrible about his face. The expression wasn't child-like at all now. And, at that moment, Beth stiffened as the revelation struck: *What I'm seeing here isn't a Vampiric boy. This is the body of a vampire that is haunted by the ghost of Tommy. The child's spirit possesses the body of a monster. Only, he hasn't realized it yet.*

Beth gazed at the gaunt face. And she asked herself: if she had the opportunity, would she end Tommy's existence? This poor, lost soul. Wouldn't it be kinder to destroy him? If a way could be found that was quick and painless? For a long time those questions occupied her mind.

At ten to five that morning the siren's 'all clear' rose up through the cold night air to reassure Whitby's citizens that the air attack wouldn't happen – at least not tonight. Any debate of where Tommy should be placed resolved itself when he climbed under the reception counter to snuggle up against Sam. The dog happily licked the boy's ear, as the pair settled down for the rest of the night.

Tommy said in a worried voice, 'I shouldn't be here. But I'm not leaving Sam.'

'Where should you be, Tommy?'

'Before the sun starts to come up I run back to . . .' He found it hard to express himself. 'The place. In the dark. It's where I sleep. It doesn't seem as if I should be there, either. It's like I dream I'm in the ground and . . . and I know I really am under the rock.' The reality of his condition obviously threatened to overwhelm him, because in a sudden change of tone he deliberately shrugged off his growing anxiety. 'I don't understand it. But my dad will explain it all when I find him.' He snuggled on the blanket until his face rested alongside Sam's head.

'Tommy,' Eleanor said gently, 'I need to lock the doors now. I have to lock the door at the top of those stairs, too. So don't try and leave this room, will you?'

He accepted all this as normal. 'I'll be good. Thank you for making Sam better. I got really frightened tonight when the soldier threw him.'

Alec and Eleanor shot Beth a glance that demanded *just what happened to you and Sally tonight?*

As for Sally, she seemed ready to fall asleep there and then in the lobby. Her clothes bore their own testimony to the night they'd endured. The poor girl still had flecks of white ash from the shed blaze in her hair.

Beth shrugged. 'No doubt we've got a lot to talk about. Only, not tonight, huh?'

Alec nodded. Even so, for a while they were reluctant to leave Tommy and his dog. However, both lay in the snug confines beneath the reception counter. The timber sides and top provided the pair with a miniature house of their own.

'Come on.' Eleanor yawned. 'We can safely leave them. I've locked the doors to the dining room, office and kitchen. And I can lock those twin doors on the first floor landing, so Tommy and Sam . . .' She could have added 'will be locked in the lobby' but, with graceful sensitivity, she concluded the sentence with, 'So both of them will be safe and sound.'

That said, the four wearily climbed the stairs. Not much of the night remained. Normally, Beth would have wondered what surprises the coming day would bring. Only, this time she was acutely aware that the next nightfall lay only a dozen hours away. This prompted troubling thoughts: *So what terrors will tomorrow night bring? What nightmares? What dread . . .*

Two

Alec Reed woke in total darkness. Luminous markings on the travel clock on his bedside table gleamed a faint spectral green. It told him it was half past twelve. Whether that was thirty minutes beyond midnight or midday he had no way of knowing.

Usually, the first sensation to reach him on waking was the itch in his injured eye. The bomb explosion, which claimed the lives of his colleagues, had sent a sliver of glass flying through the air to nearly detach his eyelid from his face. Slowly, new cells knitted themselves into his flesh. In his imagination, the pricking resulted from dozens of miniature needles that sewed the wound shut from within.

As he lay there, one finger lightly touching the swollen flesh above his eye, he became acutely conscious of the flow of blood through his own body. The stuff of life. This was the miracle liquid on which all animals depended. Alec had read somewhere that blood resembled the make-up of ocean waters to a remarkable degree. It had the same saltiness; it contained elements in suspension, such as iron, zinc and magnesium.

So – vampires?

Alec Reed lay in the darkness of his hotel room, and he replayed the events of last night. He recalled his utter disorientation from the affects of the drug (damn that woman, Eleanor, he didn't know whether to slap her or kiss her; her beauty made that red stuff in his veins flow faster. Yet what a reckless act? To add narcotic to their drinks?). *Pay attention, Alec,* he told himself, *you're letting your mind wander (and it would be nice to wander Eleanor's way; was she lying in her bed, right now?). Come on, focus your thoughts. Consider the vampires. They went berserk last night when blood spilled from the shot soldier. They crave blood like an addict craves drugs. But is it the liquid they want? Or might it be something else? The traces of metal in the blood? Or might they have found a way to feed off electrical currents in the human body?* Alec sat up. A bead of liquid trickled down his cheek in the darkness. That bloody eye again. He kicked away the blankets, then, by guess-work alone, walked to where he judged the window should be. His outstretched hand felt the fabric of the blackout curtain. Quickly, he swished it aside.

'Ah . . .' At least he'd solved whether it was just after noon, or gone midnight. Sunlight crashed into the room. Its brilliance made him screw up his good eye. At last, however, he found himself looking out upon Whitby harbour on a bright February day. Fishing boats lay alongside wharves. Hoards of men, clad in bright yellow oilskins, hoisted baskets of glittering fish ashore. The mass of houses on the far side of the River Esk climbed up the hillside, seemingly ready to float away into the calm blue sky.

What a beautiful place, he told himself. *But what an accursed town . . . considering what threatens it.* Nothing less than a tide of people flowed along the waterfront road. As he gazed on the scene, he found himself rehearsing what he'd tell the police this afternoon. Because he'd ultimately realized that this war against those night creatures wasn't his alone (or Beth's, or Sally's, or even the formidable Eleanor's). But do you mention the word "vampire" to a solidly down-to-earth desk sergeant? *No, don't tell it. Reveal it.* He'd explain he found something troubling in a cave up on the cliff top. Then he'd show the police officers the aftermath of the battle in Hag's Lung between vampires and soldiers. What then? Well, that would be up to the police. And Alec Reed would be free of this particular nightmare at least.

Three

Oblivious to Alec Reed's plan to reveal what he knew about the creatures to the police, Eleanor descended the hotel stairs a shade after half past twelve. She unlocked the doors on the first floor landing, then descended the remaining steps to the lobby.

Sam sat beside the prone figure of Tommy. The boy's face gleamed a dreadful white beneath the reception desk. His eyes were closed. Whether he breathed or not was difficult to tell. Then again, he didn't look that much different from her brother, Theo, by day. She knew full well that the substance known as Quick Salts, with which she dosed her brother every evening, had prevented his transformation after the attack by the Vampiric Gustav Kirk twenty years ago. Often she wondered if Theo would transform fully into a vampire if she stopped administering his medicine. Not that she ever intended to conduct that particular experiment. The consequences were too dreadful to contemplate.

The dog didn't resent her touching Tommy's face, in order to check that he was deeply unconscious. Nor did Sam object to being let out into the yard to answer the call of his own decidedly canine nature. Eleanor served up the remains of an old mutton stew for Sam, which he wolfed down hungrily. Clearly, the bang on the head hadn't caused lasting injury. And when she rubbed the fur on his neck he responded by wagging his tail and watching her with bright eyes.

'You do know that you've found a strange master, don't you? Tommy isn't like other little boys.' Sam pricked up his ears and tilted his head to one side as she spoke. 'Right, you go look after Tommy. I've got work to do.'

Sam quickly made himself comfortable by the comatose form on the floor – a starkly pale, boy-shaped thing. One of the clan of creatures that Eleanor had, at last, decided to burn from the face of the earth.

Four

Sally Wainwright climbed out of bed, just as the hallway clock struck one. For a while she stood at the window. Sunlight, wonderful nightmare-banishing sunlight – it cascaded through the window into her room. For a while, she watched the bustle of normality outside. Women in long skirts all seemed to be hurrying to their own personal destinations somewhere along Church Street. Nearly everyone carried a basket or bundle of sorts. Men moved more slowly, or stood in groups smoking cigarettes and talking with grave expressions. In an alleyway, a dozen clothes lines criss-crossed between houses. From them fluttered sheets that were a brilliant crisp white in the sunshine. A boy of around seven rolled a bike wheel along the roadway. Its steel rim clattered on cobble stones. When it bounced off the side of a handcart, being pushed by an elderly man, he snatched off his huge floppy cap and tried to swipe the tyke with it.

Sally watched all this. Yet memory dragged her back to last night, when the solider had attacked them. They'd been trying to hide in that shed where the fish were being smoked. Recollections of the conflagration made her flinch. When she'd opened her eyes in bed a few minutes ago, she'd hoped it all had been a terrible dream. But the tingle on her wrist drew her attention to the bite. She couldn't hide from reality. There really had been those creatures in the cave. She and Beth had been pursued by the pack of vampires. The Vampiric soldier had followed them into the shed. What's more, she knew the dog and the boy creature would be downstairs.

She checked the wounds beneath the bandage. There they were: puncture marks that formed a pattern of dots like so :::: Thankfully, they were healing. At times, she'd convince herself that she'd be transformed into one of those awful leering, ravenous things. With something close to a sob, she let her face rest against the cold glass. 'I just want to make my film. That's all. Please God, make those monsters go away.'

Because she knew that soon they would return. And next time, she and her friends might not make good their escape.

Five

Beth found there was plenty of hot water, in wartime Britain, a commodity that had become a rare luxury. The odour of the grim cave known as Hag's Lung still clung to her skin. Not to mention a sprinkle of ashes in her hair from when she'd set the shed alight. So, with growing anticipation, she ran a deep bath, added some of her precious supply of purple bath salts that she'd bought from Harrods before the war, then she gratefully immersed herself into steaming water. A sigh of pleasure gusted from her lips. Magically, or so it seemed to her, the grim odours of last night were washed away in a second. For the next fifteen minutes she leisurely, yet thoroughly, soaped her smooth skin. A hand mirror allowed her to check for anxiety lines around her eyes (thankfully, there were none). Then she fully immersed herself three times for good measure. When she finally emerged from the bathtub, it felt more like a rebirth than simply a good scrub up. After she'd towelled dry, dressed in an A-line skirt, together with a flatteringly figure-hugging yellow sweater, she felt ready to face the world – and all its nightmares.

Beth looked in on Sally. Her friend showed her that the bite wound had begun to heal nicely, which relieved them both. They chatted mainly about that, rather than the events of the night before. They knew that topic would be chewed over at length today by everyone in the hotel – everyone that could claim to be mortal, that is. And they still wondered what would become of the boy. Sally, golden-hearted as ever, hoped he could be moved to one of the big London hospitals, where some kind of cure could be effected.

Beth didn't contradict her. *Yet what cures vampirism? Those Salts of Eleanor's? Maybe.* Leaving Sally to do her hair, Beth went downstairs. Alec shouted a 'hallo' from the kitchen where, true to his Scotsman roots, he'd boiled up a huge pan full of porridge oats. 'Hot and salty – just how my countrymen like it,' he claimed with gusto. 'Want some?'

Beth declined.

Beneath the reception counter, Tommy and Sam lay on the blankets. The dog watched her with bright eyes.

'Feeling better, Sam?' She felt a surge of relief at seeing the dog so perkily alert. Tommy lay in the shadows. He never moved, or even showed any sign that he'd noticed her. Beth decided not to venture closer. Only too sharply did she recall her observations last night. *What I'm seeing here isn't a Vampiric boy. This is the body of a vampire that is haunted by the ghost of Tommy.* More than ever, Beth Layne believed that in some mysterious way that she couldn't yet explain, Vampiric flesh had replaced the skin and muscle of the boy. However, the once mortal Tommy had provided the mould that had shaped the monstrous physique. She knew if she offered her theory to Alec and Eleanor it wouldn't sound convincing. *I will try to do so soon,* she thought. *It's important that they perceive Tommy as being inhuman, not some tragic lost boy.*

Outside the front door of the hotel, lay the everyday world. One filled with sunlight, and the sounds of people living their lives. Quick footsteps, chatter, and even a peal of girlish laughter passed through those stout timbers. Yet, at that moment, Whitby and its population of human beings seemed impossibly remote. As if that step of a few inches from the hotel to the street had become a yawning gulf a million miles wide. Those men and women, with all the regular fixtures of life – gas bills, bank accounts, dentists' appointments, brothers, sisters, parents, jobs; all the rivalries, all the ambitions for the future – those people could have been simply the imaginings of a dying god; one who populated this strange town with ghosts. Even though the clamour outside the door appeared lively as it was noisy, Beth feared that if she were to pull open the door she'd find a suddenly deserted street outside. One that carried wind-blown leaves and nothing more.

A clunk of jars came from the basement door. Grateful to the sound for diverting her from some such troubling notions, Beth headed to the steps. 'Eleanor? Is that you down there?'

Beth descended into the basement. A stream of cold air carried the sound of lapping waves through the grating in the floor. Seconds later, Beth froze as a figure emerged from the shadows. Clad in glistening black, and wearing a rubber mask that concealed the entire face, it advanced, the eyes invisible behind disks of glass. It reached up and swept the gas mask from its face.

'Eleanor! You nearly scared me to death!'

'Sorry. I have to wear this, or, for me, it literally will be death.' She sucked in a lungful of air.

'It's that rubber apron. I saw it in your room.'

'One and the same, Beth, my dear.'

'What on Earth are you doing?'

'Come and see for yourself.'

'You're not making bombs, are you?' Beth tried to make a joke of it to put herself at ease. This was shocking, to say the least: the appearance of that formidable woman in the black rubber apron, with its fastening of chunky metal buckles up the back, industrial gauntlets, and to reinforce the alien creature effect: a gas mask.

'Watch what I'm doing. And, Beth, watch carefully.'

'Why?'

'Because, if anything happens to me, then you must finish the job.'

'Eleanor, don't say such a—'

'Don't smother me in platitudes, kindly meant though they are. You saw those things last night, and you saw what they can do to armed soldiers. What do you think they'd do to you, or me, or to any of our friends, if they had the chance?'

'Eleanor—'

'Watch me. Remember every step of the process. Because, if you make a mistake, it will kill you.'

Beth followed Eleanor into a disused wine cellar. Empty racks lined the walls in this windowless cell. In the middle, a stout timber table dominated the space. Standing on the table, at least twenty clear bottles that would be large enough to contain a pint of beer. Also on the table, a gallon jar. A pale blue liquid half filled it. An acrid chemical stench floated on the air; its fumes bit into the back of Beth's throat.

'Stay just outside the doorway,' Eleanor ordered. 'The air's fresher out there. And if I spill this stuff you won't get splashed.'

'What in God's name is it?'

'I'll be explaining everything to you and the others later this afternoon. In the meantime, watch carefully.'

'Eleanor? You're not making bombs are you?' Again, a desperate attempt at a joke to try to alleviate the sense of danger.

'No, not bombs.'

'Thank heaven.'

'No, these will be infinitely more destructive than mere bombs.'

Eleanor pulled the mask down over her face. The prominent rubber snout that housed a compartment for filters, which would prevent destructive gases reaching the wearer's lungs, seemed somehow wolf-like. Eleanor checked the gauntlets were pulled up over her arms, then she set to work.

The table top had been covered with a sheet of copper. Clearly, Eleanor didn't want whatever dwelt in that big glass jar to come into contact with the wood. But why? The old table looked fit for the firewood. It certainly wouldn't fetch money as an antique.

With an air of absolute concentration, Eleanor placed the spout of a grey metal funnel into a beer bottle. Then, taking great care, she gripped the gallon jar. Slowly, she tipped it so the blue fluid streamed out into the funnel. When the bottle was half full Eleanor stopped pouring, set the jar down, then picked up a hammer from the shelf behind her. She also held a metal cylinder that was the same size and shape as the cardboard tube found in the centre of a toilet roll. Eleanor placed the tube upright on the bottle, which she'd half filled, then gently, but firmly, tapped the top of it with the hammer. When she removed it, Eleanor saw that the bottle was now sealed by a metal cap. It looked the same as those flat metal caps that seal ordinary beer bottles.

As meticulous as a surgeon at work in an operating theatre, Eleanor repeated the procedure: carefully half fill a bottle with the blue liquid, then seal it shut by hammering a metal cap into place. In crates to the woman's left, dozens of empty beer bottles. In crates to her right, bottles that boasted a silver cap. Beth knew for sure that those were no simple containers of honest-to-goodness Yorkshire ale.

Beth stood at the doorway. Conscientiously, she studied Eleanor's labours. One by one, the woman poured the chemical into the bottles. The deliberate actions resonated with those of a master armourer, crafting the weapons of war.

And what kind of war? While the armies of the world clashed on the battlefields of Africa, Asia and Europe, here in this remote corner of England preparations were made for another conflict. A hidden, secret war.

Beth Layne pictured those vampires that she'd glimpsed through the cave wall. Dozens, maybe hundreds of them, swarmed in the confines of the sump cavern. Naked body slithered over naked body. They didn't have room to stand, or spend time alone – she was sure of that. Just how she knew, she couldn't say, but images of those imprisoned vampires swarmed in her mind . . . of them writhing together in the crushing embrace of the cavern. Oh, she knew what they wanted. They craved a taste of blood. For there was none in that stone prison. Their minds must beat with that single word: BLOOD. It would reverberate inside those naked skulls, like the pounding of a huge drum: BLOOD. BLOOD. BLOOD. BLOOD.

How they'd ache for just a sip. They must dream of a single drop of that exquisite red stuff on their tongue. BLOOD. BLOOD. BLOOD. A river of glorious crimson being pushed by the heart through a fantastic cat's cradle of arteries, veins, capillaries. And the sump cavern vampires must think constantly about the people of Whitby. Here are thousands of men, women and children, who are vessels to that glorious, velvety red liquid.

The hammer clanged down on the table, then Eleanor strode through the doorway, dragging the gas mask from her face. 'I'm out of bottle caps. Will you come with me for more?'

'Of course.'

'We need to be quick. The sun will set in a couple of hours. Grab your coat. I'll meet you in the lobby.'

Eleanor worked her hands free of the rubber gauntlets. That done, she closed the door of the wine cellar before snapping shut a hefty padlock to lock it.

'If you find yourself doing the bottling, keep that blue liquid off your skin. Off anything organic. Got that?'

Beth nodded. 'But what—'

'I'm giving a lecture on it later, my dear. And I'll give the three of you a vivid demonstration, too.' She turned round. 'Can you unbuckle me? Thanks.'

A moment later, Eleanor hung the apron out of sight behind a brick buttress. She stowed the gas mask and gloves there, too.

Before they headed for the steps, Eleanor turned to Beth. 'I can tell from your treatment of Sam that you're a dog lover.'

'My family have five of them back home on the farm.'

'There must have been times that you had to have an old dog put to sleep to spare it any suffering?'

Beth nodded. 'When you run out of medical options, it's the humane solution.'

'It's taken me too many years to reach the same kind of decision. I have to destroy something I love, too.' Her eyes glistened. 'And I still don't know if I can go through with it. Oh, I seem strong to those people out there.' She nodded in the direction of Church Street that thronged with people. 'But this is breaking my heart, Beth. And yet I know it's the *right* thing to do. Dear God, it hurts.' She grimaced. 'Gustav and some of his pack were my friends a long time ago. You loved the dogs that you were forced to say goodbye to. I'm going to have to say goodbye to people that made life, back in my schooldays, worth living.' She took a steadying breath.

'The universe . . . this big old universe: sometimes it can be a cruel place, can't it?'

Six

The act of stepping through the front door of the hotel into a turbulently busy Church Street felt so much like jumping into a fast-flowing river that Beth Layne found herself holding her breath. The narrow confines of the street, barely fifteen feet wide and lined by tightly packed cottages, channelled the flow of hundreds of town folk. This afternoon they all seemed in a rush. Maybe that could be blamed on the shortness of the winter's day. By late afternoon it would be dark. Already a hard sunlight cast long shadows. No doubt these people longed to finish their errands before day yielded to night.

Beth followed Eleanor in that speeding current of humanity. Children chased each other, shoving by the adults. Those adults, aplenty, carried baskets of groceries; a chimney sweep armed with sooty bristles on poles set off bad-tempered grumbling, when he brushed against the women's clean coats. Eleanor tried to toss back some comment or other to Beth but the hubbub drowned her words.

As Beth did her best to avoid losing sight of Eleanor in the crowds, she caught snatches of conversation from the locals.

A man with a fishing net over his shoulder called to his mate: 'Saboteurs! That's what they're saying. Slowitt's kipper shed got burnt down last night.'

The mate laughed harshly. 'Why would Hitler bother himself attacking a shed for smoking fish?'

'Oh, go stuff yourself, Hardacre. You always praised Hitler before the war.'

'You filthy liar.'

The men jostled, but the flow of people carried Beth away.

At last, Church Street disgorged into a broadly open area at the junction with Bridge Street, near the Dolphin Inn. Here, at last, Beth could walk without being crowded, or wincing from sharp elbows being driven into her sides, albeit by accident. Clearly, however, rumours of last night's events made the atmosphere spiky and nothing less than fraught. The army would keep facts about the attack on the soldiers a secret, considering wartime conditions made nearly *everything* a military secret. Then the authorities probably couldn't find any bodies; presumably the Vampiric soldiers would have hidden themselves in their new lairs. Nevertheless, just enough information had leaked out to spark off speculation of all sorts. As Beth crossed the swing bridge with Eleanor, she heard rumours about Nazi parachutists landing in the abbey ruins, or pro-Hitler Black Shirts trying to set fire to the town. *If only you knew the truth . . .* Beth merely had to close her eyes for the night horrors to come streaming through her head. How Gustav and his clan had pounced on the soldiers in the cave.

'Up this way,' Eleanor nodded at a steep lane that ran from the waterfront. 'As soon as we've got what we need, we'll get back to the hotel.' The woman appeared uneasy. 'The people are jittery. When they're like this it can spark of trouble.'

Here, on Whitby's West Side, the streets were a little broader. It also boasted modern stores that sold wireless sets and fashionable clothes (although availability was extremely limited due to the rationing). Through busy streets, squads of soldiers would hurry by. Until yesterday, the troops that guarded the town tended to saunter about in quite a relaxed way. Although they couldn't know exactly the fate of their comrades, they'd know that some tragedy had occurred. Consequently, the soldiers moved briskly with grim expressions on their faces.

Cold currents of air blew from the sea, as the pair climbed the steep incline. A wall poster flapped, inviting people to attend a special screening at the Whitby Picture House: *The Turn of the Tide – a portrayal of local fisher folk by Leo Walmsley.* A freshly pasted strip of paper across the poster screamed: *CANCELLED!* Up ahead, groups of boys hurled taunts at one another. A man swore at a horse that was reluctant to haul coal up the steep gradient. Down in the harbour, boats sounded their horns in short-tempered bursts. This air of fractious nerves and heightened tension added to the sense that a storm was about to break. *But what kind of storm?* Beth asked herself. *The entire neighbourhood is nervy. People are eager to dole out theories of what happened last night, then they get themselves into a flaming temper when they're not taken seriously by their friends. If you ask me, the town's set to blow its top.*

Eleanor led the way into a general supplies store to collect a bag full of bottle tops. They resembled hundreds of blank silver coins. She checked them.

'No, I ordered the plain metal ones,' she told the storekeeper, who clearly didn't like the woman from the way he eyed her with distaste.

'They are the plain ones,' he insisted.

'No, these have a cork lining on the inside of the cap.'

'So?'

'So that's not what I ordered.'

'Miss Charnwood. I don't see the difference between the—'

'There's a world of difference, Mr Filby.'

'But I don't see—'

'Mr Filby. Indulge me. I ordered metal caps without cork, just plain metal. That's all I want.'

He clicked his tongue. Obviously, he thought Eleanor Charnwood was being awkward for the hell of it. 'There's a war on, Miss Charnwood, or hadn't you realized?'

Eleanor scowled. 'I know perfectly well there's a war. But you supplied me with plain bottle tops, just two weeks ago.'

'Well, I haven't got any now. Take them or leave them.' Shrugging, he went to arrange brown earthenware bowls on a shelf. Beth noticed he also used his thumb to wipe out prices chalked on the sides. That done, he began chalking higher prices – much higher.

Beth whispered, 'Won't these do?' she indicated the silver disks in the bag.

Beth, if that stuff I'm bottling comes into contact with the cork . . . well, you'd remember the results for the rest of your life.'

Once more, Beth asked herself what, exactly, was the nature of that witch's brew that was being decanted into the beer bottles.

'Sorry, I couldn't help you, ladies.' As Mr Filby chalked inflated prices on the crocks, he smirked to himself. 'But I can order more for you. The special *corkless* ones that is.'

'You disgust me, Filby.' Eleanor's voice rose. 'You're a spiv, a cheat, a swindler. You'll sell me the ones I need at an inflated price, won't you?'

'Consider it a favour I'm trading with you at all, Miss Charnwood. Especially, as most decent folk will have nothing to do with you. Now, I will bid you good day, ladies. Please close the door on . . . wait, you're not allowed behind the counter.'

Eleanor had slammed back the timber flap, then gone to search the shelves.

'I'm warning you, Charnwood. I'll have the police on you!'

He rushed across, undoubtedly intent on dragging the woman out of the shop. Beth stood in his way.

The man raised his hands to push Beth aside.

'Mr Filby. Don't you dare touch me.'

'But that woman isn't allowed behind the counter. It's private.' This time he tried to circle Beth. Smartly, she stood between him and the counter. His face went from red to purple. 'Get out of my way!'

'No.'

'Damn you, I'll call the police.'

'And I'll tell them that you've just hiked the prices of your old stock.'

'It's my stock. Now get out of my way.'

'Aren't there laws against profiteering, sir?' Beth stood her ground. 'And it'll be the wives and mothers of the policemen who will be paying those new prices for your old pots.'

The man harrumphed, but he appeared unsure what to do next. Then:

'Ah-ha!' Eleanor pulled a paper-wrapped package from a shelf. 'These are mine.'

'What makes you think that?' The man had the air of a trapped rat; his eyes slid from side to side, as if searching for a hole to hide in.

'The name "E. Charnwood" pencilled on the side gives it away, Filby.' She tore a hole in the brown paper, then eased out a silver disk. 'Yes, my bottle tops. *Without* the cork inlay. You planned to sell these to me above their original price, didn't you?'

'Plain bottle tops! You're a lunatic.' Filby almost choked on his own rage. 'Everyone knows beer will go flat if you bottle it with those on the neck.'

Eleanor placed coins on the counter. 'What I owe you for my order.' Her tones were impeccably polite. 'I only wish I could give you a drink of what I'm bottling tonight.'

'Pah. Knowing you, it will have been boiled up in a witch's cauldron.'

'Good day, Mr Filby.'

They were back in the cold air, gusting in from the ocean. People hurried by, heads down, eager to get safely home before sunset. Eleanor carried the hefty package of bottle tops.

'In truth, I'd have paid a hundred times what he was asking for these.'

'They really are that vital?'

'Goodness, yes. Worth their weight in diamonds really. Without them, I couldn't finish bottling that witch's brew of mine.'

'Witch's brew?'

'The commercial name is X–Stock. Although it has a long chemical formula to accurately identify it.'

'What does it do?' Beth asked, intrigued.

'Better I show you than tell you. Come on. It'll be dark soon.'

They retraced their steps down a street so steep that it made the tops of Beth's feet ache. Another platoon of soldiers bustled by. Their expressions were as grim as before.

Eleanor murmured, 'I imagine the commanding officer will have called in reinforcements, while they try and figure out what happened to their men last night?'

'Could you have saved them with those powders of yours?'

'Even if I could have spirited them from the cave to the hotel, the wounds would have been too severe. Those Vampiric creatures sucked every ounce of blood out of them. Sally was lucky. She was bitten at the hotel and she managed to break away the moment the injury was inflicted.'

'Is that the same story with your brother?'

Eleanor paused, the breeze carried her hair across her face, as if it were a dark rippling veil. 'His wounds were more severe. The transformation had already begun by the time I managed to apply the Quick Salts. To be honest, Beth, I didn't really save him. I've trapped him in a kind of limbo – somewhere between being human and Vampiric. I wish I had the courage to destroy him.' She continued on her way.

Not that the return to the hotel would be an easy one.

The mood of the townspeople remained edgy. An electric tension crackled on the air. More than once, Beth recalled that dark sentence, reputedly uttered by Gustav Kirk in his youth: *Tiw strikes again.*

As they crossed the bridge over the Esk a voice snapped, 'There goes Madam Eleanor Charnwood. So high and mighty. So full of her own self-importance!'

Beth immediately recognized who'd hurled those words with the savagery of a thug hurling stones. Mrs Brady, a shawl dragged tightly around her hunched shoulders, glared at the pair of them. It was Mrs Brady that they'd encountered on the first night in Whitby, when she'd collected her strange, spectral daughter from this very bridge. Mrs Brady had uttered caustic comments that first night. Now she seemed eager to resume the feud.

'Look at Charnwood with the tart. Just look at that red lipstick. God knows what they get up to in that hotel.'

'Mrs Brady, please don't start this again.' Eleanor spoke calmly, trying to defuse the encounter. 'All we want to do is go home and cook a meal. We've eaten precious little since yesterday.'

'Eat well as a rule though, don't ya'?' Mrs Brady advanced on them. 'You don't need ration books like we do, eh? It's people like you who make sure decent folk have to go without meat and butter.'

'That's ridiculous, Mrs Brady. We have the same rations as—'

'And those fancy clothes on your backs? You got some black market men to keep you all sweet and cosy?'

The slur was as outlandish as it was untrue. Beth's long woollen coat had come with her from America before the start of the war. Equally, however, Beth knew that both she and Eleanor did dress differently from the locals. This made them stand out on this crowded bridge. And it attracted the attention of people passing by. Most had stopped to watch – dramatic events were unfolding.

Now that she had an audience, Mrs Brady gloated; she tugged the shawl even tighter. 'And have you seen this one? The stranger. She's going to be in a film about Whitby. That's right, this tart will pretend she's one of the folk from round here. We'll be a laughing stock or worse.'

A bulky man in a cap rolled his eyes at Beth. 'Is this true?'

'We're making a film to show how ordinary people in this town are coping with the war.'

'Ruddy hell. An American playing one of us.' This came from a large woman with a red-chapped face.

Immediately, a chorus of outrage rose.

'That shouldn't be allowed!'

'Some picture people are going to make us look stupid.'

'Like painted tarts, you mean.'

'You lot should go back to where you came from.'

'Tarts! Hussies!'

Instantly, the faces around Beth became masks of fury. Eyes glittered. Saliva sprayed from lips as they shouted.

Eleanor grabbed Beth by the arm. 'Come on. I told you there'd be trouble if they found out.'

'But it's part of the war effort,' Beth protested. 'Listen. We aren't going to make you look ridiculous. This film will be shown around the world. It will encourage neutral countries to – uph!'

The red-faced woman had shoved Beth. She'd have tumbled on to her back, if the bridge's fence hadn't slammed into her. Gulls cried overhead. They seemed to pick up the charge of anger. It provoked the birds into furious screeching.

'Please, let us pass.' Eleanor tried to calm an increasingly ugly situation. 'We'll go back to the hotel.'

'Don't let them through,' Mrs Brady shouted. 'It's time we stopped people like this making our lives a misery.'

The claim lacked no truth, or even much in the way of logic, yet the crowd responded with roars of anger. Beth flinched as fingers tugged a lock of her hair. More hands pushed at her. Eleanor was jostled, too. All the time, insults flew.

Eleanor shouted, 'You are good people. This isn't what Whitby folk do. I know you're frightened. It's the war that's making you act like this. We should—'

A fist flew from the crowd. Eleanor reeled back. By the time she straightened, threads of crimson were running down her jaw. Though Beth tried to help Eleanor, she couldn't move forward so much as a yard. Men and women, faces distorted with rage, pushed her back to the lattice-work fence.

Anger boiled in the mob. They shouted wilder accusations. Those at the back became frustrated, because they couldn't deliver their own blows on Eleanor Charnwood – a woman universally mistrusted, if not despised, in Whitby. They surged forward. Beth cried out as she was crushed back against the fence. Mrs Brady had, by this time, a fistful of Eleanor's hair, and did her best to rip it from her scalp. Still, Eleanor clung on to the pack of bottle tops, as if she tried to protect a baby in the melee.

Beth foresaw their fate. The crowd would pound the two women until they were bloody. Then, for good measure, they'd be paraded through the streets like a pair of enemy captives. No doubt having to brave a bruising hail of stones as they did so. After that, who knew their ultimate fate?

'Let go of me,' panted Beth. 'Stop it. We've done nothing.'

Her ribs ached from the crush. Dark splotches gathered in her eyes. She realized that unconsciousness wouldn't be far away. Once she was on the ground kicks would follow. The mob had been gripped by bloodlust. In this moment of madness, the two women could be blamed for the war, the shortages of food, the Nazi air raids. These two women were guilty. They had caused all the bad things to happen. In the grip of paranoia, it made perfect sense to the crowd to make everything right again by kicking these women until blood gushed out on to the pavement.

As Beth's knees sagged, a hand covered her face to press her downward. Grunted insults filled her ears. Just as she told herself she couldn't stay on her feet for another second, a huge voice tore through the storm of sound.

'*Hear this. Return to your homes now. From sixteen hundred hours there will be an emergency curfew. You must return to your homes. Sixteen hundred hours is four o' clock. The curfew will extend until seven o'clock tomorrow morning.*' The precisely formed words, through a megaphone, were redolent of an army officer.

Gruffer, no-nonsense voices, cut through shouts on the bridge. 'Clear the road. Go home. If you're not indoors by four, there'll be hell to pay.'

As if a switch had been flicked, the mob dispersed. Eleanor and Beth stood panting against the fence. Blood smeared Eleanor's face. The gruffer voices belonged to a dozen policemen, who didn't hesitate to shove aside any folk who chose to argue.

First over the bridge, a line of solid, large-booted Coppers. Trundling behind them, a drab green army car on which had been fixed a megaphone. The crisp officer's voice issued from this. '*By order of the regional military commander: you must return to your homes. A curfew will be in effect tonight from four, until seven in the morning. Anyone flouting this is likely to be shot. I repeat: do not venture out of doors from four while seven. Anyone breaking the curfew will be deemed to have hostile intent. You will be shot on sight.*' Behind the car, a squad of soldiers armed with rifles.

Eleanor composed herself with a deep breath. 'Just when you thought the paranoia couldn't get any worse. Now our own soldiers have us in their sights. Come on, let's get back while we can.'

'Your face is all bloody, Eleanor. Let me clean it first.'

'It can wait.' She lifted the bottle tops. 'This work can't. We've got to fill the bottles tonight.'

'What happens then?'

'All hell breaks loose.'

Seven

Sally and Alec recoiled in shock at the sight of Eleanor and Beth half falling through the hotel door.

'What on Earth happened?' gasped Sally, eyeing the dishevelled women. 'My God, Eleanor, your mouth is bleeding.'

'Here. Sit down.' Alec indicated the plush sofa.

Eleanor shook her head. 'Just a nick. I'll be fine . . . no, Alec, don't fuss.' She allowed her voice to soften a little. 'Thank you, Alec. I appreciate that you want to take care of us.' She checked the pack of bottle tops remained intact. 'But I've a lot to do tonight. I'll splash some water on my face, then I'll be ready for battle.'

Sally's eyes darted anxiously from Eleanor to the hotel door that Beth securely bolted. 'Battle? What do you mean? Beth, you must tell us what happened out there.'

Beth listened at the door. Heavy boots tramped past. Voices echoed along Church Street. Mixed with those, a commanding officer barking orders.

Alec spoke gently, 'What did happen to you? Were you attacked?'

Beth checked on Tommy and the dog in their cosy den beneath the reception counter. 'They're both asleep, still. That helps.'

Alec grew impatient. 'Tell us!'

Eleanor's delivery was matter-of-fact, 'The townspeople are frightened. They know something bad happened last night, only the military have suppressed news of their troops going missing.'

'Now the authorities have imposed a curfew,' Beth added. 'If anyone even pokes their nose beyond their door tonight, the soldiers will shoot on sight.'

'But you've been attacked,' Sally wailed. 'Who did that? The soldiers?'

'No, they saved our necks,' Beth said.

'Like I say,' Eleanor told them crisply, 'the locals are frightened. So frightened that they've become paranoid. Because we dress and behave a little differently to them, they decided to gang up on us.'

Alec flared, 'They should be reported. I'll telephone the police.'

'You'll do no such thing,' Eleanor told him. 'We don't want policemen nosing round here.'

'Why?'

'For obvious reasons.' Eleanor nodded across the reception area. She might have been indicating the sleeping place of Tommy, their Vampiric guest – then again, she might have been indicating the basement entrance. Beth knew that's where this formidable woman had stockpiled her arsenal of weapons. The ones that took the form of beer bottles half filled with that pungent chemical. Either way, Beth Layne understood perfectly that Eleanor didn't require any inquisitive policemen stomping about the place. Eleanor touched the corner of her mouth, where the blood seeped, and winced.

'The long and the short of it, Beth and I were jostled by some very frightened, paranoid people. For them, it was out of character. Ascribe it to the madness of war. Now, I'll go give this old face of mine a scrub.' With that gesture of bravado, she sailed through the doorway to the kitchen. Always, but always, she clasped the bag of bottle tops – for her, they were more precious than gold coins.

Ascribe it to the madness of war? Beth wasn't so sure. *Ever since we arrived here, I've noticed that the locals avoid you – as if you'll infect them with some dirty little bug. They fear you, Eleanor. Do they have some inkling about the nature of your old childhood friends? When Whitby folk are in their own homes, do they whisper rumours of vampires roaming the neighbourhood?*

'Beth . . . Beth, are you alright?'

'Hmm? Sorry, I was miles away.'

Sally hugged her friend. 'They didn't hurt you? The mob?'

'Hardly a mob, Sally. A few people got jittery; that's all.' Beth deliberately underplayed the incident to put her friend at ease. 'I could do with running a brush through my hair, though. That would be nice.'

Alec pressed a finger to the eyepatch, as he regarded her with his good eye. 'Nevertheless, you've had something of a shock. I'll bring you a cup of tea with a hefty shot of rum. That'll have you firing on all cylinders again.'

'Thank you, Alec.' Beth saw that the man cared for her, as he did for Sally and Eleanor. She would allow him his role of avuncular doctor, even if the medicine he prescribed was a shot of strong liquor.

The clock chimed three.

'Not long until nightfall.' Alec headed for the kitchen. 'These damned winter days. They're gone in the blink of an eye.' He pushed open the door. 'I'll have the tea ready in five minutes, Beth. I want you to drink it while it's hot.'

'Yes, doctor.'

The joke, small though it was, cheered the man up. 'Then be a good patient. Have your wash and brush up, and be down here in two ticks.'

Beth headed for the stairs.

'I'll come with you.' With each moment that passed, Sally became increasingly anxious, and when the army car passed along Church Street she gave a gasp of fear.

'There is to be a curfew.' The metallic voice pierced the door. *'From*

four this afternoon, until seven tomorrow morning. During that time, you must remain indoors. There are no excuses. Observe the curfew. Those failing to do so will be shot on sight. I repeat: Shot on sight.'

In sheer despair, Sally wiped away a tear. 'It's like the voice of a monster, isn't it? Now we're trapped here.'

Three fifteen. Shadows grew longer, somehow more skeletal, on the roads as the sun neared the horizon. Beth made quick work of washing her face and brushing her hair. Sally remained with her, afraid to let her friend out of her sight. Beth appreciated that the woman, despite her carefree, happy-go-lucky manner, could suffer bouts of nerves that left her frightened and childlike.

Once Beth had finished repairing her make-up and self-confidence, she and Sally headed for the kitchen. Alec Reed had brewed up that strong tea of his. In each of the mugs, he added sugar and rum.

'No doubt you'll detest the taste.' He boomed the words, as if trying to dispel anxieties of his own. 'But I guarantee it will restore you to the rudest of health.'

After forcing the concoction down her throat with shuddering politeness, Beth left Alec and Sally talking in the kitchen, while she delivered Alec's restorative to Eleanor. The open basement door provided a telling clue to the woman's whereabouts. In the old wine store Eleanor had already unpacked the silver bottle tops; now she was in the process of donning the heavy rubber apron that covered her from chin to toes.

'This is Alec's special cure-all?' Beth held out the steaming mug. 'Oh?'

'Tea strong enough to hold a roof up, and a mighty shot of rum.'

'That's good medicine.' Eleanor smiled. Taking the mug, she downed it in one. 'Phew. If we ever run short of aviation fuel . . .' She scrunched her shoulders, as the potent cocktail hit her stomach. 'Phew again. That's the kind of pick-me-up that could take a bomber to Berlin and back.'

'I'm here to help,' Beth announced.

'If you're going to work in this bomb factory of the damned – forgive my purple prose – you're going to need protective clothing.'

'You've got a spare gas mask and rubber gloves.'

But if this stuff splashes you . . .' Eleanor indicated the jar of blue-ish liquid on the table. 'Boof.'

'There must be something I can do to help.'

'Very well, my dear. Thank you. Another pair of hands would be extremely useful. I'm going to need at least a hundred of these bottles filling.' She shot Beth a telling look. 'Don't worry, I will explain what this stuff is later. For the time being, consider it as a cure-all for vampires.'

They set to work. Beth donned rubber gloves and the spare gas mask. Because of the dangerous nature of the chemical, and because Beth lacked full protective clothing, she set out the empty bottles on the table for Eleanor to half fill with the blue spirit. When the bottles were relatively safe, with the metal cap in place, Beth then dunked each bottle into a tub of fresh water to ensure that any chemical on the outer surface of the bottle was washed away. In the confines of the vault, acrid chemical fumes accumulated to such a degree that a blue haze formed in the air. Despite the gas masks both women developed sore throats, their eyes watered. Yet neither paused in their labours. Beth knew this work had all the importance of a holy quest. She pictured the vampires in Hag's Lung. The soldiers' rifles had been useless against the creatures. If these bottles of blue were some kind of answer to that Vampiric menace, then Beth would do her utmost to help make this weapon – whatever it was, and whatever effect it would have on the blood-thirsty monsters.

The time: three forty-five. Alec had left Sally to gaze out through the dining room window at the sunset, while he ventured into the office that he'd been using to revise the film script. The streets were emptying of people; dusk fell over the town. Even the car with the megaphone had retreated into the distance. That unsettling, even menacing word, 'curfew' had become a faint noise that seemed to shimmer in a ghostly fashion on the cold winter air.

Alec sat down at the desk. When thinking hard, he'd developed a habit of resting his finger lightly on his eyepatch. The good eye focused on the black telephone on the desk. This had become the only link to the outside world. The wire that ran from the body of the phone would carry his words to a world beyond Whitby. Even though he'd only been in this mysterious, isolated town at the edge of the sea for a few days, it seemed, weirdly, as if he'd spent most of his life here. Alec found it hard to visualize the faces of his family in Scotland. The country beyond the barrier of high, moorland hills could have been on the other side of the world. Alec was gripped by a powerful notion that he would spend the rest of his life in this seaside town – a dreamlike realm, where the normal laws of nature

no longer existed. This was the kind of place where the impossible
not only might happen, but MUST happen. *Whitby: a town of miracles and nightmares.*

This telephone provided his only means of escape. Alec strove to
marshal his thoughts. If he picked up the handset and dialled the
number for the local police headquarters, what then? Did he possess
the eloquence to describe what had befallen him and his three
friends? Would they believe him, when he revealed that Vampiric
creatures prowled this windswept port? He thought hard. Surely
there would be an elegant, yet simple way to convince them?

'The child.'

What if he delivered Tommy to them? One look at the Vampiric
boy would prove to the authorities that he told the truth. Now . . .
if he called the police and told them he'd found a lost child. *So, not
exactly the truth, is it? But what does it matter?* All he required was a
couple of constables at the Leviathan Hotel, then to say in quite a
straightforward manner, 'Good evening, officers. If I could ask you to
step through to the other side of the reception counter? Now . . . if
you take a little peek at what's lying there on the blanket . . .'

Yes, that would do it.

Alec picked up the telephone.

The clock's ponderous tick . . . tock tightened Sally's nerves. That
gulf between the tick and the tock became a silent vacuum that
seemed to beckon demonic creatures into it. The echo of the tick
and the thudding of the tock could have been a fist slowly pounding
the door of a tomb. The occupant wanted out. It knew where it
could find new companions.

Tick . . . Tock.

Every swing of the pendulum tightened that nerve inside her
head. She paced the dining room. The white light, which had
flooded over harbour waters to cascade in through the windows,
had slowly transformed into a buttery yellow. Now, at last . . . the
dying sun bled crimson rays into the room. Once the tables had
been clearly illuminated; now a deepening pool of shadow drowned
them.

Sally hated the sun. She hated its cowardice. It hadn't the courage
to shine down over the town. It would slip beneath the blue hills,
then it would slither around the globe to illuminate other people,
in other towns, on the other side of the planet. Traitor sun; treach-
erous orb.

Tick . . . Tock.

Sally slammed her fist on to the table. A voice in the back of her head told her that this wasn't logical. Sunset is entirely natural. Yet she hated the setting of the sun. She cast enraged glances at that blood-red ball. She rubbed the sore wound on her wrist. And she longed for nothing more than to grab hold of what remained of the daylight. She would keep her grip on the beams of radiance. They wouldn't slip from her fingers. They wouldn't leave her to the darkness.

Just half the sun remained. A ruddy dome sitting on the hilltop. *The light's leaving you, Sally, hang on to it — don't let it run away. You need the light.*

'Come on,' she hissed at the sun. 'You can stay for longer. Don't leave us. I don't want it to be night.' She repeated the last sentence. This time, not a hiss, but a full-blooded yell. *'I don't want it to be night!'*

Sally Wainwright pelted through the dining room to the office. Alec sat at the desk, phone in one hand, he dialled with the other.

'*Alec!*' she yelled with such ferocity that he almost dropped the handset. 'Alec. Come and see it. Hurry! It's starting to go!'

'Sally? What's wrong?' Startled, he replaced the handset. 'Sally?'

But she'd raced out of the office into reception. Instinct told her not to venture too near to the counter (because *he's* under there). She shouted in the direction of the open basement door, 'Come and see it! Eleanor! Beth! Come and see what's happening . . .'

Panicked, struggling to draw air into her lungs, she ran wildly back into the dining room. Light the colour of blood filled it. All that remained of the sun, a bitten sliver of crimson.

Alec, Eleanor and Beth rushed through the doorway.

'Sally?' Beth called. 'What's happening?'

'You can see it for yourselves?' Sally pointed at the tiny nugget of light on the distant hilltop. 'It's going . . . the sun's leaving us.' A sound erupted from her throat. No one could tell whether it was a peal of fraught laughter, or a yell of terror. 'I — I tried not to let it go. I wanted to stop it. I — I . . . oh, God help us, I tried with all my heart to stop it setting.'

Alec spoke softly, 'Sally, my dear, it's sunset. Just the sun going down at the end of the day, like it always does.'

Sally crashed both fists down on a table top. 'Don't you see? We can't let it get dark tonight. As soon the night comes *they'll* come, too.'

Eleanor said, 'We can't stop the sun from setting. We have to accept there will be darkness.'

'But I don't!' Sally howled out in fury. 'I won't let the sun set! I won't let it get dark. Because I don't want the night to come!' Her wild eyes raked their faces. 'Don't you see? The curfew means we can't even run away. We're prisoners in the hotel. We're stuck here . . . we might as well be sacrificial offerings.' She pointed a trembling finger at each one. 'We were lucky to escape those creatures last night. I'm telling you that we won't be so lucky again. They'll have our blood. Then we will be like them. We'll be monsters.' She caught her breath, as a terrible fact reached into her head and seared her mind. Softly, she murmured, 'It's gone . . . it's gone.' The soft pulse of words bled into still air. 'It's gone, it's gone . . .'

They all turned their eyes to the faraway hills. The sun had gone, indeed.

And the night had, at last, come down upon them.

PART SIX

{From The Monastic Testament *of St Botolph – AD672}*

Wicked spirits flew at the towers of Whitby Abbey. Their appearance forewarned and foretold the coming of the Blood-Storm.

One

No. They didn't creep out of their lairs. They didn't slither from their crevices in the rock face. There was no shuffling out into the night. They arrived as a storm. They were hurricane of movement. The ravenous creatures plunged down the cemetery steps into Whitby town.

There they raced along the canyon of houses that is Henrietta Street. They smelt the incinerated bones of one of their kind in the shed that had burnt to the ground, just hours ago. With no prey to be found there, the pack of vampires turned, then swept back into Church Street. The wartime blackout meant total darkness in the roads and alleyways and closes. The vampires were lords of this lightless place.

The pack consisted of Vampiric soldiers, the pilot, still wearing goggles, Mary Tinskell in her white nightdress, and creatures that had once been Eleanor Charnwood's childhood companions. The monstrous, pale figures gushed through the narrow passageway into Benson's Yard. A few cottages clustered around an open area barely larger than a pathway. From an open window, a woman looked out, wondering if her soldier lover had come to call.

The pilot didn't even slow down. Effortlessly, he scaled the outer wall of the cottage, with all the agility of a cat. Before the woman even cried out in shock, he'd scooped her from the window, then flung her down to his companions. The sound of their teeth puncturing female flesh sounded like surprisingly loud clicks in the otherwise silent yard. The woman kicked her bare legs as waves of agony engulfed her. A moment later, she lay still. Bloodless. Apparently lifeless. But not a state of affairs that would last for long. Even as the vampires withdrew from the body, still tasting her fresh blood on their lips, the woman's eyelids fluttered open. Colour from the iris faded. By the time she rose to her feet, her body pierced by dozens of teeth-marks, her eyes were white – a blazing, soulless white. The mark of the Vampiric.

Still hungry for blood, the vampires rejoined the main thoroughfare to scour the town for fresh prey. Tonight, hell would be a street in Whitby. The only people to be wholly safe were the ones that were already at peace in their graves.

At the front door of the Leviathan Hotel, the pack of rapacious vampires encountered Gustav Kirk. Yet they advanced on the building: the fierce gleam in their eyes screamed their intent.

'Not here,' Gustav implored. 'Leave these people alone.'

Mary Tinskell snarled, 'The boy's in there. He'll betray us if we don't get rid of him.'

The Vampiric soldiers were inebriated by the draughts of blood they'd downed. 'There's more in there,' one of them breathed. 'We've got to drink. We need it.'

'Not here,' Gustav insisted.

'Why should we listen to you?' hissed the pilot. 'We don't recognize your authority over us.'

'Please,' Gustav begged. 'My friends are in there. Theo and Eleanor.'

'They're no friends of yours,' Mary sneered. 'You're as deluded about that fact as you are about your precious Viking gods.'

The vampire pack moaned with hunger. 'We've got to have more.'

'We need it.'

'Blood. I want to taste it.'

'Just to open a vein . . . to drink.'

They surged forward, ready to break down the hotel door. Like a pack of hungry wolves, they pushed Gustav back. They wanted to get through. Nothing else mattered. Blood. They could smell it on the air. And, oh, how they yearned for its soft, velvet heat on their tongues.

'Not here,' Gustav implored. 'I won't let you hurt them.'

'Push him out of the way.' Mary tossed her head with contempt. 'I don't know why we ever let that weakling lord himself over us.'

A voice cut through the cold night air: *'You. Yes, you lot. Stand there. Raise your hands. No sudden movements.'*

A pair of soldiers moved purposefully along the street towards the creatures, their rifles at the ready. The pair of young mortal men couldn't yet properly identify what menace they confronted. The gloom here in Church Street blinded them.

The vampires saw what approached alright. They saw a pair of blood-filled vessels. The creatures could smell the red stuff inside of them. They could even hear the enticing pulse of it as it gushed through their arteries. And the sweetest blood of all is in the heart.

One of the men barked, 'Your hands! I told you to raise them. Don't you know there's a curfew?'

Forgetting the hotel (at least for now), the pack fell on the two soldiers before they could even fire a shot. Teeth opened arteries.

Vampiric men and women sighed with pleasure as fountains of blood struck the backs of their throats. The night was theirs. And so were these living sacs of hot, nourishing liquid – the elixir of life.

Gliding over Whitby, a lone raven defied its nature to fly by night. Beneath it, blacked out houses didn't reveal a glimmer. The dark squares that were the buildings imitated perfectly the squares of stone in the cliff-top graveyard. The raven circled over the hulking shape of the Leviathan Hotel. Sharp avian senses detected that human beings occupied the structure (as, likewise, it could divine the presence of vampires in the street. Moreover, it sensed the ancient vampires that were trapped in the sump cavern – those naked creatures that burnt with hunger so much that they couldn't stop their ceaseless, turbulent movement in the confines of the cave). In ages gone by, the raven's instincts could foretell when a battle was imminent. Then the birds would fly high over the battleground, waiting for the time when they could move in and feed on the fallen warriors. Tonight, that same instinct flared in the brain of the raven. A battle was coming. A huge conflict. Many would fall. The carrion would provide rich feasting grounds.

The bird cried out to its companions, gathering in the darkness above the night-clad hills. It called its brethren to the feast.

Two

Beth Layne heard the cry of the raven high above the hotel; she could also hear scuffling from the street. Now the curfew had come into force there should be no one out there, other than the armed patrols. Beth, however, made out the sound of feet lightly, and swiftly, padding along the cobblestones. Not the usual thud of army boots.

Standing there, in the centre of the reception area, Beth gazed at the timber door to the outside world. It was resolutely bolted against intruders of any shape or form, yet that barrier seemed absurdly flimsy. At any moment, she expected it to fly open to reveal those pale creatures she'd encountered last night. The ones with the colourless eyes and widely spaced teeth set in swollen crimson gums. She shuddered.

The dog slipped out from behind the reception counter to stand just in front of her, as if he sensed she needed reassurance. The animal's coal-black face turned towards her, his bright eyes met hers, and the jaws parted slightly to reveal a pink tongue. Sam's senses were heightened to an unusual degree. He sensed the threat beyond the doors. No doubt he knew that whatever moved in Church Street didn't possess a mortal heartbeat. Sam turned his eyes back to the locked door. His ears were pricked upright. They twitched slightly, reading the rich information contained in those light scuffling sounds that Beth could only barely hear now.

'They're out there, aren't they, Sam?'

He swished his long black tail.

'Good boy.' She crouched to put her arm round his sleek neck. 'You aim to protect us, don't you?'

'Sam's brave, Miss. He's the bravest dog ever.'

Beth glanced back. She tried not to flinch at his appearance. But it was no good. The sight of Tommy standing there did come as a shock. *I know what to expect,* she told herself. *He is one of those Vampiric creatures, but he's not dangerous. He wouldn't harm us.*

Even so . . .

Just to see the diminutive figure, standing there in front of the desk, still as a figure carved from gleaming white bone, tested her courage. Yes, the voice that came through the dark lips could have come from any boy in Whitby – a child proud as anything of his pet dog. But it was the dreadful reality of that short figure. The pale skin. The white eyes. A pair of fierce black pupils staring into her face. The inhuman posture. The dark tracery of veins in the neck. Once more she told herself that what had entered their lives wasn't human. *This is the ghost of a boy that haunts a monster's body.*

She steeled herself with a deep breath. 'How are you, Tommy?'

'I'm very well, thank you, Miss,' he responded politely.

'Can I get you anything to drink, or eat? That is, if you're thirsty or . . .' Her voice failed her in the presence of this Godless scrap of flesh and bone.

'I'm not hungry. I'm never hungry these days. How's Sam? He looks alright to me, does he look well to you?'

'Your dog is made of tough stuff, Tommy. He seems to be over that bump.'

'Sam. Here boy! That's a good boy!'

Sam rushed to Tommy, tail wagging happily. Tommy fussed over the boy, gently checking the wound on the dog's head, then giggling when he realized the animal hadn't suffered lasting harm. Once more, the actions and the voice were that of a human boy.

Yet Tommy's face possessed that stone-like expression of a corpse. Beth shivered.

'I'd like to hear that box again,' Tommy declared. 'Can I use the wire loss?'

'The wireless? Of course you can.'

'Come on, Sam. We're going to the wireless.' Before he ran to the dining room, he sped across to Beth. Quickly, he took her hand, then kissed the back of her bare wrist. His lips were chill as butter from a fridge.

Beth tried to force herself to believe this was just an ordinary boy. *Try,* she told herself. *He saved your life last night. Not once, but twice.*

Then Tommy, followed by a skipping Sam, hurried to the dining room.

'Don't open any curtains, Tommy,' Beth told him. 'We're not allowed to let any light out. It's the law now.'

Tommy accepted this without question. Before she could switch on the lights in the pitch-black room, he wove through the chairs and tables. *Another of his talents. He sleeps all day. He doesn't need food or drink. And he can see in the dark.*

Quickly, he crouched by the radio to turn the shiny brown knob. Seconds later, valves glowed through the vents. Voices burst from the speaker. It seemed like a comedy show. There was something garishly out of place about the play's banter. Beth realized that her tense-ness of mood, and the disturbing situation she found herself plunged into, made the broadcast grate on her nerves.

A Scottish husband and wife were arguing.

'So, Peggy, where do you expect my uncles to sleep the night afore the wedding?'

'They can sleep in the blinking coal-hole for all I care.'

'There's a war on, Peggy.'

'Well let them kip down with flipping Hitler. He's as mad as a hatter – he won't mind.'

Tommy knelt before the radio, his arm round the dog's neck. Those alien eyes of his fixed that brown Bakelite box full of voices. Once again, she recalled family dogs from her childhood that had to be put to sleep when they were too ill to continue with their lives. She knew it would be a kindness to release whatever remained of Tommy from that cold shell. But when? And how? And did she have the courage? Those were the questions that plagued her when Alec put his head through the doorway.

'Beth. Eleanor's ready for the demonstration.'

'I'll be right along.'

Beth watched Tommy stroking Sam. *The boy is suffering, too. It would be cruel not to.*

Three

Beth Layne left Tommy listening to the radio. Thoughts weighing heavy on her mind, she descended the steps into the cellar. Alec and Sally were there. The man kept adjusting the eyepatch, as if he found it impossible to find any degree of comfort with it. Sally shot frightened glances in the direction of the iron grate in the floor. A cool draught, which carried odours of the sea, oozed from it. Beneath the grate, a pit of shadow. A blackness that suggested that ghostly forms would find it to their liking. A lair from which to strike.

Eleanor stepped into the light of the single, naked bulb. She had donned the rubber apron and was fastening the buckles up her back. 'Ah, good, everyone's here. Then let's make this quick. We might be running short of time.'

Sally appeared happier that Beth had joined them. 'Here, let me, Eleanor.' She fastened the buckles for her.

'Thank you, Sally, you're a dear. Will you bring me the gauntlets, too?'

Alec said, 'You don't have to do this, you know?'

'Of course, I do. You must learn the vicious nature of this chemical.'

'No, I mean you don't have to fight this battle yourself.'

'What do you suggest?'

'The police.'

'Even if the police believed me, there is a curfew.'

'So? Wait until morning?'

'My dear Alec. We don't have the luxury of waiting until morning. Those creatures attacked last night. They'll do so again tonight.'

Alec clenched his fists in exasperation. 'Damn it, woman. Why didn't you go to the authorities before now? You've known about those monsters for twenty years.'

Sally finished buckling the apron. 'Don't be hard on Eleanor, Alec.'

'Don't be hard on her? Ye Gods. Why wait until now, Eleanor?

Were you frightened of telling the truth? Did you think the police would arrest you?'

Eleanor's eyes flared. 'Alec. I'm afraid of nothing! Yes, I prevaricated. But until recently Gustav and the rest were, to all intents and purposes, inactive. They didn't attack people. Yes, they might have slaked their thirst on animals, but humans? No. Absolutely not.'

'What changed them?'

Beth knew the answer. 'The war – that's what changed them, Alec. Temptation was placed in their way. I know, strictly speaking, they're not like movie vampires: they don't fear crucifixes or sleep in coffins, but they do crave blood.'

'And they suppressed that craving,' Eleanor added. 'But when men are tumbling out of the sky from exploding aircraft, or sailors being washed ashore from wrecked naval ships, with the blood still in their veins, then what are the wretches supposed to do? How would an alcoholic cope with a crate of whisky being delivered to his door every day?'

'They're monsters, Eleanor. Not humans with addiction maladies.'

'Gustav Kirk is, at heart, a good man. He tried to stop the others attacking innocent people. He denied himself human blood.'

'But it was Gustav Kirk who attacked the army sergeant in Hag's Lung.'

'That was when he was sprayed with the man's blood. Momentarily, he lost control.' A tear rolled from Eleanor's eye. 'Gustav tried so hard.'

'As you tried so hard with Gustav,' Alec murmured.

'What do you mean? Tried so hard with Gustav?'

'Tried *not* to fall in love with him?'

'I don't love him.'

'No?'

'No!'

Alec gave one of those if-you-say-so shrugs.

Eleanor took the rubber gauntlets from Sally. 'I know that I can't just sit back and hope the danger will go away. The reality is this: vampires have invaded our world. There are more trapped in the sump cavern. Soon they will escape. If they do, the town will be overwhelmed. Whitby will become Vampiric. My parents accused me of being timid, of lacking courage. I proved them wrong. I will prove to you that I will act, without concern for my own safety, to destroy the vampire menace. But I need your help. So I will demonstrate the weapon I have devised.' She stepped back into the shadows. 'Wait here for a moment, please. But *do* stand well back. This will be dangerous.'

Eleanor headed through a doorway into the basement wine cellar.

Beth whispered to Alec, 'We're in this together. We've got to stand by Eleanor.'

'We could still phone the police.'

'During a curfew?'

'Yes.'

'You really think they'll send men here to the hotel?'

'If they won't, then I'll go to authorities in the morning. I'll tell them everything.'

In the cold tones of a prophet of doom Sally uttered, 'By then, who will be left among us to reveal anything?'

Beth pressed her lips together. A chill that seemed unearthly in its intensity forced its way up her spine. The breeze blew harder from the grate. With it came the whisper of the sea – a sound like conspirators drawing up plans of attack.

A moment later, the strange silhouette of Eleanor in the long rubber apron appeared. Although she wore gauntlets, she didn't bother with the gas mask this time. In both hands, as if she carried an offering for the gods, she approached with a glass bowl, the kind you might eat strawberries from on a summer's day. In the bottom, a little of the blue liquid. Eleanor set the bowl on the stone floor. She noticed that Alec had glanced at the table, and now clearly wondered why she'd gone to the trouble of putting the bowl at her feet.

'This is X-Stock.' Eleanor indicated the blue liquid. 'In chemical terms, it's a cousin of Hydrogen Peroxide. Alec, you asked yourself why I didn't put the dish on the table. If I had, and spilled it on to the wood, you wouldn't live long enough to know the answer.'

Sally ventured, 'The chemical will react with the wood?'

Both Alec and Eleanor showed surprise at Sally's knowledge of chemistry.

'I'm not all about make-up and movies, you know.' She blushed. 'I remember my chemistry lessons at school. Mr Patterson dropped a tiny piece of potassium in a bucket of water and it sort of danced on the surface, flashing and shooting out sparks. It burnt a hole in Mr Patterson's necktie.'

'This stuff is volatile . . . incredibly volatile,' Eleanor told them. 'It's what scientists would describe as hypergolic. Meaning it reacts with organic matter. Wood, cotton, wool, skin, muscle, bone.'

Alec nodded. 'Hence the rubber apron and gloves.'

'And they have to be a specially treated synthetic rubber at that.'

Beth eyed the blue liquid. 'So you've put X-Stock into the bottles? You plan to use them to bomb the vampires?'

'Forget wooden stakes and crucifixes. The only way to deal with our Vampiric friends here in Whitby is by beheading, or dismemberment, or incineration.'

Sally shuddered. 'And I don't expect you'll persuade one of those things to stand still long enough for you to chop off its head?'

'Exactly.'

Alec frowned. 'Are you sure this chemical will work?'

'Once you see it in action you will agree wholeheartedly that X-Stock is the perfect vampire killer.' Eleanor adjusted the apron's rubber collar so it was raised high enough to cover the bottom of her jaw. 'I read the kind of books that my contemporaries don't. I love books about ancient civilizations, exotic islands, faraway places, and I like to read about experiments in rocket travel. I came across a journal of the British Interplanetary Society; they planned to build a rocket fuelled by X-Stock. There would be a tank of this blue liquid, which would be sprayed into a combustion chamber; there it would hit another spray of fluid; this would be kind of organic soup. The resulting chemical reaction should blast a rocket into space. Anyway, enough of the theory. Sally?'

Sally shrank back. 'You don't want me to touch that blue stuff, do you?'

'Hardly. But I'd like one of the hairs from your head.' Eleanor gave a grim smile. 'Or at least one that's already adrift.'

Sally, wide-eyed and apprehensive, plucked a stray hair from her sleeve, then handed it to Eleanor.

'Everybody stand back,' Eleanor warned.

Then she released the hair from her gloved fingers. It drifted down towards the bowl of blueness. The whisper of surf, echoing up the tunnel, grew louder. Did some unseen intelligence experience their sense of anticipation, too? *Beware, one and all, Tiw is watching.* The impression of being spied upon whispered along Beth's taut nerves, as her gaze fixed on that single hair floating down towards the bowl. Everyone held their breaths. Apart from Eleanor, nobody knew what would happen next.

The second the strand touched the X-Stock its molecules attacked the organic molecules of the hair. With a loud pop that hurt Beth's ears, the hair vanished in a ball of white flame. Sparks shot from the bowl as far as the basement ceiling. By the time the pungent smoke had cleared there was no sign of the hair. Only that deceptively tranquil blue liquor remained.

'Imagine half a pint of that fluid hitting a human being,' Eleanor told them. 'Or, rather, one of the vampires. It doesn't just melt flesh – the stuff ignites it.'

'Ignites?' Sally exclaimed. *'It explodes it!'*

Eleanor gave another of her dry smiles. 'My dear, I couldn't have put it better myself. Now, if you'll excuse me, I'll put this dish somewhere safe.'

Soon Eleanor was back. She eased off the heavy gloves.

From Sally's expression she only too clearly envisaged the damage the X-Stock could inflict. 'Eleanor? Are you sure you can't use those white powders of yours to cure the vampires? After all, they worked on that bite on my arm.'

'It's far too late, I'm afraid. The physiognomies of the infected people have changed too much. The vampirism is embedded into their bodies at a cellular level. Sally, would you be a dear?' Eleanor turned her back in order to display the buckles running down her spine. Sally quickly went to work, unbuckling the garment. With a sigh of regret, Eleanor explained her plan. 'Tonight. The vampires will return to the hotel. I'm sure of it. I'll open the gates to the backyard. They will try and enter through there. We station ourselves at the upper windows. Once the vampires are inside the yard, we throw the bottles down on to them.'

'Will that work?' Beth asked.

'You saw what the X-Stock does to organic matter. Whatever the vampires really are, biologically speaking, I can't say for sure, yet they are still bones and meat covered with skin.' She shrugged herself free of the apron. 'Now, I suggest you go to the kitchen and make plenty of coffee. It's going to be a long night.'

Sally and Alec went upstairs, leaving Beth alone with Eleanor.

'You go along, too, Beth. I'll just finish up here.'

'I've been thinking about Tommy.'

'Oh?'

'We have to do the same to him, don't we?'

Eleanor appeared shocked. 'Douse him with X-Stock, you mean? But he's harmless.'

'Yes, harmless, but Tommy is trapped in that monster. Don't you see it? There's the ghost of a little boy locked inside that thing.'

'You do know what the chemical will do to his body?'

'Tommy is a prisoner inside an abomination. If we are humane, we will stop him suffering.'

'You are a brave woman with a good heart.' Eleanor squeezed her arm. 'I wish to God that you'd come here years ago. I could have done with a friend like you.'

'So? Tommy?'

'You're right.'

'When shall we do it?'

Eleanor crimped her lips together until she reached a painful decision. 'Go upstairs now. Ask Tommy to come down here. Say we want to show him something.' Her voice became more strained as she added, 'Beth, I'm warning you. The effects of this chemical on the boy will be . . . well, I don't have to describe how terrible, do I?'

Four

'Tommy. I want to show you something I've found in the basement.'

Tommy sat on the lobby carpet, where he rolled a ball for Sam. Both boy and dog had been so engrossed in the game that she'd watched for a while. That had been the moment when the dreadful enormity of what she'd planned became a reality. Soon he'd walk down the basement steps with her. Somewhere down there Eleanor would wait for him. What then? Dash a bowlful of the X-Stock into his face? Strangely, Beth felt absolute calm. *This is what I must do.* The child would be free of the monstrous body. No more searching for parents who were long dead. No longer spending his days lying in some hole in the earth. To release the boy would be humane.

So, when she uttered the words: *'Tommy. I want to show you something I've found in the basement'* they left her lips as normally as telling someone supper was ready. Yet, in the back of her mind, she wished that she was so distraught that she couldn't continue with this plan to escort the boy downstairs to his destruction. However, she acted as if nothing was amiss, and she found herself hating her cool single-mindedness. *Is this how those Nazi fanatics feel when they line up innocent civilians and shoot them? That it's just a job of work?*

She held out her hand. 'Come on, Tommy.' *Oh, and the words spoken with such a pleasant smile on my face. Just who's the monster here?* 'Leave Sam there with the ball.'

'What have you found?'

'You'll see.'

The slight figure ran gladly towards her. He trusted her and suspected nothing.

'Wave to Sam.'

'Bye, Sam, see you soon.'

'Lead the way, Tommy. Careful with those stairs. They're steep.'

She closed the door after them. In the basement, Eleanor stood facing the wall. Her arms were in front of her; she must have something in her hands. That 'something' would bring this existence of Tommy's to an end.

Keep going, Beth. Stay strong. Don't stop now. Tommy won't suffer any more.

Tommy and Beth descended to the floor level. Beth found that she held her breath. Her chest tightened. One hand went out to rest on Tommy's shoulder. She might have to physically guide him to the centre of the basement.

She had taken no more than two steps when Eleanor turned her head slightly towards them.

'Don't come any closer,' she hissed.

'Eleanor?'

'Get out of the basement.'

'What's wrong?'

'He's back.' Although she didn't turn around fully, her eyes slid sideways to indicate the grate.

Tommy continued walking. 'Wasn't there something you were going to show me?'

Beth whirled to the shelves. She darted to an old toy truck, lying amongst a jumble of bric-a-brac. 'Here, this is it. I found this wagon and thought you might like it. It's got all dusty, so take it to the kitchen and give it a wipe with a cloth.'

Eleanor still didn't turn around fully. She growled, 'Beth, get him out. You, too.'

Beth whispered to Tommy to go back upstairs. But Beth didn't leave. As soon as the boy had gone, she approached the grate.

Eleanor groaned, 'Oh, Beth, for God's sake . . .'

A starkly white figure stood beneath the iron grate. The single light bulb gleamed on the skin; shadows from the bars formed a heavy black + pattern on the face of the man. He stood panting there. Some enormous passion gripped him. His eyes could have been eggs planted there in the sockets. They bulged with manic intensity. The pupils were tiny black dots – nothing less than a mad ferocity blazed from them.

'*Eleanor . . .*' he hissed. '*Eleanor . . .*' The whisper of the ocean fused with the voice, sustaining it, and transforming into something that seemed to ghost from a tomb. 'Eleanor . . . look at me . . .'

Eleanor remained with her face to the wall, not looking back; in fact, at that moment, it appeared no force on Earth could make her turn around to gaze on that abomination.

'Eleanor. It's me: Gustav. I need you, Eleanor.' He raised his hand through the grating, until the bars were level with the wrist, and the fingers flexed gently, as if they were sensory organs that could taste what emotions stained the air of the vault. 'Eleanor. I'm here to warn you. The others believe you intend to harm them. Their instincts tell them there is danger . . . and that you are the source of that danger . . .'

Beth found a similar trait in Gustav as she'd glimpsed in Tommy. It seemed to her that the ghost of a tender, intelligent man now haunted that ghastly carcass. He waged a war with the monstrous side of his nature. A war he was slowly and oh so surely losing. Yet in this desperate moment he reached out to an old friend.

'Eleanor.' His whisper joined with the murmurs of the sea. 'They will try and reach you tonight. And your friends, too. Please take my hand. I'll try and help you. But I need to feel your touch, because if I have something human to hold on to it might stop this thing inside of me. It's taking control . . . I can feel it . . . I want to taste blood. I am trying to resist, but the animal inside of me is getting stronger. I know I am a vampire . . . but if I try, with all my heart, I might not succumb absolutely to bloodlust. But I must confess: I've taken human blood. You saw as such in the cave. I couldn't stop myself. But your hand in mine will help so much.'

Eleanor stood absolutely still, as if hewn from cold granite.

'Eleanor, please . . . don't let this devil inside of me win.'

Beth's heart surged. 'Do as he asks.'

Eleanor shook her head.

'If we can help him, then maybe he really can stop those things.'

Still Eleanor refused to even look at the man beneath the grate. All she would do was mouth the word *no*. This rejection struck Gustav hard. He sagged; the strength bled from his limbs. The white face, with the colourless eyes, suddenly became more alien, more terrible – the emotion that flickered across the features was one of utter desolation. Here was a man that had almost lost his final battle.

Beth urged, 'Go to him. I know he won't try to hurt you.'

The woman closed her eyes. She did her utmost to pretend he wasn't there.

'*I'll do it!*' Beth threw herself to her knees beside the grate. Beneath the iron bars the vampire stood there, the ocean tide had turned, water swirled around his ankles. It poured along the same tunnel that Gustav would have used to enter that pit beneath the basement floor. Expressions flitted over the man's face. Hunger. Desperation. And, more than anything, such a sense of loss that it hurt Beth to witness it. 'My name is Beth Layne. I'm Eleanor's friend.' She clasped the man's hand in hers. Such coldness possessed it. It felt like plunging one's hand into a mountain stream. The moment she did take his hand, his fingers closed over hers, a grip so tight she gasped. By this time, Eleanor had turned to watch the pair. On her face, an expression of pure shock.

The man's eyes glared up through the bars. The tiny black pupils were fierceness themselves. In those points of darkness, the raging passions that burnt within him. She saw his Vampiric lust for chaos, destruction, and above all blood. He wanted hers now. He longed to feel that torrent from her vein – for it to flood through his lips, to play on his tongue, before slipping so delightfully down his throat.

Eleanor gasped, 'You shouldn't have touched him. He'll bite.'

'No, he won't.' Beth didn't try and pull free, instead she gripped his hand firmly. 'That's right, Gustav, isn't it? You won't attack me. I trust you, Gustav. I believe you are fighting the vampire inside of you. And you've fought that life and death struggle every night. A terrible battle inside your heart. You've done everything in your power not to hurt a human being. Don't I speak the truth, Gustav?'

The grip tightened. She wanted to scream at the intensity of it. Yet she didn't allow the slightest trace of that pain to alter her expression.

'Gustav, if need be, you'd give your life to save Eleanor, wouldn't you?'

'*Yes!*'

The gust of air from his vampire lungs blasted into Beth's face. It smelt of nothing, yet its coldness evoked eternal despair.

When Gustav spoke again the tone and the phrasing had become that of a normal young man. 'I don't want Eleanor to be like me.'

'But she never will.' Beth shook her head. 'Twenty years ago, those creatures in the cave bit Eleanor on the wrist. The wound never healed, but she was never infected. Isn't that true, Eleanor?'

Eleanor clenched her fists. 'Yes, but what does that make me?' The woman groaned. 'Oh, look at his eyes.'

Colour returned to the man's irises. A pale blue. The pupils lost that fierce aspect.

Eleanor laughed, but it was a defeated sound. 'Beth. I hate you. For twenty years I've turned my back on Gustav. Now you come here and you've made him at least half human again.'

'Then if we help him fight this thing?'

Gustav pushed his other hand through the bars. 'Eleanor. Take hold. There's a chance I might get well again.'

Eleanor, shaking her head, tears streaming down her face, raced up the steps, back into the body of the hotel. Beth remained crouched there, her hand grasping his.

The colour leeched from Gustav's eyes. The black pupils became prominent once more. Yet a human lilt remained in his voice. 'Look after her, Beth.' On the vampire's face a ghost of a mortal smile played. 'I've a confession. Though I was afraid of Eleanor Charnwood, when I was young, I had a crush on her. She was the loveliest girl in Whitby. Her intelligence shone as bright as the sun. I could warm myself beneath it. Since I stopped being the flesh and blood Gustav Kirk, I'd still pretend to myself that one day I'd become well again. And I'd no longer be forced to live like a snake in that hole in the cliff. That, eventually, I'd climb out into the bright sunlight. I'd stand up straight. Then I'd walk through the graveyard to the long flight of steps down into town. Feeling human, a big smile on my face, pleased and happy, I'd come here to the hotel. Instead of creeping through the tunnel into this basement, I'd march into the lobby. There I'd find Eleanor standing at the reception desk. She'd be so pretty in the brightness of a spring day. And I'd say to her, "Eleanor. I've never dared confess this before. But I've loved you since I was ten years' old. And I'm here to ask if you'd be my wife." That dream stopped me from doing awful things, Beth. But if it had come true, and I became mortal again, do you think she would have married me . . . or does she find me repulsive? After all . . . did she find me repulsive when I had human blood in my veins?' The dreamy smile became lost to the shadow. Sighing, he released his grip on her hand. The pallid shape retreated into darkness.

Earlier, it had seemed as if Eleanor had successfully formulated a plan that would get them through the night. *Now it's all unravelling,* Beth told herself. *Eleanor isn't as strong as she thought. And I don't know what the next few hours will bring.*

Five

Eleanor stumbled into her rooms on the upper floor. There, she raged at the reflection in the mirror: 'You ineffectual, idiot. You coward. It took a stranger to do what you daren't.' Tears came. 'Beth Layne! She's an actress. One of those glittering angels that's all make-up and make-believe. You even saw her serving a cocktail to Cary Grant . . . up there . . . on the silver screen. Ha!' She laughed at her tear-stained reflection – a harsh, mocking laugh. 'Now she steps into your hotel here in Whitby and she takes hold of Gustav's hand, and she makes him human again. Or . . . or at least something akin to flesh and blood.' Eleanor threw her arms in extravagant movements. A personal melodrama that she wanted – really wanted to hurt her. 'Because I deserve this.' She loathed those watery eyes in the mirror. 'Scaredy cat. You never even spoke to Gustav all those times he crept through the tunnel into the basement. All he wanted was human contact, but you were afraid to even engage him in conversation. It's not as if you wanted him in your bed, is it?' She ripped back the sleeve to expose the never-to-be-healed wounds on her wrist. Yes, oh yes, it seemed insane – yet she had to sink her own teeth into her flesh – into the puncture marks with their pink edges that resembled tiny roses. Though she bit hard, the pain in her wrist couldn't match the sensation of her heart being torn in two. *If only the pain of a broken heart could be negated by mere physical agony.*

'Ah, yes, that's the old Eleanor.' She whirled away from the mirror, drunk on her own misery. 'You make clinical observations on your own sorrow, on your own mucked up life, like your some psychologist observing the nervous breakdown of some godforsaken patient. Nice work, Eleanor.'

Laughter vied with sobs. Instead of returning to the mirror, she threw a punch at her shadow, which the bedside light cast on the curtains.

'When are you going to take control of your life? Are you going to hide in this hotel forever, Miss Haversham. Because that's what you became. A lonely Miss Haversham. Forever hiding away from the world. And you were bitten by the vampires. But you never became one of them. Why? Does that mean you were never ever human, too?' She lashed at her shadow on the curtain. This time the fabric didn't yield softly beneath her fist. The impact, however, didn't suggest contact with the wall or window pane.

As Eleanor recoiled, the curtains were swept aside. A stark, white face erupted from the darkness behind the fabric. Gleaming eyes locked on hers. The pupils were like spikes being driven into Eleanor's brain. The attacker shoved her with such power that she left the ground before bouncing down on to the bed.

That's when Eleanor recognized her attacker as Mary Tinskell. Or what had been Mary Tinskell until just days ago. The vampire leapt on her in an absolute fury of violence to wrestle her down on to the mattress. Black veins wormed beneath a blue-white skin. The creature's mouth yawned wide to reveal white teeth in thick red gums.

'Go ahead,' Eleanor stormed. 'Bite me. Here, I'll make it easy for you!' She tore open her blouse at the neck to reveal her throat.

But that whirlwind of a creature held Eleanor down on to the bed. Clearly she had other plans for the woman. Then maybe Mary knew that Eleanor didn't have the kind of blood that vampires lusted after. Perhaps Eleanor would provide something else that Mary required so desperately.

Eleanor tried to struggle free of the cold body that sat astride her, icy thighs nipping tight against her hips. Swiftly, the vampire grabbed the bedspread at each corner, then drew them together. Soon Eleanor found herself in a cocoon of thick Yorkshire wool. Panting, striving to draw oxygen from the stuffy atmosphere inside this impromptu sack, Eleanor tried to call out, but this choking confinement pushed her chin down into her chest; she could barely grunt never mind shout for help. She knew that the vampires had plans for her. Whatever those were, they'd be far from pleasant.

Unable to see, unable to move, barely able to breathe, Eleanor sensed motion. The creature carried her as easily as in life it would carry fresh meat home for dinner in a shopping bag. Briefly, Eleanor felt a hard flatness beneath her and to one side.

My God, she thought in horror, *I'm being pushed through the window. It's a thirty foot drop to the street.*

Then came the dizzy whirl of rapid motion. The direction was downward. And lethally fast.

Six

The instant Gustav retreated through the subterranean passageway to the harbour Beth hurried upstairs. Tommy sat on the floor with the toy truck. Sam watched on, with bright, interested eyes. Beth found Sally and Alec in the kitchen. Quickly, she told them what had happened in the basement. When Sally heard about the return of Gustav she rocked back on her heels as if she'd faint.

Beth said, 'I've never seen Eleanor so upset.'

Alec's single eye gave her a shrewd look. 'Because you have a greater power than Eleanor Charnwood over her old boyfriend?'

'I don't know if Gustav ever was her boyfriend.'

'But you made her jealous. You succeeded in making him at least half human again, whereas she consistently failed to even face him.'

'Alec. Please.' A nervous tremor ran through Sally's voice. 'This isn't the time to accuse Beth of getting the better of Eleanor.'

Already, Beth hurried to the stairs. 'Eleanor must have gone to her rooms.'

Alec called out, 'Leave her be for a while. You've clearly given the woman something to think about.'

Racing up the steps, Beth heard the pair following. *Dear God, tonight isn't the night for tantrums and sulking alone. If what Gustav predicts comes true . . . if the vampires attack?* By the time she reached the upper floor, where Eleanor's apartment was located, she realized something was amiss. A cool breeze blew along the hallway. The door to Eleanor's quarters swung in the breeze.

'Hurry!' she shouted back at the pair. *But I know we're too late* was her unspoken thought. Without considering that vampires might be lurking in the room, Beth charged through the door. 'Damn it, no.' Her eyes raked the turmoil. Chairs were upended; the bedside lamp lay smashed on the floor. Bedding had been ripped from the mattress. She raced to where curtains flapped in the breeze. Sweeping them aside, she leaned out through the open window. Church Street lay thirty feet below her. In the gloom, the long, thin stripe of its cobbled surface resembled the back of a serpent, the stone blocks the cold scales.

In this dreary blackout there wasn't much to see. Just the line of the road, flanked by tall, narrow cottages that looked so much like upright gravestones in a cemetery. But then . . . Yes . . . She leaned out further. Her eyes adjusted to the night, allowing her a glimpse of a terrible sight. A figure in a nightdress scaled the steps to St Mary's graveyard on the cliff top. The Vampiric figure carried a bundle on its back. Though her eyes watered in the cold air, Beth knew that in the bundle lay a figure. The blanket deformed as someone struggled within it.

'What's happened to Eleanor?' Alec panted.

Beth turned to stare at the bed. She saw that the bedspread was missing.

'Those things have taken her.'

Alec rushed to the window. 'I can see someone, they're carrying a sack, or something like . . . but how can you tell they've got Eleanor?'

'Oh, believe me, they have. They've bundled her into a blanket like she's a ragbag of stolen clothes.'

Sally sagged against the wall. 'The poor woman . . . the poor woman. Oh God, I don't even want to imagine what they'll do to her.'

Alec ran his hands through his hair. 'But she can't be infected. Yes, she's got that bite wound that doesn't heal. However—'

'However nothing,' Beth snapped. 'If they want to hurt her, they will. And if they chose to kill her . . .'

Sally groaned. 'They've got the upper hand, haven't they? We can't stop them, any more than we can stop this awful war.' Hysteria crackled on the air. 'They've beaten us. The vampires are going to come and take us whenever they like.'

Beth seized her friend's hands. 'Listen, Sally. I told you I'd look after you.'

'But that was against lecherous men.' Sally's laugh sounded dangerously unbalanced. 'You'd chase suitors away with a sweeping brush!'

'We *will* win. Eleanor has made those bombs of hers. We can use them.'

Alec agreed. 'Then we best keep them nearby at all times.'

Sally appeared calmer, yet her teeth clicked together as she trembled. 'But . . . we . . . we aren't s—safe here. The windows . . . They could just force the latch. And this place is all windows. There are dozens and—'

Beth tightened her grip on the quaking hands. 'I've thought of a solution. We'll go to Theo's cottage. Those windows are covered with iron bars.'

'But it's across the yard. We'd have to go outside.'

'Worry not Sally, dear.' *Beth forced herself to smile. I just hope it's a reassuring one – not a mad grin.* 'When we cross the yard we'll have bottles full of that volatile, fiery, and oh-so-destructive X-Stock. So – vampires beware!'

'Yes . . . I . . . ah, guess . . .'

Beth realized she'd nearly managed to help Sally recover her nerve.

Alec closed the window against the dangerous night. 'We might be safe in the cottage. However, that doesn't help us save Eleanor.'

'That's why we need the help of her brother.' Beth nodded with certainty. 'Theo's going to be our ally.'

Seven

For Sally Wainwright, the hotel could have become a nightmare castle. In her overwrought mental state, her senses became distorted. Walls appeared to slope inwards, perilously close to her head. Corridors transformed into impossibly long tunnels that vanished into shadows. And in those places engulfed by darkness vampires would lurk. She was sure of it. Doorways resembled gaping mouths that longed to swallow her. Ornamental plasterwork around light switches appeared to be diseased things that bulged out through the wallpaper. Down the stairs they went to the lobby. Tommy sat on the carpet beside his faithful dog. He played with a toy truck. A monster with the voice of a little boy.

The creature sang out happily, 'Thanks for the wagon, Beth. It's really good.'

They descended into the basement. Chill currents of air sighed up through the grate. Alec and Beth walked alongside Sally – yet, to her, they seemed far away. She wondered: *if I talk to them will they hear me? Have we entered a dream world, where normal things aren't normal any more? Where boys are vampires. And they run with black dogs. Will we turn into what Tommy has become? Will we sleep during the day, then roam at night? Forever lost.* Beth had begun to speak, although Sally found it hard to understand the words. *Maybe I'm having a nervous breakdown? Yet I must still look normal to them. I think I must be answering their questions when they speak. I'm just not sure of anything any more . . .* Beth's voice echoed from the basement walls. Beneath the iron grate, water swirled around the bottom of the pit. White bubbles, brown weed. *Do all of Whitby's houses have tunnels that connect them to the sea?*

Alec's voice shimmered in this tomb of a place. '. . . then we must be careful with the bottles. The X-Stock has more pep than TNT.'

Beth: 'The bottles are only half full of the chemical, to make sure they're light enough to throw easily.'

'These are nasty bombs, Beth, very nasty indeed. They might be more dangerous to us than the vampires.'

'Nevertheless . . .'

'I know. We don't have an alternative, do we?'

Beth touched Sally's arm. 'You stay here. Keep an eye on the basement door.'

At that moment, Sally couldn't say why the pair acted in such a way. They brought crates of bottles from a storeroom. They set them down, then returned for more. The breeze made the light bulb swing on the end of its flex. Sally watched the shadows. Ghosts, marching as if to war. She tried to catch her breath, because she'd become light-headed. Legions of tramping shadows held her gaze. While in her mind's eye, she pictured that silent building above her; the dozens of empty quarters. Rooms as still as graves. And through the windows . . . those fragile, so easily broken windows . . . the vampires would enter. Then, fleet of foot, they'd pad down here. *They'll grab me with those ice-cold hands. They'll enjoy the fear on my face. Then they'll bite and keep biting . . . until I become one of those monsters, too.*

Beth and Alec's voices whispered from the storeroom. The pair were out of sight. What wasn't out of sight were the two vampires in the pit beneath the grate. A young man in a soldier's uniform, and a woman with thick, red hair. Both had stark, white faces that matched the whites of their eyes. Black veins wormed beneath the flesh of their necks. As they leered at Sally, they both raised their arms, then began to heave at the cast iron grate. Though it possessed an enormous weight, those creatures gloried in a formidable strength. Expressions gloating, mouths opening to reveal white teeth set in tumescent red gums, they pushed upwards.

Sally found she could do nothing but watch them. She couldn't move her limbs. The echoing voices of Beth and Alec seemed impossibly distant. What had once been a soldier stared up at her through the bars with such intensity he already seemed to be drawing the life force from her body. Slowly, the grate began to rise. Dirt flaked from the edges, where it parted from the frame.

Sally pictured her parents grieving over the loss of their daughter. Her ambition had been to act in films. Yet it was more than that. Her parents lived a poor life in a damp house. Her father was an invalid. This film had been Sally's big chance to change her family's life for the better. Now the dream was being stolen from her. Suddenly, she thought: *No, you're not taking my life from me. I won't let you!* Her hatred for those life-robbing monsters powered her limbs; it gave the woman renewed strength.

Sally grabbed one of the bottles from the crate; she raised it in her clenched fist. Then, like Zeus hurling thunderbolts, she threw the bottle. The glass container struck the ironwork. Shattered. Blue liquid gleamed in the electric light, spraying downwards through the gate's bars — and into the faces of the vampires.

Then the volcano erupted.

Or so it seemed to Sally. A column of fire spewed from the pit in the floor. It struck the brickwork of the vaulted roof with the power of a blowtorch.

And in that crucible of fire . . . in that furnace . . . two figures screamed in agony. Though they still gripped the bars above their heads, the hands were those of skeletons. Flesh ignited, muscle exploded from the bone; veins were burning fuses.

Then the blazing wreckage of the two bodies dropped into the seawater at the bottom of the pit.

Sally panted as she stood there, her eyes fixed on the dead vampires. Then she realized that Beth and Alec had entered basement. Both stared at her in astonishment.

Sally took a deep breath. 'I enjoyed that. No, I didn't.' Her voice rose to a full-blooded shout. *'I loved it! I hurt them! And it feels wonderful!'*

Eight

The pace quickened. Beth found canvas satchels in the wine cellar where the X-Stock had been kept. Clearly, Eleanor intended these to carry the bottles in at least relative safety. That resourceful woman had adapted each satchel by inserting a thick, inner layer made from blue velvet. This had been stitched to form cells that would house individual bottle bombs. The velvet would at least stop the bag full of bottles clashing together. For, if one broke in the bag, the results would be too terrible to contemplate.

Six of these had been prepared. Alec claimed two. As they loaded the home-made bombs into the bags, they discovered each satchel would accommodate ten bottles.

'The bags will be heavy,' Alec told them. 'Don't make sudden movements, or the weight could topple you.'

'We'll be careful,' Beth told him. 'Are you sure you can carry two, Alec?'

'What a big hairy Scotsman like me? It'll be no more arduous than carrying a pair of lace handkerchiefs.'

They'd been working in the hotel lobby for a matter of minutes when Tommy approached the locked front door. Those white eyes of his stared at the timbers. The black dog stood alongside him and gave a faint whimper.

Alec put the strap of one satchel over his shoulder. 'What's the matter, son?'

'I should be going home, sir. My mother and father will be wondering where I am.'

'You best stay here with us.'

'But I need to see them.'

'Tommy—'

'I want to go home.' The voice of a little lost boy came from that Vampiric mouth.

'It's not a normal kind of night, Tommy,' Beth told him. 'We need to stay together.'

'I haven't seen my parents for a long time. Or my sister. It seems like years. Only . . . I forget how long. Sally, why is it I lie in the ground when its daylight? What's gone wrong with me?'

'Don't get upset,' Sally said gently. 'We're your friends. We'll look after you.'

Beth couldn't bring herself to look Sally in the eye. Beth had vowed to end Tommy's suffering. She still intended to do just that.

Quickly, Beth said, 'Tommy, play with the truck.'

'I'm too het up. I need to go home.' He held her gaze. 'There's something worrying you, Beth. What is it?'

Alec shouldered the second satchel. 'We might as well tell him the truth.'

'*Pardon?*' Had Alec overheard her and Eleanor discussing the need to kill Tommy. That would be the humane thing to do, after all . . . nevertheless . . .

'I'll tell him about Eleanor,' Alec said. 'He isn't a child, Beth. Not really.'

Beth nodded. When Alec went to explain that Eleanor had been kidnapped, she helped Sally slip the bottles, containing the X-Stock, into the velvet housing within the bags.

'We'll have forty in all,' Sally told her. 'Is it enough?'

'Say a prayer that it will.'

Alec joined them at the reception counter. 'Tommy wants to look for Eleanor.'

'He can't,' Beth said.

'Tommy knows places where they might have taken her.'

Sally rested her palm on Beth's hand. 'Let him go. After all, as Alec said, Tommy's isn't really a little boy. He can take care of himself. And those vampires won't be after his blood, will they?'

'They can still hurt him.' Beth pushed the last bottle into the bag. *Yes, Tommy should have his misery ended. But in a humane way. Or at least as humanely as possible.* 'Alright. Tell him to find out where Eleanor's being held . . . if she's still alive.' *Dear God, did that sound as cold to them as it did to me?* 'Tell him to keep himself and Sam out of harm's way.'

From upstairs came the sound of breaking glass.

Sally's eyes flicked in the direction of the staircase. 'I guess we've got new guests.'

Alec nodded. 'Then this is the perfect time to decamp to Theo's cottage.' He called across to Tommy. 'We'll use the back door to the yard.' As Alec led the way through the kitchen, collecting the cottage key from its hook on route, he commented, 'Careful, remember the curfew.'

Sally watched the boy slip through the door into darkness, sure-footed as a cat at night. 'I imagine the soldiers won't even notice Tommy; never mind try to catch him.'

'Take care,' Beth called softly after the boy and his dog. However, they'd already vanished from sight.

'Alright,' Alec said. 'Stick close. Walk, don't run. We don't want anyone falling over in the dark. Not carrying this devil's brew. Head directly for the cottage door. Stop at nothing.' He pulled a bottle from one of his satchels. 'If we encounter trouble, I've got just the remedy. Go.'

They went out into the night.

Nine

Tommy moved along Church Street. Beside him loped Sam. His claws clicked on the stone paving blocks. Though the blackout held Whitby in a totality of darkness, the boy saw perfectly. Right down to the black pitch that cemented the blocks into the road, and the spent match broken into a V shape, and the mouse gnawing on a grain of wheat by the baker's door. Tommy sensed that those night creatures, which had tried to attack him before, flowed through the alleyways – fast, predatory shapes. He sensed their hunger. Sometimes he even caught a faint trace of their thoughts. It puzzled him, when he realized that they longed to sink their teeth into human skin, then suck blood from the body. Although Vampiric, Tommy had never craved that gory feast. All he ever yearned was to return home. This bloodlust seemed an utter mystery to him.

Sam suddenly paused, hackles on his back bristled upwards. From an alleyway, a pair of men in uniform chased a cat with greedy glints in their eyes. Soon they'd gone. Tommy and Sam continued along the street to the cliff-side steps. He would find Miss Charnwood. Tommy wanted Beth, and the rest, to be pleased with him.

Ten

Panting, the three bustled through the doorway into the cottage kitchen. They didn't pant with exertion. Instead, the fear of being so vulnerable outdoors had propelled their hearts, until blood hammered through their arteries faster than any mountain rapids.

Alec made a point of checking and rechecking that the bolts were pushed home. 'A good stout door,' he declared. 'Though I don't know how long it will keep those devils out.'

Beth lifted the heavy satchel from her shoulder and placed it on the kitchen table. 'There's Theo's medicine all measured out.'

'So he hasn't taken it yet?' Sally picked up the glass that contained a spoonful of the white Quick Salts – the drug that, in certain cases, somehow suppressed the Vampiric infection.

'Good,' Alec stated. 'Then Theo should be waking up.'

'So he must be upstairs?'

Sally set her bag down, then headed for the staircase. 'I'll sit with him until he's awake.'

'Are you sure?'

'I've done with hysterics. I'm going to be as tough as a commando.'

Beth nodded. 'And so you are. You're our vampire killer.'

'And we'll be right here, if you need us.' Alec eyed the door. 'That's the weak point in our little fortress. Beth and I will guard it with our lives.'

Sally mounted the steps to the upper room. In near darkness, she found Theo lying on the bed. Just as before, when they saw him here in the cottage, he was in the thrall of coma. Then they'd had to bide their time as he emerged from that passive state. Sally perched herself on the end of the bed and waited. A clock ticked in the shadows. It had the slow beat of a man's heart, one who waited at death's door. She hoped it wasn't an omen of things to come.

Beth switched off the light, so she could peek out through the blackout curtains. The iron bars appeared solid enough over the windows. Just thirty paces away, the bulk of the Leviathan Hotel soared upwards. Across the flat face of the building, dark shapes moved with the swift grace. Quickly, they slipped in and out of the windows. The vampires had made short work of breaking in. No doubt their frustration mounted as they discovered all the rooms were empty of victims. She carefully covered the window again to ensure no light escaped, then flicked the switch to flood the room with that reassuring wash of electric light.

Alec stood by the door with a bottle of X-Stock. The "crab-claw" of a right hand wasn't at all dexterous, but he managed to hold that home-made bomb without any problem. Cocking an eye at the window, he asked, 'I take it they wasted no time before entering the hotel?'

She nodded. 'There's no going back there until daybreak.'

'Not that we'd want to. Soon we'll be heading outdoors anyway. After all, we've got to find Eleanor.'

'How do we know they didn't kidnap her in the full knowledge that we'd try and find her?'

'And then leave the relative safety of this wee cottage?' He gave a grim smile. 'I rather suspect they did, Beth, my dear. But I warrant they don't know that Eleanor prepared these lovely hellfire bombs first.'

'We also have to run the gauntlet of the curfew. Soldiers will shoot on sight.'

Lightly he rested his fingertip on the eyepatch. 'Just a couple of weeks ago, I picked myself up out of the ruins of that café when the bomb struck. My colleagues lay dead. All I suffered was this nick to my eyelid. Maybe there is a divine intelligence at work, which believes I will somehow now see more clearly through one eye. After all, throughout my adult life, I saw precious little of my common sense through two.' He rolled the bottle in his hand. 'So maybe a higher power decided I should come here to Whitby and confront evil.'

'You believe you were spared to fight the vampires?'

'Beth.' His tone was grave. 'I don't believe my life was spared. I rather suspect it was taken by the explosion in the café. Now I have it back on loan, until the job here is done.'

'Alec. Are you suggesting that when you go through that door tonight it will be on a suicide mission?'

'We shall have to wait and see.' He smiled. 'But if I can fight our little war here on the coast, and win . . . then the loss of this beer-sodden, indolent life of mine, will be worth it, don't you think?'

Sitting in the gloom, she suddenly straightened when she heard movement on the bed. Her eyes had adapted sufficiently to allow her to see Theo kneel up.

'You're not Eleanor.'

'I'm Sally. We've met before, Theo.'

'Beautiful Sally. Yes, I remember you.'

He swiftly climbed out of bed, then immediately swayed, dizzy. Rising to her feet, she caught hold of the slim form. Fast as a striking cobra, he encircled her with his arms.

'You know something, Sally? This is the first time I've embraced a woman.' His breath blasted into her face. 'The poets are right. It really does make one's heart race. Kiss me.'

Instead of pressing his lips on hers, they brushed her neck. Sally tensed, ready to fight for her life. The man's mouth pressed hard against her shoulder. Then his entire body sagged, so she had to grab hold of him to stop him falling to the floor.

'Help me!' she yelled. 'Beth, Alec! Theo's dying!'

Eleven

For the first time they caught Tommy by surprise. He'd reached the foot of the celebrated one hundred and ninety-nine steps that ascended to the graveyard when a figure swung itself over the iron railing. It grabbed hold of Sam in both arms before racing away.

Tommy heard the dog snarling; no doubt he would be biting the vampire that had snatched him, but the vampire's bloodlust overwhelmed any discomfort that dog bites might inflict. Immediately, Tommy pursued the creature that had stolen his dog. The figure in a soldier's uniform glanced back at the boy. The sheer look of greed and downright pleasure in snatching this compact vessel of hot, living canine blood incensed Tommy. The boy ran full pelt along Church Street, past the Leviathan Hotel, and by those silent cottages. When Tommy charged through the marketplace, he surprised a pair of soldiers who stood by the old town hall.

'Hey! Stop! Stop, or we'll fire!'

The second one grunted, 'Damn, where did he go?'

'He was moving like lightning. I haven't seen a kid run so fast . . .'

The voices faded as Tommy sped after the figure along Sandgate. The vampire that had stolen Sam no doubt wanted to carry him across the bridge to some quiet hideaway where he could feed in peace. However, the gates at the end of the bridge were closed, and the swing bridge lay open, with all the seductive promise of a yawning portal to a magic realm. Shining waters flowed through it to a silver sea.

Thwarted at crossing the river to the other side, the vampire searched for somewhere else to secrete himself with his prize. Sam, meanwhile, still snarling, darted his head at his captor's face, inflicting bite after bite. Yet the thing felt no pain; at least, he showed none. As the night-creature struggled to formulate another plan, he paused there in the deserted roadway.

Tommy knew he didn't have the strength to fight this towering demon. Instead, he bounded up on to a wagon parked in front of the Dolphin Hotel. So quiet was he, the vampire didn't notice the boy. From the vehicle's roof, Tommy looked down on to the roadway that ended at the bridge gate. A gap of five yards separated the now severed road from the main body of the swing bridge. Sam yelped in pain as the vampire tightened his grip.

Senses sharp, muscles tense, Tommy judged the distance. Then he leapt. His dive ended with him smacking into the top of the vampire's head. No way would he kill the vampire, or even hurt him – however, he did knock the giant off balance. Sam seized the chance. He wriggled free of the man's arms.

'Run, Sam! Go on, boy, run!'

The dog sped into the night. Enraged at losing such a sweet morsel, the vampire sought vengeance on Tommy. He seized the boy, flung him against the bridge gate, then pounced.

Tommy scrambled from beneath the figure then, using that terrific agility of his, swung himself over the gate at such speed the momentum carried him across the gap between the road and the bridge itself. Instantly, the vampire followed. Clearly, he intended to rip Tommy apart at the earliest opportunity.

Now Tommy had reached the bridge, he was effectively on a man-made island in the river. He wouldn't be able to leap the fifty yards or so to the other side of the Esk. The only solution, to find a place to hide in the latticework of iron beneath the structure. Tommy swung himself over the high fence. River waters swirled some ten feet below.

Nimbly, he lowered himself through the iron struts beneath the vast bulk. Yet once more the vampire closed in. The creature's huge fist slammed into the boy's back. Tommy wove in and out of the ironwork. Behind him, boots clattering on girders, the Vampiric soldier followed.

The structure juddered. Tommy felt motion. The bridge-keeper was now closing it again. Several hundred tons of metal rotated slowly, as it swung backwards in order to align itself with the far bank. The powerful creature that pursued him didn't know exhaustion. He would pursue him to the ends of the earth if need be. All that registered in the vampire brain was that Tommy had cheated him of the precious red stuff. The vampire wouldn't rest until he hurled shreds of the boy into the river.

Tommy reached the huge steel cog on which the bridge rotated. At fifteen feet in diameter, it lay flat on a platform of wooden timbers. A second cog, this one upright, and with dozens of teeth six inches long, connected the drive shaft to the electric motor. Slowly, the cog turned about its axis, those six-inch teeth meshed, winding the bridge round towards its closed position. Tommy leapt on to the big turntable of a cog, then ran across its spokes. The vampire pursued him. A second later Tommy felt fingers slash at his back. Tommy sped towards the smaller vertical cog. Then he dropped into a crouching position, head tucked down, arms holding his body into a ball shape.

The momentum of the big vampire kept him moving. He stumbled over Tommy to slap down hard on to the rim of the cog. He tried to scramble to his feet, but Tommy clutched his ankles. Before the creature could kick free, the upright cog, still mechanically engaging steel teeth with the corresponding teeth of the horizontal cogwheel, took hold. The vampire's head entered the intermeshing cogwheels. He still kicked his legs in fury. Only the machine devoured him now. Like a garment fed between the rollers of a mangle, the body from head to hips passed between the formidable steel wheels. As it emerged from the other side, the cog teeth left deep indentations, a regular crimp pattern along the back of the head, then between the shoulder blades, and down the spine.

Leaving the twitching form to continue its slow revolutions on the rotating bed of steel, Tommy scrambled back on to the bridge as it reconnected with the mainland. Now he must find Sam. And Miss Eleanor Charnwood. Fast. Very fast.

Twelve

Beth ran into the upper room of the cottage to find Sally cradling the still form of Theo on the floor. His eyes were closed, his expression somehow deathly. The man wore a plain white shirt, open at the neck, and black trousers. As before, his skin had the same pale gleam. She glimpsed the masses of puncture wounds on exposed flesh. Unlike Eleanor's wrist wound that never healed, these spots of glistening scar tissue were a pale grey.

Sally hugged the man, as if simultaneously trying to comfort him and wake him. She kept repeating, 'He's dying, Beth. I can't wake him.'

Alec gripped the man's wrist. 'His pulse is strong as an athlete's.'

Beth added, 'It must be an effect of the drug withdrawing from his system.'

'Well, he's not getting his dose of that stuff tonight.' Alec lifted Theo on to the bed. 'We need his help.' None too gently, he slapped Theo's face. 'Wake up, laddie. Come on, join the living for once.' He slapped harder.

Theo's eyes snapped open. 'Ah, pain . . . you don't know how good it is to *feel* again.' He smiled. 'So, what have they done with my dear sister?'

Beth asked, 'Do you know what happened tonight?'

Smiling, he shook his head. 'Eleanor hoped the vampires would simply go away if she ignored them. It was only a matter of time before they came for her. After all, I know Gustav has been obsessed with my sister ever since they went to school together. Unrequited love . . . that makes all hearts ache, whether mortal or not.'

'This is serious,' Beth snapped. 'Those monsters have kidnapped Eleanor.'

The gaunt man bounded to his feet. 'Then we should save her from those filthy bloodsuckers. But who will save her from herself? That's the insoluble conundrum.' From a corpse of a man, to this restless figure that crackled with energy, had only taken seconds. Despite the predicament of his sister, he appeared to be enjoying himself hugely. 'Just give me a moment to find some shoes . . . do you know, I haven't donned a pair of shoes in more than a decade? I don't know if I own shoes any more. After all, for year upon year, I've existed in a cold, loveless, painless, senseless zone between life and death. My dear sister, Eleanor Charnwood, maintained that perfect status quo with aplomb. She's quite a woman, isn't she?'

Beth shot Alec and Sally glances that said, *Are we doing the right thing here? This guy's crazy.*

Sally gripped the gaunt man by the arm. 'Eleanor's in real danger. We all are. Those horrible creatures have broken into the hotel.'

'Fantastic!'

Beth shook her head. 'You're not going to be much use to us, are you, Theo?'

'On the contrary. I've got the vampire *germ* in my body . . . oh, don't look at me like that, my friends. You know I have. Vampiric tendencies are crawling through these veins of mine. Eleanor's witch potion merely froze the transformation.' He paced the room with restless energy. 'I share some of those vampire instincts.' His eyes swept up to the ceiling. 'High above the roofs of the town are ravens, flocks of them, black clouds of them, all wheeling round and around.'

'Ravens don't fly at night,' Alec stated coldly.

'Not normally, no! But these aren't normal circumstances. And Whitby never has been a normal town. Whitby is where land meets the ocean. Yet it's more wonderful than that: Whitby is where the world of humanity overlaps the realm of the gods. So, ravens fly at night. They are carrion eaters. They sense a huge battle is to be fought here. Moreover! Ravens are the eyes of Odin. Whatever the raven sees, then the mighty Viking God sees. And, by the feasting halls of Valhalla, he is very, very interested in what happens tonight.' Theo ripped aside the curtain so he could gaze upon the night-shrouded buildings. 'Out there, across this sorry planet, the armies of the Nazis and the Allies clash. Here in Whitby, the clash of the vampire and human.'

'We have weapons,' Beth began. 'Eleanor has—'

'Oh! The X-Stock. I know about that. She talks to herself as she tucks me into bed. How much have you got?'

Alec said, 'We've brought forty bombs with us.'

'They work?'

'I'll say.' Sally refused to be daunted by this firecracker of a man. 'Hit one of those vampires with a bomb and boof!'

'Boof?'

Beth explained, 'Two vampires tried to break into the basement. Sally burnt them to ashes.'

'Good for you, Sally.' Theo headed for the stairs. 'You are a warrior. And I think I'm falling in love with you.'

Sally blushed. Beth couldn't say for sure whether her friend was angry or flattered.

'Hurry up,' Theo shouted. 'Let's toast us some monster meat.'

They followed him down into the kitchen. He tore boxes from a cupboard until he whistled in triumph. 'Got 'em.' He drew out a pair of black shoes into which he slipped his bare feet. 'Now, to bring Eleanor safely home.'

'Wait a moment,' Alec told him. 'We don't know where they've taken her.'

'Or what they plan to do with her,' Beth added.

Theo ran his fingers through his hair. 'They'll know that Gustav pines for her. Maybe they've delivered her to him as a gift . . . as a bride.'

'Tommy is looking for her.' Sally's expression was hopeful. 'Maybe—'

'Maybe,' Theo said quickly. 'Maybe not. Though should we rely on a vampire boy?'

Sally retorted, 'Tommy's saved us before. I'd trust him with my life.'

Theo took a deep breath. Ever since he'd come fully awake he'd been a whirling blur of movement. Now he stood absolutely still, as if feeling a sudden pain.

Beth studied his frozen expression. 'What's wrong?'

'You won't feel it. But it's those creatures in the sump cavern. They're like old wine in a cellar. Something so intriguing about them. Utterly beguiling. They cast a spell . . . even on a part-vampire like me.'

'You can sense them?' Alec asked.

'Oh yes! Indeed, yes! It's like a domestic dog that picks up the scent of the wild fox. For them, there's something so alluring about the scent. The smell of fox; it drives a pet pooch to distraction. It fires up its nerves. Fox odour proclaims what it's like to be able to run free, to hunt, to feed on living prey. It can drive a dog to howl at the moon, and to mourn its own prison of domesticity. Those ancient vampires in the cavern are like that fox. The new vampires want to have their power and strength.' He inhaled deeply. 'The sump vampires are trying to break out. Soon they'll succeed. Then they will pour out into the world. They'll make Hitler's battalions seem as harmless as children playing in a field. That's when planet Earth will know eternal chaos. Take me to the bombs.'

While Alec showed him the satchels, with the bottles of X-Stock nestling inside, Beth murmured to Sally. 'This might not be a good idea. Theo's too unstable. Heck, he's downright manic.'

'He's not crazy, Beth. He's fully alive after who knows how long.'

'Just be careful. Eleanor kept him drugged for a reason.'

Theo studied one of the bottles that contained the blue liquid. 'Beth's right, Sally, my dear. I've never gone without my evening fix of Quick Salts. Who knows what I might become before morning?' He handed the bottle to Alec. 'So reserve one of those for me . . . just in case.'

Once more, he paced the room, as if the soles of his feet were itchy. 'Stage Door Johnnies,' he blurted. 'You've heard the phrase?'

Beth shrugged, puzzled. 'We're actresses, of course we have.'

Theo smacked a fist into his palm. 'Stage Door Johnnies. What are they?'

'Men who hang around the stage door at the end of a show in the hope of picking up actresses. What's this got to do with—'

'So — Stage Door Johnnies. They're drawn to the theatre's back door. Thespians are an allurement.'

'Yes.'

'Our latter-day vampires are a lot like that. They're drawn to the ancient vampires in the cavern. They want to be close to them. If they weren't driven down into the town to find victims, they'd spend all their time at Hag's Lung Cave; there they'd simply bask in the glow of those old beasties. Remember my comparison with the domestic pet dog finding the scent of the fox so enticing?'

Beth said quickly, 'You mean we can exploit this fascination that Gustav and his friends have for the ancient creatures.'

'Absolutely. But we shouldn't waste time here.' He gazed up at the ceiling again. 'The sump vampires. Their excitement. Their anticipation. I can taste it!'

Sally asked, 'Are they really close to breaking out?'

'They are indeed. And the ravens are massing over Whitby. They know what's to come.'

Alec shouldered his pair of satchels. 'We still need to find Eleanor. And how, in practice, can we kill the vampires? Even though we've got these bombs, the creatures are scattered throughout the town. We can't track them all down in one night.'

Theo smile's was a wild one. 'I'm working on it.'

A clatter sounded from outside; much like crockery being hurled on to the ground.

'Was that a window?' Sally hazarded.

'Roof tiles,' Theo replied. 'The vampires know you're in here. They're up there on the roof, stripping away the tiles.' Cheerfully, he added, 'They'll break through any minute. Time to move on out.'

Alec grabbed the man's arm. 'This is no laughing matter.'

Beth launched in. 'Alec's right! You're treating this like a game. As if you're some giddy child who's been let out of school early. Listen to me, Theo, your sister is in danger, we're in danger. I looked through that hole in the cave and I saw the damned monsters for myself. If we don't stop them, innocent men, women and children will suffer. Not just here in Whitby. But across the entire world. So quit the melodramatic performances; stop being so damn happy about all this. It's a tragedy; there is pain and trauma. People have died. Or worse, they've been transformed into vile creatures. Now's the time to prove you're a man – not a ridiculous caricature!'

Theo took a deep breath. 'Alright. I may sound deranged. But you don't know what it's like to rot in this tomb of a place. I've never been out. I haven't talked to anyone but my sister, not until I met you three, just a few hours ago. For years I've been a corpse – well, as good as. I spent my days asleep, or stumbling about the cottage, not knowing who I am. My nights pass by in a drugged trance. Just a lethargic half-man. Yes – I don't know what tonight will bring. Or whether or not I will turn into one of those monsters. After all, I won't have the drug in my blood. It could all end horribly for me.

Or for you. But . . .' He flexed his hands. 'I feel life inside of me again, Beth. It's roaring through my veins. My heart's on fire.' He gave a grim smile. 'So, don't worry. I have two quests tonight. To save my sister. And to kill the vampires. Trust me.' Solemn, he extended his hand.

Beth shook it. Then Alec and Sally did the same.

From outside came another loud clatter.

Theo nodded at the satchels. 'We need more of that stuff.'

'There are gallon jars in the basement.'

'I'll be right back.'

'What about those things on the roof?' Sally's anxious gaze roved over the ceiling

'They've still to break through the boards in the attic. That should give me enough time to collect more of Eleanor's vampire killer. Lock up after me.'

With that, Theo was through the door. Quickly, Beth shut it, then pushed the bolts home.

'Can we trust him?' she asked.

'Yes.' Sally spoke firmly. 'Absolutely.'

Alec nodded. 'The man cares about his sister. He'll be fine.'

'Great God, I hope so,' Beth said with feeling.

For a while, they stood there, listening. From the roof came scrabbling sounds; then there'd be a rattle as a tile slid off the roof to shatter in the yard outside.

Sally gave a strange little giggle.

'What's so funny?' Beth asked

'We never told Theo about the curfew.'

Alec sighed, then with a touch of gallow's humour added, 'Somehow, being shot by soldiers is the least of our worries.'

Beth cocked her head to one side, as she listened for sounds outside. 'Of course, has anyone thought what we'll do if Theo doesn't come back?'

Alec grimaced. 'You mean, he might decide he's more vampire than man, and decide to go hunting with his pack?'

'He won't.' Sally showed no doubt. 'Theo will stick by us.'

At that moment, a swift tapping on the door. Beth put her hand on the bolt then hesitated.

A whisper from the other side, 'It's me . . . Theo.'

Beth opened the door. Theo's bone-white face blazed in the darkness. His eyes were alive with excitement. In his arms, he hefted a gallon jar full of X-Stock. 'Time to go,' he announced. 'Our friends are in the attic.' From above, the sound of splintering boards confirmed his statement.

Sally and Beth grabbed their satchels of home-made bombs.

'Stick close together,' Alec warned. 'They'll pick off stragglers.'

Beth nodded at the jar of blue fluid. 'Be careful, Theo. If you drop that it will annihilate half of Whitby.'

Theo's nostrils flared. 'Danger of death. Those three words are guaranteed to make you feel truly alive. Am I not right?'

A groan sounded deep in the night. It seemed to rise up through the ground beneath their feet. Up, up, up the note climbed into the sky. That groan became a rising wail. One that cried out to the world that a fresh danger approached.

Sally paled. 'The air-raid siren!'

'There's no sheltering from what threatens us.' Alec's expression was dark indeed.

'Just listen to it.' Theo quivered with ecstasy. 'Can't you hear the very note of doom pouring through that sound? Doesn't it sound like the symphony you'd hear at the death of the universe?'

Beth's voice rose over that despairing wail of the siren: 'Curfews, Nazi warplanes? Forget them, we've got our own battle to fight.' Taking a deep breath, she walked into the cold night air – and prepared to greet whatever dangers lay in wait.

Thirteen

This is it. Beth saw the end was in sight. *But how will it end?* She walked quickly along Church Street. In this narrow lane, flanked by unbroken lines of cottages, she could have been in the bottom of a deep canyon. Darkness would have been total, if it weren't for the searchlights that probed the night sky for enemy aircraft. The low cloud reflected some of that glow to earth. Windows glinted. The square stones that paved the street were as knobbly as the scales on a crocodile's back.

Alongside her, Sally and Alec. They wore their satchels of bombs. Theo, the gaunt man in the white shirt, didn't feel the cold. He carried the flask of blue liquid. More than once she imagined its destructive force if he were to drop it. The explosion would wipe those cottages from the Earth. And in those cottages would be innocent people.

Already they must have taken refuge in cellars, as the mournful cry of the air-raid siren called out that death and destruction were on their way.

Every so often, Beth would catch a glimpse of the sea down to her left. Dark waters surged through the harbour mouth. The chill breeze would have had its genesis somewhere over the Russian Steppe. It might have been her imagination, but with those scents of brine came hints of dark forest. Then this was Whitby, a town that lingered on the borderland between this world and realms stranger than she could imagine. Might those scents of fern and leaf and animal musk have drifted from some other sphere? At one point, a group of soldiers hurried along the street. Beth and her companions sought refuge in one of the alleyways. With the siren screaming, as if it were hell-bent on being heard beyond the grave, the soldiers didn't hear the curfew-breakers as they ran for cover. However, the moment the four stepped out into Church Street again they immediately encountered a figure.

'I've found her.'

Beth found she looked into Tommy's colourless eyes.

'Miss Charnwood's at the abbey ruin. They've put her in a grave.'

The dog stuck close to his master. Both appeared anxious. Then the siren penetrated Beth's skull. That rising-falling note could have been a drill bit boring through. Tommy appeared to accept Theo's presence without any concern. No doubt he divined that the gaunt man's nature shared similarities with his own.

'You must be quick,' Tommy called.

Theo asked, 'Is my sister still alive?'

Tommy already hurried back along the street. Sam moved with effortless grace beside him.

Beth gripped the satchel strap tight to stop it swinging danger-ously against the cottage walls. Then she and her friends followed the boy. Soon they scaled the long flight of steps up towards the cliff-top cemetery. Theo's energy appeared boundless. For the others, this climb proved a tough one with their burdens. Beth gulped cold air into her lungs. Her calf muscles burnt. A stitch dug into her side. Yet nobody paused, nobody complained.

As they climbed the steps, they left the main body of Whitby behind. Cottages thinned out. Searchlights shone upward from so many different angles that the glow reflected by the cloud layer conjured shadows that danced across the ground. Even the shadows of stationary objects, like trees and lamp-posts, darted madly. Restless, shape-shifting phantoms, or so they seemed to Beth.

When they reached the graveyard, they continued along the path towards the abbey ruins. Two miles beyond them, yet more searchlights. The rods of white light could have been unearthly columns that held the night sky aloft. And as they hurried to the abbey, the siren finally stopped. A sudden silence pressed down on them with an ominous force all of its own. They entered the ancient cliff-top ruin. Gothic walls, pierced with vast arched windows, towered over them. The abbey lacked a roof, so the searchlight's reflected gleams lit the grass where a tiled floor would have once lay. Masonry poked from the ground, like giant fists pushing through from beneath the earth.

Tommy held up his hand. Then he pointed.

Beth followed his outstretched finger. There, crouching on the ground, a figure in white. But Tommy claimed that Eleanor had been put in a grave? Besides, the figure wasn't the proprietor of the hotel. This was a vampire. The woman who, in life, had been Mary Tinskell. The creature appeared interested in what lay beneath her. She leaned forward to pick at something.

Theo gestured for them to take cover behind a curtain of masonry. He set down the jar of X-Stock, then climbed the pitted wall, until he could look through one of the stone window frames. The weathered stonework provided easy handholds, so Beth joined him. From this vantage point they had a plain view of what Mary found so fascinating.

Eleanor had been placed in one of the disused stone coffins. The anthropomorphic tomb consisted of an oblong stone block, which, centuries ago, had been hollowed out to form a human shape. Into it, Eleanor had been partly concealed. The artefact lay buried in the earth almost to its rim. Clearly, the vampire had dragged a stone slab across it, so it formed a partial lid on the tomb, covering Eleanor's chest. However, it left her head exposed. The vampire took pleasure in digging her fingers into the mortal woman's face.

'What's she doing?' Eleanor whispered.

'Mary knows Gustav is in love with Eleanor. If you ask me, the spiteful creature is torturing my sister, because it will hurt Gustav when he finds out how she died.' Theo spoke so matter-of-factly that Beth shuddered. 'Remember, vampires don't operate to normal rules of logic. Mary will take great pleasure in producing Eleanor's head to Gustav, so proving how strong she is. No doubt she wants to rule the vampires.'

'We've got to get Eleanor away from there.'

'We can't use the bombs. The explosion would kill my sister, too.'

'Then I'll lure Mary away.'

'No.'

'Theo, I've got something in my veins that Mary wants.'

Beth scrambled to the ground. In whispers, she told the others what she'd found, then urged them to stay out of sight. After plucking one of the bottles from the satchel, she set the bag down so, when the time came, she could move fast. As stealthily as she could, she crept through the skeletal edifice. Its ruined towers flickered in hues of brown and gold in the searchlights' glow. Shadows conducted an eerie, undulating dance across the walls.

Beth moved along the wall to her right, in order to ensure that the vampire's back remained to her. However, the creature took so much delight in tugging hard at the rings in her victim's ear lobes that she didn't notice the intruder. What's more, Eleanor's groans of pain drowned the whisper of Beth's feet through the grass.

Sliding along the wall as quickly as she dared, Beth glanced ahead of her. She knew what she wanted. A moment later she found it. In that eroded masonry she found a Gothic archway that led to the steps of the tower. These only ascended a few feet before they reached an iron fence – a barrier to anyone foolhardy enough to desire to climb the unsafe structure. In those swarming shadows lay ancient stone slabs. Monks' feet had passed over them for more than a thousand years. Bit by bit the sandals had worn the stone slab away until it had formed a shallow concave.

Perfect!

Beth Layne glanced out through the door. The vampire plucked hairs from Eleanor's head, chuckling with glee as the woman cried out. Beth thought: *Careful now. One slip and you'll blow sky high.* Hands shaking slightly, she used a lip of stone beside the doorway to force the metal cap from the bottle neck. That done, she gently tipped its contents into a floor slab that had been worn into something resembling a shallow bowl. As she did so, she prayed there'd be no moss on the slab, otherwise the X-Stock would react so aggressively it would blaze her face from her skull.

When the last drop had been poured (fortunately with no detonation), Beth went to the doorway that opened into what would have been the interior of the abbey.

She whistled. Vampire Mary's head came up, senses alert; she turned with savage speed. When the white eyes fixed on Beth, they burnt with utter ferocity. What the creature would have seen was

an oh–so–vulnerable victim filled with fresh blood. Confident that
her prisoner in the stone coffin couldn't escape, Mary leapt to her
feet. Her white nightdress billowed in the breeze.

Then she ran at Beth. A blur of movement. A shocking spectacle
of aggression fused with bloodlust.

Beth retreated through the doorway into the base of the tower.
There was no exit here. Her plan must work, if she was to escape
with her own life intact. Taking great care not to step into the X–
Stock, Beth hopped over to the other side. Then she moved as far
as she could from the shallow depression in the stone slab that
contained a pool of liquid explosive, which was perhaps an inch
deep and eighteen in diameter. Pulses of radiance from the searchlights made that puddle of death flicker an iridescent blue.

Mary darted through the archway, hands stretched out, fingers
hooked into claws; an expression of greedy anticipation deformed
her face.

Her bare feet splashed into the fluid. Instantly, her feet exploded.
Amazingly, she regained her balance, so she stood on ankle stumps.
Yet the expression of bloodlust on her face had changed to one of
confusion. Those uncanny eyes glanced around her; she knew something had gone wrong, but couldn't identify the problem.

The X–Stock was relentless. Each time the vampire's flesh and
bone touched the chemical it reacted explosively.

Beth watched a machine gun–quick series of explosions devour
the monster. The bursts of white flame set the nightdress alight. Each
explosion destroyed five inches of limb. With each one, the vampire
became shorter. To Beth, it looked as if the creature sank through
the stone floor into the ground. When the detonations reached
Mary's hips she suddenly opened her mouth to let forth a huge
scream of pain.

The explosions quickened. Hips, stomach, chest: all vanished in
a flash of fire. Incendiary jaws devoured the vampire's body. From
start to finish, it took maybe ten seconds. And after those ten seconds
all that remained resting on the slab, like a mask, was the flesh of
the face. Still its eyes rolled in the sockets. An expression of someone
desperately searching for an escape route.

But there was no escape. Soon even the face melted.

Beth stepped over the smeary remains of the creature, then hurried
through the cavernous body of the ruin to free her friend.

Fourteen

Eleanor's a formidable woman. Her speedy recovery, however, surprised even Beth. As they left the abbey, she told Eleanor what had happened since the kidnap.

When Eleanor saw her brother with the group, she nodded at him, a strangely formal greeting. Then, with smiles of relief, she hugged him – then the rest of the little band of vampire killers.

'So you brought my home-made bombs,' Eleanor observed. 'Good. Let's put them to the test.'

Alec said, 'But we can't run around in the dark, trying to pick off vampires one by one.'

Beth retrieved her satchel. 'You said you'd devise a plan, Theo. Have you?'

'It's got to be something that involves Hag's Lung Cave,' Sally ventured.

'You are my favourite.' Theo took a firm grip of the gallon jar. 'And I am falling in love with you.'

Beth started walking. 'So it's the cave, then?'

'I'll go first,' Theo told her. 'We don't know what might be waiting for us.'

Fifteen

Searchlights stalked the night sky; rapiers of pure silver. The church on the headland tolled midnight. The sound ghosted over the grave-yard and the ruins of the ancient abbey to die amongst the hills.

Seven of them walked across the meadow. The dog stayed close to Tommy. Maybe adrenalin gave her renewed energy. Beth could hardly feel the weight of those bottles of instant death in her satchel. She glanced at the faces in the dappling glow of those restlessly probing searchlights that skated the underside of the cloud layer. Everyone wore expressions of determination. White gusts of breath blew from their lips. Their eyes were locked tight on the low mound ahead that marked the entrance to Hag's Lung. Eleanor had recovered from her ordeal remarkably quickly. The bloody scratches on her face didn't appear to bother her. Then no doubt her veins were flooded with adrenalin, too.

'The authorities might not have connected the disappearance of the soldiers with Hag's Lung Cave,' Alec told them. 'If they have, they might have sealed it back up again, and we don't have any tools.'

'We've got to get into that cave.' Theo hugged the gallon jar to him as he surged through the grass. 'If it's the last thing we do.'

Beth knew that Theo's plan would be torn to pieces if they couldn't enter. Though she didn't know exactly what he planned, she figured it was connected to the ancient vampires trapped in the sump cavern that adjoined the cave.

Alec grunted. 'Keep a look out for soldiers. There's still the curfew, remember.'

Sally asked, 'Do you really think they'll shoot on sight?'

'They'll know that some of their comrades have vanished hereabouts, so they'll be jittery.'

Eleanor's clear eyes regarded the mound. 'We don't have to worry about the doors, anyway. Just take a look at them.'

Even in the unsettling, shifting glow of reflected searchlights, it was plain to see that the doors had been brutally torn open. Sections of timber a foot long and six inches wide had been ripped from those once formidable structures.

Theo crouched to examine the doors. 'My plan also involves these being intact.'

Beth crouched, too. 'The timber-work's taken a mauling, but they're still sound.'

'And the lugs are in place, too.' He fingered the O-shaped iron work set in the planks. Through these heavy-duty loops an iron bar would be slotted before being padlocked. Amongst the debris, scattered about the turf, he found the bar. It even bore the teeth-mark of one of the vampires – a mark of its hatred of humanity and everything that belonged to it. He handed the bar to Alec. 'Keep this safe. You'll need it later.'

'Are you going to share your plan with us?' Alec asked.

'Spill it, Theo,' Eleanor told him sharply. 'We don't have time for your theatrical quirks.'

Sally added, 'Stage Door Johnnies – that's what Theo told us would stop the vampires.'

Eleanor cocked an eyebrow. 'Stage Door, Johnnies? Theo, are you *compos mentis*?'

'Absolutely. Never more so.' A grin flared. 'And since that witch potion of yours leeched itself out of my body I've never felt so alive. Now, let's see if anyone's home.'

Eleanor stopped him. 'You know this can't last. As soon as this is over, you will have to start taking the drug straightaway.'

'I was afraid you'd say that.' An immense darkness seemed to flow into his eyes. He knew that he'd return to that comatose state he'd endured for the last two decades. He tried to dispel that melancholy expression with a shake of his head. 'Each of you take out one of your bombs. You never know, there might be a welcome party waiting for us.' Theo appeared to have no need for illumination because he lightly ran down the steps into the shadows. Alec pulled the torch from his bag, switched it on, then followed the gaunt figure.

To Beth's relief she found the cave was empty. However, it had changed . . . and changed profoundly.

'It's hot,' Sally exclaimed. 'Can you feel the heat?'

'I told you the vampires in the sump were getting excited.' Theo set the gallon jar down in a corner of the cave. 'That's body heat you can feel. And smell that.'

Beth inhaled. 'It's an animal scent. Tell me I'm wrong, but I think those creatures trapped in the next cave are in a different kind of heat.'

'The heat of bloodlust.' Theo all but shouted the words. 'That excitement of theirs! The knowledge they're going to break out and rampage through the town! It's contagious, isn't it?'

Even Tommy's eyes burnt; he sensed some great change in the air. Sam whimpered, his ears flat. He sensed danger, too. The dog's eyes were fixed on the hole in the rock that connected this vault with the sump cavern. When air gusted out from it, the heat made steam, like the exhalation from a whale's blowhole.

Eleanor grabbed her brother's arm. 'Alright. Tell us why we're here.'

He held out his hand to Sally. 'If I can have one of your bottles, my dear.'

She passed him one, its blue contents sloshed inside.

'Listen up.' Theo sounded excitable. His eyes darted from the bottle to the blowhole in the wall. 'My Stage Door Johnnie theory works like this. The vampires out there in the town are attracted to the ancient vampires imprisoned in the sump. More than that! They are obsessed. Gustav's pack broke in here, so they could soak up their scents. They crave to be close to them. They worship them. And they long for the day when the sump vampires break out. And, after years of inactivity, they are no doubt striving to do just that.

Imagine them digging a route to the surface with their bare hands. No doubt that accounts for the generation of all that body heat you're feeling right now.' He carefully slipped the bottle into the five-inch wide hole in the wall. Then he picked up a long twig from the floor. 'Now let's stir up some mayhem.'

Alec's eyes went wide. 'You're going to kill the creatures on the other side of the rock?'

'No, not kill, my friend . . . I plan to make them howl the place down.'

Beth nodded. 'So the other vampires come running.'

'Absolutely.' He used the stick to push the bottle further in. Yet he held off from shoving it through the mini-tunnel to the other side. 'Please listen very closely.' His face became serious. 'There isn't enough X-Stock in the bottle to kill every vampire in the sump. After all, there must be hundreds of the things. But it will hurt them – they'll call on their own kind for help.'

Alec said, 'So, minutes from now, this cave will be flooded by very angry vampires.'

'Indeed so.'

'We can trap them in this cave.' Sally's eyes lit up. 'Then we can use the bombs to kill them all.'

'Almost.' A note of sadness flowed through Theo's voice. 'What you must do is go to the steps. When I push the bottle through it will explode in the sump. The vampires will howl. The other vampires will hear, then they'll come running. By then, my friends, you will be outside, and in hiding. When all the vampires are in here that's when you close the doors. You, Alec, will use that bar I gave you to lock them shut.'

Eleanor's expression was one of pure shock. 'Theo. Don't you dare.'

Sally's eyes filled with tears. 'Theo, you're going to stay in here with the vampires, aren't you?'

'You're smart,' he told her with a sad smile. 'That's what's made me fall in love with you tonight.'

Beth's heart pounded. 'This isn't a joke!'

'No.' Theo's smile was grim. 'No. At last, I'm deadly serious.'

Eleanor shook her head. 'No, no, no. Give me a few minutes. I can come up with another plan.'

'For one, dear sister, that new plan of yours puts me back in the cottage. Where I'll be under the spell of the drug for another twenty years. A husk. A half-man, existing like some poor prisoner. No, thank you. Tonight I'm alive . . . so alive I feel as if I can reach across the universe and play with the stars.'

'That's lunatic talk.'

Calmly, Theo made this statement: 'The gallon jar will be enough to kill the vampires in this cave. When they're dead, and it's safe to enter again, keep feeding those bombs of yours through that hole in the wall until all the devils in the sump cavern are dead, too.'

Alec was clearly appalled. 'Theo, Eleanor's right. Let's talk about this. We can come up with another plan that doesn't involve any suicide missions.'

'Thank you, Alec.' Theo smiled. 'Only we've gone and run out of time.'

Before anyone could react, he drove the stick into the hole. It pushed the bottle through into the sump cavern beyond, where dozens of vampires clawed their way through the rock to the surface.

Exulting, Theo yelled to his friends, 'Get back!'

Eleanor screamed. 'Damn you, Theo. Damn you!' Yet she knew she had no choice other than flee to the far corner of the cave.

Her companions sheltered with her, as the bottle exploded somewhere down in the sump. Not only flames jetted through the narrow blowhole. With that leaping tongue of fire, came screams. And such screams. A nerve-stripping howl of anguish. It vibrated the ground beneath their feet. The screams of burning vampires rose with even more power than that air-raid siren had possessed earlier. The cry of the ancient vampires tore through the night sky. It echoed through the streets of the town. It shook windows. The cry of agony rolled in a wave across the harbour.

In her mind's eye, Beth saw the vampires that roamed Whitby. They'd instantly hear that outpouring of misery. And they'd know where it came from. And exactly who had made it. From wherever the creatures scuttled, whether alleyways, or in the undergrowth along railway tracks, or in hidden walkways beneath the harbour pier, they'd immediately race back to the cave. *Protect their own kind! Destroy the intruder!* That would be the imperative on their lips.

Theo was a whirlwind of energy. 'Hear them scream? That will bring every one of those monsters back here!'

Alec shouted over howls of pain and fury, 'We're staying to fight them with you.'

'That's noble and loyal of you, Alec. What I need from you, however, is to lock those doors tight shut the moment the vampires are inside. That, and a handshake.' He extended his hand.

Alec shook it.

Eleanor's eyes bled sorrow. 'I'll be with you, Theo.'

'No, you won't. If a single one of you are in here with me, I won't be able to smash that damn flagon over their heads. Go!'

Tommy and Sam went first, scrambling up the steps to the night air. Sally flew at Theo, clasped his face in her hands, then kissed him on the lips.

Theo sighed. 'Take care, my Sally, you sweet thing.'

Quickly, he hugged and kissed Eleanor and Beth. She felt the fire in his lips. This man was truly alive.

'I wish there was another way,' Beth told him.

'There isn't.' He smiled. 'This, however, is perfect . . . for everyone.'

Tension put steel in Alec's voice. 'The creatures will be here soon. We must go now.'

Sally took hold of Eleanor's arm and guided her up the steps. Beth followed. Outside, Tommy and Sam waited for them. Beth put her arm round the boy.

'We must hide. Also, there will be an explosion, so be ready to reassure Sam.'

'I'm not frightened any more.' Tommy spoke softly. 'I know what's coming.'

Beth nodded. 'Hide over there in the bushes. I'll join you in a moment.' As the boy and his dog walked across the grass that seemed to pulse emerald green in the reflected glow of the searchlights, his thoughtful sentence echoed inside her head *I know what's coming.* The child's tone possessed a haunting resonance.

'Beth,' Alec called. 'When the time comes, be ready to give me a hand with the doors. Until then, make sure you're out of sight.'

Beth adjusted the satchel's strap on her shoulder. Soon they'd need those home-made bombs of Eleanor's. She raised herself on her toes, so she could look across the meadow to the churchyard that lay beyond the abbey. Searchlights, striking the underbelly of low cloud, generated enough of a glow to make the gravestones clearly visible. In the main, they were upright slabs of dark stone by the hundred. They formed a bristling mass, somehow reminiscent of teeth jutting from a monstrous jaw. But those gravestones did something that defied God.

They were moving. Shapes darted over the churchyard wall. They sped towards the abbey ruin. A second later, they flowed around the shattered walls. How could tombstones move? What malignant power was at work here? Then her eyes adapted to the gloom.

'They're here,' she yelled. 'Hide!'

She glanced down the steps into the cave. Theo's eyes met hers. He was smiling.

Alec grabbed her hand. 'Come on!'

Together, they rushed for the cover of bushes that sprouted from a scatter of boulders. Chest heaving, Beth had chance to reappraise what she'd interpreted as running gravestones.

No gravestones.

These were the vampires. Dozens of them. They rushed in nothing less than a wolf pack towards the cave. They'd heard their ancient brethren scream. Now they were here to protect them. And no doubt help free them from the sump cavern.

The pounding of feet made the ground tremble. As if their Vampiric touch caused revulsion in the earth itself. Beth shrank back into the deepest shadows. Closed her eyes. Held her breath.

And waited.

Sixteen

Darkness . . . a deep, velvet darkness, filled Hag's Lung Cave. Yet Theo possessed certain attributes of the vampire, for he saw it in all its cold detail. The stalactites, the scattering of twigs on the floor, a glint of crystals in the rock. The screams had, at last, stopped and there was silence.

Twenty years ago a vampire had attacked him. Eleanor had applied those Quick Salts of hers to the wounds. The ancient alchemy had only been a partial remedy. Theo's blood had become tainted. Days were a vacuum of nothing. If he did move, it was akin to sleep-walking. At night, he only came partly awake, because the potion he drank dampened down his vampire tendencies. Now, however, he had clear sight and a wide-awake mind; it allowed him to examine the cave in this silent interlude between making the sump creatures howl and the arrival of their brethren.

Theo placed the gallon jar of X-Stock in a rocky hollow beside the steps. He'd need to hurl that as soon as the vampires were inside – and, the saints willing, Alec had locked the doors back in place. The success of his plan depended on all those roaming vampires being imprisoned in this vault with him.

'Any regrets? Anything left unsaid?' His whisper echoed softly back at him. 'I should have told Eleanor to get married. The woman's been a prisoner as much as I have.' He listened to the silence for a moment.

The creatures would be here soon. He sensed their angst. The screams of their kinsfolk in the sump must have shocked them to the bone. 'I wish I could have talked to Sally. I could have told her that this thing called Life is the most powerful force in the universe. Weeds will fill a garden if they get the chance. Bacteria, the human body. The vampire is just another creature that's driven by the life force to conquer. Human beings have been doing so for a hundred thousand years. Only we've never had any real competition.' He smiled. 'So, you're right. I am strange, aren't I? A strange child, I was, too. One who devoted all his time to his daydreams. But it made me feel good inside. I wouldn't have changed myself for the world.'

Shivers ran up his spine. Instinct told him that the fabric of reality had just sidestepped into a realm where other laws apply. He divined that a legion of evil charged towards this hole in the ground. A split second later, the sound of hammering poured through the blow-hole. In his mind's eye, he saw them: the surviving sump vampires (and there must be hundreds) had seized hold of rocks and were furiously battering at the wall that separated this cave from their prison vault. They were hell-bent on smashing a way through with their makeshift hammers.

'I hear you,' he murmured. 'I know what you want.'

As the pounding reverberated through the cave, he sank back into deeper shadow. For a figure darted down the steps. After that came more. He saw some of the vampires wore military uniforms. One, clad as a pilot, still wore his goggles, which only reinforced the inhuman aspect of his eyes. Theo pressed himself further back against the wall. The jar of X-Stock appeared to glow with a blue light all of its own. The contents of that jar could have been the fires of hell in liquid form. Soon it would have its release.

Seventeen

Sally crouched alongside Tommy and Sam in the bushes. Through the spiky branches she'd glimpsed the arrival of the vampires. They'd poured in a grim tide up the cliff steps to the graveyard, then across the meadow to the hole in the earth that was the entrance to Hag's Lung Cave. One after another they raced down the steps. One, two, three, four, five . . . soon she'd lost count.

Tommy and Sam watched, too. The dog had grown so tense she felt his body quiver against her thigh.

Branches crackled behind her. Then a huge concussion. It sent her rolling forward across the grass. To her horror she saw a vampire in a soldier's battledress burst from the bushes. Any second now his teeth would find her throat. Sally clenched her fists in anticipation of that agonizing bite.

Yet the man ran on. All that mattered for him was to reach the cave. More creatures charged through the bushes. The cry of the sump vampires must have drawn their kin for miles. Another vampire, this one with fiery red hair, raced by without giving Sally a second glance.

Winded, Sally struggled to her feet. Alec and Beth already ran to the cave's doors. The last vampire plunged into that rock mouth. Alec and Beth didn't delay. Each grabbed a heavy timber flap, then slammed it shut. Alec drove the iron bar through the lugs.

'It's done,' Beth shouted. 'They're trapped!'

Eighteen

'They're trapped!'

Theo clearly heard Beth's triumphant shout. He also heard the tremendous clash of the heavy doors being slammed into place. Theo had his captive audience. And he found himself enjoying this special moment.

Thirty or more vampires clustered at the blowhole. Their faces were distorted with nothing less than fear. These things were absolutely terrified that their Vampiric clan in the sump were being harmed. None of them spoke. They listened to the clatter of rocks at the other side, as the creatures tunnelled through. At last, their expressions of fear melted into one of relief. Some of them picked up stones in order to attack the wall. Now vampires on both sides of the stone divide were determined to break through.

As Theo stooped to pick up the jar, one of the vampires in military garb happened to glance back. The moment he saw Theo he let out a howl of rage. Others turned, too. In a blur of movement they rushed the man. Before he could even touch the jar, they dragged him into the centre of the cave. Theo could have wept with frustration. The jar of X-Stock remained against the steps. Now it could have been on the far side of Mars for what good it could do. He fought to free himself from the mass of hands.

'Go on – bite me,' he yelled. 'You'll get nothing but a bitter drink from these veins.' Freeing his hand, he punched a vampire's face. In fury, it snapped at his hand. His little finger vanished into its jaws.

That pain . . . it raced up his arm like lightning. And, dear Heaven, it felt so good.

'Go on, more! You're only making me feel more alive.' He struggled to break away from those grasping hands, but they were too strong.

Then a familiar face emerged from the masks of hatred.

'You shouldn't have come,' roared a voice. 'I can't protect you.'

'Gustav?'

The stark, white face possessed those colourless vampire eyes. Twin black pupils locked on to Theo.

Gustav forged through the mass of bodies to his old friend. 'They've gone berserk. They know that those monsters in the sump are close to breaking out. Nothing can stop them. They'll tear Whitby apart. Everyone will be infected. Then they'll cross over the moor. All the world will be taken – they'll suck the lifeblood out of humanity itself.' The man's eyes rolled; his prophecy of global doom overwhelmed him.

Another set of teeth sank into Theo's shoulder. They couldn't extract blood to their liking; however, they'd make sure he was torn to pieces.

'Gustav, help me.'

'I can't save you.'

'I don't want to be saved.' More jaws gripped him. Teeth crunched through skin. 'But for the love of Eleanor I want you to save her . . . her friends . . . the entire world.'

The vampires' exultation surged through their throats. On the other side of the rock divide, the creatures in the sump beat the wall harder. A furious drum roll of sound.

Gustav appeared grief-struck. 'I can't do anything, Theo. They don't listen to me.'

'See the jar? Over there by the wall. Open it, Gustav. Release the genie.' They bit harder. Theo let out a yell that was as much laughter as hurt. 'Old friend, release the genie and all will be well!'

Gustav pushed his way through the vampires, who clamoured for Theo's flesh. The creature picked up the jar; he studied the blueness within.

'What is it?' he called.

'It's what we've both longed for this last twenty years.' Teeth pierced his side. 'It is peace everlasting.'

'But I need something to make me human again. I want to be with Eleanor.'

'Not in this life, Gustav.' Jaws ripped his flesh, but Theo felt no more pain. Almost dreamily, he sang out, 'Gustav. Just throw the jar. Then everything will be good. After all, you can't save these creatures, but you can free their souls.'

Finally, Gustav understood. Two old school friends faced each other and smiled. Gustav swung the gallon jar upwards. The glass shattered against the rock ceiling. Then the liquid fell back down, a gentle, blue rain.

Theo raised his face to it. He felt sleepy – at peace. Drops of sky-blue alighted on him; for an instant, they felt as cool as morning kisses, a refreshing tingle, a sense of release.

And then . . .

Nineteen

And then . . .

The ground rose up. The shock wave blurred the air above the cave doors; a concussion displaced the air around Hag's Lung with such force it stripped grass from the ground. Then came a sound louder than a thunder clap.

Beth reeled before the huge sound. It seemed as if some invisible barrier tried to contain the explosion.

And failed.

For a torrent of flames shot through the holes in the timber flaps. A second later, arms appeared in the column of white fire that towered above them. The arms extended through gaps in the doors, fingers out splayed. And all the vampires shrieked in agony, and the despair in their voices rolled away over the distant hills to die amongst the barren moor.

Beth watched as the X-Stock exploded the flesh on those raised limbs. The iron banding on the gates glowed yellow. Timbers were incinerated in seconds. Yet not one creature emerged.

Shielding their eyes against the brilliance of that tower of fire, Beth and her companions approached the cave entrance. A succession of smaller explosions warned them not to get too near. They hung back from that mouth in the earth that spewed fire. Sparks darted into the sky. At times, the incendiary tower rose as high as the clouds, making them glow white.

The flames abated. As quickly as if a lever had been thrown. Smoke rolled up the steps. What remained of the metalwork still glowed orange from the heat. Then a flurry of movement. A figure. A charred man-shape raced towards them.

Beth recognized the remains of melted pilot's goggles on the man's face. The demonic form charged at her, hands outstretched, a fury of movement, intent on destroying her.

Alec threw the bottle. It struck the figure in the chest. Instantly, X-Stock reacted with flesh. The running vampire became a fireball. All it managed was another ten paces before the thing was rendered down. A conglomeration of shambling bones; a skull denuded of skin; the glass lenses of the goggles melted to run down the cheek-bones; huge glittering tears.

The vampire collapsed, becoming a smear of dark ash on the ground.

They waited another four minutes. Nothing else emerged. Overhead, the circling ravens dispersed into the night. When the smoke had cleared enough, and the heat within the cave had dwindled sufficiently, Alec descended the steps. Beth followed. Then Eleanor and Sally. Alec swept the torch around; its light revealed scorch marks on the walls. Of the vampires, of Theo and Gustav, there remained only black dust.

From the other side of the cave wall came the clatter of rocks on stone. The sump vampires still worked in all their vengeful fury to break out.

Eleanor recovered her composure. With a steely glance at the blowhole that connected the cave with the sump cavern, she said, 'We've one last job.'

Alec began to feed bottles into the narrow hole. When he'd pushed three inside, he retrieved the iron bar from the entrance of the cave. He grimaced. The metal was still hot enough to sting his palms. Nevertheless, he inserted the bar into the hole, then used it to push the bottles right through to the other side.

'Stand back,' he ordered.

As the bottles fell into the sump, he flung himself down. The explosion on the far side of that rock face produced a jet of flame that shot from the blowhole into the heart of the cave. Its heat made Beth's face smart. The inferno within the sump must have been unspeakable. She pictured the ancient vampires writhing in agony. Dozens must have been obliterated.

Yet, seconds later, the pounding of stones continued. The monsters weren't defeated yet. Alec repeated the process. Three more bottles of that liquid hellfire. Again, flame erupted like a blow torch. Screams vibrated the stone beneath their feet.

Eleanor plucked more bottles from the satchel. 'Keep going. We can't stop until their all dead.'

After the next batch of bottles entered the sump, the rap of stones against the cave wall stopped. Screams faded to groans.

'More,' Eleanor said.

After the next brace of bombs had been shoved through the screams stopped. And after that, even though they pushed more bottles through to the other side, there were no more explosions.

Beth stopped Eleanor from inserting more bottles into the hole. 'That's enough. There isn't any organic matter left through there to react with the chemical.'

Eleanor sank to her knees. Beth looked at the faces of her companions. Soot-streaked, exhausted, yet a spark of triumph shone in their eyes.

'We've won.' Alec coughed. 'They're all dead.'

Then Sally's gaze roved around the cave. 'Has anyone seen Tommy?'

Twenty

Tommy lay beside the bushes. A half-buried boulder appeared to form a pillow on which he'd rested his head. Sam sat beside him so closely the sides of their bodies touched. The dog watched them approach, then he turned his eyes to his master that lay so still on the ground. Beth ran to the boy. She crouched down and lifted him into her arms.

Tommy opened his eyes. He appeared drowsy; his eyelids were almost too heavy to keep raised. She hugged the light frame to her. Sam moved a little so he could press his body alongside that of his companion's. Beth could sense the dog wanted her to help the child; those canine eyes were so expressive. In the reflected glow of the searchlights, she couldn't see anything amiss. Then she noticed a dark stain on the boulder. She touched the back of Tommy's head.

Beth felt wetness on her fingertips. 'It's when those vampires came charging through the bushes. One must have knocked Tommy off his feet so hard he hit his head on the stone.'

Sally's eyes watered. 'He'll be alright. I mean, he's not a human boy.'

Alec crouched down. 'He's one of the vampires; they're not easy to kill.'

Eleanor shook her head sadly. 'He never hurt anyone. If you ask me, he wasn't quite the same as the vampires. He'd not transformed like them.'

Beth stroked his face. 'I'd always seen Tommy as a boy that haunted the body of a vampire. I can't see that now. Something's changed.' She lowered her head so Tommy had a clear view of her face. 'It's alright. We'll look after you.'

His voice came as a soft sigh, 'I'm not afraid.'

'I know you're not. You're a hero. We all love you.'

Tommy rested his hand on the dog's back, then that slight body that had seemed so light in Beth's arms grew heavy. Even so, the lad raised his head a little so he could look over her shoulder.

'That's funny,' he murmured. 'All that time I spent trying to find my mother and father –' his eyes glinted – 'and now they've found me.'

Beth glanced back in the direction he was smiling. She saw the underside of the clouds, and nothing more. Then she felt Tommy relax in her arms; this time the weight pulled her downwards.

'Let me help,' Sally whispered.

Together, they rested the body on the ground. Tommy lay, as if in a deep sleep. Eyes closed, serenely still.

And finally, from the distance, came the rising call of the siren. This held a different sound to the one that warned of imminent attack. That distinctive note signalled the all clear. The threat of enemy bombers was over. The siren's sweet voice sang out to a night-time world: *The danger has passed. You're safe. All is well. All is well.*